THE DARK ORDER

The wizard lifted his arms above his head and broke into a chant. The staff gleaming from between his hands shone with an angry glare.

A breeze sprang up, and Rogue could hear the sighing sound of laughter across the square. Along with the eerie sound, the breeze carried a growing smell, the stench of rotting fish.

Then iron plates set into the square's cobblestones heaved up, and black openings yawned. From each hole slithered a huge, taloned black hand, rising on a tentacle arm, like some charmed snake out of an unholy basket.

Rogue looked up to find the wizard's eyes boring into his own. The wizard spoke: *"I know who you are—and I will destroy you!"*

By Dennis McCarty
Published by Ballantine Books:

FLIGHT TO THLASSA MEY
WARRIORS OF THLASSA MEY
LORDS OF THLASSA MEY
ACROSS THE THLASSA MEY

THE BIRTH OF THE BLADE

THE BIRTH OF THE BLADE

Dennis McCarty

A Del Rey Book
BALLANTINE BOOKS • NEW YORK

A Del Rey Book
Published by Ballantine Books

Library of Congress Catalog Card Number: 93-90178

ISBN 0-345-37713-3

Manufactured in the United States of America

First Edition: August 1993

The author dedicates this volume to his younger daughter, Colleen, who brings music and laughter to his days.

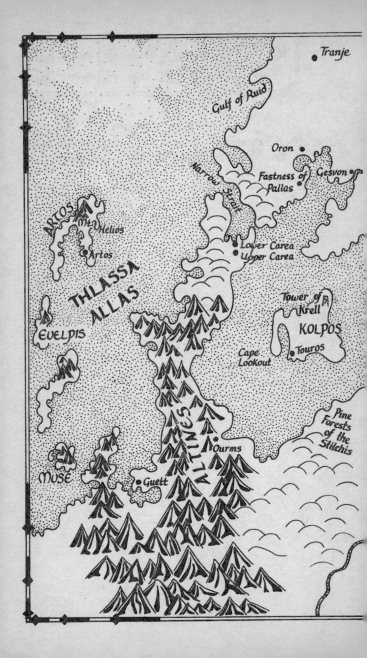

Chapter One:
In the Streets of Oron

THE REALMS ABOUT the Thlassa Mey are ancient lands, with roots sunk deep into the soil of history and tradition. Over the centuries, times and ways shifted like windblown sands. Sometimes people sought light, while at other times they lived lives of darkness and decay.

There was a time across the Thlassa Mey when the great feudal nations of Carea and Buerdaunt had not yet formed. Palamon the Peacemaker was not yet born, nor was Lothar the Pale. Back in this time, men did not even worship the civilized gods of Carea or Buerdaunt, but followed dark and greedy deities, beings that thirsted for human blood and human sacrifice.

It was an evil time, when no kings or queens or princes held order. The world struggled feebly in the grip of dark gods and their dark minions. It was a kind of theocracy, a loose network of hard-hearted priests called the Dark Order. More often, it was known simply as the Order.

These priests had bathed not even their little fingers in the milk of human kindness. They extorted gold and food from the wailing masses. It was rumored they even practiced blood sac-

1

rifice in their secret temples, but no one could stop them. They ruled by their own hard laws.

Disorder bared its teeth everywhere. Where the priests did not hold sway, bands of thieves and cutthroats took what they wanted. The wealthy and the powerful hired soldiers to protect them. The meek could only struggle and suffer and die in poverty and despair. Even in the priestly orders themselves, violence was the way of life. If a priest felt ambitious, the most certain path to advancement was to murder those in higher position. Trust became unknown and every churchman surrounded himself with a bevy of private bodyguards.

There were no real armies and no constables or town guard. Thieves roamed freely, unhindered as long as they paid a share of their booty to their Local Order. Thugs, cutthroats, and murderers plied their trades openly. The poor gave the best portion of their goods to the Local Order and lived in fear of being pillaged or worse. While thieves, mercenaries, and the wealthy found matters to their liking, all good people seethed and smoldered.

In the midst of this chaos a male child was born in the slums of the city of Oron. His parents were no one of account, two shadowy figures in a shadowy time. Neither of them survived until the youth had hairs on his chin.

His given name vanished with them. He grew larger than the average street-boy to young manhood in the fierce slums of the city, roving with street gangs, extorting food and copper coins from street vendors, prostitutes and pimps, even pickpockets and cutpurses. No one dared stand against this young ruffian and his companions. He grew tall and strong, and his friends knew him only as Rogue.

For all his fierceness, strength, and skill with daggers and clubs and hurled stones, females did not favor Rogue. He was anything but handsome. He stood head and shoulders above most men his age. But his nose was narrow and hooked and his eyes were colored a nondescript hazel. His lips were full almost to the point of being grotesque, and his lower jaw stuck out beyond his upper.

He knew all the alleys, all the cesspits and stinking passages of Oron's waterfront district. He knew all the places a rough young man could have a good time. He knew every inn that sold strong drink to youths, and he knew where every party took place.

He kept beside him a huge, black and white mongrel dog he had named Boofer. This canine possessed the unusual characteristic of being so ugly he made his master look comely by comparison. The animal had been blinded in one eye. The socket hung open, a black, gum-filled void surrounded by pink, puffy scar tissue. It looked like a carbuncle about to burst. One ear was missing. He sported a wide mouth filled with long teeth and drooled so badly that Rogue's friends called him "the walking sponge."

Boofer could not bark. Someone had kicked him in the throat when he was a puppy, and now the only noise he could make was an evil sound, something halfway between a cough and a hiss. He had a good disposition for all that. He licked his master and all his master's friends with great spirit. Every one of them sported damp spots from the beast's tongue.

On a warm, wet evening during Rogue's twentieth summer, the young tough found himself walking toward the shadowy corner where he would meet his friends. It had been an average day, and he had no reason to think it would be other than an average night. Nothing much ever changed in Oron—you just fought and survived, that was all.

He strode forcefully with his thumbs hooked into his belt. People stayed out of his way. He slowed, however, as he noticed something glittering in the open sewer that flowed down the center of the street. He stopped, glanced about to see no one watching, then bent closer. Surrounded by filth, with a trickle of water running over it, lay a gold coin. Again Rogue glanced about, then plunged his hand into the smelly water and picked the coin up.

He sneered with disgust as he shook foul water from the coin. But the coin was a full talent piece, more money than he had ever seen in one place in his life. It shone darkly as he turned it over; then he swore loudly as it slipped from his fingers. It rolled down the street, bouncing merrily over the cobbles.

He leaped after it, bowling past a couple of surprised bystanders. It slowed and toppled, and he snatched at it, but felt only cold stone at his fingertips. He blinked in surprise: the coin lay a few cubits away now, glinting as if laughing at him. A talent was a great deal of money for a street youth. He did not even consider the joke being played on him as he scrambled after it again.

Again he missed, then saw the coin lying in the shadow of a building a few cubits farther on. This time he leaped more quickly, snatched it up, and clutched it tightly. He felt its shape hard against his palm. Then the hard touch vanished. When he opened his hand, he saw nothing there. "Gone again," he said to himself.

Laughter floated to his ears—a woman's laughter, sounding like little bells on a crisp morning. He looked up and found himself at the mouth of a narrow, dark alley. Back in the shadows stood a woman dressed in light-colored robes. He could barely make out her pale form against the darkness. "Gold does that," she said with a smile.

"Does what?" Rogue said. He walked toward her.

"Disappears, like mist before a wind." She was an unearthly beauty, with light hair, brilliant skin, and eyes gray as smoked glass.

"Who are you?" he asked. "Why did you trick me?"

"I did nothing of the sort. You have that golden talent—here." She touched him on the forehead, and her touch sent an unearthly tingle through him, a kind of exalted, drunken feeling.

He stared at her. She was a beautiful woman, and beautiful women—any women—had never had any use for Rogue. "Who are you? What do you want?"

"I want to tell you that you're special," she said with her smile. "You have never known that, have you?"

Now it was his turn to laugh. "Whoever you are, you're full of it," he said. But whatever he thought of himself, Rogue knew *she* was special, and he regretted the remark as soon as it passed his lips.

"I've watched you," she said. "You are chosen—what will come to you, is meant to be. You have the strength and I am with you."

He could only stare after her as she faded back into the alley and disappeared in the darkness. He stood for a long time and puzzled over what had happened. Finally, he shrugged his shoulders and went on his way. An hour later, he had all but forgotten the incident, and he joined the band of some two dozen street toughs as they walked along a busy lane in search of pleasure or adventure.

Sundown found them in a large market square. The place was quiet as things went in Oron. Fewer vendors than usual had set up stalls and the crowd was sparse, so most of the area's sneak thieves had left. Only one man had been knifed during the day, and he had lived.

Many of the bazaar's merchants had hired guards. The mercenaries had no problem keeping order with such a thin crowd. With so little to attract their attention, the youths began to banter back and forth with one another, the odd elbow flew, and one young man swore at the fellow next to him. Rogue frowned. The band always grew restless when things were this quiet.

There were two youths, named Kenn and Shonn, who were no friends to Rogue. They always caused trouble—more trouble than was good for anybody. On this night, the two of them split away from the group and made their way to a fruit vendor's stand. While the man watched them suspiciously, they eyed the baskets full of figs, pomegranates, and quinces. "My produce is the best you'll see this side of Kruptos," the vendor said grumpily.

The taller youth, Shonn, grinned and snickered. "We didn't come to buy anything," he said. "We thought you might want to buy something from us."

The vendor looked from one to the other and sighed. "Come on, boys, I don't need trouble from you."

"I'm serious," Shonn said. "We can help you. Everyone else has his own guards. We want to work for you."

"How often do you come into this square?"

"Every day." Shonn kept a smile fixed on his face.

The old man shrugged. "Then you know no one ever bothers me. I don't make trouble for anyone; they don't bother me. Don't you bother me, either."

"We wouldn't dream of it," Shonn said, lifting his hands. He turned to his partner. "Would we, Kenn?"

"Not us," Kenn answered with a smile.

"We just want to work for you," Shonn said. "We understand some people are planning to cause you a lot of trouble, and we'll put the word out on them. We'll stop them. It'll just cost you a couple of coppers a day."

The stallkeeper sighed, and a bearded fellow wearing a breastplate walked toward them. "What's going on here?"

Kenn stared at the mercenary with theatrical, feigned shock. "It's him," he cried.

"Him who?" the stallkeeper cried back.

"One of the troublemakers," Shonn offered. He leaped to the armed man, kicked him hard in the shins below the man's chain-mail protection, then pulled the loose-fitting chain-mail hood down over the bearded face. "We'll save you from him." The two of them struggled and wrestled about, swayed back and forth, then finally toppled onto the stallkeeper's vegetables. The stand splintered and smashed to the cobbles. Pulp, juice, seeds, and rind sprayed in all directions.

Before anyone could lay a hand on either of them, the two roughs rolled the guard over, kicked and stomped him, then upset cartons of fruit. Kenn smeared the stallkeeper's face with smashed tomato, and the two lads dashed away with their pockets full of produce.

"Robbery," the hapless vendor cried. He tried to run after the two and so did other people. Their feet slipped on scattered produce, and their efforts came to nothing. Kenn and Shonn scrambled away from pursuit, down an alleyway, and to safety.

"Next time he'll pay a couple of coppers to keep trouble away," Kenn said. He bit into a quince. "Faugh. This thing's hard as goat meat." He tossed it into the shadow of a building.

"That guard wasn't worth an old shoe, that's for sure." Shonn laughed.

By now they had met with a half dozen of their fellows, who had also raced from the square as the commotion had begun. There was laughter and jeering, and some of the young men jostled back and forth as they walked. The rest of the group joined them by twos and threes, and Rogue and Boofer caught up with them, as well.

"That wasn't a classy thing to do," Rogue said to Shonn. "That old fellow's never done us any harm."

"This whole world's done me harm," Shonn said with a sneer. "And everything in it. Piss on 'im, I was bored."

"And broke," Kenn added with a laugh.

"It still wasn't classy," Rogue said. "It was small."

"Then show us something better," Shonn cried. He whirled and stood nose to nose with the leader. "Show us something classy if you're so superior. If you can't find us something to do, shut up."

Rogue's face flushed. He shoved Shonn backward so hard the smaller youth staggered. The gang formed a circle as the two of them squared off. "Don't tell me what to do or how to do it," Rogue shouted. He and Boofer wheeled on Shonn, and the dog released a hissing growl.

"Let's have a contest," Kenn cried. "Whoever can think up something to do, he's the leader. Whoever can find us the most fun."

"I'm boss," Rogue shouted.

"That ugly dog doesn't make you boss." Shonn faced the rest of the group. "Come on. I'm going to find you a good time. Stay with Rogue and his stupid dog if you don't want to do anything; otherwise, come with me."

Rogue glared at the youth. He ought to shake him, throw him onto the cobbles and squash him like an insect. He didn't, though. He could answer this challenge with skill, not force, and enjoy some excitement in the bargain. "All right," he said with a laugh. "You're going to show us how to have fun? You know so much? Do it, then. I'll come along, just for a laugh."

"Follow me, then," Shonn cried with a wave of his arm. He turned down the alley and led them down the slope toward Oron's riverfront docks. Like an aggressive avalanche, thirty young men washed down streets, between grimy buildings. Residents and street beggars scrambled out of their way, leaping into doorways or around corners to avoid the rush of young muscle. Youths shouted, laughed, and elbowed one another for more room as they swept through the darkest section of the city.

A narrow avenue led along the river, dotted by wooden mooring bits. Barges, galleys, and skiffs bobbed against the stone quay. As the youths surged from the alley, the evening's last light turned the river blue and red, gold and silver. Greasy cobblestones shone, metal fittings flashed, and waves sparkled. Then, as quickly as it had come, the golden light vanished. The sun dipped behind the rim of land and the city passed from gold and pink to gray and shadow.

"Where we going?" one youth cried.

Once more, Shonn swept his arm forward. "Just follow," he yelled back.

A hundred cubits down the avenue lay a wide, low galley with ports for a single bank of oars. Shonn led the company that way and leaped from cobblestone to wooden decking, nimble as a goat. He pulled out his dagger and faced his fellows. "Here we are," he cried.

Kenn laughed. "You're crazy. What do we do now?"

"Anything we want," Shonn wheeled and yelled. "Hey, who's aboard this scow?"

A man in leather breeches and a ragged jacket popped up from belowdecks. "You there. What are you doing on my ship?"

"Whatever we feel like," Shonn shouted. He leaped at the mariner and slashed at him with his dagger. The older man reeled back. The fellow snatched up a curved sword and squared off against the youth. Kenn scooped a stone from the pavement and winged it at the man, striking him above the eye, causing him to stagger.

"Murder," the man cried. "They're killing me." Sailors boiled from below, and youths vaulted onto the ship to meet them. More sailors showed up in tavern doorways, then scrambled toward the fray. Mercenaries came to the causeway at the same time. They also drew swords and rushed toward the riot.

Rogue and Boofer leaped onto the barge and joined the fighting. Men and youths surged back and forth across the deck, fought with fists, knives, swords, even stones and clubs. Boofer sank his teeth into one sailor's leg. The fellow screamed and writhed. A mate took a swing at the great dog with a wooden pole, but Rogue's fist caught the man in the middle. The fellow doubled up with a gasp. The huge youth then picked the sailor up and heaved him down to gang members still on the dock. Fighting surged everywhere.

From the corner of his eye, Rogue spotted the guards, who were coming at a dead run. All his gang together would be no match for them. "Jump aboard," he cried to the boys who remained ashore. "We've got real trouble." He snatched his dagger from his belt, then ran to the ship's bow and slashed at the mooring lines. "Get the other end," he cried.

The vessel lurched as the current caught it and the bow swept out toward midriver. Youths ran to the stern and tried to cut it free. Before they made it, the first guardsmen reached them. The tumult doubled. Some guards, intent only on quelling the riot, swung swords and clubs at youths and seamen without heed for who might be right or wrong. The melee turned into a free-for-all. The air filled with cries and the sound of club impacting against sword and stone, or stone against shield. In a blind fury of battle, Rogue got his hands on a fallen sword, then hacked the last mooring line in two.

The ship swept free of land and moved downstream, crosswise to the current. As the deck lurched, men screamed and fell into the dark water. Other men ran along the avenue, shouting and waving weapons as they tried to keep up with the drifting vessel.

For a moment, the ship fouled another vessel tied along the dock. More guards scrambled aboard, until Rogue and a couple of other youths hacked and shoved their way free and pushed back into the current.

There still weren't enough guards to defeat the young roughs. Some gave up and leaped from the deck; some surrendered and were thrown off. The youths overwhelmed them one by one. By the time the drifting ship cleared the city wall, Rogue's gang had won it as gloriously as some band of sea pirates.

Shonn ran the length of the deck, leaped to the low sterncastle, and threw his fists toward the sky. "This is great," he shouted. "We're kings of the river, now."

"Sure, great," Rogue shouted back. "Now you have a ship, and I've got cuts and bumps all over me. Who knows how many of us are hurt worse than I am? What do you think you'll do now?"

"Find food, find wine," Kenn shouted. "There's got to be something worthwhile on this tub. Let's go." He scrambled down a gangway that led below, and several youths scrambled after him.

Rogue sat down with a sigh and rubbed his forearm where

a club had struck it. It really hurt. It would be black as a bucket of rotted slops in a day or two, he suspected. While he sat, Boofer ambled up and ran his warm, canine tongue over a cut on the young man's other arm.

The lads who had swarmed belowdecks soon reappeared, hauling up cured meats, wine pots, and leather goods. A celebration began, even though the vessel still drifted. The main road from the city paralleled the canal until it passed through a low range of hills that lay between Oron and the sea. There, the road swept to the south and the angry guardsmen, weary from their hot pursuit, gave up the chase.

Rogue stood up. "We've got to do something," he shouted. "We'll be to open water before long, and none of us knows how to sail this thing."

"He's right," another lad shouted. Some had already sucked down too much wine to be any use, but others leaped to the tall youth's side. Together they released the ship's heavy bronze anchor from the cathead and dropped it into the dark water. Down the great grapnel plunged, while rope hissed from the rope locker.

None of the boys knew enough to tie off the rushing anchor line. The barge swept downstream until the last fathom paid out. By their good fortune, the line's bitter end lay tied about a great timber in the rope locker. The barge lurched as the line came taut. Hemp thick as a man's arm sang like a lute string, and boys staggered for support as the vessel heeled over.

The anchor caught fast and the craft swung about, straight with the current. So great was the scope of their anchor line that they swung back and forth, first touching one canal bank, then the other, like a clumsy pendulum in the darkness.

"Bravo, bravo." Kenn and Shonn both clapped and cheered. "You're not much of a boss but you might be a sailor someday."

Rogue glared at them. "I ought to throw you two over the side," he said.

"Not them," another youth shouted. He wore a new set of finely tanned leather breeches from the ship's hold. He had topped that with a new leather vest, and his chin dripped red from the wine he had gargled down with his friends. "This is the greatest thing we've done since I joined. Shonn ought to be boss, not you."

"No way," another youth shouted. "If it hadn't been for Rogue, those guards would have thumped the life out of us. Rogue is boss, as far as I'm concerned. Shonn is nothing but a screwup."

A lot of youths shouted agreement with that, easily as many as had cheered for Shonn. Still, the debate caused Rogue to hesitate. He had always been the strongest and most adventurous, but now he had been outdone. He had been outdone by a lad two years younger than himself.

"Enough," he roared. "This isn't a social meeting. Shonn, you are a screwup. You didn't know what you were doing from one end to the other, you just let things happen and I had to pull your nuts out of the fire. I'm boss."

"A pretty dull boss, then," Shonn said with a laugh. The taunt galled Rogue to the point where he lunged at the younger lad, but Kenn and a half-dozen others blocked his way.

"Is it a challenge?" Rogue cried. "Fine. Pick your knife, your club, sword, spear, whatever you want to use. You challenge me; it's to the death, little boy. I'll cut your liver out and feed it to the fish in this canal."

For an instant, Shonn's face showed fear. Then he forced his devil-may-care expression back into place. "You're too big to fight," he said. "Everybody knows it. You just don't have any imagination, that's all."

Several lads laughed. Rogue glared at them. "I don't, eh? No nerve, eh? All right, let's get off this thing and I'll show you some sport—if you have belly enough for it."

Many youths eyed him uncertainly. His eyes blazed, his lips had curved themselves into a snarl. He had always been the most adventurous of the company; any lad who didn't believe he would come up with a truly dangerous escapade hadn't known him for long.

"Look, Rogue," one began. "You don't have to get angry."

"Don't call me names, then," Rogue said. "I'm going ashore and back to town. Some of you have pretty big mouths as long as you don't have to bite anything. Fine. Those who are with me, come with me. If you're with these two"—he waved at Shonn and Kenn—"go home to your mothers."

He made his way to the vessel's rail, timed his leap, and vaulted to the canal bank. Boofer took a little coaxing. At last, the great hound threw himself over. He landed in the canal, then splashed water over Rogue and a dozen square cubits of canal bank. "Come on, whoever's coming," Rogue shouted. "Do we have to do it by ourselves?"

"What's the game?" one lad called.

"I'll tell you when it's time," Rogue shouted back. The fact was, even he didn't really know what stunt they would pull. He only knew it would have to be something spectacular, unheard of.

One by one, most of the gang followed their leader, some splashing into the canal's muddy water, some lighting on the bank. Even Kenn and Shonn came. "You've got a deal," Shonn said. "I've got balls enough to do whatever you do. If it shows enough spark, then fine. You're the boss. But if it's something milquetoast, then we have an election. You and me, and whoever gets the most votes runs things."

Rogue glared at him. Boofer growled. "Fine," Rogue said. "You've got yourself a deal. I hope you can live with it." He turned on his heel and walked away. He didn't even glance back, just walked toward the city with Boofer trotting at his heels. One by one, wondering what was in store, the others straggled after him.

Chapter Two:
The Temple

ONLY ABOUT TWENTY of the band went with Rogue on the walk back to Oron. The rest faded into the brush to nurse bruises and cuts. Still, the twenty made a nasty-looking band. A group of peasants walking beside a produce wagon scattered at their approach, leaving the vegetable cargo to the youths' mercy.

Rogue strode right past the wagon with Boofer trotting along beside him. A couple of youths grabbed the odd potato or tomato as they swept past, and most of them dropped the item they had taken before they walked twenty paces.

"You must have a mighty good plan," Shonn said with a snicker. He munched a carrot and looked sidelong at his tall rival.

"We'd better get off the road," Rogue said, ignoring the comment. "Those mercenaries could turn up any minute, and we don't need their hassle." He stopped walking and began to shove the fellows into the trees. "Come on, off the road."

Young men stared at him, but most headed for the trees before he had the chance to shove them. Their eyes showed puzzlement. That was the look Rogue wanted to see. In all truth, he still had no idea what he would do to best Shonn's caper— but if the band thought he had some intense plan, so much the better.

They made their way through trees and brush. Boys stumbled in the dark and swore. Some even said things under their breaths. Maybe they were cursing him, Rogue thought. It didn't matter. He didn't want to meet any patrolling soldiers.

They finally reached Oron as the half-moon began its rise out of the hills. That made the walking better. Sometimes some wealthy merchant in the city would get wind of marauding thieves, and send his housecarls to bar the city's gates. Not on this night, however. The gates stood open in the moonlight. No one moved in the streets beyond the dark entrance.

"We're where we want to be, now," one boy murmured. "No one will ever find us—we know these streets a lot better than we know the hills and roads outside."

"Wait," Rogue said. "Do you hear something?" Downhill, toward the canal basin, a low grumble traced its way to their ears. He led the group down back alleys in that direction.

The sound became louder as they made their way down the stinking streets. Human voices: shouts, screams. The din of metal pounding metal. All at once, Kenn laughed. "It's a riot," he cried. "A riot down by the basin. What a pickle we got everybody into, and we're not even there to pay the price. That's rich."

Someone else laughed. "We ought to go see," he said.

"Not on your life," Rogue said. "If everyone's there, we can play anywhere we want to. We can do something special." He turned toward his charges and grinned. Boofer grinned, too, and slobber dripped from his dog lips.

"Get rocks," Rogue shouted. He still didn't know what he was about, but a queer kind of thrill ran through him. Something grew inside him, some sense that this was a night for doing things they had never done before, never even dreamed of.

They turned away from the canal district, toward the more wealthy part of the city. Rogue didn't know these streets as well as the slums, but on this night, he didn't care. As they walked, boys kicked cobbles and bits of street paving loose, or snatched objects from the gutter. The ones who had knives fingered their weapons.

All at once, the street widened into a broad square. At the center stood a towering building, a high, looming shadow in the darkness. Even the torches that burned in brackets along the front and sides did not seem to brighten the ancient stone. All they did was send up an oily smoke that sooted the gargoyles under the eaves and made the shadows edge back and forth as if waiting for something.

Rogue's grin broadened into a grotesque leer. "Yes," he breathed. "This is the place."

Kenn stared at him. "The Local Order? You've got to be kidding."

"What," Rogue said, "are you going to shrivel up at the thought of something really major?"

"You're going to try a caper here? Those priests will have your crotch cut out."

Rogue laughed. "I don't care if they try," he said. "I don't care about anything tonight." He grabbed Kenn by the hair. "I'm in a mood tonight, and you're the one who put me there. You can come into this with me, or you can crawl away with your tail between your legs. But if you chicken out, don't ever talk to me again about class, or about what real men do."

"All right, all right. Get your hands off me." Kenn writhed out of Rogue's grip and staggered away a few steps, his feet scuffing on the cobblestones. "This isn't such a deal, after all. Throw some fruit, that's not class." Quick as lightning, he snatched an overripe tomato from one of his mates. "See this?" He whirled, and his hair flew as he hurled the thing at the high stone wall. It struck with a splat, and a dark stain smeared its way down the marble. "To blazes with you, Rogue. This is nothing."

Rogue only laughed, because he knew the other youth was bluffing. He himself grabbed fruit and garbage from the open sewer that wound its way through the dark square. He threw the objects, then grabbed a loose paving stone. He threw them all at the building like a human hurling machine. The others watched, including Kenn and Shonn. "Piss on you all," he finally yelled. "A fat lot of little flowers you are."

Shonn glared at the taller youth. Then he, too, threw a stone.

Others followed suit. In a moment, the square filled with shouting and the sounds of hurled filth splattering against stone.

A white-robed man appeared atop the high stone porch that surrounded the temple. "Here, here," he shouted. "Stop this." A wet rag caught him in the mouth, and he hurried out of sight, to the sound of laughter and jeers.

They went on until some of the youths' arms grew tired. They stopped throwing things and fell silent. The whole square went quiet then; not a thing stirred. Even the water hurrying along the sewer's course seemed afraid to make a sound.

Footsteps whispered to them; then someone else appeared on the temple porch. This was a different fellow from the first. He was taller, and his robe was a much purer white—so pure it almost glowed. He looked out at the young men, and they stared back at him. He walked toward them and turned and looked at the vandalism they had done to the building. The stones had done little, but the fruit and debris had left marks and stains all over the walls and columns.

The air lay so quietly that they could hear the man's breath as he turned back toward them. "It was bravely done," he said in a soft voice. "You have all proven your wisdom and courage. Now you will all form a line and follow me."

"Where?" Rogue asked in a brazen voice.

The man stared at him as if he had asked a very stupid question. "Why, to the place I take you. You are all under arrest."

"Kiss my dog's ass." Rogue spat, then grinned his most insolent grin. Other youths snickered.

The man shrugged. "Guards," he called softly. No one answered.

"Your guards are all off at the waterfront, in another fight," Rogue said. "We sent them there." There were more snickers from the boys.

"Very well. So much the worse for you." The man lifted his arms above his head. Something gleamed from between his hands. It was a staff, a staff so dark they had not noticed it. Now it shone with an angry lantern's glare. The man groaned, then broke into a chant in some arcane language that Rogue had never heard.

A breeze sprang up and carried the sighing sound of laughter across the square. The youths stopped their own guffaws and looked about for the source. They could see nothing. Along with the eerie sound, the breeze carried a growing smell, a stench like a million rotting fish. "Damn you," Shonn said to Rogue. "What have you got us into?"

"You'll be a coward till you're dead," Rogue shot back, then added a sound he hoped was a guffaw. But the priest's laughter and the stink chilled him to the center of his belly.

"Let's get out of here," one youth yelled. He wheeled and ran, his footsteps echoing across the square. His back faded into darkness; then they heard the sound of metal scraping on cobblestones. The youth screamed, they heard a scuffling sound, and then there was a gargling cry that was beyond a scream. The cry choked away into the night, followed by the hideous crackle of bones being crushed.

"Oh, help us," Shonn whispered. "We're all dead as mallets." He started to run and so did the others, colliding against one another in their panic. Here and there within Rogue's view, iron plates set into the square's cobblestones heaved up and black openings yawned. One youth plummeted down a hole with a scream.

From each hole slithered a huge, taloned black hand, big as a man, rising on a barrel-broad tentacle arm like some immense, charmed snake out of an unholy basket. One caught Shonn with viper quickness and squeezed him until blood squirted between the hellish fingers.

Rogue stared at the temple porch, and his eyes met those of the priest. The man stood motionless now, the glowing staff held above his head. On his face rode a look of joyous fury, and his eyes bored into Rogue's. *"I know who you are,"* the look said to the young man. *"I know how this started, and I want to destroy you more than any of the others."*

Rogue heard a sound and dodged to one side. A hand crashed down on the spot he had just left, and slime splattered his face. The hand surged toward him again, but he dropped and rolled to one side while the stinking fingers closed on empty air. He ran, but he knew it would be useless to run away. Already a dozen youths who had tried were twisted, crushed heaps lying on the cobbles.

He rushed to the temple porch, up the steps, and threw himself into the astounded priest. He knocked the man down, and the glowing staff clattered on the stone. The two made a mad scramble for the piece of arcane wood. It was Boofer who snatched it up in his great jaws and scrambled across the temple's broad landing. Rogue hurled the priest into a column and ran after his canine friend.

Along the side of the temple they ran, one after the other, their breath hot in the night. All across the dark square they could hear iron scrape on stone, could hear the monstrous slithering of the Order's minions, and could glimpse torchlight's gleam off shiny, black scales. Torn youths screamed death agony into the night. Rogue and Boofer ran all the way to the temple's rear porch, then down the steps, across paving, and between a couple of stone buildings that stood near the temple's rear entrance.

The alley swallowed them in blackness. They both ran in terror, into a lightless void where they could not even see the cobblestones beneath them. It was so black that Rogue suddenly lost his balance and fell head over heels. Boofer collided with him, and they rolled themselves into a scrambling heap that was all arms and legs.

They bounced off a wall, and something huge and stinking swept past them in the darkness. Rogue heard himself scream and struck at the darkness with the priest's staff. The enchanted wood struck something, and sparks flew. The sudden burst of light showed a huge, clawed hand looming over them, a hand supported by an immense tentacle that trailed back down the alley toward the temple. The hand snatched itself back, reared up like a cobra, then shot down at them.

Rogue held the staff pointed up, with one end against the paving. The hand impaled itself in an explosion of light, then went into a frenzy of sweeps and cartwheels across the narrow passage. Scales clattered on stone, fire gushed from the hole the staff made, and glowing silver liquid pumped from the wound like magma. The glare showed the looming buildings on both sides, locked doors and shuttered windows, and piles of garbage on the paving.

The glare also showed two more hands slithering into the alley like huge serpents. Rogue threw himself against one door but it held against his lunges. The next building had two casement windows, both shuttered. In desperation, he threw himself against one of the shutters, and it gave way. He scrambled through it, and Boofer followed after him just as the flames in the alley went out as if doused.

Rogue had no idea whether the one hand had survived the wound the priest's staff had made. He made no attempt to find out. He darted the length of the dark room, stumbled over a series of sleeping bodies, and cried out as he collided with another closed door.

Chapter Three:
The Grotto

ROGUE'S HEAD FILLED with stars, and he felt sick and giddy from his collision with the door. Someone coughed and a voice yelled, "What's going on?"

"A thief," a second voice shouted back. "A thief has broken in." The shouts turned into angry cries as Boofer trampled over the man, snatching at the trailing edge of the quilt covering him.

The room's shuttered window caved in with a crash and shards of glass flew everywhere. A black, squamous hand, smelling like garbage from hell, grabbed the first thing it touched. A man screamed, the scream choked off, bones cracked. Squirting blood splattered across Rogue's back as he fumbled with the door latch.

The latch did not give. The hand dropped one mangled body and grabbed another. Perhaps more than one hand had broken into the room; Rogue could not tell. Boofer's barking added to the crazy din. A half-dozen people clawed at the door and screamed till they all but deafened him.

In desperation, Rogue stepped back from the door and sent

a devastating kick at the wood. The latch splintered and gave way, the door swung outward, and all the people left alive in the room surged into the darkness beyond. The place looked like a starlit cave and smelled almost as awful as the hands behind him: stale bodies, foul breath, and excrement.

He stumbled and fell, and people ran over the top of him. He crawled frantically, hitched himself along until Boofer ran by, then grabbed the huge dog's long hair and used the beast as a handhold so he could haul himself to his feet.

The place was full of couches and sleeping mats. The candles and the acrid odor of the smoke told him it was an opium den, a lair for living scum and human monsters. But on this night, the humans were no match for the inhuman monsters that invaded the place.

He and Boofer stampeded through, knocking over tables, trampling smokers and sleepers stretched out on rugs. A man yelled and threw a knife at them. Another tried to block Rogue's way, but the youth bowled him over like a doll and kept running. As he reached the steps that led up to the street, he heard more screams behind him and guessed the hands were still in hot pursuit.

A stitch clamped his side as he ran down the street. The cramped muscle stole his breath away and caused him to cry out with the pain. Then he rounded the corner and yet another of the hands reared up in front of him like a monstrous serpent. He tried to stop, but his feet slid out from under him.

As he fell to the pavement, his heart sank. He had come full circle: in front of him lay the square that held the Local Order's temple. The hand formed a fist and struck down as if to smash him, but he rolled out of the way just in time. The fingers opened out and groped for him.

Boofer snarled in a fury. The huge dog launched itself at the scaly wrist, buried teeth, ripped hide and flesh. The attack could not stop the hand, but it distracted it from Rogue. The thing whirled, uncoiled like a viper, and struck the big dog, knocking him several cubits. He attacked again, harder than the first time.

This time, Boofer's teeth ripped at the web between finger and thumb. The dog's great head shook and again tore away squamous hide and flesh. But the rest of the fingers closed around the doomed animal, even as he tore at them.

Rogue's heart all but stopped. He heard Boofer's bones break even as the dog ripped one finger out at its base. The hand shook, and the whole street seemed to tremble. Liquid flowed out of the wound like molten silver. The hand dropped, and Boofer's cries ceased. The dog lay dead atop the dead monster.

Tears flooded Rogue's face. He kicked the paving. "Damn you. Damn you, damn you." He didn't know whether he was cursing the Dark Order, the hand, or Boofer for his foolish bravery and loyalty. He didn't care if another hand might catch him and smash him in his grief. Boofer had been the only real friend he had known in all the world. "Damn you." This time, it was the hand he kicked.

The hideous thing sagged and crumbled in on itself. The silver liquid stopped flowing. Then the hand dissolved completely, turning to little globules, which beaded up on the paving stones like quicksilver.

Rogue stepped back. None of it looked natural. The globules quivered on the pavement, took shape, glowed, shined, then turned into silver scorpions. They were scorpions the size of house cats, with long tails and huge poison glands on stingers shaped like assassins' daggers.

The things scrambled about aimlessly, but when Rogue ran down the alley, they scuttled after him. He ran past the endless, snakelike arm, and the scorpions chased him all the way. His steps took him back toward the temple.

Suddenly, he found himself falling. He knew even as he landed that he had fallen through the grating from which the dead hand had issued. He flailed about, rolled over, then crawled on, terrified that one of the scorpions would catch up with him.

The softness of the ground was all that had saved him from broken bones. He could tell he now was in a grotto, a huge, underground chamber, which had a glow all its own. As his eyes grew accustomed to the dark, he could see stone monuments, tombstones, even mausoleums. Every little way, from an open grave, one of the snakelike arms extended up through another grating, like the stem of some plant.

The place was a cemetery, an underground cemetery, and it was huge. It was a natural cavern with a soft floor, where bodies could be buried. Maybe that was why the temple had been built in that place generations ago. The whole thought gave him the chills.

The combined stench of blood, corruption, and death attacked his nostrils. This place was more than a huge underground graveyard. For the first time in his life, Rogue sensed evil—not just the badness of the young men he had run with, that came from unchecked anger and simple high spirits. No, this place was evil. The secrets it contained were evil.

He found a walkway paved with flagstones and worn smooth by generations of feet. He followed it downhill, all the while eyeing the blasted underground scenery. Once, as he approached within a few cubits of one of the serpent-arms, it retracted from the grating far above and slid back into the open grave from which it had sprouted, like a vine magically returning to the seed pod. As the huge, dark hand loomed into view, he quailed and looked for a place to hide himself. But it ignored him. It lowered back into the yawning crypt, and the stone cover slid back into place. Apparently, its work for the night was done.

He walked ever downward, through semidarkness. Always, the eerie glow of the place gave him just enough light to see. He could not guess how many cubits below the temple he now was.

The huge building's weight must have put an unbearable strain on the cavern's roof, because he came to a place where looming granite menhirs supported the stone overhead. It was like a great underground temple down here, too, and this was where the cold and wet and stench gripped him strongest.

He heard a blast of trumpets and dove behind a stone slab. When he peeked out, he saw lights descending into the chamber, down a central staircase carved from a pillar of pure stone. Robed figures carried torches and chanted in wailing voices as they marched toward him.

Among them, shackled by heavy chains that clanged against the stones, walked four slender figures. Rogue recognized them as members of his own gang. His heart all but stopped. He could easily be sharing their fate—perhaps even should be.

The raid on the temple had been his idea. But at that moment, no force on the shores of the Thlassa Mey could have made him show himself.

One hooded figure bellowed unknown words in a deep voice. The others replied with a new chant, then came to a halt in front of a flat stone slab. The four youths set up their own wail, a piteous sound of terror and helplessness.

"Help me," one of them cried as a half-dozen hooded figures grabbed him and stretched his struggling body out on the slab. The leader lifted a knife, a blade that looked like cunningly chipped stone rather than iron or bronze. Rogue watched in awe as the blade struck. It did its bloody work, and the young man's screams died away.

Rogue slid to his hands and knees and began to sob quietly. In his worst nightmares, he had never thought up anything to compare with this. He turned away from the rite. He wished he could be dead, but did not wish it badly enough to show himself.

Then he opened his eyes and looked up. A figure stood above him, grim and silent, with a sword lifted high. Rogue scrambled to one side and the blade clanged off stone amid sparks and flying chips. The robed man cried out in the unknown tongue as Rogue leaped and ran.

The swordsman blocked his retreat, so he bolted straight toward the altar. Three of his former partners had been executed and the fourth lay on the slab. "Come on," Rogue yelled as he charged past. "Don't die without a fight."

He grabbed the young man by the collar and hauled him after him. The maneuver so startled the priests that the two of them actually made it a little way before the howling pursuit started. Rogue pounded along the stone walkway, and the other youth ran after as best he could, chains rattling. But he could not keep up. Spears clattered off the stones, and Rogue heard the fellow scream as one struck him.

The stone tower now loomed before Rogue, but he spied an opening in the base of it. He ducked through and ran into pitch darkness, tripping over rough places in the floor, bouncing off angles in the irregular wall, picking himself up and running on like a crazy man. His body felt as if it had been in a thousand fights, as if he had been wounded over every little bit of his skin. But he did not stop.

He heard the crash of pursuit behind him, but could go no faster. Then the surface over which he ran changed and grew smooth and sandy. He ran down the slope and into water. The place felt like a beach. The water got deeper with each step until he lost his balance and fell with a splash.

Torches poured into this new chamber through the opening by which Rogue had entered. Priests spread out along the sandy beach, cursed at him in their strange tongue, then threw more spears. He swam away from them, then dived to avoid the sharp shafts.

In the depths, a sudden current pulled at him and sucked him downward. Again, he felt himself jolted off rocks until he wanted to scream. This new force sucked him through a hole, sucked him down until his lungs fought him, bursting with desire to breathe in, to breathe anything, even the water from this underground abyss.

The current shifted. As strongly as it had pulled him down, it vomited him into a new chamber like a piece of garbage thrown into a sewer. Only slowly did he understand. He had reached an underground pool that fed some underground river. He could not tell where he might be going, but it had to be better than the horror grotto he had just left.

He swept madly on, through the blackness. He did not worry about priests now and did not worry about the hands of horror or of rivalries among the members of his gang. He remembered his beloved Boofer and how the great hound had died, and he wept his own tears into the torrent. Thoughts came to him, half-dream and half-real, of the four youths who had died underground. He groaned.

But all that really mattered now was the rush of this racing river, the rocks he scraped past or bounced off, and the roar of the waters. He had no idea where he might be going and no longer cared where he might have been.

Chapter Four:
Rinna and Lissa on Artos

FAR TO THE west of Oron, outside the Narrow Strait and across the Thlassa Allas, lay a pleasant island called Artos. No cities lay on Artos, and there was only one village of any size at all. The village bore the same name as the island.

Leagues north of Artos the city, at the center of Artos the island, stood Mount Helios, which was not a mountain at all. Rather, it was a steep, pine-topped hill surrounded by lower hills. Rain washed these hills every few days during the summer, and the soil lay rich and deep. For the few farmers who lived in this region, a summer's hard work would bring a rich fall harvest.

On one farm at the base of Mount Helios lived a young woman named Rinna. She laughed often, cried on occasion, and wondered at least once a day about love. She had lived only sixteen summers and had never experienced that emotion, at least not in the form poets sang about.

Rinna loved her parents, of course. She loved to walk among the pines and birches of Mount Helios and listen to the rattle of the leaves and the creak and groan of the swaying trees. But she did not seriously know any young men, not eligible ones, at any rate, and she knew for a fact that she was missing the best of what that emotion had to offer.

She could wait. Her father and mother kept telling her how young she was, so she granted herself the luxury of at least a couple of years to wait for love. If it did not arrive by that time, then she would call herself an old maid and live the rest of her days in misery.

The night that found Rogue fleeing through the streets of Oron found Rinna crawling cozily into her bed of straw. The bed sat in the farmhouse's loft and was a favorite sanctuary. Many times had the canvas-covered straw, her down pillow, and her wool blankets heard the secrets of her soul.

There were no secrets on this night, though, only smiles. Tomorrow would be a glorious day. She and her best friend, Lissa, would take a basket of food to Owras, who lived on the north slope of Mount Helios.

For all that the day behind her had been pleasant and the day ahead of her promised to be even better, bad dreams invaded her sleep. Wild, hairy beasts tore at her with long fangs. She and her mother and father fled, but the beasts with their fierce eyes blazing pursued, knocking down the farmhouse where she lived and uprooting trees.

She tossed and rolled and thrashed at the blankets that covered her. All at once, when it seemed she must release sleep entirely, she heard the bell-like laugh of a young woman. A soft palm laid itself across her brow and the fierce dreams faded. "Sleep well, O human child," a woman's voice said. "No matter what may threaten, I will guide and guard thee."

After that vision, Rinna's sleep became peaceful. When her eyes opened in the morning, she found herself lying on her stomach with her head buried beneath her pillow. She yawned, stretched with her arms and legs, then reached up and pulled the pillow away. She felt wonderful, except that something heavy pressed down on the small of her back.

She looked over her shoulder and saw a round black head with two huge, yellow eyes that gleamed back at her. "Oh, it's you," she said. "I hope you slept better than I did, Fuzzy Waddles."

Fuzzy Waddles, being a cat, did not reply. Its mouth gaped in a huge yawn as it stretched, unlimbering claws that looked like small daggers. It was slate gray, almost black, and spectacularly huge. It was supposed to live outside—Rinna's parents didn't approve of cats inside the cabin—but it often climbed up to her window and slept in her bed. But it was *so* heavy. Rinna's back ached from its weight. She made an impatient sound and shoved the pet off the bed.

Fuzzy Waddles hopped back onto the bed and lay down against her leg. It gazed at her out of its silent yellow eyes as she spoke to it. "If you want to get into trouble, it's your business," she said. "You know Father doesn't allow cats in the house." She stroked its smooth back. It purred and rolled over so she could rub its belly.

The shutters stood open at either end of the loft. It surprised her that any cat as heavy as this one would climb that far just to sleep with a human. A playful smile lit her face. "Were you the one who spoke to me in my dream? Are you here to protect me? If you are, Sir Cat, what is it you're here to protect me from?"

The cat only looked at her out of its yellow eyes as if she were the most foolish thing in the world. Just then, her mother's voice sounded from below. "Rinna, you'd better get up. I've cooked you breakfast."

"I'm coming," Rinna said. The cat grudgingly walked to the foot of the bed as she sat up. "Will you let me pick you up?" she asked. The cat did let her pick it up. Its weight was a comfortable burden as she carried it to the nearest window. "I don't know how you got in here," she said as she set it on the windowsill. "But you'll just have to go out the same way. Father will hang your hide on the wall if he finds you up here." She petted it again, and its back arched against her palm. "He'll probably hang mine next to it."

She dressed and went down to breakfast. The cat must have gotten to the ground somehow, because it leaped up onto the kitchen windowsill as she ate. Her mother knocked it off a few times, until it finally stayed outside. That made Rinna sigh. She knew all the farm's cats were supposed to stay outside and catch mice, but this cat was so handsome and so friendly, she wished it could be an inside pet.

After breakfast was over, Rinna's mother gave her two baskets covered with muslin. "These are for Owras," the woman said. "This one has pastries and a skin of last fall's wine. There's also dried beans for him. This one has a ham your father cured, along with a skin of water if you two get thirsty. I know they're heavy, but when Lissa gets here, she can help you carry them."

At that instant, a knock sounded on the farmhouse door. "Hello, hello," came a voice. "Is anyone in there?"

"You're just in time, Lissa. I'm just giving the baskets to Rinna." Rinna's mother lifted the door's bar and in walked a sixteen-year-old girl, exactly Rinna's age and height. The newcomer looked a bit slimmer and her hair shone a degree lighter, but her face was not quite so fair as Rinna's.

"Good morning, cousin," Rinna said. "Here, take this basket. It's heavier." She handed Lissa the basket with the ham in it.

"You old hag," Lissa said with a smile. "You always make me carry the heavier one."

"I don't either. And you're more of a hag than I am."

"Foof."

"Skeek."

Rinna's mother smiled at the two girls. They always talked to one another that way. "Get along, you two," she said. "Owras is waiting. You can argue while you carry those two baskets to him."

As soon as they stepped outside, the gray-black cat came walking along the side of the house and rubbed up against Rinna's leg. "What in the world's that?" Lissa said. "It looks big enough to eat someone."

"It's just a cat," Rinna said. "It climbs through my window at night. We're friends."

Lissa laughed. "Cats don't climb through windows."

"This one did. It's my pet."

"You better not feed it or let it into the house," Lissa said. "Your father will kill it. He hates cats, I know."

"I may not feed it or let it into the house, but it's my pet, all the same."

"What do you call it?"

Rinna looked down at the cat. "I call it Fuzzy Waddles, that's what."

"That's silly," Lissa said. "You can't call it that. It's a silly name for a pet. I can tell you've never had one before."

"It's not a silly name," Rinna said. "You've never had a pet, either, so how do you know what's a good name and what's a bad one?"

"Foof," Lissa said.

"Skeek."

They walked along beneath the sun of Artos, joking and laughing and playing with the cat. When they got tired and thirsty, they stopped, sat down beneath a shady tree, and drank some of the water Rinna's mother had given them. All that time, the cat stayed with them and let them pet it. It didn't seem to mind which one did the petting. But it stayed by Rinna's side when they walked, like a dog on a leash.

Their pace slowed as they started up the tree-shrouded slope of Mount Helios itself. Sweat popped from their smooth foreheads, their banter slowed, and Fuzzy Waddles looked so hot and miserable that Rinna finally picked it up. The girls took turns carrying it, along with their baskets.

They were all out of breath by the time they reached the stone fence that marked Owras's cottage. On the other side of the fence they saw the old man working away in his garden. Once Rinna had asked her mother why he didn't just live on things grown in his garden, instead of eating the food people brought him.

"He doesn't grow food in his garden," Rinna's mother had said. "He grows herbs to heal sickness and cure hurts. Now, don't ask any more questions, just do as you're told."

What Rinna and Lissa both barely understood was that Owras was not like the rest of the people who lived on the forested highlands of Artos. He was a very wise old man, and people often came to him for counsel. It was not just Rinna's parents, or Lissa's, that visited either. Several other families they knew also sent him food and asked his advice. Sometimes the old man performed marriages or funerals, too.

On this day, he had taken off his brown robe and spaded his herb garden in baggy leather breeches and a linen tunic. Sweat poured off him just as it did from the two girls. "Well, well," he cried when he saw them. "It's my two princesses, come with good things to eat. Come in and listen to a story or two. The gate's not locked." He drew a handkerchief from his breeches and wiped his face. The skin had gone all ruddy with his work, making his long beard look as white as snow.

"You should move off this mountain," Lissa said as they pushed the gate open. "It's too hard to climb up here."

"Ah, no," Owras replied. "Hard work is good for you."

"It's not either. Look at you. You look as if you might fall down dead any minute."

Owras laughed until his thin shoulders shook. "That won't happen. I'm old enough, I should have died long ago. But I just don't have the time."

"You don't mean that," Rinna said. "You always have time to tell us stories."

"That's because storytelling is important." He frowned and looked over Rinna's shoulder. "What's that?"

"Oh." Rinna set her basket down and lifted Fuzzy Waddles in her arms. "It's my pet."

"A cat? It's a monstrous large one."

"It's friendly, though. And smart, too."

Owras and the feline eyed one another. "It is handsome enough," Owras said. "All the same, I'd just as soon it stayed outside my cottage. Cat hair makes me sneeze."

"That's all right," Lissa said. "We can sit in your garden." The two maidens didn't really like Owras's dwelling, because a lot of it consisted of a cave. Long, long ago, he had found the hollow half-concealed behind trees. He had just built a stone front on it.

"Suit yourself," Owras said. "Now, what have you two princesses brought me? I always like to see you—not just because you're lovely, but because your mothers are the best cooks on this island."

Lissa smiled. Even more than Rinna, she loved to be told she was pretty. "I have a ham for you," she said. "And some beans."

"And my basket has wine and some pastries," Rinna said.

"Mother told us we could help you eat lunch."

"Oh. I don't see why you should—can't you get beans at home?"

"No," Rinna said with a laugh. "She meant the pastries."

Owras smiled. He was always teasing the two. "I don't know about the pastries. They may be too good for someone as young as you."

The two maidens knew his teasing for what it was. The three of them laughed and bantered as they walked to a corner of the garden that looked out over a steep slope. They could sit on a bench Owras had built here and see all the way down to the sea, leagues away.

The three of them sat down, talked, and Rinna opened the pastries. They tasted rich and flaky and crumbled in the mouth before the pieces melted away on the tongue. Inside, each one held a dab of berry filling, just enough to tantalize. The two maidens gobbled them down so rapidly that Owras managed to get only a couple. "Here, here," he finally said. "How can you two eat so fast?"

"It's easy," Lissa said. "You just put them in your mouth and chew."

"Well, stop it," Owras said huffily. "They're almost all gone, and you two won't bring any more for a fortnight. You've each had a half dozen already."

"I'm sorry," Lissa said, blushing. She put down the pastry she had been lifting to her lips. It was, indeed, her seventh. "Foof."

"Oh, dear," Owras said. "I didn't mean to sound angry. It's just that I'm jealous, you know. At my age, those pastries turn to lard about the middle. At your age, they turn into curves young men like to look at."

"Then it's all right," Rinna said brightly. "You need us to eat them all up for you."

"No, it's not all right. You can get your mother to make more, and I don't know how to make them."

"She won't make them just for us."

"All right, tell her I said for her to make some for you so I can keep a few of mine. Is that fair?"

Rinna smiled. "That's fair. Now tell us a story."

"Yes," Lissa said, forgetting her earlier shame. "A story with princes and knights in it."

"Very well," Owras said. He took a sip of wine from the skin and began a story, one of the many endless tales he told the two young women. He did tell of knights. He told of nobles and courts and gentle heroes and brave heroines. The stories all had lessons to them, the two knew that. They knew instruction in proper behavior was the reason the old man told them. But the stories were so pleasant they loved to hear them anyway.

When the story ended and virtue had triumphed over evil once more, Rinna leaned her head on the back of her hand and smiled up at the old man. "That was wonderful," she said. "The places you tell about are so beautiful. Has there ever been such a place in the world?"

"Does it matter?" Owras said with a smile.

"Of course. I'd like to know."

Owras leaned back and looked up at the sky. "It might be a place that once was, or a place that someday will be. They're both the same."

"That's silly."

"But they are. The past and the future are one and the same as far as you're concerned."

"How can that be?"

Owras looked at her. "My little princess, there are at least two reasons, maybe more. But if I tell you those reasons, you'll swallow them down as quickly and as thoughtlessly as your mother's pastries. Then, just as quickly, you'll forget them. Go into your mind and into your heart, journey there as far as you can—and find the reasons yourself."

Rinna looked down at the endless sea and frowned. "Skeek."

"Owras," Lissa said. "Why do so few people live on this island?"

The old man smiled. "Because most people live somewhere else."

"Then why do you live here? Why do we?"

"Ah, you pursue your question well." Rinna was usually the one who asked the hard questions. He looked slowly from one young woman to the other, then back. "You are both very young and very beautiful," he said. "You were born into a world which is ancient—and which holds much ugliness." He pursed his lips and paused. "If you ever lay eyes on strangers among our little community of farms, you must run up this mountain and tell me without delay."

"But you didn't answer my question," Lissa protested.

"Oh, yes I did." He rose and put on a businesslike face. "But it's time for you to go. I'm an old man and there's a lot of work for me to do. Give my best to your parents and thank them for all the wonderful gifts."

He took the food out of the baskets and handed them back to the two young women. "By the way," he added. "Tell your parents they need to come see me in person. They haven't been up here in a long while. As for you two . . ." He smiled and tousled Rinna's hair. "You two sweet maidens must climb this mountain and enchant me again, soon."

Rinna and Lissa rose, for they knew the visit had ended. "We won't be away too long," Rinna said. "We promise."

"That's good," Owras said. He went with them as far as his garden gate and watched, a wistful smile on his features, as they started back down the rocky path. The huge black cat walked haughtily beside Rinna, its thick tail stuck straight into the air.

Long after the two maidens had returned home and night had fallen, Fuzzy Waddles stayed awake and lurked in Rinna's parents' garden. Like any cat, it loved to lurk. But as the sun set and the stars spread across the night sky in a smear of diamond brilliance, the animal stretched lazily and walked toward the cabin. Its feline eyes easily made out the track its claws were starting to wear into the wooden wall below Rinna's window.

Suddenly, its eyes flared, its back arched, and it spat furiously. A broad, black shape flapped down from the night sky, with leather wings and lizard scales. The cat's ears lay back. The thing leered at the cat and black, rubbery lips pulled back from needlelike teeth.

Too quickly for eyes to follow, the monster leaped onto the pet. It covered the squalling, writhing form like a dark, doughy blanket until the cat became still. Then it seemed to turn liquid, to flow into the cat through every opening. A moment later, Fuzzy Waddles stood once more, and continued on its way toward the house. The pet looked just as it had before.

Chapter Five:
The Stranger

THINGS WENT ALONG as they always had around Rinna's home. Warm, moist breezes blew across the spring fields. Rains fell, her father plowed and weeded, and her mother cooked and washed. Rinna had many chores, but she also had time to cavort with Lissa and to teach Fuzzy Waddles to do tricks. It really was a remarkable cat. It could count, for one thing, and she had never had to train it to do that. It would look at her when she spoke, as if it knew exactly what she was saying. And it came into the loft to sleep with her each night, though it did not always stay until morning.

Rinna's father took sick one day. Not terribly sick, just a runny nose and a rash, and he was tired all the time. He worked in the fields despite that, which was like him. Still, the sight of him sniffling away at night with his feet propped up in front of the hearth unnerved Rinna. He had never been sick a day in his life. Then Rinna's mother took sick, too. She plainly felt too poorly for cooking. When the next time came for the two maidens to take food to Owras, Rinna's mother made only biscuits instead of the fancy pastries the old man loved.

Rinna and Lissa felt well enough, however. On this day, they took a new route to Owras's cottage, a path that led down along the beach, then up the steep hillside to his cottage. It would be hard walking the last couple of leagues, but they were young and did not mind, especially as long as the climb lay well before them.

The beach sand lay warm under the sun, so they pulled off their sandals and walked barefoot. They laughed and sang songs and danced in the waves that rolled up from the Thlassa Allas. Fuzzy Waddles looked disgusted with all that nonsense and kept to the uppermost part of the beach, where the water was sure not to come.

All at once, Lissa stopped. "Look, there's something lying by the water," she said.

Rinna looked. A long, dark shape lay far up the shoreline, at the water's edge. A wave would push it up the sand a little way; then it would slide back down the slope. It had the loose, floppy look of something dead. "Ugh," she said. "Probably a dead fish, or maybe a seal."

"I don't care," Lissa said. "I want to look at it." She ran along the shore and Rinna walked after her. Fuzzy Waddles walked down from the edge of the grass, too, to help investigate. When they got close, Lissa let out a cry. "Oh. It's a man."

"It can't be," Rinna said. "Where would he come from?" But when she caught up, she saw that it was, indeed, a human being, a man somewhat older than themselves. When they rolled him over, they saw that salt water had matted his hair and reddened his skin, and white crusts of salt had dried all over him. He wore leather breeches and a thick leather jacket, studded with iron plates.

"Armor," Rinna said. "Leather armor, I've read about it. He must be some kind of warrior."

Lissa beamed at her. "You mean like the warriors Owras talks about?"

"Maybe. And I think he's still alive."

"Yes, he's warm, isn't he? And handsome, too. This is wonderful."

The face was, indeed, comely, though the man was older than either of the two maidens. He had reddish brown hair, and a few days' beard covered his jaws. He looked to be tall, broad of shoulder, and his arms bore the burning from much time spent in the sun. "He's barely breathing, though," Lissa said.

"Let's roll him over and get the water out of him," Rinna said. "It's a miracle he isn't drowned." They dragged him up the beach, rolled him back onto his stomach, then rubbed and worked at his back as best they knew how. He only stirred enough to cough up a little water and mucus. The eyes did not open, and his breathing did not improve.

"We have to save him," Lissa said. "What are we going to do?"

Their heads lifted and their eyes met across the prostrate form as the same thought came to both of them at once. "Owras. We have to fetch Owras down here." Like two gazelles, they were up and running along the beach, sand flying from their heels. Up the steep path they flew, mindless of their bare feet, laughing with excitement. Owras would save the stranger, just as certainly as the sun would set and then rise again. Then the mysterious man would owe the two maidens his life.

"I think I'm already falling in love with him," Rinna said. "I wonder if he's a warrior from some far land, or maybe a shipwrecked mariner off some treasure galley."

"He's not yours, he's mine," Lissa said. "I saw him first."

"So what. I was the one who knew he had to have the water drained out of him."

"Some job of draining you did. All he could do after that was throw up."

"Throwing up was good for him just then. Shows what you know."

"Foof."

"Skeek."

"It doesn't matter," Rinna said with precise logic. "He's beautiful and he came from some faraway place, so we just have to save him." Having agreed on that point, the two redoubled their pace up the rocky path and finally arrived at Owras's gate, panting from the hard climb.

They did not bother rapping at the door, as they would normally have done. Rather, they barged right into the cottage. The inside of the place looked black compared to the brightness outside, and the air smelled heavy with spices and incense. The soft shadows stopped the two until their eyes adjusted. A shadowy form rose from its knees, turned, and faced them. It resolved into Owras, his face white and angry. "Why do you interrupt my prayers?" he asked.

"We're sorry, we're sorry," Rinna replied. "But there's a man washed up on the beach below us."

"A stranger," Lissa added helpfully.

"A stranger?"

"Yes. He's just about drowned, but you have to save him."

The old man pursed his lips. "Very well," he said after a moment. "You did the right thing. We have to bring him up here, right away."

"But he's all the way down at the beach," Rinna said.

"And he's a very large man," Lissa added.

"We'll deal with that, we'll deal with that." Owras rubbed his beard and glanced between the two. "And you left your baskets in your haste, didn't you?"

"Well, yes, we . . ."

"We left them so we could climb the path faster," Rinna said.

"Ah." Owras nodded. "That was for the best, wasn't it? Let's hurry then. We don't want your stranger to expire, and we don't want any of your mother's wonderful cooking to go stale." He hurried them outside, dragged open the door of a small shed, then rolled out a barrow. "None of us happens to be very brawny, so this might come in handy."

They started down the path, taking turns pushing the barrow. Its wooden wheel creaked and rattled off rocks and left a trail in wet places as they went. "I suspect this will be heavier on the way back up," Owras murmured.

"It'll be worth it," Lissa said with a laugh.

"What does that mean?"

"Oh, well," Lissa said. "I don't know. I just said it to be saying something."

"Is that right?"

Rinna shot Lissa a dirty look. "It just means he's come from some faraway place. Surely he'll have some wonderful tales for us."

"If he hasn't drowned," Lissa said.

"Oh, I see." Owras frowned. "I'm sorry to say this, my fine young princesses, but I didn't grow so old without learning a little. You two are young and you're pretty and you want to explore all of life's mysteries as quickly as possible. That can be dangerous."

He looked straight down the path as he spoke. "There's a man down there. Perhaps he's comely. You two don't have any boys in your life out here, do you? So you want to explore this strange new man the same way an explorer would explore a new island."

"That's not true," Rinna said.

"Oh, yes it is, and you know it. You've come to an age where your body tells you magical stories—stories an old tale-teller like me can never match. Your bodies give you ideas and entice you into things. That in itself isn't bad. It only shows that you're developing into young women. But remember, the body is a trickster—it will lie to you whenever it wants something. Strangers can be bad. Strangers among us can threaten our very existence."

"We couldn't just let him drown," Lissa said.

"That's true. You did the right thing in coming to me. But you must know, if this stranger threatens me or the people I serve—most of all, if he threatens the two of you—I will destroy him the way a cook would destroy a cockroach."

Rinna stared at him. "What are you saying? You can't just kill a person."

"I didn't say I'd kill him. All I am saying is, don't try to make friends with him."

Neither Rinna nor Lissa said anything. They did not look back at Owras as he spoke, and they did not look at one another. Each kept her own counsel as they walked down the path beside the old man.

They came to the beach, and Owras did not try to push the barrow out onto the dry sand. Rather, he left it in the shade of a tree, and they walked to where the body lay. It had not stirred since the two maidens had left it.

Owras knelt beside the man and felt the arms, legs, and

throat. He rolled the limp form over and studied the face. "This is bad," he said softly.

"He won't die, will he?" Lissa asked.

"I don't know. He's very close to it. Did you drain the water out of him?"

"All we could."

"You did well." He rolled the body back onto its belly and began working the arms and rubbing the back. As he worked, he looked up at the two maidens and his expression softened. "You two did very well, really. It's always good to save a life, even if you don't know just whom you're saving. It's a very pure instinct, kindness to strangers. It shows a high and pure nature in both of you."

The two smiled but did not speak, so he went on. "It's just the harsh time we live in that makes me so suspicious of this man. In better times, there would have been no stern words for you, no lectures. Still, times are what they are, and we must be careful."

Rinna nodded and dropped her eyes. "We will."

Owras wore a packet at his belt, a little pouch like a richly embroidered coin purse. He opened it and pulled out the thick leaf of some plant. He crushed the leaf between his fingers until they were wet and smelly from the juice, then held the pulp under the man's nose. The fellow coughed, then groaned, but did not open his eyes.

"He's in bad shape," Owras said. "These leaves would revive most anyone. Let's get him into the barrow and haul him up to my cottage."

The three of them worked like galley slaves to drag the body to the barrow and dump it in. As an afterthought, Owras also took along the two baskets of food, which the maidens had once again left on the beach. The three of them took turns pushing the heavy load up the steep path, stopping several times for breath.

"This is the hardest I've ever worked in my life," Lissa said at one point, mopping her brow with her sleeve. "I hope he's rich or a prince or it won't be worth it."

"Most likely, he's neither," Owras said dryly.

Rinna looked down at the half-drowned man and at the scraggly growth of beard and the skin beneath. The face looked dirty and dark from lack of air. "Please don't die, stranger," she said. "Wherever you come from, you have tales to tell and secrets to share."

"Perhaps," Owras said. "Lets get going."

After a long time, they made it to Owras's cottage. They dragged the man in and laid him down on Owras's cot. Then the two maidens found themselves banished outside to fetch water from a spring that trickled a few cubits from the dwelling.

"I know what he's doing," Lissa said. "He's just getting rid of us." Maybe that was true, too, because as soon as they brought in the pail of water, Owras sent them outside to wait. They lounged on a little patch of grass at the front of the cottage, wiped the sweat from their foreheads, and finally fell asleep.

A scream and a crash woke them up. "What in . . ." Rinna started to say. She stopped in dismay.

"No, no," a voice cried. "Not the spurs, not again. Don't, don't." The shouts trailed off into a stream of sobs.

"That's not Owras's voice," Rinna said. "What's he doing to the poor fellow?"

They leaped to their feet and ran inside, to find Owras trying to hold the stranger down on the bed. "Get rope," the old man shouted. "He's hysterical."

They ran back out to the storage shed and found a length of new hemp. By the time they came back, the stranger had writhed to the floor. He and Owras thrashed back and forth, knocking over chairs and bookshelves. "Don't," the man shouted. "Don't, don't."

"Don't what?" Rinna shouted back.

The stranger stopped fighting. His eyes popped open, and he sat up and stared at her. For a long time, their gazes met. Then he looked at Lissa, then at Owras. Finally, his eyes landed on Rinna again. "Who are you?"

"What business is it of yours?" Owras shot back.

The stranger ignored him. "I've not heard your voice before, not when I was changed, nor gaffed and dying, nor changed back. But still, you're like . . . you're like . . ." He stopped and stared again. "Who are you?"

"I'm Rinna, a maiden," Rinna said. She could see Owras's

and Lissa's faces. One showed worry. The other showed fascination and a measure of jealousy.

"Rinna, a maiden," the stranger said. "What is this place?"

"It's the cottage of Owras," Rinna answered before the old man had a chance to.

"Am I in danger here?"

Rinna glanced into Owras's eyes before she answered. "I don't know. Who are you?"

The question was the most natural in the world, yet the stranger's face looked as if it were an amazing thing to ask. "Who am I?" he said back. "Who am I? I guess I don't know."

"Do you have a name?"

He thought for a moment. "I think so."

"What is it?"

He thought again. "Geryam, I believe."

"Geryam." Rinna breathed the name. "Where are you from?"

"I don't know where I'm from."

"What are you doing here?" Owras asked in a suspicious voice.

"Where am I?"

"The island of Artos," Owras said curtly.

"I'm—I'm running away."

"From what?"

The stranger shook his head. "I don't know." He sat silently on the floor for a long time. "I don't know what I'm running from. Then again, maybe I'm running to, instead of from. Maybe I'm looking for someone."

Owras's face darkened. "For whom?"

"I don't know." The stranger shook his head and started to say something else; then an awful growling sound interrupted him. They all followed his gaze and saw Fuzzy Waddles in the cottage's doorway. The cat's eyes blazed, its back arched, and from its mouth came a cat's howling moan of pure hatred.

Chapter Six:
Priests, Cults, and Questions

GERYAM DREW HIMSELF up and felt at his side. A puzzled expression seized his face. "My sword," he said. "Which of you took it?"

"No one took anything," Owras said. "Rinna, what's the matter with that cat of yours?"

"I don't know. It's never acted that way before." Whatever its reason, Fuzzy Waddles's eyes burned like yellow flames. It didn't try to come through the door. It just crouched at the threshold and arched its back with its fur straight out, and its cries and growls made the blood run cold.

"Get it away from me," Geryam said. "Or I'll kill it. I have a right to defend myself."

Rinna ran to the door and swung it shut with Fuzzy Waddles on the outside. "You leave it alone," she cried to the stranger. "It's my pet, and if it doesn't like you, it's because there's something wrong with you." As soon as the door latched, the cries ceased. Fuzzy Waddles would usually leap into the window nearest its mistress and watch her, but this time it did not appear.

"You're not going to kill anything," Owras said to the stranger. "You're not going to defend yourself from anything, either. For one thing, you're too weak. Now lie back down before you get dizzy and fall over."

Geryam and the old man glared at one another before the stranger climbed onto the cot and lay back. "Damned cats," he said. "No one should ever have invented cats."

"Maybe, maybe not." Owras put a protective arm about Rinna's shoulder. "Then again, maybe my young princess has a point. Maybe the fault lies in you, not in the cat."

Geryam sighed as if in surrender. "All right. I'm a guest—or a prisoner. I won't make a fuss. You said you didn't take my sword?"

Owras shook his head. Lissa said, "You didn't have one when we found you. You just had the clothes on your back."

"I should have my sword," Geryam said wearily. "I'm a warrior. I should have my sword."

"So you're a warrior," Owras said. "For whom do you make war?"

"For . . ." Geryam fell into silence. "I don't know," he finally said. "For someone, though."

"Ah, for someone. That doesn't tell us much." All this time, a small cauldron of the water Rinna and Lissa had fetched had been heating in the fireplace. Owras dipped some into a copper cup and broke dried leaves into it. He looked thoughtful as he stewed the brew. "Here, drink this," he said to the man. "It'll give you strength."

Geryam took the cup and held it in one big hand. He studied it. "Can I trust you?" he finally asked.

"Exactly my thoughts about you," Owras replied. "Drink. If we wanted you dead, we would just have let you lie in the surf and finish drowning. Would have saved us the trouble of hauling you up here." He ignored the disapproving sound both Rinna and Lissa made at the idea of letting the handsome stranger perish without even getting to know him.

Geryam drank the hot brew. "Tastes like mint," he said noncommittally.

"Drink."

Geryam finished and handed the cup back to the old man. Then he lay back. "I thank you for all you've done," he said.

"Don't get me wrong. It's just that . . . It's just that a fellow doesn't wake up every day in a strange bed in a strange cottage." He looked at Rinna and Lissa. "You say these girls found me?"

"We're not just girls," Rinna said sharply.

"All right, I'm sorry." Geryam sighed. "I'm tired."

"You have a right to be," Owras said. He watched with sharp eyes as Geryam's head rolled to one side. Then a snore escaped from the stranger's lips and the old man frowned. "Rats," he muttered.

"What's wrong?" Rinna asked.

"I gave him an herb. Lactin, it's called. It'll relax his defenses and make him tell the truth. But I gave him too much for his weakened system, and it put him all the way to sleep." He pursed his lips. "There's no doubt he almost died in the surf—a man that size would have to be very weak to react that way."

"You gave him a drug?" Lissa asked.

"Yes. I want to know where he came from. I want to know what he's doing on this island. And I want to know he's telling me the truth when he talks to me."

"That stuff won't hurt him, will it?" Rinna asked.

Owras smiled. "No, little princess. I won't harm your handsome stranger. I just want to see that you're not harmed by him, either. A handsome face can hide an evil heart just as easily as a fair one." He sighed. "We'll just have to wait. He'll sleep for a time and that'll do him good. I won't try to question him today."

Just then, a knock sounded at the cottage door. When Lissa drew it open, a middle-aged man walked in. "Master Owras," the man said with bowed head. "There's a gathering in the village south of us this afternoon. A priest from the Local Order at Helios is going to speak to the people. Or so I hear—that's what the banns say. Everyone's supposed to be there."

"Faugh," Owras said with a disgusted face. "What have I to do with any Local Order?"

The man took off his cap and rolled the fabric between nervous fingers. "All the folks thought . . . well, we don't want you to get into trouble. Besides, we thought you might want to know what the Order was up to."

Owras stood in thought a moment. "There might be something to that," he finally said. "And I suppose there are no concerns here to keep me from going."

"What about him?" Rinna gestured toward Geryam.

"He'll be just fine. He's going to sleep for a while, that's all. No need to watch him." He rubbed his chin. "Though it might do to make sure he doesn't go anywhere after he wakes up." He stepped to a chest on the far side of the room, rummaged around in it, and drew out a set of shackles. Despite protests from the maidens, he brusquely shackled one of Geryam's ankles to the bed frame.

"That's mean," Lissa said.

"Not mean, just careful. I want to know everything in this place will be here when we get back." With that, they put some of the maidens' biscuits into a bag, took a flask of water with them, and left.

Only on the pristine island of Artos would such a little place have seriously been called a village. Three or four cottages nestled about a common area, and a little smithy stood off to one side. A maypole on the common doubled as a meeting place on fair days, and soldiers sometimes posted notices there in hopes someone would read them.

It took half the afternoon for Owras, the two maidens, and the old farmer to reach the place. By the time they got there, two or three dozen people had gathered. All except Owras were plainly farmers. They looked at one another with puzzled eyes and concerned faces while they waited for the official speaker who was supposed to come.

Rinna's parents had come, too, even though all could see they were not healthy. Rinna's father's face had turned pale beneath his tan, and her mother had lost weight. "Karral and Emm," Owras said with a look of concern. "You don't either of you look well."

"Something that's going around, I guess," Karral said. "Makes it hard to do the things I have to do." He shrugged. "These things happen, but I'll be glad when we're all over it." He and Emm spoke awhile with Owras. The old man promised to brew a helpful remedy and send it to them as quickly as possible. After that, the old man spoke to several other people.

After a while, a train of horsemen rode into the crowd. They wore dark leather armor covered by heavy iron studs that looked like starbursts. "Mercenaries from the mainland," Owras muttered. "The Local Order hires such men to crack heads because the priests know how much their message is really worth."

"Be careful," Karral said. "They might hear you."

Owras grunted. At the center of the horsemen, eight bulls pulled a heavy wagon, which rolled along the rutty road like a ship at sea. It finally groaned to a stop, one of the soldiers pulled aside a curtain, and a heavyset man in white robes climbed to the ground. A murmur ran through the crowd as he walked to the center of the people.

He had long since gone bald, so it was hard for Rinna to guess his age. To her, all old people—from her parents on to Owras—looked pretty much alike. But this one was not only old—he was mean-looking. He scowled as if angry at having to come on an errand he considered beneath him. A tall soldier walked with him and bent as the robed man whispered into his ear.

"Stand close and listen," the tall man shouted. "Arlogos, high priest of the Local Order of Artos, is going to speak to you. All hail the high priest, bend your ears, and learn the true word."

Arlogos cleared his throat and spoke in a high voice. "You citizens of Artos must repent," he cried. "Backsliders are everywhere, the common people fall away from the true word, and lose their souls. Strangers come and preach false prophecy. Simple heads like yours are turned by pretty words. As your high priest, I will not permit this to happen."

He spoke a long time. It seemed that a new cult had sprung up on the banks of the Thlassa Mey and he warned everyone to be very wary of it. He threatened the people with loss of their souls, confiscation of property, and even imprisonment if they were caught harboring members of this heresy. "Beware of strangers," he cried. "Beware even of your own neighbors, and beware of yourselves, lest you be false to the Order. Trust in the Order and follow us down the true path."

Owras stood expressionless through all this. In the middle of it, Fuzzy Waddles, Rinna's cat, came walking into the crowd.

It sat beside her foot and licked its paw, all the while looking as if it understood as much as anyone.

While Ariogos spoke, his mercenaries walked through the crowd and studied each face. Rinna watched them and felt glad the handsome stranger had not been well enough to come. He was plainly not from the village. His leather armor would have marked him instantly as an outsider. She wondered what people like this would do to him if they caught him. Then again, was he one of the cultists the priest was shouting about? He certainly didn't look like a person who would have something to do with any religion, let alone a cult. She sighed and decided she didn't know a thing about this whole mess.

The high priest spoke for a long time, and everyone looked tired by the time he was done. When it was over, he and the soldiers didn't just ride away. Rather, the armed men mounted their horses and roughly dispersed the crowd, shouting that they should go straight home and ponder the things the high priest had said.

"Ponder, maybe, but don't discuss," Owras said as they hurried away. "They don't want us thinking too much about all this. They just want us to follow orders."

"What do you think about it?" Karral asked in a grave voice.

Owras looked back at Rinna's father just as gravely. "I think this may soon turn into a hostile land for small people like us. The Order doesn't have much use for people who just want to live their lives and be left alone."

"Where is this Local Order?" Rinna asked. "Why don't we ever see more of them? What do they do?"

"We see all of them we want to," Owras said.

"Hush, Owras," Rinna's mother said. "Don't get yourself into trouble. We all need you."

"I'm sorry. It's just that they're more interested in gathering up gold and land and victims than they are in saving souls. If souls were all that were at stake, you wouldn't see this Arlogos fellow worrying about cults, as he calls them."

"Mother, what's a cult?" Rinna asked. "You never answer my questions."

Emm put her arm about the maiden's shoulder. "They're all hard questions, my love, and I fear you'll have more answers than you want sooner than you'd like." She looked over at Owras, because he was watching them carefully. "Owras is very wise and he can answer you better than I can."

"In due time, in due time," the old man said. "For now, it's time for you to go home and rest and be well. Send Rinna and Lissa in a couple of days and I'll have an elixir brewed for you. It might help."

"Thanks," Karral said.

"And take good care of Geryam," Rinna said.

"We'll see," Owras replied.

"Geryam?" Emm looked at the old man. "Who's that?"

"I don't know," Owras said. "But I have every intention of finding out. Fare you all well. Rinna, my little princess. I expect to see you in a couple of days." They parted company and Owras turned uphill, toward his cottage. It was a long walk, and he felt tired. He had put in a long, hard day.

By the time he reached his cottage, the light had almost faded away. He felt too weary even to cook his dinner. He would go in, eat some of Emm's biscuits, and rest a while. His weariness faded, though, when he saw the cottage's front door standing open.

He peeked through cautiously but the place was as they had left it—except for one thing. His cot stood empty in the corner of the chamber. His brows knit as he looked it over. The blankets lay on the floor, the straw tick mattress was scewed to one side, and the chain from the manacles hung limply from the wooden frame.

He lit a lantern to study the scene better, then whistled in surprise. The chain had not simply been broken. That would have been remarkable enough, given Geryam's condition. Rather, one link had been burned in half as if heated in a forge. "What have we let into our midst?" he asked himself.

He glanced about the cottage. Other than the rumpled bed and the melted chain links, the place looked tidy. He debated whether to pick up a pointed iron rod he used for hooking the kettle that hung in the hearth, but thought better of it. He was an old man. The rod would do him no good against anything that could melt chain.

He carried the lantern with him and peeked out the door. The evening had grown dark by this time and the lantern's light formed a half circle in front of the cottage. The stone wall was a shadow a few cubits away, and the shrubs looked like dark spirits.

A groan caused him to turn. He stepped toward the garden and found Geryam stirring between rows of plants. The stranger lay in a pool of his own blood, the manacle still locked about his ankle. Owras could see the burn the heated metal had caused.

"By the good gods, what happened to you?" the old man shouted.

"Horrible, horrible," Geryam said in a slurred voice. "Wings, jaws, eyes that were fire." He rolled over and coughed. "Where did you go?"

Owras studied Geryam. A deep gash had laid the man's upper arm wide open. He was lucky he had not bled to death. "We all had to go listen to a speech. Where did it go, this monster of yours?"

"I don't know. It burned me and hauled me from the cot. I struggled, of course. It would have killed me, I think, but a man fights hard when he's getting the piss scared out of him."

"Yes, I suppose. Let's get you inside, and I'll have a look at you. Can you stand?"

"I think so." Geryam made it to his feet, and the old man helped him back inside. "My head feels like someone has been dancing on it."

Owras made no answer. The lactin herb he had given the stranger was doubtless to blame for the headache. He looked the man over and found a couple more wounds like the one in the arm, only much more shallow. They looked like they had been made by a razor. "I'll give you something for the headache," he finally said. "It won't be much, but it'll help."

"Thanks."

"Maybe your warrior's training helped you against whatever attacked you."

"Fear helped me. Do you have many animals like that around here?"

"None." Owras noted that Geryam seemed just as suspicious of his new host as Owras was of him. Perhaps that was good. And the stranger seemed candid; at least he had not been afraid to admit his fear. Perhaps that was good, too. Even so, the old man had no real idea how to treat him. After all that had happened, it was hard to judge whether to protect the man or imprison him.

Chapter Seven:
Bad Tidings

AFTER GERYAM FELL back to sleep that night, Owras sat awake for a long time and studied him. All the wise old man's instincts told him the stranger's arrival on the island was no accident, that it was an event woven into place by the Fates. But to what end—was Geryam a friend or an enemy? Even Geryam himself did not seem to know.

Owras studied the slashes in Geryam's flesh. Beside the deep cuts, there were lighter ones, one in one wrist and one inside each elbow. They looked as if they had been put there by the most expert surgeon.

Owras finally fell asleep in his chair before the hearth. When he awoke, bright daylight had spread through the house and the fire burned down to embers. He stretched and found himself as stiff as an old board. "Oh, me," he said with a wince. "Tonight, I make a cot for the stranger and take my own bed back."

Geryam still slept. Owras prepared a breakfast for the man, then woke him. The old man found the stranger much stronger than he had been the day before. They ate, then Owras gave

Geryam some more tea laced with lactin. When he questioned Geryam this time, the stranger's answers never quite outstripped the new questions that flew into the old man's brain.

Geryam's condition improved steadily. After a day or two, he was able to help with chores. He acted polite though distant and made no attempt to leave. And whatever Owras's suspicions might be, he could not fault the stranger as a worker.

Two days after Geryam had first arrived, Rinna and Lissa arrived at Owras's door. The maidens looked worried. "Why, my little princesses," he said. "You're right on time. I have a nice, tart-tasting brew prepared. Your mother and father can be sipping it, gagging, and getting better by the end of the day."

"If they can sip anything," Rinna said sadly. "They're very sick."

"My parents, too, now," Lissa said. "They just keep getting weaker and weaker."

"I see," Owras said. "Then the brew I made may not be enough."

"Please help us," Rinna pleaded. "They can barely move."

Owras's face fell. "This is very bad. I'll go down with you, and we'll do all we can." He turned and looked at Geryam, who was making the morning fire. "Would you like to come for a walk? I'm sure you're strong enough, now."

"Sure," Geryam said. "I wouldn't mind seeing a little of the island."

Rinna and Lissa both looked a little happier at seeing him up and about. "My," Lissa said. "You look healthier than you did when we first saw you."

"Yes," Rinna said. "You looked all wet and sandy."

Geryam smiled back, which made both the maidens laugh. "I'm glad to hear it, then," he said. "Are you the two who found me?"

"We are," Lissa said. "You'd just as well say we saved your life."

"I thank you, then." He smiled at them, glanced between them, then turned back to his fire.

Rinna and Lissa eyed his back, then eyed each other, then looked at Owras, who had watched it all without a word. "Might have been a little friendlier," Rinna muttered to herself.

Owras hurried to lace up his boots and leggings. He fetched

a satchel and stuffed it full of herbs and drugs. Some he had grown in his garden, and some he had processed from plants he had found on the slopes of Mount Helios. He didn't really know what to take but hoped something he might load into the satchel would do some good.

When they stepped outside, they found the path blocked by Rinna's cat. As it had before, it took one look at Geryam, and its back arched and it spit and growled. "Fuzzy Waddles," Rinna said. "Don't fuss so."

"I don't like that cat," Geryam said. "I don't trust it."

"Apparently, it feels the same about you," Owras said. He bent to stroke the animal, but it hissed and raked the back of his hand with razor claws. "By the gods," he said as he put the wounded hand to his mouth. "Whatever the matter is, it's in no mood to be tampered with."

"Any cat that did that to me would be flybait in a hurry," Geryam said. His hand went to his side. His face registered surprise, then reluctant acceptance that there was no sword there. Owras marked the motion.

"Don't you dare talk mean about my cat," Rinna said. "Mister big man mysterious stranger lost-at-sea. You're not on some ship now, you're with civilized people. We aren't children you can bully."

Geryam looked at her in amazement, then smiled. "Yes, my lady," he said. "I promise I won't attack it unless it attacks me first."

"That's better," Rinna said.

"Yes," Lissa said. "That's better. I'm glad to see you're a gentleman after all."

Owras frowned. "Let's get going," he said. They started off. Geryam walked behind them on the trail and plainly avoided so much as touching either of the two maidens. He ignored the cat. For its part, Fuzzy Waddles settled down once they started walking. It frisked between Rinna and Lissa but would not even walk on the same side of the trail with Geryam.

Once they emerged onto plowed ground, they spied a posse of riders far off. The riders must have seen them, too, for the horses turned toward them. Owras kept a steady pace without turning, and in moments the horses thundered near. Owras recognized them as the guards who had ridden with the high priest of the Local Order days ago. The lead rider reined in his horse and looked them over. "I've seen you before, old man," he finally said to Owras. "What are you doing out in these fields with these two girls and this fellow?" He eyed Geryam as he spoke.

"I might ask the same of you," Owras said. "These are no more your fields than mine."

The man scowled. "I'm Erwin, marshal of the Local Order at Artos. I belong anywhere on this island I choose to go. What's in that bag you're carrying?"

"Vegetables from my garden. I picked them for the parents of these two maidens."

"Um. How about I have a look-see."

"You don't want to do that." Owras's gaze locked into that of the rider. They glared at one another for a moment, then Erwin the Marshal dropped his eyes. He looked angry but he did not look into Owras's face again.

Instead, his gaze swung to Geryam. "And who's this? I've never seen him on this island, and his clothes aren't what you'd find on a farmer." He eyed Geryam's studded leather jerkin suspiciously.

"I'm just a wanderer," Geryam said quietly. "A wanderer who appreciates the kindness these people have shown me."

"Kindness to strangers can be a mistake," Erwin the Marshal said. He swung down from his saddle and faced Geryam. Owras glared at him as if to peel the whiskers off his face, but the mercenary seemed careful not to look at the old man again. "Are you here to start trouble?"

"No, sir," Geryam said, though he plainly resented the other man's attitude.

Erwin the Marshal stood so close he actually put his chest against Geryam's. The stranger stepped back. "Strangers aren't welcome here," Erwin the Marshal said. "There's a lot of religious sedition going on. Men are out to steal people's souls and the Order's on the lookout to protect the flock. I wonder if I should put you under arrest."

Geryam set his jaw, plainly angry. But though his face flushed and his jaw worked, he stared at the ground. "I wish you wouldn't," he finally said.

"Say that again."

"Please don't arrest me."

Erwin the Marshal laughed. "You're a regular rip snorter, aren't you? I'll tell you what—you don't look as if you're even worth arresting. You don't look the type to preach false prophecy or any prophecy at all. So I'm going to let you stay out of irons for the time being." He swung back up into his saddle.

"Thank you," Geryam said.

"You'll do well to thank me," Erwin the Marshal said. He and the other horsemen laughed at Geryam. "See that you behave yourself. You won't always have those two girls and that old man to protect you." He laughed again; then the lot of them rode away with a rattle of hooves and a spray of flying clods. Geryam took a breath and watched them go. His face had gone as pale as paper.

"A fine show," Rinna said. "Mister warrior, always looking for your sword. You didn't even try to stand up to them."

"It was well done," Owras said. He put a hand on Geryam's shoulder. "I could see it was hard for you."

"What hard?" Lissa asked. "He didn't even argue with them; he just stood there. You stood up to them, Owras, why couldn't he?"

"I have techniques he doesn't have," Owras said. He advanced to the two maidens, stood between them, and took each of them by the shoulders. "Oh, my princesses, don't let's argue among ourselves. You both have good heads on you. Believe me, you'll know things someday that you don't know now. Let's go look after your parents."

Rinna and Lissa each gave Geryam a hard look. Then they tossed their heads and walked on. Rinna's cat paraded at her heels, its head and tail held as if it thought even less of the stranger than she did at the moment. For his part, Geryam sighed, shrugged, then followed.

When they reached Rinna's home, they found things had come to a sorry pass. Rinna's parents were too weak even to get out of bed. Owras examined the people and found they were not hot with fever nor marked by any pox. Rather, they looked pale, their skin was cool to the touch, and they had numerous scratches about their wrists and the insides of the elbows.

The old man scratched his head. "This is like what you had

that one night," he said to Geryam. "Only there are no deep cuts like yours, just little ones."

"But I got over it after a day," Geryam said.

"That's true." Owras pulled open his satchel and went to the farmhouse's hearth. He mixed a tonic and paste for a poultice, though he had no real faith in either. He simply didn't know what to do.

"Owras, we have to talk." It was Rinna's mother calling from the bedroom. "Bring Rinna, too."

"I'll wait out here," Geryam said. "I won't push into a family conversation."

"I'll wait, too," Lissa said.

Owras and Rinna went into the bedchamber and looked down at her parents. They looked sick enough to bring tears to the eyes: her father, once a burly, robust man, had wasted away to half his old bulk. Rinna's mother beckoned the maiden to sit at the bedside. The older woman stroked her daughter's hair, then let her hand fall. "It's time for Rinna to leave us," she said quietly.

"Mother," Rinna cried. "I can't just leave you. Not when you're sick like this."

Owras looked from one female to the other, then at Rinna's father. The man just lay silently, his breaths coming in shallow gasps. "No, little princess," Owras said. "Your mother's right. The strife we've seen lately, this sickness. It's no place for you."

"I won't get sick. I would have done it by now if I were going to. Look at Geryam—he got well."

"You can come back when we're better and things have quieted back down," Emm said. "But you must go away with Owras, and you must do as he says."

"What about Lissa?"

Owras cleared his throat. "It's for her parents to decide. But I suspect they'll agree." He gazed sadly at the two people on the bed. "One thing. I think we should bring Lissa's folks here, to stay with you. We can bring their supplies, too. You'll do better with the four of you together."

That was how they agreed, even though Rinna and Lissa argued. They quickly set out for Lissa's home with a handcart. The place was not far off, and they were soon making their way back with two more patients, plus some flour, a few barn-yard animals, and some other goods. Lissa's parents were too sick to walk, so they rode in the pushcart with the flour.

As the party forded a creek midway between the two farms, three men came riding along. They wore studded leather armor, and Owras recognized them as three of the men who had ridden with Erwin the Marshal earlier that morning. They reined in on the far side of the creek and laughed at the party, now standing in the dancing water. "Well, if you ain't a sight for sore eyes," one of the three said. "You peasants are everywhere today."

"We're not doing any harm," Owras said.

"Maybe, maybe not. How do we know what you have in that cart?"

"There's nothing there," Owras said. He glared at the man much the same as he had glared at Erwin the Marshal earlier.

But another rider spurred his horse forward. It struck Owras with a flank as it passed and knocked him onto his seat in the water. "No more of your tricks," the rider yelled. "In fact, you're coming with us. You're under arrest for practicing magic and false religion in the domains of the Local Order of Artos." He leaped from his mount and hauled Owras to his feet.

"You leave him alone," Lissa shouted. She jumped onto the man's shoulders, scratching at his cheeks and pummeling him with her fists. Rinna joined her; then the other two horsemen leaped from their mounts and joined the fight. Lissa's parents tried to get out of the pushcart, but it rolled over in the water and they had all they could do just to keep their heads above the surface.

Geryam leaped to help them, but one of the horsemen got in his way, faced him down. "Back, you dog," the man shouted. "They're all going to the cells, you with them." He drew his sword and forced Geryam back onto the bank.

"Don't even think it," Geryam said. He dropped, rolled to one side, and snatched up a fallen tree branch as he sprang back to his feet. He swung before the horseman could overcome his surprise, knocked the sword from the man's grip, then broke the branch over the fellow's head. The man fell as if his legs had turned to powder. Geryam snatched up the sword and leaped at the other two men, who still struggled with Owras and the maidens.

The men shoved their former adversaries away, drew their swords, and faced Geryam. Even two to one, though, they were no match for him. His own blade flicked like a viper's tongue, rattled off their two, then drew blood in a half dozen places. He forced them back and back, across the stream, and out onto the far bank, until they threw down their weapons and ran for their mounts. He whirled and faced the third man, who had come to and was struggling to his feet. The fellow didn't want a fight. He spread his arms, palms out, and scuttled away. Soon he, too, was on his horse, riding hard to catch up with the others.

Geryam tossed down the sword he had captured and ran back into the stream to help rescue Lissa's parents. "You've told me more about yourself with that blade than you ever did with your mouth," Owras said. "You were a warrior indeed and not just a common spear carrier."

"I suppose I was," Geryam said. He didn't seem to care about what he had done. "I couldn't have told you I would be able to do that before it happened."

"I never saw anything like it," Rinna said. She stepped toward the sword Geryam had thrown down. It lay on the ground, and Fuzzy Waddles sat beside it, licking blood from the blade. Rinna picked the weapon up and carried it back to the stranger. "Here, you should carry it from now on. It marks your station. You're not just a farmer or a sailor, you're a warrior."

Geryam laughed. "I'll not carry it, little lady," he said. "I've no scabbard to put it in."

"At least take it along with you," Lissa said.

He looked at her, then at Rinna, then at Owras. "You'd better hang on to it," Owras said gravely. "The other two, as well."

Geryam nodded. He took the blade, then bent to pick up the two the other men had thrown down. He put all three into the cart beside Lissa's parents. "You fought well," Lissa's father said. "But I wonder how long it'll be before they come back with others. Those riders have been all over this valley the last few weeks."

"They'll come back, but we won't be here," Owras said. "This is all the more reason for us to see you to Karral's farm and be on our way."

They started up again, with Owras and Geryam pushing the cart up over a low hill and toward Rinna's home. Behind the four adults, Rinna and Lissa followed at a distance and argued in whispers. "He was *gorgeous*," Rinna said. "I knew when I first saw him that he was something special."

"Says you. You didn't think so much of him this morning. You'd hardly even talk to him."

"You, either."

"I did, too. I stuck by him while you were being fickle. We sat and talked by your parents' hearth while you were all whispering away in the bedroom."

"You didn't do it because you liked him. It was just because the two of you happened to be there."

"Did too."

"Did not."

"Doesn't matter. He's a hero and he's going to fall in love with me."

"Me."

"Me."

"Foof."

"Skeek."

Chapter Eight:
More News

RINNA AND LISSA soon packed their crucial belongings into a couple of cloth packets and set off with Owras and Geryam. They bade a tearful farewell to their parents, mitigated by the promise that they all would rejoin once the two couples had gotten well enough to travel. As to where they would travel, Owras would only reply, "We will see. And we will send a message once we get there."

They struck south, toward the coast and a little fishing village Owras had heard of. This boggled Rinna's mind. For the wise old man to so casually leave everything in his cottage was beyond her belief. Surely, they would come back to Artos before long.

They did not get far before night fell. They only reached the range of hills that formed the valley's south edge. There, they stretched out their bedrolls and made camp. They lit no fire and ate only some bread Rinna's mother had sent along.

When they awoke the next morning, Rinna's hand went to her mouth when she saw plumes of smoke rising from the valley floor. "Owras," she said. "What's happening?"

The old man eyed the smoke grimly. "I was afraid of this."

"Those horsemen," Geryam said. "They came back and took revenge, didn't they?"

"More than just that. They would have come in any event."

"Mother and Father," Lissa cried. "They're down there. Your parents, too, Rinna."

"We have to go back," Rinna said. "Owras, we can't just leave them. Mother and Father and Lissa's parents, too—something awful's happening."

Owras just shook his head. "Whatever awful thing it is, it's already happened."

Rinna stared at him. "You knew, didn't you? You knew it was going to happen and you left them. Left them too sick to even walk, at the mercy of those . . . those thugs."

"Not just the ones we saw," Geryam said. "Look." He pointed downhill. On a trail below them rode a long column of men. They did not ride as orderly troops might ride, but helter-skelter, whooping and capering, each one at his own pace in his own place. "Mercenaries. Someone's hired them to burn people out."

"The Local Order hired them," Owras said.

"And you knew it would happen," Rinna said. She began to cry, then rushed to Owras and pounded on his chest. "You knew, you knew." Lissa stood and stared at them, the back of her hand pressed to her lips.

"Not now," Geryam said. "They'll see us." He grabbed Rinna and hauled her toward the center of the grove. She kicked and struggled, then finally got a hand free and slapped him. He shoved her roughly away, glared at her as though he might strike her. Her cat bristled its fur and spat at him.

Owras and Lissa hurried up. "Not now," the old man said. "Geryam's right—they'll notice us. If they do, it's death."

"What's happening to the world?" Lissa said in a sobbing whisper.

Owras's face crumbled into sadness. "Oh, my little darlings," he said. "Life is hard beyond words and you have to taste the full measure of that, now. For years, ever since you were both little girls, I've called you my little princesses. And princesses you are, though of the spirit and not of the blood. Haven't you heard the things the priest and the marshal said?

The Local Order rails against the new religion. The priest comes to investigate our village. Now they've hired soldiers to root out the threat."

"What has that to do with us?" Rinna cried.

"Shh," Geryam said. "Haven't you been listening? You *are* the new religion."

"What?" Rinna and Lissa stared at him, then back at Owras. "What's he talking about?"

"You listen well, my friend, and your mind catches my drift instantly. Yes, my princesses, you are both born and dedicated as priestesses of the true gods. Your parents dedicated you in love for the true faith, but kept all that hidden under the mantel of their farming. Long ago, before either of you were born, we worshipers traveled to this island so we could escape the Order where we lived. It took them a long time to find us, but they have."

"This can't be," Lissa said. "We're just girls."

"Not quite," Owras said. "You are one with the beings of the earth. You are one with the beings of the heavens. You will ask the hard questions, you will seek the hard truths, and people naturally follow you. You've neither one of you ever felt special—special people never do. But all who know you have seen it."

"And now the Order's out to get you," Geryam said softly.

"And you just let my parents be killed?" Rinna cried. Again, she struck Owras, then fell to her knees before him in a sobbing mass. For her part, Lissa stood and watched dumbly, as though in shock.

Owras knelt beside her, soothed her, stroked her hair. "Ah, my darling, my little one, it was as it had to be. Your parents knew, and Lissa's as well. They knew the Order had found them, knew it was practicing magic on them. They were doomed, all doomed, and they knew it. Perhaps the mercenaries killed them, perhaps not. It doesn't matter. You two are all that matters."

Now Lissa began to cry. Geryam stood by, embarrassed, while Owras comforted both the maidens. He spoke many soft words, held each of them in turn. Geryam walked to the edge of the grove and kept a lookout for soldiers.

At last, Owras pulled the two maidens to their feet. "You

have a right to each tear, my princesses," he said. "You have a right to mourn. But you must also live, and to do that, we have to travel. So put tears away for a while, for we have to hurry south. The soldiers will look for us and they will surely find us if we stay here."

Rinna and Lissa did as he said, though they moved like sleepwalkers. They picked up their things and set out again, and by afternoon they had traveled far to the south. As they walked, they met a few people they knew, who had been burned out. By the end of the day, the total party numbered over twenty people.

Neighbors they soon met confirmed the awful truth: both maidens' parents had perished in the raid. Many others had died, as well, and when the pilgrims at last made camp that night, the whole scene was one of mourning and misery.

Owras, the maidens found out, was old and wise and very learned. He was a priest of the true gods. He could speak the truth to men and women, but he could not hope to receive guidance from Hestia or any of the other twelve great deities. One had to be born into the priesthood and dedicated to Pallas or Hestia or Artemis or another of the Twelve to do that. And that was the fate of Rinna and Lissa, their fate since birth, even though they had never suspected it themselves.

How could it happen? How could they live lives, sing, dance, and hope, and never dream of what they were being trained for from the time they first learned to speak and listen? They talked of it together in low whispers, staring into each other's faces with uncomprehending eyes. But their conversation was punctuated by long silences and confused sighs.

For all their own griefs and cares, they found themselves thrust into the unfamiliar role whether they understood it or not. Pilgrims, refugees, whatever one called the people who had lived in the valley, they all needed comfort and guidance through that next awful night and day. The two maidens found themselves listening to the troubles of people they hardly knew, found themselves comforting men and women older than their parents. They, in turn, went to Owras for advice, until the old man was also frayed to the last nerve. It was a tough time, indeed.

Through the next day, the party trudged south, one foot before the other, exhausted and mindless. They hardly had any food, and they watered themselves at every stream they crossed. When prayers were needed, it was Owras who gave them. The two fledgling priestesses had yet to learn how.

Worse, a couple of the pilgrims woke up weak and dizzy. When Owras looked them over, he discovered marks in their arms like the marks he had found on Rinna's and Lissa's parents. The only ones he told about this were the two maidens—he even kept the information secret from Geryam. "This is serious," he said. "Let me know if you see anything the least bit strange, especially at night."

"How will we know?" Rinna asked. "We posted a watch and he didn't see anything out of the ordinary."

"That's what worries me," Owras said. "It's all very strange. Maybe this is just a sickness, or maybe it comes somehow from the Dark Order. Either way, it's serious—perhaps a disease that could wipe us all out, or at least make us so weak the mercenaries can catch us and kill us. And if it's the Order's work . . ." His voice trailed off into a troubled sigh.

"What about Geryam?" Lissa asked. "Maybe you could have him keep a special lookout."

"I haven't told him," Owras said.

"Why not?" Rinna asked.

Owras hesitated. "I still can't be sure about him. In fact, he did have the watch for a while last night. There's still so much I don't know about him—and most of that happens to be things he doesn't even know himself." He shook his head. "I shouldn't burden you two with this—you've already got more on your shoulders than is fair. But to me, he's just another part of the puzzle. How can I give him extra responsibility when he might be part of the problem?"

"If he works for the Order, why didn't he just kill us when he had us alone?" Rinna asked. "From what we've seen him do, he certainly knows how."

"That's a very good question," Owras said. "But I know he's hiding things—that much I know for sure. How can I trust him when I know that?"

Rinna nodded and sighed. "That's a good question, too." The conversation ended, and the three of them went back to their labors, sorely troubled.

Owras did not assign Geryam any part of the watch that night. The stranger eyed the old man as if surprised, but said nothing. He shrugged his shoulders, unrolled his blanket, and stretched out on the ground with the other pilgrims. Beside him, he kept one of the broadswords he had taken from the riders.

For her part, Rinna curled up beneath her blanket and closed her eyes. But she could not get to sleep. She felt Fuzzy Waddles lie down beside her leg like a lead weight to hold the blanket down, but even that did not comfort her. She lay for what felt like ages, squirming to keep away from hard spots on the ground, tossing her head back and forth, the events of the past days marching to and fro through her brain.

Her constant movement must have been too much for Fuzzy Waddles. After suffering repeated shifts of position, it finally stood, stretched, and walked off into the darkness. Finally, after a long time, Rinna fell asleep.

Almost immediately, it seemed, screams woke her up. As she sat up and stared about, she realized that what she heard wasn't screaming at all. It was the cat. "I caught you this time," a voice roared. "You'll never do that again."

The campfire had burned low, but there was still enough light for her to make out Geryam, tall and broad-shouldered against the smoky glow, clutching her cat by the scruff of the neck. "Fuzzy Waddles," she cried. "What's he doing to you?"

"I'm going to kill it, that's what. It bit me clear to the bone."

"No." Rinna screamed, and threw herself against Geryam. The man staggered from the impact, then shoved her so hard she fell onto her rear. For its part, the cat seemed to need little help. It twisted, spat, and squalled, and when Rinna distracted Geryam's attention, the beast tore at the man's forearm with teeth and claws. Blood spurted everywhere, but Geryam did not let go.

Geryam snatched his broadsword from the ground even as he clenched his teeth from the pain of the cat's claws. By now, everyone in the camp was awake, and the place was chaos. Just as Owras came running up, the cat finally tore itself free and Geryam struck it with his sword.

The blade described a glittering arc against the darkness as it met the cat's black fur. The blow should have cut the animal in half, but it only spun as if struck by a stick, then landed on the ground. Again, Geryam slashed at it. This time he pulled back a blade that was bloody and knicked, but the cat scrambled away across the ground.

Rinna and Lissa were both tearing at Geryam's neck and shoulders by this time, pummeling him without mercy. Still, he swung at the cat one more time as it tried to get away. Then laughter filled the air, laughter as cruel and taunting as a demon's mirth. "Stupid, stupid man," a high-pitched voice giggled. "You only postpone your fate. You hurt me, hurt me, you did. But you'll bleed enough for it before I'm done." The voice went faster and faster, then merged into a high-pitched squall.

The cat grew before their eyes and turned into a hideous shadow. Teeth became curved fangs, silver against the darkness. The body grew till it was the size of a big dog, and wings sprouted from the back. The eyes turned into glowing holes into hell.

"You're all as good as dead," the voice screeched. "I'll drink all your blood before I'm done." It rose onto its hind legs, flapped its demon's wings, and lifted into the air. The force of those wings blew into their faces like a gale, scattered into the fire, and sent sparks everywhere. Some people cried out in pain as coals lit their clothing. Others coughed from the smoke that blew into their faces.

"Fuzzy Waddles." Rinna choked on her own astonishment.

"It was the cat all the time," Owras breathed as the wings' steady beat faded toward the south.

For his part, Geryam knelt on the grass and clutched his forearm. Blood streamed from beneath his fingers. "He left me plenty to remember him by," he said through clenched teeth.

"Quick," Owras cried. "Get bandages. Bind his wounds."

People scattered in every direction. Rinna grabbed Geryam's sword and used the blade to hack at her own petticoat. Shock still made it hard for her to speak. "I'm so sorry," she managed to say. "I never dreamed . . . I mean, you were trying to kill it, and it was just a cat. Just a cat, a little pet." The sword dropped from her fingers and the torn tassel of petticoat trailed away over the grass. She buried her face in her hands, sobbed, and slumped to the ground.

"Hush, lass," Geryam said in a voice soothing as a caress. "You couldn't have known. Who could've?"

Lissa wrapped her arms around Rinna's shoulders. "No one could have known. By all the gods, how could we be in such a world?" Her own lower lip quivered and tears traced her cheeks.

With the last drops of wine from a skin Owras had in his bag, the old man washed the crisscrossed lines the claws had left in Geryam's arm. Geryam grimaced from the pain. Then the old man wrapped bandages about the muscular arm. Blood soaked through the first layer, so he went back over it. "How did you find out, Geryam?"

"I caught the little bugger," Geryam said. "Opened my eyes and there it was, licking away at me. It'd sliced me with a claw, I guess, just like before, and was licking the wound, using me for a drinking cup, you might say."

Owras stopped wrapping and stared at him. "The way you were wounded the night after we hauled you off the beach," he said. "That was it, too."

"I remembered it all when I woke up and saw it drinking me," Geryam said. "Remembered why I hated it so much, and why I was afraid of it, too. It'd tried to kill me. It'd hauled me outside."

"How?"

"It was big, then. Just as when it flew off. Only you came back, and I guess you scared it away."

Owras sighed. "You're a mystery to me, Geryam. Mysteries follow you like a dog on a leash."

Geryam looked at the old man with a blank face. "I'm a mystery to myself, too."

"It's not that easy. You're hiding things. You always have hid things."

"Easy, old man. If you think I had anything to do with that animal, you're crazy. That thing hated me even more than I hated it. My life is mine, I don't ask you about your past."

Owras looked as if he was about to say something unpleasant, but he thought better of it. "Let it rest. You're wounded, and we need to treat you, not argue with you."

Every pilgrim in the camp had gathered around by this time, along with Rinna and Lissa. Owras turned to a couple of them. "You. Fetch my satchel. You. Build up the fire, fetch water, and set it boiling. This man's wounds aren't serious—yet—but they need prompt attention.

"As for you," he said to Geryam, "lie back and try to sleep. You need rest—you're the one real warrior among us, and we can't afford to lose you."

"Sure," Geryam said. There was no real telling what he meant by the single word, but he lay back and closed his eyes. Rinna brought her own blanket and put it over him.

"Take care," Owras said to her. "There's still a lot we don't know."

"Oh, Owras, isn't there anything in this world we can be certain of? I thought Fuzzy Waddles was the most pleasant, the most harmless pet in all the world. Please don't tell me I can't trust Geryam either."

"I don't know what to tell you," Owras said. "But I do know I'm going to find some things out about him this night, or I'm going to get very weary trying."

"What are you going to do?"

"The lactin again."

She looked at him. "Why should that work? It's never worked on him before."

"The one time I gave him a strong enough dose to loosen his tongue, he was very weak and it just put him to sleep. After that I just tried weak doses, which couldn't do much at all. Plainly, he's strong enough now, and I'll find out what he's hiding if I have to boil down every leaf in my satchel."

"Please don't hurt him."

"You needn't look so frantic about it. The worst it could do is put him to sleep again and leave him with a nasty headache in the morning. Either way, it'll help his wounds heal. But here comes my satchel." He took the satchel, left her side, and knelt beside Geryam again. "I'm going to make you some of the potion I gave you when you first came, a strong dose. It'll take time, but it'll be worth it."

Geryam nodded at the words, but he did not say anything.

Owras stood and whispered to Rinna and Lissa. "Keep him company while I'm brewing the stuff." He smiled a wry smile.

"I've seen the way you both look at him, so I'm sure you won't mind."

"I feel like a traitor," Lissa said.

"It'll do him no harm if he's a friend," Owras replied. "And if he's an enemy, we have to know. Don't worry, it's on my shoulders, either way."

The two young women nodded. They walked to Geryam and knelt one on each side of him while Owras made his way toward the campfire. A couple of pilgrims had filled a small cauldron with water and suspended it from a tripod over the flames.

Chapter Nine:
Fish and Fancy

THE UNDERGROUND TORRENT swept Rogue along, pummeled him without mercy, bounced him off stones, and scraped him through narrow passages. More than once, he had no doubt he would drown. Each time, he managed to get his head into an air space, coughing and gagging, and sucked down enough precious wind to survive for a few seconds more of the torture and tumult.

Then the torrent hurled him through one last hole like spit between two loose teeth. He felt himself rising through some broad, warm body of water. He wondered for an instant whether he had simply died. Then he broke the surface, where the feel of waves and the taste of salty water told him the underground river had carried him to the sea.

His arms had grown so weak he could swim only a few strokes. That was enough to carry him up against a shore of rock that stood above the gentle surf the height of a man. He felt too dizzy, weak, and battered even to attempt a climb out, but he found the water shallow enough to wade. The footing felt rough and treacherous, but the night was calm, the sea all but flat, and he was able to make his way to a stretch of sandy beach.

He knew he was on the shore of the Thlassa Mey, but could guess nothing more. Were the mad priests of the Local Order still after him? He could not begin to guess. But even if they were not, he knew they would be hunting him before long. The underground river could not have carried him beyond the Dark Order's reach, he knew, even if he had spent a day and a night in the torrent.

He plodded along the water's edge for a long way; then a dark shape loomed before him. He circled around it, but found another, then another. Fishing boats they were, drawn up on the sand, just beyond the reach of high tide. He slumped against one of the dark, stinking hulls, exhausted. He quietly sobbed because he felt so weary.

He heaved himself over a gunwale and into the bottom of one boat. The decking felt polished by years of feet and nets and scaly bodies. The smell of fish seemed to have soaked into the wood's grain, and he guessed that even if the hull burned, the ashes would still stink. It didn't matter. He crawled to the boat's stern, where the hull was decked over and rolled nets and a sail were stored.

He pushed the heavy sailcloth out of the way and crawled back under the decking like a tick crawling under a rich man's collar. Hide, his mind screamed. Hide where they'll never find you. He crawled clear back to the boat's transom. Then, although the air was close as a crypt and reeked of fish, he fell asleep.

He might have slept a wink or a day or a year, there was no telling. He slept without dreams, and ever after, he would never be able to swear he had even kept breathing. When he finally did wake up, it was because he felt himself getting wet.

Water lapped at his sides and his ears. He tried to sit up, cracked his head on the decking above, and almost cried out in panic before he remembered where he was. Then he lay back and kept quiet. The boat's rolling motion told him he was at sea, and he could hear feet moving along at the vessel's waist.

He lay there and listened for a long time. Again, it might have been a day or even a night and a day. Sometimes the water in which he lay would rise to the point he feared he would be forced out; then the fishermen would man a bilge pump over his head, and he would be almost dry for a while.

The boat seemed to stay at sea forever. Hunger gnawed at him; then the rolling of the boat made him so sick he could not even think of food. He faded between wakefulness and sleep, starvation and seasickness for what seemed an eternity. He grew so famished that he felt as if he could eat the very planking of the deck above him, so he finally crawled from his hiding place.

Night had fallen. The fishermen had stepped the mast and raised the sail, but the canvas hung limply in the dead air. A lantern hung from the mast and thumped against the smooth oak with each roll. Rogue could make out a pair of bodies sleeping in the bow. "I say," a voice cried. "What are you doing here?"

Rogue wheeled about, fell on his rump, and found himself staring up at another man, who had apparently been manning the tiller at the stern. The fellow stood and yelled, "Farrel. Kael. Wake up, we've got a stowaway."

Rogue's instinct was to silence the fellow, but between the boat's rocking and the time he had gone without food, he could not even stand. When he tried, he pitched forward onto the deck and landed at the helmsman's feet.

"Not so fast, you," the fellow shouted. He dodged to one side and picked up a piece of wood the length of a man's arm. "I'll take a club to you if you want to get frisky."

Rogue lunged at him again, but the man dodged to one side and brought the club down on the deck with a whack. "The next one'll be on your skull, my friend. I can bash the life out of a shark with one swat from this thing—gives the last rites, it does—and I'll bash the life out of you if I have to."

Rogue tried to rise to his knees just as two men piled onto him from behind. They pinned his arms behind his back, ground his face into the hardwood deck, and one yelled, "Get some line. Tie his wrists." They wrapped cord around his wrists and cinched the knot tight without mercy, until Rogue cried out.

"Don't like it, do you?" the helmsman said. "Well, don't show up on our boat in the middle of the night. You won't do it again, will you?"

"Untie me, you fool," Rogue yelled. "I'm not going to hurt anyone."

"No, you're not," the man called Kael said. "Because you can't."

"Who is he?" the one called Farrel asked.

"Who cares?" the helmsman said. "From his clothes, he looks like a street tough. Let's just throw him over the side and have done with him. No one'll ever know."

"Oh, Leek, hush," Kael said. "You're always talking big."

"Cut him up and use him for bait."

"Kael's right," Farrel said. He knelt and peered into Rogue's face. "What are you doing on our boat, stranger? You'd better tell the truth because we don't have time for games."

"I was hiding."

"From who?"

Rogue's mind raced. "Street toughs, like he said. I wouldn't go along with them—they were too rough for me, they wanted to rob some people."

"All right, that's enough," Kael said. He grabbed Rogue by one leg and dragged him toward the gunwale.

Rogue kicked and struggled. "What are you doing?"

"Putting you over the side. I told you I didn't have time for games."

"I'm telling the truth."

"Sure you are. Grab him by the arms, Farrel, and let's put him over. Leek was right in the first place. Make him into shark feed, no one will ever know."

"Let me bash him first," Leek yelled, waving the priest.

"Wait, all right," Rogue cried. "I'll tell you. Oron's Local Order is after me."

"Say, what?" Kael asked.

"The Dark Order. They're trying to kill me."

"I'd rather have him telling us lies than a story like that," Farrel said. "What do we do with him now?"

"Put him over the side anyway," Leek said. "Then the Order'll never know we had anything to do with him." The club hung at his side, and his face showed shock, even in the feeble light.

"We can't—we don't know what they might know or might

not know." Kael slumped onto the deck. "Oh, me. If that's the truth, then why did you have to pick our boat to hide in?"

"No wonder we've had lousy luck," Leek said.

"We'll have to go back in when it gets light," Farrel said. "We'll have to turn him in."

"Piss on the lot of you," Rogue said. "Is that what you'll do, give me back to the Order after I nearly killed myself getting away from them? I've been under their temple, I watched them cut my friends' guts out just for fun. If you're going to give me back to them, you might just as well throw me off this stinking tub the way you threatened."

Kael looked at Rogue. "Stars above. You're that afraid of going back?"

Visions of that awful night still filled Rogue's head. He slumped against the gunwale. "Don't take me back. Anything but that."

"We can't keep him," Farrel said hastily. "He's bad luck. Besides, someone might find out."

Just then, the fishing boat shook as if something had bumped it from below. The prow swung about, and the craft heeled over until the three fishermen staggered. "The nets," Kael said. "Something's in the nets."

"I'll swing out the lantern," Farrel said. He unleashed the boom that supported the ship's lantern and swung the light out over the water. The light gleamed off endless bright flashes that rolled like a silver river just beneath the sea's surface. "Bonny chubfish," he cried. "Big ones, and there's a million of them."

"Man the windlass and pull them in," Kael said.

"What about the stowaway?" Leek said.

"Leave him. He won't go anywhere and we have more important things to do."

So Rogue lay tied in the bottom of the boat and watched the men labor to bring in the net. In moments, an avalanche of gleaming, wriggling fish the size of his forearm poured into the craft, spilling over his legs and coating the planks with their slime. He wriggled to get away from the creatures, but the fishermen ignored him. They emptied the net as quickly as they could, then let it out again. Again, it filled with fish until the boat heeled over. Again, they winched it in and emptied their catch into the boat until Rogue was all but buried.

Two of them finally grabbed Rogue under the arms and hauled him out from under the pile. Then they went back to their labors and brought yet a third netful of fish in over the side. "We can't haul any more in," Kael shouted. "We'll founder ourselves."

"Look at this," Farrel shouted back. "We've never filled this tub in so short a time." They laughed, whooped in glee, and clapped one another on the backs. "A glorious catch, and all of them beauties," Kael said at last.

Rogue lay there and watched them celebrate their catch. At least it was good he had crawled out from belowdecks. Had he stayed down there, he would have been trapped, probably smothered, by the mountain of fish.

"Hey, what about the stowaway?" Kael finally said. "Maybe he's not such bad luck after all."

"Not now that he's showed himself at any rate," Farrel said. "We might hang on to him for another day or two."

"We don't dare take him back to the mainland anyway," Leek said. "We've got to head for the nearest land. This boat'll swamp if a wind comes up."

"I'll turn her about." Kael clambered over the mountain of fish and made his way back to the stern. He manned the tiller while the other two reset the sail. The vessel slowly swung about. A gentle breeze came up, and they ploughed through the gentle sea. By looking at the stars, Rogue guessed they were headed south.

Kael pulled a whetstone out of a pouch in the bow. The three men pulled their knives from their sheaths, took turns spitting on the stone, and sharpened their blades. Then they set about cleaning fish. Rogue marveled at the deft way each grabbed a fish, smashed its head against the gunwale, then slit it open and dumped its guts into the sea. They did it all in one fluid motion. The cleaning emptied the animals enough that the pile shrank noticeably.

They worked at the endless task until the lantern began to flicker. Then they refueled it and started up again. After a long time, the sky off the boat's port side began to glow. Rogue lay and watched. Even though the smell of slime and blood overpowered his senses, he felt as if he would perish without something to eat or drink. "What about me?" he finally yelled. "Are you just going to let me lie here and croak on you? I haven't eaten or had a drink for days."

Kael stared at the youth as if noticing him for the first time. "Oh, you. Tell you what—can you clean fish?"

"I don't know. I guess I can learn."

"Here's an extra knife." Kael used the blade to cut Rogue's bonds, then handed it to him, handle first. "Get to work, then we'll talk about food and drink. And no funny stuff—you're weak, outnumbered, and I can tell you don't know how to get about on this boat."

"You can't give him a knife," Leek said.

"Don't worry about it. He brought us good luck, and maybe he can help get these things gutted." Kael looked back at Rogue. "Now get to work."

"Can't I at least have something to drink?"

"Work first."

Rogue picked up one of the fish. Most of them had long since suffocated in the boat, so at least he didn't have to worry about how to kill the thing. But the knife felt large and clumsy in his hand, the belly scales stood up against the iron blade like plate armor, and the fish flopped in his hand almost as badly as if it had been alive. He finally did manage to cut it open, rip some of the insides out, and throw them into the water. By this time, the air had come alive with seagulls. They squawked, dodged and whirled in the lantern's light, or just bobbed about on the water and wolfed down the banquet of fish parts.

Rogue threw the badly cleaned fish onto the pile and picked up another. "Ow," he yelled as the knife's keen blade dug into his hand. The blood flowed over his wrist and mixed with the fish blood already there.

"For the love of anything," Kael said. He dropped the fish he was cleaning and took Rogue by the hand. "You're just about helpless, aren't you?" With a deft motion of his knife, he slashed the sleeve from Rogue's shirt and bound the hand with it. "Sit there. No sense having you clean fish tonight if you're going to kill yourself doing it."

The man stepped to the bow and brought back a wineskin. "Here," he said, and offered it to Rogue. "You just as well take a drink. When you get done, you can start salting the fish we've gutted. The wine may not make your hand feel any better, but at least you won't slice it off."

"Thanks," Rogue said huskily. He tilted his head back and drank deeply. The wine was the first nourishment of any kind to pass his lips in days, and it fell into his empty stomach like a load of rocks. Still, once he had begun, he could not stop drinking until he had drained the skin. He handed the empty container back to Kael. "I needed that," he said.

"I can see," Kael said. He threw the empty wineskin back into the bow. "The salt's stacked in the bow, too," he said. "Get a bag and start rubbing it into the fish we've gutted. We'll make landfall in a few hours, but it won't hurt to get a head start on the job."

Without a word, Rogue stood and made his unsteady way toward the front of the boat. But the rocking made him dizzy. His feet turned numb, then his calves, then his thighs. Weariness, hunger, and wine seized him like a chicken snatching a bug. His head filled with clouds and he collapsed on the deck.

Chapter Ten:
The Old Prophet

WHEN ROGUE WOKE up, he found himself lying in the sand. A warm sun beat down on him, and his clothes reeked of fish. He coughed, rolled over, and sat up. Kael, Farrel, and Leek labored like ants uphill from him, where grass sprouted from the dunes. This was apparently an old base for them, for he could see a weatherbeaten shanty and row on row of wooden racks for drying the fish in the sun. The wood was polished to a shining silver from endless use.

Kael glanced in his direction. "I see you're back among the living," the man said. "Are you finally ready to become useful?"

"Where are we?"

"We're on the island of Kolpos. Our fathers dried fish here before we were born. I suspect we'll do it till the day we die and then our sons will take over after us. Pitch in, and we'll give you something to eat."

"Fish?" Rogue made a face.

"Without a doubt. But it's salted down and smoked in our smoke pit. We may not eat anything but fish from the sea, but

of those fish, no king eats better than we do." He shrugged.
"It's up to you. If you want to starve, you can always do that.
You won't find friends on this island—the Order is strong
here."

Rogue sighed, then stood. He joined the others, rubbing salt
into the moist flesh of each fish, then hanging them on the
wooden racks to dry beneath the summer sun. Salt got into the
cut on his hand and it hurt like sin. Still, he learned quickly.
By day's end, he could salt as well as any of the others, though
his hands had turned redder. The cut eventually stopped hurting.

As for the smoked bonny chubfish they gave him, he was
amazed at how good they tasted. He ate until he was ready to
drink down a wellful of water. They refused to give him any
more wine, but showed him the water of a little freshet that
danced down to the sea not far from there.

So it was that Rogue became a fisherman. Kael, Farrel, and
Leek fished off Kolpos's shore for several days. During that
time, Rogue learned much about the fisherman's trade. He
learned to dry and repair nets, he learned to clean the fish and
hang them in the sun, and he even learned a few things about
handling the fishing boat. It was backbreaking work, this fishing. Still, he had broad shoulders and few years to weigh him
down, so he adapted well.

He even learned to eat fish: dried, baked, smoked. The
beach and the sea seemed as foreign as another world to him
after a life spent on the poorest streets of Oron. The only fish
he had ever eaten before had been what he and his friends had
stolen from vendors' stands.

Drying made the fish lighter, so the boat could haul three
times as many dried fish as it could hold when they were
fresh. Once they had caught all they could carry and the drying
was well begun, the fishermen had to return to their home port.
"You're free to go with us," Kael said to Rogue. "You're a
strong lad, and you catch on fast."

"Besides," Farrel said, "you brought us the best luck we've
ever had."

"Smashing good luck," Leek agreed.

"That's right," Kael said. "So it all comes down to this:

you'll always have a job with us if you want it. There'll always be a boat willing to take you on."

"Thanks," Rogue said. "But I don't dare go close to Oron. They're after me there. You don't know what it's like once you've offended the Order."

Kael shrugged. "No, I don't suppose we'd know about that. But that was something you chose to do and we don't mix with that sort of thing."

"What are you going to do if you don't go fishing with us?" Farrel asked.

"I don't know," Rogue replied. "There's a city on this island, isn't there?"

"Clear on the south end," Kael said. "It's a long hike."

Rogue shrugged. "Doesn't matter. I've come a long way already. I guess I'll hike south and see what turns up." He looked about. The beach and the waves were all the world he knew outside Oron. "I'll find something."

"Help us load our catch, then," Kael said. "We'll give you some smoked fish and a skin of wine."

"Oh, sure. *Now* you let me have wine." They all laughed, and Rogue helped them as they started loading their catch into the boat. They stacked the fish in like cordwood, row on row of bonny chubfish, mackerel, and ling. They stacked the first night's catch lowest in the hold because it was driest, then the others above until the freshest lay on top. It took most of the morning. When they were finished, less than a cubit of the gunwale remained above water.

"Be careful," Rogue yelled. "Don't swamp that thing."

"Don't you worry about us," Kael yelled as the tide drew them toward open sea. "We'd rather sail home with a boat full and risky than a boat empty and easy."

Rogue laughed, waved one last time, then watched as the little vessel set sail and plowed north toward the horizon. When it was just a dot, he stood, picked up the packet the three fishermen had made for him, and started up the dunes that lay beyond the beach.

Beyond the dunes lay leagues of grassland, and beyond that were rocky hills and a carpet of trees. He knew the wild olive trees because of the fruit they produced, but city lad that he was, he could name no other kind. Still, he enjoyed walking through the forest, whistling and listening to the birds, which seemed to whistle back.

He had gone quite a way when he realized the only sound in the forest was himself. The birds had stopped singing, and the squirrels had stopped chittering. Even the breeze seemed to have stopped blowing. His pace slowed; he looked about, suddenly alert. Even though he had spent his whole life in the city, his instincts told him what the changes meant: danger.

He stepped into the shelter of a tall pine tree and fingered the dagger the fishermen had given him. He did not even know what he was watching for: large animals, evil men, or even a posse of the priests who had pursued him in Oron—nothing would have surprised him.

What he did hear surprised him, though. Someone was singing softly at first, then growing louder in tones that wafted up the hills and between the trees. It was a song of celebration and joy, interspersed with handclapping and the sound of a stick being rattled against tree trunks. "Hark, the solstice comes apace, The days are long and full of grace, Eat bread and drink the merry mead, 'Tis time the flesh and soul to feed." Rogue had heard that song on feast days in Oron, but had never dreamed he might hear it in this forest.

He circled behind the tree that sheltered him and never stopped watching down the hill. At last a man appeared, a strange, crazed old figure who wore flowers and twigs in his hair, a breechclout and mantle made of filthy rags, and white hair and beard both so long they swayed as he danced along. "Celebrate a winter's night, Let mirth and spirits bring aright, All things that pass from year to year, Let sorrow change to song and cheer."

Rogue could only scratch his head at this apparition. The old fellow must have noticed the motion, because he stopped and stared at the tree where Rogue hid. "Bless me," he said. "Is somebody there?" Rogue did not answer, but the old man must have possessed some sixth sense. Laughter shook him all over and he danced toward the young man's hiding place. "You can't fool me," he said gleefully. "I know you're there."

Rogue looked about wildly, but there was no way for him to haul himself up into the branches or run away without being seen. Besides, it seemed crazy to run away from this funny figure. "All right," he said impatiently. "I'm right here. What does it matter?"

The old man's white hair had drifted into his eyes. He parted it and peered at Rogue. "Why, there you are," he said happily. "I don't know what it all means, but you're a pleasant-looking fellow."

"Me?" Rogue said. "Pleasant-looking? You must be blind."

"You're just the kind I'm supposed to find."

"Supposed to find? For what?"

"The Brethren send me into the woods to find people." The old man looked puzzled. "Don't know why they want me to do that, really. But I do it—and I'm good at it, if I do say so myself." He chuckled.

"I'm leaving now. I don't want anything to do with your brothers or whatever."

"You don't have any choice," the old man said. "Once I've found you, they'll find you, too. It always happens. They say I'm their prophet."

Rogue looked at him narrowly. "You with the Dark Order?"

"The what?"

"The Dark Order. The church."

The old fellow laughed gaily. "Youngster, I *am* the church, that's what they told me. But the church of the brothers, not any particular order. We're all equal as squirrels scampering up a tree." He laughed again, and turned a pirouette in front of Rogue. "Up a tree, up a tree, ti-ra-la-la. Say, *that's* a question. Do you climb trees?"

"If I have to."

"Good plan. Get you closer to heaven."

Rogue felt ready to tear his hair out. "You're crazy," he said.

"Indeed, I am. Crazy as a bedbug. Crazy as a loon. Crazy as a cat in catnip. Crazy as a bug in batter. Crazy as a mouse in ale." He laughed and laughed. "But it works. I'm happy. Better than that, I'm the Old Prophet and I know the Way."

"Fine. What's the Way?"

The old man sidled up to him with a glint in his eye, and stood up as though to whisper into Rogue's ear. "Search me," he said in a whisper. "But it always sounds good to say it— gets your attention. Here, now, the Brethren will come along any time now and they'll explain it all to you." He reached out and pinched Rogue's arm. "Oh, my, you'll do well."

Rogue pushed the Old Prophet away. "Stay back," he said, and drew the dagger the fishermen had given him.

"Put that down," the old man said in a stern voice. The sound rang through the forest, full and brassy, nothing like the tones the old man had used before. Without thinking, Rogue let his hand droop to his side. "Oo, you liked that, didn't you?" the Old Prophet cried. "You'll make a fine member of our church. Hale and hearty you are and broad of shoulder and thigh. You could use a little more fat on you, but times are strained." The old face turned cunning. "You'll be a welcome addition to the body of the church, yes you will."

"I'm not joining your stupid church," Rogue shouted so loud the leaves nearly rattled. "I just want to find some town on this stupid island."

"Too late, too late. I hear the Brethren coming."

Rogue could also hear the sound of something moving through the trees not far away. "The induction ceremony will begin as soon as they get here," the Old Prophet said. "In fact, I have salt with me, so we might just as well get started." He drew a little pouch from inside his flowing robe. He sprinkled what looked like salt over Rogue's head.

"I don't want your salt, I don't want your ceremony," Rogue said. He flinched as a couple of salt grains lit in his eye. "Stop that. What's that for?" Though he had his hand over his face, he heard bodies moving toward him. The footsteps broke into a run.

"The salt? Can't take you into the Brethren without salt. Parsley, too, and garlic."

"This is crazy."

"You foolish fellow. What better way for you to join the body of a church? Now, you just hold still . . ."

"You're crazy. Your church is crazy." Rogue knocked the Old Prophet down before the old fellow could finish. Through his one good eye, the youth glimpsed a half-dozen men running toward him, faces gleaming with religious zeal. They all looked as crazy as the old man or worse: they wore robes that were more rags than cloth, their faces filthy as stable sweepings, and they had hair and beards that swung with every step, they were so long.

He burst between a pair of them, running so hard he knocked them down when they tried to grab him. Because of the salt in his eye, he could barely see. He couldn't tell how many there were. He stumbled on a fallen log and went down hard, but scrambled to his feet before they could catch up with him. "Get him," one shouted. A rock struck Rogue between the shoulder blades and knocked the breath from him.

"Don't do that," the old man shouted. "You'll hurt him."

Rogue ran like the wind, leaping stones and stumps, arms and legs pumping wildly, breath coming in gasps. They all looked nutty. Were they really as crazy as they looked? It really didn't matter—he only knew he wanted nothing to do with them.

He paid no attention to which direction he might be going, just thudded over the hilly ground as the sound of pursuit faded behind him. At last, when he could hear it no more, he slowed.

He sank to his knees, his chest heaving like a bellows. A little stream danced between the trees downhill from him, so he rose and staggered toward it. He knelt, drank, then used the pure waters to bathe his irritated eye. It quickly felt better, and he looked around. He had no idea where he was now. The forest looked dense in this area; thick canopies of leaves blocked out the sun until the place looked dark as a basement.

Leaves rustled up the hill from him and he heard a rough voice say, "He came this way. See how the leaves are kicked up?" He didn't wait to see who was coming. Instead, he took off once more, like an arrow shot from a bow.

He ran like the wind along the stream's course, then leaped the little waterway and took off up the hill. These men seemed to be expert trackers, so he would be more careful this time. He would put plenty of distance between himself and them, then take to the trees to throw them off his trail.

A fallen log lay ahead of him. He leaped it with room to spare, but his feet struck the fallen leaves on the far side and the ground gave way. It fell in beneath him and he plummeted into the void beneath. He struck the bottom of the hole, and his momentum carried him against the far side, all at the same time. The blow drove the breath from him, he saw stars, and the smell of moist earth filled his nostrils.

Chapter Eleven:
Geryam's Tale

THE MOON SET, and the night grew dark as the inside of a cave as Owras sat before the fire and boiled his serum. At last, he poured the steaming brew into a stone cup and brought it to the place where Geryam lay. The stranger had dozed off by this time, but he stirred and his eyes opened as Owras knelt beside him. "Oh, there you are," he said. "Am I supposed to drink that?"

"Yes," Owras said. "The girls will help you sit up."

Geryam's brows knit. "I don't need any help. I'm not cut up that bad."

"You don't know that for sure," Owras said as Rinna and Lissa each held one of the warrior's strapping shoulders and helped lift him. "That was no knife or sword or spearpoint that cut you, it was the claw of a magic beast. Probably a servant of the Dark Order. None of us can know what mischief those wounds might cause."

"I suppose," Geryam said. "Well, that stuff did help me sleep last time. And my wrist hurts like sin. So serve away, and much good may it do me."

"There's a good lad," Owras said with a little smile all his own. He handed Geryam the cup and watched as the stranger drank the liquid down to the last drop.

"That's a stout brew," Geryam murmured once he had gulped down the last steaming swallow. He lay back down. "I'd forgotten how hard it hits a fellow." He tried to hand the cup back to Owras but missed the old man's hand and dropped the cup into the grass. "I feel dizzy."

"It'll pass," Owras said. He exchanged glances with the two maidens. "Do you feel well?"

"I feel, well . . ." Geryam swallowed. "Hardly anything," he finished.

Owras gestured toward the two maidens. "Cover him," he whispered. As they fetched extra blankets and pulled them over the drugged man, Owras dabbed the broad forehead with a cloth. "You're sweating."

"Is that so?"

"Aren't you glad to be with us?"

"I don't know," Geryam said dreamily. "You have troubles, it looks as if you're in real danger. That's the way it's been everywhere I've ever gone. But you're decent." His speech slowed and he closed his eyes for an instant. It looked as if he might fall asleep.

"We're decent?" Owras asked, plainly to keep the man speaking.

"Decent. Yes, you're all decent people. And I've been in more danger than this. That makes it all easy, doesn't it?" He smiled and chuckled to himself.

"Where have you been in danger?"

"Oh. Here, there. Other places. I shouldn't even be alive, by all rights. Who knows? I have my mission to perform, that's all. That's why I'm alive, not because I deserve it."

"What's your mission?"

Geryam's eyes fluttered open, and he gazed up at Owras as though he thought the old man was a silly fellow. "To find him, of course."

"To find whom?"

A pause followed that question. "I'm not sure. How can I remember when I don't remember?" He looked about dreamily. "How, how, how. I keep wondering how it all happened to someone like me. He transformed me, you know, and she transformed me back, and I have to confront him. That is the mission—there was the lesson and the mission, and that is the mission."

Owras exchanged glances with the two maidens once more, then sighed. It would take a long time and many questions to get to the bottom of all this. But while the maidens watched and listened in fascination, he set to his task. Bit by bit the tale unfurled, a tale as strange and terrible as any the old man had ever heard. And it was a tale still incomplete, because there were many things Geryam himself honestly did not remember.

He had been a warrior somewhere, that much was certain. He told what it was like to sleep in a barracks with straw on the floor, to get up in the cold or the heat, and to wear the same sweaty leather armor day after day. He had followed the mercenary trail. He talked about street riots he had suppressed, bandits he had chased down and caught, and fights he had broken up in wealthy churchmen's foyers. But he said little about pitched battles between armies.

He talked about cities, but never named them. Owras could recognize some of the places by Geryam's mention of a noble's name or a landmark. Many, however, he could not guess. That didn't matter. The point was, Geryam had served many masters in many places. And he mentioned enough details of enough fights, enough techniques he used to save his own life or take the life of another, that any listener would have known him as a master at his trade.

Then there were the women, more women than masters and cities together, women almost beyond number. He had been young and strapping, tall and reckless. Women had looked on him as misers looked on money, and he had enjoyed his share. He entertained them with stories, then by playing on the lute, then by pleasures of the body. Owras looked uneasily at Rinna and Lissa as the drugged Geryam mumbled sensuous secrets, but the old man did not send the maidens away. They were as deeply involved with the stranger as he himself was, and their paths were linked. It was just as well they heard every sordid detail and knew with whom they dealt.

There was one woman in particular. Geryam called her Nyala, but he wasn't even sure that was her name. She was tall, and had auburn hair, an insolent smile, lithe muscle, and green eyes. Her laughter on the outside hid the anger that festered on the inside—and that made her dangerous to any man.

That was all the same to Geryam, though. He never saw any woman as a danger to him, because he allowed none to mean enough to him for a danger to be posed. Nyala was one more conquest to him, albeit a young and lively one. He knew he was not the only man in her life and knew she had a husband. He did not know the husband's name, nor did he care. On the nights she came to him, she was available, and they could laugh together at the poor fellow they were cuckolding. That was all that mattered.

The affair mattered much to the husband in question, though. He was, it turned out, a priest high in the Local Order and rich in secret lore. He ordered Nyala packed away into some cell in some hidden place, there to pass out her remaining days in lone anguish. Geryam he had arrested and brought before him, bound and naked.

The priest was an older man, tall, broadly built, and bald. He looked the mercenary over with a cold eye and a calculating smile. "You think you're something, don't you?" he said. "You've killed men with weapons and with your bare hands, haven't you? And you've slept with many women."

He did not allow Geryam to answer. He only spoke as if musing out loud, as much to himself as to his prisoner. "You are one of those foolish fellows who thinks success in copulation makes you a wise and sophisticated man. Yet you know nothing of talking and listening to people, you know nothing of the art of learning. You do not know how nations exist— nations copulate, too, you know, yet you know nothing of that. You know nothing of the secret worlds that lie between all we see and all we do."

The priest smiled. "You expect me to kill you, I can see it. You tell yourself that by facing death bravely, you can wring some kind of victory out of your own stupidity. You will have somehow won over me, even though I have you executed, because you knew my silly little wife and did not flinch when I cut you open."

The priest laughed loud and long. He drank liquor from a bronze cup, smiled to himself, then went on. "Your only victory was that a man like you could even be noticed by a man like me. In that, you did gain above your station. But I tell you, that is your last victory. I will not kill you, at least not in a way you can comprehend."

His face showed rage and triumph, all in the same expression. "I will turn you into what you have already become," he said. "I will turn you into what you dedicated your life to being. You'll go on living, but you'll look . . ." He laughed a nasty laugh. "You'll look a little different from the way you look now." Another laugh, then, "You'll be even better suited to your new profession than you were to your old one. You can celebrate and thank me later."

The priest turned away with the wave of an arm. Slaves shackled Geryam to brass rings set into the chamber's metal wall. The priest lifted his arms, chanted, sang, danced, and whirled in a frenzy of action. At the last, he snatched up a clay pot from the floor and threw the contents of dark liquid and fluffy things over the condemned man. Geryam saw even as he clenched his eyes from the impact that the stuff was blood and feathers.

The blood splashed over him while the feathers fluttered down and stuck. The blood burned like boiling tar. It stank, made him vomit, and scream with pain. The room whirled around him, his joints cramped, his head ached, his neck grew stiff. He hardly knew what happened as the slaves hauled him from the room.

When he awoke, he found himself in open grasslands. Everything looked strange, larger, farther away, until he realized the world had not grown larger. Rather, he had grown smaller. And the feathers still covered him like a blanket.

He inspected himself as best he could. He had broad, strong wings with bright auburn feathers. To straighten them with his beak seemed the most natural thing in the world, now. He could see colors he had never noticed as a human, and he heard new sounds, too. And bugs began to look tasty to him. Without even thinking about it, he danced down the streambank, snatched a beetle with his beak, and swallowed it before it could even wiggle.

His legs had scaly skin now and had turned a reddish yellow. He had three forward toes with little claws at the ends, and a heavy, powerful spur that faced backward from his ankle. Not lovely, he supposed, but adequate for his new life's needs. If nothing else, he did not have to buy clothes now, or crack the heads of young ruffians, or risk having his own head cracked.

He went toward the first farm he saw.

He smoothed his feathers and looked about, and that was when he saw the black rooster running at him, its wings spread. His own hackles lifted, he tensed himself, and before the rooster could attack he leaped from the ground and kicked his feet forward. He drove his spurs against the other bird's neck. It squawked and fell kicking, tangling Geryam's feet. They rolled about in the dust; then Geryam spurred the rooster again, drawing blood this time.

It scrambled to its feet and ran away just as fast as it had come. Geryam ran after it a little way, then stopped and let it escape, secure in the knowledge that he now ruled the barnyard. Then a man, the farmer, ran up and caught him between calloused hands. "By the stars, d'you see this bird? As fine a gamecock as I've ever seen—drove old Chanticleer off, and it wasn't even a match."

The man carried Geryam into the farmhouse and called his wife. For as long as the woman would listen, he raved about what he had found. "It just came into the barnyard and took over. I never seen anything like it." Then he took Geryam to another part of the barnyard, to where cages stood in rows, each one with a rooster in it. He summoned his son, and together the two of them wrapped cloth around Geryam's ankles and covered his spurs. They pulled a rooster from one of the cages and did the same for it.

The farmer held Geryam, the boy held the other rooster, and positioned them both so they could peck at one another's comb and eyes. Geryam saw red with anger. When the farmer set him down, he flew at the bird, knocked it over, spurred it without mercy. When he became too tired to spur it, he pecked at it with his beak, pulling feathers until that bird, too, gave up.

Again, the farmer snatched him up. "As I said, that's the best bird I've ever seen. You'd expect him to run off a barnyard rooster. But this time he beat another gamecock, and a good one. He's going to make us some money, I'll swear to that."

So it was that Geryam learned he was not just a rooster, but a gamecock. It wasn't a bad life at first. He was given the best feed and put in with the hens from time to time and had his own cage. In a way, the priest had spoken the truth. His life did not change much from what he had been. He was still a mercenary, just a different kind. Though he still knew who he was, enough of his instincts had changed to a birdlike nature to make life pleasant for him.

One day, the farmer put him and some other gamecocks into smaller cages and loaded them onto a cart. They traveled to a village and for the first time, Geryam knew he was going to fight other roosters in matches his master would bet on. He looked forward to it. He had beaten without mercy every other gamecock on the farm and knew he would do just as well in these matches.

The farmer and the boy took him out of his cage and held him while they put long iron gaffs over his spurs, then fastened them in place with pine gum and linen. Geryam did not wonder what that might mean until he fought his first match. Then, when he and the other gamecock flew at each other, his new iron spurs sank deep into flesh every time he used them. Before he knew it, the other rooster lay dead in the dust before him, bathed in blood.

But he had been wounded, too. In its losing effort, the other bird had still found him a couple of times with its own gaffs. His wounds hurt him all night, and in the morning he felt stiff, sore, and dizzy. Then he realized his punishment. He would fight and be wounded, fight and be wounded, all the time winning bets for the farmer, all the time fighting the toughest gamecocks. And no matter how well he fought, he would be wounded—there would be no end for him until he died from his wounds. It was a death sentence, and he would be a long time watching that death approach.

He fell into black depression, yet he still had to fight his best or die. When he did not fight hard enough, the farmer would grab him and cuff his head between those two rough hands to make Geryam angry. And Geryam could only take that anger out on another rooster. Once he won, the farmer would treat him kindly for a few days while his wounds healed and his strength came back.

He fought several times that season, and the next. But he could feel his body getting stiffer from the scars the other gamecocks' gaffs left. He got slower and found it ever harder to escape more damage. He had to use strength more than skill as he went on, and that left him more hurt and bleeding after each match.

Finally, it happened. He was fighting in a special pit cordoned off before a noble's castle, against the fastest gamecock he had ever seen. The bird came at him, nimble and lucky. They leaped together, feet foremost, and one of the other rooster's gaffs caught Geryam behind the ear. Roaring filled his head and he could feel the blood flow over his feathers. When he scrambled back to his feet, he felt so dizzy he could barely stand.

He did not really understand how the match went after that, though it seemed to last a lifetime. He became wearier and wearier and bled from a half-dozen deep stab wounds. When the judge lifted him up and the people shouted, Geryam had no idea whether he had won or lost. He only knew the farmer's boy took him from the judge and that Geryam's blood was dripping on the lad's hands.

"He's done for," the boy said to the farmer. It sounded to Geryam as if the lad was about to cry.

"That's how the sport goes," the farmer said. "He was a good one while he lasted, and he won me some good money. But now it's over. Take him out behind those sheds over there and throw him on the dunghill."

Geryam felt the motion as the boy carried him; then he passed out. When he came to, he was lying amid the filth and rubbish of the dunghill, shivering from the cold and too weak to stand. He tried to get to his feet, tried to even crawl down the hill to somewhere where he could be warmer. But he could barely move.

His breathing became shallow; he could feel his lungs filling up with liquid. He thought of the woman and of her husband. It seemed a lifetime ago when all that had happened. Now the priest's moment of revenge was at hand. Geryam wondered, did the priest know what was happening to him? Did the man know Geryam was breathing his last on some dunghill?

Geryam hated the farmer. He hated the way the man had used him. He had fought well, had given his all, had given much excitement, and had won the man many bets, but he had never shared the wealth. He had deserved better than to die on a dunghill, he thought bitterly. The farmer had been wrong, wrong to use Geryam for his own pleasure and gain.

"That's true, Sir Geryam," a woman's voice said.

Geryam felt too weak to turn his head toward the voice. But he felt the woman's hand slide under his bloody feathers and turn his eyes toward hers. "You were once a very handsome man. I saw you. Oh, yes, I watched you often. Even as a gamecock, you were striking. How your feathers shone out in the sun, as if they had gold threads in them."

Geryam had no idea what woman would hold a dying chicken, but it didn't matter. Good looks didn't do me any good, did they? he thought.

"No, they didn't. You were a skillful warrior and that didn't do you any good, either."

How a woman could read his very thoughts, why she would even speak to him, did not matter to Geryam. All that mattered was that he was dying—what else *could* matter beside that? It was the farmer's fault, he thought. He treated me well enough, but when all was said and done, he just used me. He just used me. The bitterness filled him. It wasn't right.

"In that, you are correct." Though he could sense that she was nodding, Geryam also sensed mockery in the woman's tone. That made him angry.

It's easy for you to laugh, he thought. I'm the one who got used. I'm the one who's dying.

"Are you the only one who ever got used? When you were a man, what of the women you knew? Did you treat them any better than your farmer treated you?"

Geryam stared at the woman. The setting sun framed her face in the roses of its glow, yet by contrast made the gray-blond of her hair even more silvery than it might otherwise have been. She was—and he had kept careful track, so there could be no doubt of this—the most beautiful woman he had ever looked upon. She had an aquiline nose, fine, high cheekbones, and eyes as gray as waves on a cloudy day, as gray as the eternal void that awaited him.

Totally feminine was her nature, yet without a trace of wantonness. Geryam had looked on women of every shape and size, of every station, in every state of dress and undress. Yet he had never seen anything even to rival this maiden, let alone to match her. The look of her so shocked him that he forgot all they had spoken about.

His stare plainly amused her. Her fine lips parted and she laughed, a laugh that sounded on the air like dozens of little bells. "Oh, foolish man," she said. "Have you not learned a thing from all that has befallen you? I ask again: Were you the only one who was ill used—an object just for sporting?"

He swallowed. "I see your meaning," he said. "I admit it."

"Then rise, Sir Geryam," she said. She looked as if she were about to laugh at him again. "Rise to your feet and follow me."

For the first time since her voice had awakened him, he looked at himself. He was no longer a gamecock. To his amazement, his eyes swept over himself, a self scarred and bloody and naked as the day he was born, but a man once more. For the first time in his life, he felt shame at his nakedness and tried frantically to cover himself in the garbage of the dung heap.

The woman frowned, and the frown terrified him. "No," she said. "I see you to the center of your soul. Don't think some scrap of fabric blocks my vision. More than once, you've tried to clothe yourself in garbage, when you didn't want to look upon the real you. And I suppose that you succeeded for a while. Don't try to cloud my view that way, or I will be offended."

"I don't understand," he said. That was the truth with a vengeance.

"It doesn't matter," she replied. "But rise up and come with me."

Chapter Twelve:
The Maiden's Quest

To Geryam's amazement, his body no longer ached and his wounds no longer bled. He was a man once more, whole and healed, and when he rose to his feet, he found the old, familiar strength and spring in his limbs. "How did all this happen?" he asked in wonder.

"Don't try to understand," she replied. She took his hand and led him away from the dung heap. "Don't fear the gaze of men while you're with me."

They walked for a while, until they were far from the town. Where Geryam's hand touched hers, his skin tingled as though something were flowing from her into him. He felt stronger with each step.

After a time, she turned and faced him. "You've lived a foolish life, Sir Geryam," she said, then placed a finger over his mouth. "Don't make excuses. There are many kinds of people: one kind lives life, but another kind dreams up excuses for the life they've led. Of those, you are the latter."

Again he tried to protest and again she hushed him. "I've restored your body. There has always been a strength in you and goodness you don't yet see within yourself. You owe your life to me from now on."

"I understand," he whispered.

"Your task is to become what you should be. At no time will you ever use another human being for your pleasure—that's the first condition of my gift. The second is that you must find the priest who altered you."

"Am I supposed to kill him?" Geryam asked.

She smiled a sad smile. "You still don't understand. Someday, perhaps you'll know more than you know now. No, no, Sir Geryam, you shall not kill him—for yourself or for my sake. But still you must confront him when you find him—and the Fates will spin the tale from there. That is the quest I give you." She dropped his hand.

He stared at her and swallowed. His throat filled with emotion, his eyes filled with tears, but he could not think of a word to say. He reached for her and tried to give her an embrace of thanks, but she faded like smoke. She was gone before he could blink.

Owras looked down at Geryam as the warrior paused for breath. For all the old man could tell, the effect of the lactin leaves had worn off, and the stranger was telling the story now because it was time for him to tell it. Owras glanced at Rinna and Lissa. Amazement opened their eyes wide in the firelight. Their faces had turned pink in the glow.

"Not much to tell from there," Geryam said. "A peasant found me. He let me work for a few days and gave me food and clothes. Finally, I made my way to the nearest seaport and shipped as able-bodied seaman aboard a cog bound for the outer islands."

"Why?" Owras asked. "Is this where you'll find the priest you're after?"

"I've no idea who the priest is, or how to find him. He could be anywhere by now. I don't know the name of the city where I met him, or even the port I shipped from. There's a lot I don't remember."

"All right," Owras said. "Go on."

"The ship called me, you might say, so I joined the crew. We stopped at Oron and Lower Carea, then sailed through the Narrow Straits. Then a terrible storm hit, we foundered, and I was swept overboard." He looked up at Owras, then at the two maidens. "You found me. That's all."

"It's a miracle, a fantasy," Rinna said. "How can we believe you?"

"For my part, I believe him," Owras said. "Sometimes there's more truth in some fantastic story than in an everyday one." He stood up. "Besides, Geryam, your description of your vision—that has a strong ring of truth."

Geryam sat up. "That maiden—you've seen her?"

"I've talked to those who have. The description is pretty much the same. You've had a vision, young man, and a powerful one. You've been part of a miracle. You should have told me all these things right from the first."

"I couldn't." Geryam made a face and turned his head away. "I just couldn't. These maids, these sweet and innocent maids who go with you everywhere." Rinna and Lissa glanced at one another. "They saved my life, didn't they? And they look up to me. All the women I've known in my life—not many of them did that." He shrugged. "For the first time, maybe I've learned to look up to myself. And they trusted me. How could I tell them the things I've done?"

He glanced at Rinna, then away. "How could I tell them about the women—some just girls like them—I've had for breakfast, lunch, and dinner?" He sighed. "How do I tell them, even now?"

"That doesn't matter. It's over," Rinna said. "We don't care what you did."

"That's right," Lissa said. "We all make mistakes."

Geryam looked at her with an odd expression. "You two don't even know what to name the things I did. Don't try to sound old and wise and magnanimous. It doesn't wash with me."

Rinna and Lissa both looked hurt and insulted. Owras glanced between the three of them, frowned, then spoke. "You saw the goddess Pallas," he said to Geryam. "Others have had similar visions and have come to me in the same way. It's a great honor."

"Thank you," Geryam replied coldly.

"You must do as Pallas tells you. You have to seek this

priest of the Order. And since she has sent you to us, we'll help you."

Rinna and Lissa stared at the old man. "Why?" Rinna finally said. "We don't even know where to find the man. We don't know where to go."

"We'll find out," Owras said with a smile. "When the time comes, Geryam will know. And we'll know, too. That's what faith is for."

"I'm not sure what good faith does," Rinna said. "My father and mother are dead. What good did their faith do them?" She burst into tears. Owras tried to hold her, but she turned away from him. "We're supposed to be born priestesses, but what good does it do?"

Geryam sat and looked at her with oceans of feeling washing over his face. But he did not move. Finally, Lissa put her arms around Rinna. "You're right, you know," Lissa said. "How do we know any of this is true? How do we know anything? How do we know the gods we follow are even worth the trouble? How do we know they'll keep their promises?"

"My poor, dear princesses," Owras said sadly. "Those are hard questions, and yet you have a right to ask them. Will you listen to an answer? I don't ask you to just obey without thinking, or even to understand without a lot of thought. I only ask you to listen."

Rinna and Lissa nodded. "Come sit with me," Owras said.

They sat one on either side of him, as they had all the times he had told them stories or taught them how to sing songs. "There are many gods in this world," he began. "There are as many gods as there are different ways for people to believe in them. There are gods which exist to serve mankind, or at least to help mankind serve himself, just as there are people who live to grow and serve others.

"But there are other gods, too. They exist to be served. That's just as there are people who believe everyone should serve *their* needs, that the world should hew the line *they* mark. Such people will tell you they serve true gods, but the gods they serve stand for darkness and slavery. They set rules without end and demand endless monies and services from their worshipers.

"The gods of good and evil will always come into conflict,"

Owras said. "Both will always tell you they are right and their opponents are wrong."

"How do you tell the difference?" Rinna asked.

"It's simple, yet very complex," Owras answered. "But remember this: Evil gods make men serve them, all the while telling men that is the way to true freedom. They will tell you of free agency, then threaten you with dire punishment if your free decision varies by a thin hair from their prescription.

"The gods that help people grow will tell you to seek the truth within your own bosom. And if your truth does not match theirs, so be it—for all truth is good to them."

"I don't understand," Lissa said.

Owras nodded and smiled. "It is hard to understand," he replied.

"If our gods, if the Twelve, exist to serve men, then why do they ask us to take on the Dark Order?" Rinna asked. "Why don't they just destroy the Order themselves, and make the world a safe place for good people?"

"That's another good question," Owras said. "But if you accept that there are gods which smile on people and gods which enslave people, this logic follows: If we would have the former rather than the latter, perhaps, we must work to earn them."

"I understand that part," Rinna said. "I'll have to think about the rest."

"Me, too," Lissa said.

"Your thought is all I ask," Owras said.

The girls rose and went to Geryam. "We're going to help you on your quest," Lissa said. "What do you think of that, stranger?"

"I guess that's good," Geryam replied with a smile. "I only wish I knew where my quest would take us."

"That's the nature of all quests," Owras said. "But it's very late. The fire's burned low and most of our friends have long since gone to sleep. We'd better sleep, too, for the little time left before dawn." He looked at Geryam's arm. "Your wound is much improved already. By dawn we'll be able to wrap you with a proper bandage." He turned from the warrior with a yawn. He and Rinna and Lissa found their blankets and stretched out on the damp ground to sleep.

Morning found the group bustling on its way toward the

coast. Now that Fuzzy Waddles had been driven away, no one woke up weakened by cuts. That sent new optimism through the pilgrims. They ate a meager breakfast, then started on their way.

Geryam walked ahead of the company, always on the look-out for mercenaries or bandits. Usually, he would range as much as a half league ahead of the party. Sometimes he would rest while they straggled by, then watch after them for pursuit before he caught up with them and scouted ahead once more.

At one point, he heard a noise behind him and turned to see Lissa peeking from behind a tree. She snatched her head back as he turned, but it was plain he had seen her. "Oh, brother," she said. "We had just as well come out, we won't be able to hide anymore."

"Thanks a lot, Lissa," came Rinna's voice. "You had to go and let him see you."

"He'd have seen you if he hadn't seen me. You were sticking your head out like the prow of a ship half the time."

"Oh, foof."

"Skeek."

Geryam smiled and watched the two of them approach. "I should have my eyes put out, for all I've used them. I should have seen both of you. If this were a proper company, my commander'd have had me beaten for being a bad lookout."

"No beatings, please," Rinna said. "Enough has happened. How's your arm?"

"Well enough. It stings a little, but Owras says that's a sign of healing." He looked at the two maidens. With all the resiliency of their youth, they had recovered from the strains of the night before. They showed no sign of what had passed. Fact was, in their innocent pursuit of him as he scouted, he could see a forgiveness and acceptance of him that they never could have expressed with words.

They followed him noiselessly, taking care to stay out of his way, not talking, walking so quietly he could not help being impressed. "By my newfound faith," he said at last. "You two would make good scouts yourselves."

"We've been watching you," Lissa said proudly. "We know how you get around so quietly."

"Plainly, you do," Geryam said. "If I ever need guardians, I'll hire the two of you."

"We have questions for you, though," Rinna said with a swallow.

"That's right," Lissa said. "We daren't ask Owras. Besides," she added with a look at Rinna, "he's old and I don't think he'd remember the answers."

"If he ever knew them," Rinna said with a giggle.

"Ladies, I'm no match for any question Owras can't handle."

"You are this time," Rinna said, blushing.

"Take our words for it," Lissa added.

"Didn't you ever feel ashamed after spending the night with some woman?" Rinna blurted. "Didn't it go against what your parents taught you?"

Geryam looked at them, speechless. He saw no guile, no attempt to give offense, so he did not take any. "I never thought about it that way," he finally said, trying to be completely honest. "I don't suppose my parents taught me much of anything. No, it never bothered me, at least not in any way I ever noticed."

"Does it bother you now?"

Again, he studied the two. "What's done is done," he finally said. "I steered one course and now I steer another, that's all. But it became boring in a way, which is too bad. And there's always the threat of disease, you know." He eyed them, then shrugged. "Maybe you wouldn't know about that. At any rate, I wouldn't live that way again. I wouldn't be a mercenary, either."

They both nodded. "We understand," Lissa said. She turned to Rinna. "Ask him."

"No, you ask him."

"I can't. You'll have to."

He almost laughed at their little argument. "Ask me what?"

"What's it like?" Rinna blurted out, her face going as pink as rose blossoms. "The act of love, that is."

"Ladies!"

"We could never ask Owras that question," Lissa said. "Or our parents, either." She blushed, too.

"So you have to answer us," Rinna said in a businesslike voice.

Geryam stared, not knowing quite what to say. In such a question lay a kind of trust and faith no human being had ever before given him. But he had no idea how to answer. He suspected he was blushing just as much as Rinna. "It's not like anything," he finally said. "If your body were a tongue and the world were sugar, perhaps you could say that's what it's like." He hesitated. "But you've trusted me and asked a hard question, so I'll be honest. I don't know—I think there's more to it than even I know. I've never loved another, nor been loved. I've been told there's more than I've ever experienced, and I believe that." He lowered his voice. "And that much, I *am* sorry for."

"I don't understand," Lissa said.

"Me, either," Rinna chimed in.

Geryam looked away. "How could you? I'm not sure I do. Why don't we go back and join the main body."

"No," Lissa shot back. "We're asking you questions. We want to learn things."

"Oh, you two are a pair," Geryam cried. "You're made up of questions."

"No, not at all," Lissa said.

"We only have one more," Rinna said.

"Then ask away and let's have an end to it."

"Very well," Rinna said in a businesslike voice, as though she was the one who had been appointed this task. "We listened to you last night and we've listened carefully today. We're not stupid—we know you're not as wise as Owras is, or as spiritual as our parents were. But all the same, there are things you know that they would never tell us."

"I daresay that's the truth," Geryam murmured. "But heavens forbid that you should ever learn them."

"Don't interrupt," Rinna went on. "Now, before I ask this, I have to get your promise that you'll be totally honest. No lies, no deceit—even if you think you're doing it for our own good. We're grown up, and we don't need to be protected."

"I'm the one who needs protection," Geryam replied with a smile.

"Just get to the point, Rinna," Lissa said. "Quit beating around the bush."

"I'm asking the question my own way," Rinna said. "If you don't like the way I ask it, then ask it yourself." She looked at the other maiden and received silence as a reply.

Satisfied she made her point, she went on. "You're very experienced, by your own words. So I expect a truthful answer. Who's prettier, me or Lissa?"

"Say what?"

Rinna frowned impatiently. "I spoke plainly. We want to know—who's prettier? Me . . ."

"Or me?" Lissa chimed in.

"Oh, no," Geryam said. His face lengthened into a desperate expression. "There's no fairness in a question like that. You're both lovely and pure and good in my eyes and there's an end to it."

"Then we can go by categories," Rinna went on matter-of-factly. "First, who has the prettier eyes, Lissa or me?"

"You maidens," Geryam said. "I'm supposed to look for danger and instead I find myself pelted with impossible questions. If I'd known this was part of the bargain your divine Pallas forced on me, I'd rather have stayed a chicken on a dung heap."

Chapter Thirteen:
The Brethren

TRAPPED IN THE dank pit, Rogue jumped for his life. He leaped like a game fish on the end of a line and grabbed for the lip of the hole, but all he could grab was handfuls of dirt and a severed root or two. At last he grew so tired he could only gasp for breath and wait for whoever had caught him.

They soon arrived, filthy and awful—the ones he had escaped earlier. They surrounded the pit, looked down, babbled like excited children. "He's a fine lad," one man said. "He'll be a fine new member."

"You'll never take me alive," Rogue cried. "I'll never be one of your sacrifices."

"By all that's righteous, you're not a sacrifice," a man yelled back indignantly. His hair trailed to his shoulder blades, long and shaggy and infested by bugs. Rogue could actually see them crawling on him. Bugs crawled in his beard, too, for the beard hung just as far down his chest as the hair hung down his back, and was just as matted and unkempt. It gave him the look of a person wearing a hideous mask.

The Old Prophet reached the pit and looked down. His

white hair and beard streamed in the breeze. "No, no," he cried. "We're the true church. We don't sacrifice people the way the Order does. The Order is nothing but lies and black rites and footsteps in the dark." He laughed at this, though Rogue could not see any joke. "No, we are the only true order."

"I don't trust you," Rogue began.

"We're just glad to have you with us," the Old Prophet replied.

"Then why do you dig traps for people?" Rogue yelled up.

"Oh, ho, that's precious." The lot of them laughed as if their ribs would split. "We dig pits so that something will run in to them." More laughter. "The heavens will provide, the heavens will provide." The Old Prophet started dancing, his white hair and robe trailing out behind him until he had moved out of Rogue's view.

"The Dark Order drove us out," another man shouted. He was a big, black-bearded fellow even taller than Rogue. But he was no cleaner than any of the others. "They knew we held the secrets to saving men's souls, and they were jealous. They drove us from our cloisters and our studies, drove us out of the city and into these hills. They hounded us day and night, and bandits robbed us until we had no more for them to steal. Vagabonds came and beat us. Some of us went mad from it, I can tell you."

The Old Prophet danced back into view. "But we still have the secret to your salvation, yes we do."

"I don't want any secrets," Rogue said. "I just want to get out of here."

"You're trapped in that pit just as your soul is trapped in the pit of eternal damnation," the black-bearded brother cried. "To rise out of one, you must rise out of both—there is no other way."

"Then what do I have to do?"

"Become one with the Brotherhood," the Old Prophet sang. "It's the only way, the only way." He stopped dancing his circles and stared Rogue in the face. "It's a hard path for you to follow, but you'll gain glory by it. What better can any young man ask than a promise of glory?"

"Whatever," Rogue said in a sour voice. He had to get out

of the pit to survive. He might just as well say anything he had to. "Whatever it takes to get me out of here."

The Brethren raised a shout and threw their hands into the air. A couple of them shinnied up a nearby tree and fetched a rope from the crotch of two branches, then leaped back down. They ran breathlessly to the pit and threw one end down. "Catch on," the Old Prophet cried. "Catch hold and we'll pull you up." He laughed joyously and the rest of the Brethren exploded into mirth with him. Rogue had to join in, the laughter sounded so contagious.

The rope had been twisted out of vines and bark, and it hung all stiff and angular. He grabbed the knotted end, and the Brethren hauled him out of the pit as though he were a fish on the end of a line. Once he had clambered to his feet, the Old Prophet embraced him in a powerful hug. "Now you are one of us," the old man sang. "You're a brother, a brother, a brother of our very own."

They set the leaves aflutter with their shouting. Then they formed a group around Rogue and hustled him back the way he had come. There was no way he could escape, so he walked along with them for the time being.

"Where are we going?" he asked.

"To our cathedral," one answered. "There to make you a member of the Brethren."

This looked like no group of churchmen Rogue had ever seen in his life. They had tatters for clothes, with flies buzzing about their ears, their eyes wide and wild, and their nostrils flaring. Only the Old Prophet looked clean, yet he was the wildest-looking of the bunch with his songs and his dances and his white whiskers floating in the breeze.

They came to a place where the trees stood thick and tall, and one huge dead hulk of a stump towered over lesser growths. A mighty tree in its day, it had been consumed by fire and now stood like the blackened ruin of some castle. There was a low opening, which one brother knelt and crawled through. The rest then pushed Rogue through and followed on their hands and knees.

He found himself standing in a cavelike space. Sunlight glimmered in through the top of the trunk, twenty cubits above his head. Candles glowed from niches carved into the wood.

The brothers formed a circle and made Rogue stand at the center. "Will you pray for us before we initiate you?" the Old Prophet asked.

"I suppose so," Rogue answered. The Old Prophet set up a giddy, singsong chant the likes of which Rogue had never heard before, a series of whines, giggles, and moans, sounds from the throat without any apparent reason or meaning. "Now you sing the response," the old churchman said with a smile.

"What do I say?"

"The spirit will direct you." The Old Prophet broke into another long series of snorts, whistles, coughs, and snickers. The other brothers joined in until the tree's interior sounded like a cage full of wild animals.

Rogue still had no idea what to say. But he could see eyes lift and peer into his face, so he knew he had to do something. He coughed, then belched, then screamed at the top of his lungs.

"Bravo, brother," the Old Prophet cried. "The spirit is with you indeed. Tra la, tra la, sing a song of happy days."

For Rogue, the whole thing turned into a bit of fun. He whistled through his teeth, then whinnied like a horse. No matter what crazy sound he made, these strange people ate it up. They clapped and smiled at him as if he were some sort of long-lost savior. He forgot his earlier fear and loathing of these people—he was having fun, now.

In the midst of the tumult, the Old Prophet disappeared into a shadowy hollow at one side of the dark chamber. He came back an instant later, holding his hands behind his back. All the Brethren broke into song just then, a chant that had no tonal quality and that made no more sense to Rogue than anything that had gone before.

Though the whole proceeding might have been a matter of grave religious import, none of the Brethren seemed to take it any more seriously than anything else they did. Some still drooled and giggled insanely and some picked fleas and cooties from the filthy rags they wore. Many stared at Rogue and rubbed their hands together.

Each of them stepped to his right once, then again, so they began to circle Rogue. They moved slowly at first, then faster, forming a chain of shadows that confused the young man's eyes. They stepped toward him, the circle closed in on him, then they all stepped away. The whole ritual had an almost hypnotic effect. Rogue could no longer tell which of them was which. Light played on shadow, voices droned in his ears, and he found himself growing dizzy and confused.

He heard a sound behind him and turned his head. The Old Prophet brought a huge dagger down toward Rogue's back, and the youth wheeled away. The blade drew blood as it sliced along the youth's jerkin.

"Stand still," the Old Prophet yelled. "It's time to make you one with the body of our church."

"By chopping me up?"

Rogue backed away, though he had nowhere to go. From the corner of his eye, he saw other brothers duck into the alcove the Old Prophet had vanished into before. They, too, came out with knives. The droning, dizzying chant went on as they circled toward him, blades lifted.

"Some things have to be done," the Old Prophet said in a childish voice. "Roasts, hams, a few chops. The small pieces go for pies."

"What?" Rogue yelled.

"How better to make you one with the body of our church?" the Old Prophet cried. He rushed at Rogue, but the young man kicked at him, knocked him down, and the huge knife rolled away into the shadows. Rogue could not turn before one of the other Brethren struck him from behind, a glancing blow that did not draw blood. He pivoted, knocked that man down, then wheeled toward the entrance.

That was hopeless. A dozen men blocked his way. Even if he reached the little opening, they would be on him long before he could crawl through. He wheeled again and dashed toward the chamber's far wall. He bowled two men over in his rush, then made a desperate leap. In niches set above the level of his head, candles glowed weakly. At the top of his leap, his clutching fingers found one niche. He hung there, scrabbled desperately against blackened wood, then cried out as hot wax poured across his fingers. At last his other hand found a hold, and he hoisted himself up.

Men caught at his feet, but he kicked them free and hauled himself out of reach. The inside of the tree was rough and pieces of charred wood rained down on him as he dug for another handhold. He finally found one, though, a large knothole where the base of a limb had once grown, and hauled himself up another cubit.

The brothers shouted and cursed at him. The Old Prophet babbled and screeched, then began to blubber like a baby. Another brother hurled a knife, which thudded into the charred wood a finger's width from Rogue's elbow. Hanging precariously, his feet in candle niches and his hand hooked to the wrist in the knothole, he wrenched the knife out with his free hand and hurled it back down. One man screamed and collapsed; the others backed away and cursed him even more loudly.

Flinging his arms and legs up like a man possessed, Rogue managed to climb a few more frantic cubits. More knives struck the wood around him. One even struck him in the back—the spinning handle, not the blade—and though it glanced away, the impact was enough to make him lose his grip.

He fell screaming, clutching frantically at air, and struck the chamber's dirt floor with an impact that drove his breath from his body. Dirt and stone gave way, and he found himself falling farther down, glancing off rocks and tree roots that hung into open air. The shouts of the Brethren echoed behind him as he landed on a sandy slope and rolled down it. At last, more astonished than hurt, he came to rest on a flat, sandy floor. A dropped knife pelted down next to him, and he instinctively snatched it up.

His arms and legs had received a score of scratches. The sandy stuff hurt like sin where it touched a wound, and when he ventured to taste it, it turned out to be salt. He lay for a bit, then ventured to stand. This new chamber was too low for that, though, so he found himself plodding along on his hands and knees.

He did not hear anyone chasing him, but he was too frightened to stop crawling. He blundered ahead in the darkness, hissing with pain at the salt, which worked itself into his open cuts and scratches. Then he saw a light ahead and halted. He held the knife stiffly.

The tunnel he found himself peering along looked nothing

like the one he had caved his way into. It had been carefully shored with heavy timbers. Torches flickered from sconces set into the walls, and the light was dim. Still, it seemed a divine blessing after the darkness he had faced before. He made his way slowly and carefully, remembering with every step the caverns beneath the Dark Order's temple at Oron.

He walked carefully along until he heard sounds of digging ahead of him. Advancing slowly, he found himself opposite a low chamber in which a group of men hacked away at the wall with picks, singing as they worked.

> "We dig the salt by night and day,
> With a hey, ho, bring it down smartly,
> It's softer than gold and cleaner than clay,
> Bring it down smartly, my boys."

That chorus finished, one man sang above the rest in a high-pitched voice:

> "I dig all day with fingers and toes,
> Hey, ho, bring it down smartly.
> The salt bites my eyeballs and tickles my nose,
> Bring it down smartly, my boys.
> I'll dig forever, no story, no lie,
> With a hey, ho, bring it down smartly.
> The salt's got my body too pickled to die,
> Bring it down smartly, my boys."

The man had apparently made the verse up as he went, because the others laughed to hear it. The humor didn't matter to Rogue, however. What mattered was his hope of tiptoeing his way past the chamber's opening while the salt miners—it was plain that was what they were—dug and sang. He had all but made it when he heard one of them shout, "Hey, there's someone in the tunnel."

He didn't wait for the sound of picks being thrown to the cavern's floor. He ran as hard as he could, with the tunnel's fine salt kicking up in little puffs with each step. Down the tunnel he ran, past twists and turns, down a steep incline, until he ran full into the arms of another half-dozen men. He struggled, bit, and cursed, but there was no getting free of them. They wrenched the knife from his hand, grabbed his arms and legs, and forced his face down to the tunnel's floor.

Chapter Fourteen:
Salt Mines

ROGUE STRUGGLED LIKE a wild man. He writhed, fought, kicked, and scratched, but too many men held him for him to get free. "Hold him down," one man shouted. "We've got you, you scoundrel. Belikes a salt thief you are, and got no more brains than to sneak right into the mine itself. You'll pay for it, now, you will."

"I'm not any salt thief," Rogue shouted back. "Nobody'd steal your stupid salt anyway."

"That's him," another voice shouted. More men thundered up from the tunnel Rogue had just fled. "I just caught him out of the corner of my eye. He'd all but made his getaway."

"Where's your sack, son?" a man asked. "You might just as well tell us. We'll find it anyway."

"I don't have any sack. I'm just trying to get away from the Brethren."

"What Brethren?"

"A crazy old man and a bunch of his friends. They were going to eat me."

The man laughed. "That's a good story, I'll credit you with

that much. But I've never heard of anyone who eats people in these parts. Salt thieves, yes, bandits, yes. Cannibals—no, I don't think so." The man looked Rogue up and down, rubbing his wrinkled face and twisting a long mustache that was white and droopy. "Still, you don't look as if you're from these parts." He turned to one of the others. "Adam, Kaylan—you two take a couple of torches and search back down the tunnel. See if he's dropped a salt bag anywhere. That'll tell us something."

"How'd you get into the tunnel, lad?" another man asked. "It takes a lot of nerve for a man to sneak right past guards and cook's hut and sleeping hut and all."

"I fell in," Rogue said. "Let me up." The miners who held Rogue looked to the tall man with the broad mustache. He nodded, and they released the young man's arms and legs. Still, they watched with grim eyes as he rose and dusted himself off.

"Where'd you fall from, son?" the man asked.

"From the Brethren's cathedral," Rogue said. "It's an old, burned-out tree." He told his story then. Even though some of the miners smirked openly, they heard him out.

Adam and Kaylan came back while he was finishing. "No bag," Adam said. "And there's a new wash tunnel formed off the last shaft. That's where he came from—we saw the tracks."

"Wash tunnel?" The mustached man stared at Rogue. "How'd you find that?"

"I don't even know what one is," Rogue said. "I told you what happened."

A group of miners took him back the way he had come. When they reached the tunnel he had come down first, a couple of them went in with rope and torches while the rest waited in the shored area. "A wash tunnel is a natural passage," the man with the mustache told Rogue. Rogue understood by now that the man was the miner's leader. "Usually they're formed by water, which is where the name comes from."

The two men came back after a little while. "It runs about the way he says," one of them said to the leader. "And it goes through some of the best mineral salt I've ever seen." He held out a pouch and poured a sprinkle of colored crystals over the leader's palm. The crystals were red, green, all colors mixed with white. "You hardly even have to break it up—it's all ready to ship."

"Well I'll be . . ." The leader turned to Rogue. "You've brought good luck with you," he said. "We can start working this seam right away." He held out his hand for the young man to shake. "My name's Mallor, by the way."

"Pleased," Rogue said without much enthusiasm. He had brought luck to the fishermen, now he brought luck to the salt miners. He only wished he could bring luck to himself. "Look, all I want to do is get away from here. I mean, it's nice you believe me about this tunnel, but I want to get as far as I can away from those crazies up above us."

"Yes, I suppose." Mallor scratched his head, then talked for a moment with the men who had explored the tunnel. "They did find where you broke through, but they couldn't climb up because the salt crystals are so loose," he said. "But if you've told the truth about everything else, I suppose we might just as well believe you about this."

"Then what are you going to do about the Brethren?"

Mallor shrugged. "Nothing."

"Nothing?"

"Nothing. If they've avoided us this long, it's because they know there are too many of us for them to harm. Once we start mining under their headquarters, they'll probably move on."

"You're pretty casual about it."

Mallor shrugged again. "Our mineral salt gets used at the most noble tables across the Thlassa Mey. It's prized like jewelry, worth its weight in silver. It tastes like something out of a dream, brings health to those who taste it." He smiled. "Rich men believe it makes them more virile, though I doubt that."

"Wait. Back up," Rogue said. "I salted fish 'til my hands turned white, so I know a little about salt. It costs money, but it's not as valuable as you say it is."

Mallor smiled. "This isn't just any salt." He bent and picked up a handful of crystals from the floor. They were square, the size of lentils, and glimmered in the torchlight with a dazzling array of colors. They looked like little jewels.

"They look like you could set them into rings and things," Rogue said.

"That's right," Mallor said. "They're prized at the most noble tables—and this mine is the only place in the world they're found. That makes the stuff almost priceless." He tossed the salt crystals away. "The rich will pay a king's ransom for the stuff. We deal with bandits and thieves all the time. We're not worried about your mad priests."

Rogue frowned. "You might want to change your mind. Nobody likes to get robbed, but if you got chomped by that bunch, it'd *really* ruin your day."

But for all his misgivings, he decided it was better for him to stay with the miners for the moment than to move on. He had no idea where the Brethren might be lurking and decided he would be better off with friends than by himself. So he helped them mine, ate with them in their cook hut, and slept with them in their long, low sleeping hut.

He learned that the mines wound like moles' tunnels almost a league back into the rising uplands at the middle of the island of Kolpos. That was why the miners and the Brethren had never met—because the mine's entrance was far from the burned-tree cathedral, even though the tunnel now passed under it.

He also learned about different grades of mineral salt. The highest grade—like what he had stumbled over when escaping from the brotherhood—looked like a collection of little jewels and was almost as valuable. The tiny, square crystals gleamed every color a man's imagination could conceive, reflected light in a million little sparkles. Yet it tasted simply as salt on the tongue. He wondered whether the stuff really aided digestion or did any of the other wonderful things reputed to it. But it was lovely to look on, and that was enough to make it priceless, whether it performed the wonderful things it was reputed to do or not.

Rogue found it strange to think about. Twice he had stumbled onto groups of workers and twice he had brought good fortune with him. Perhaps it was merely coincidence, or perhaps it was a gift he had. Either way, it proved useful for smoothing his way in the world.

The miners needed all the men they could muster to widen and shore the tunnel Rogue had discovered. He found himself helping with the task, chopping down trees, lugging the tim-

bers down the endless tunnels, knocking them into place and
pinning them together, hauling out baskets full of dirt and rub-
ble.

They opened the tunnel clear to the end. It had apparently
had its beginning in rainwater, which traced its way down the
root system of the ancient, burned-out tree the Brethren called
their cathedral. But the wonderful layer of mineral-salt crystals
extended beyond that point and overlaid a layer of hard stone.
None of the miners had ever seen anything like it. "Our fortunes are made," Mallor said as they labored in the new tunnel.
"I always wondered if there would be enough mineral salt in
this hole to make work for the rest of my days, but there's
enough in this new tunnel to provide for us and our children,
too."

"Yes," Kaylan said. "The first time I laid eyes on Rogue, I
thought 'That man's come to take my livelihood. Maybe my
life if he gets a chance.' " The young miner grinned at the tall
youth. "Then I found out you brought a ripping good gift.
Life's strange."

At that instant, the whole tunnel shook and dirt and stone
rained down on them like big hailstones. Shoring timbers
groaned and snapped; one man screamed as a section of roof
collapsed on him. Fibrous tentacles of wood writhed from the
overhead and crushed through the narrow space.

Rogue dashed for the main tunnel, but it was too late. A
section of roof gave way and a great weight of dirt and rock
sloughed down, trapping the fleeing miners. "The tree," he
shouted. "It's that tree. It's so big and heavy, it's crushing the
tunnel."

"Brace it up," Mallor shouted back. Men scurried like rats,
grabbed timbers, and propped them under the biggest roots.
The groaning and cracking finally stopped. Pebbles and grit
rolled down between the roots, and men breathed harshly from
the strain of their struggle. "At least we're not going to get
squashed, but we're trapped down here," Mallor said.

"Maybe we can crawl up through the roots," Rogue said. "I
got down here that way."

"Aha, so there you are." An eerie cackle followed the loud
words. Then the Old Prophet stepped from between the dark

roots, carrying his broad knife. "Our cathedral itself chased you down after you defiled it."

Rogue stared at him, then at the other Brethren, who clambered down through the ragged roots. Many carried knives. They looked dirtier and crazier than ever. "It's time at last," one said. "You will join us now."

They leaped at him, but miners snatched up picks and shovels and fought back. Rogue kicked the wild old man in the groin and snatched the knife when the old body crumpled. The youth buried the blade in the belly of the next man who came at him, snatched it back, and used it again. Cries and shouts rang through the narrow space, along with screams from the wounded.

The fight quickly turned against the attackers. Mining tools knocked knives from hands, shovels clanged off skulls. Some of the Brethren tried to scramble back up the way they came, but the root-lined hole made hard climbing. Miners snatched at them, caught them, and hauled them back down. "Tie them," Mallor shouted. "We can't afford to have them loose down here."

Men snatched up rope that had been intended for use with shoring. In moments, they bound the mad cultists hand and foot. The pitiful band lay screaming and wailing along the sides of the tunnel. "So much for them," Mallor said to Rogue. "That part of your story was also true, it seems."

"What are you going to do with them?" Rogue asked.

Mallor shrugged. "Once we get this tunnel opened back up, I suppose we'll have to let them go."

"What?"

"We can't just kill them."

"We can haul them to Touros with the next shipment of salt," Kaylan said. "At least do something to get them far away from here."

And so it was done. The miners labored for hours, and finally one was able to exit by way of the burned tree's roots. He quickly returned to the entrance, and men brought more ropes and timbers. By the end of a couple of days, they had built an alternate entrance and were working on the cave-in from both sides. They cared well for their captives, but also watched them closely. And as quickly as they could make preparations, they loaded bags of refined salt onto packhorses. They pulled their captives out of the hut they had housed them in, bound their hands and strung them on leads together, then set off.

It was a brisk downhill walk from the hills. They came to a stream after a while, then followed its course toward the valley below. The trees stood more sparsely here, but many rock outcroppings and narrow spots lay along the trail. Rogue, who had been brought along to help guard the captives, enjoyed himself thoroughly. Before much longer he would be at the waterfront in Touros. While Mallor bargained away his salt, Rogue would sign as an able-bodied seaman aboard some ship. Then he would leave for faraway lands, perhaps even someplace beyond the Narrow Strait. No longer would he have to live in fear of the pursuing Dark Order.

The sun's chariot climbed high in the sky; the day grew warm. The prisoners stopped begging and cursing and plodded sullenly along. The horses grew stolid and their heads drooped. If not for the fact that they were still clopping along, Rogue could have sworn the animals were asleep on their feet.

As they followed the stream down a narrow defile, a scream froze Rogue's blood. Heads popped up behind boulders and from behind fallen logs, and men leaped up and ran toward the packhorses. These were not simple crazies, either. They carried swords and spears and attacked like experienced campaigners.

"Quick," one of the miners shouted. "Up into the rocks. We can hold them off there." But the onslaught cut off the retreat. Men screamed and fell or screamed and fled, and the clang of weapon off weapon echoed through the hills. A rock struck Rogue from behind and his brain exploded into bright lights. The last thing he remembered was the feel of his knees giving way beneath him.

Chapter Fifteen:
The Tower of Krell

WHEN ROGUE CAME to, he found himself lying in the dirt with his hands bound behind him. The dust tickled his nose and made him sneeze. As soon as that happened, he heard a voice yell, "Hey, the big ugly one's awake."

"Good," another voice answered. "Finish tying the others and let's get out of here."

Strong arms jerked Rogue to his feet. When he looked around, he saw the miners, all bound hand and foot and sitting neatly in a row along the trail. The robbers tethered him to the last of the still-tied Brethren.

The familiar white head in front of him turned and the Old Prophet smiled. "So you're back with us at last," he said with a giggle. "I knew you wouldn't be able to stay away." His eyes glinted hungrily.

Rogue groaned. "I'm not here because I want to be," he said. "Besides, you're tied up the same as I am. I don't see how you can be so happy about that."

"Those of the true faith are always persecuted," the Old

Prophet replied matter-of-factly. "Humiliation is our portion in this life, but we will receive our reward in the next."

Rogue turned away from the crazy old man and studied his captors. He counted more than twenty bandits. All were large men, well tanned and healthy-looking. Their weapons were in good condition; their clothes looked new and well cared for. "You don't look like the usual run of thieves," he said to the nearest one.

"You're an insolent snot," the man replied. "For what it's worth to you, we're not thieves at all."

"You could have fooled me."

"Tell 'im, Gar," another man shouted. "We work under contract, don't we? In the hire of someone special, ain't we?"

"That's the truth," Gar said. "Get along, now. It's time we should be going." He drew his sword and prodded a captive in the back with the tip. They started off down the trail, along with the miners' packhorses.

"Where are you taking us?" Rogue asked. "You can't sell this salt in Touros."

"Don't have to," Gar said. "Our . . ." He smiled. "Our patron—he'll take care of it all. He knows how to get rid of the salt at a profit, or maybe he just wants it for himself. At any rate, he'll pay us for it and there that ends."

"What about me? What about the rest of these men?"

"Oh, you're all ours to keep. That was the deal. There's people who'll want the services of a big lad like you."

"You're slavers, then?"

"That's a nasty way of saying it, yes." Gar grinned.

"What about the miners? They'd make better slaves than these men."

"Maybe, but who'd mine the salt? No, our master, he says anyone in mine garb we leave alone. They'll wiggle free in a day or two and then they can go back to their work. They'll do well enough without this one little load—sort of like bees, don't you know. They always make more honey than they can use." He and his fellows guffawed at this dab of wit.

"And I'm wearing city boys' breeches so you grabbed me, is that it?"

Gar nodded. "You might say that."

Rogue went silent. Maybe that was the reason the slavers

had grabbed him. Then again, maybe there were other reasons. He didn't want to think about such things. He followed the Brethren along the trail and tried not to think of anything at all.

They stopped for water where the stream emptied out into the valley; then the captors ate a lunch from packs they carried. When they started off again, they turned east and followed the valley's length. When Gar got close again, Rogue caught his eye. "You're not going to Touros at all, are you?"

"Nope. That's south."

"So where are you going?"

"To the Tower of Krell," Gar said. "You ever heard of Krell?"

"No," Rogue said. "I'm not from around here."

"He runs the Local Order in Touros. But he spends most of his time in his tower. Sort of a home away from home for him, you might say."

Rogue groaned so loudly that Gar stared at him. So the Dark Order had recaptured him at last. He should have known he couldn't elude them for long. Again he lapsed into silence and walked along buried in his thoughts for the rest of the day. Either these men knew who he was and what he had done, or they didn't. It didn't matter. He had no choice but to attempt escape every chance he got.

Not that there were any chances as the troupe walked along. He worked furiously at his bonds for an instant; then the Old Prophet said, "Quit jiggling back there. You'll just have to wait your turn, like everybody else." Then there came a giggle and a snatch of a song.

One of the guards—not Gar, but another—came up and checked the knots. He retied a couple, cuffed Rogue across the cheeks for trying, then they moved on. Rogue tried working at the ropes more carefully, but the result was no better.

For the rest of the day, they marched northeast, then made camp beside a little pond. The thieves bound each captive hand and foot, then relaxed and ate biscuits and dried meat from their packs. "Aren't we getting anything?" Rogue yelled.

"Shut your face," one man shouted back. "Where you're going you won't need food."

"Shut up," another man said to the first in a loud whisper. "Don't stir them up."

"Doesn't matter," the first said with a shrug.

"What do you mean?" Rogue asked. "Where *are* we going?"

"You're too full of questions for your own good," Gar said.

"That happens when I'm hungry," Rogue retorted. "Feed me and I'll be quiet."

Gar got to his feet, belched, then picked up a waterskin and walked to the pond. The campfire made shadows on his back as he squatted and filled the skin. Then he brought it back and dropped it into Rogue's lap. Even though his hands were tied, the young man was able to tip the skin up enough to take a long drink.

"That's a little better," he said as Gar took the skin away and handed it to another captive. "But you never said what's going to happen at this Tower of Krell."

Gar smiled grimly. "That's because I'm a lowly mercenary." He waved his arm in a broad gesture at the well-fed, well-clad men who lounged in the firelight. "All of us, we're just vassals of the ones who make the decisions. Ain't no way in the world we can know what the high-muck-a-mucks are going to do with you."

The loudmouthed man by the campfire snickered, so Rogue knew Gar was lying. It didn't matter, though. Whatever Krell or any other member of the Order might have planned for him, it would certainly be bad. Once the camp settled down and most of the guards went to sleep, he tried again to get free. The mercenaries had tied the ropes expertly, though. Besides, a guard with a torch would come by every little while and check his bonds. Plainly, Rogue thought as morning came on, these men were highly paid, well-trained experts.

That gave him another idea, though. "Hey," he said to Gar as they walked along the next morning. "You ought to let me join you. I'm big, I'm strong. I've been in some pretty nasty scuffles. I'd fit right in."

Gar looked at the young man out of the corner of one eye. "You're no dummy, either, are you? Sorry, but it's not for the likes of anyone here to decide what happens to you. Krell makes all the big decisions on Kolpos."

Rogue nodded. He felt disappointment but no surprise. "When do we get to this tower of his?"

"With luck, we should get there sundown today."

"I'm glad of that. I'm hungry enough to eat an ox."

Gar looked at him. "Enjoy that hunger," he finally said, then turned away.

Rogue thought about that for a while. There could be no doubt, the mercenary knew more than he was letting on. Rogue hung back, walking as slowly as he could get away with, and racked his brain for some way to escape. Meantime the group marched over hill and grassland, through terrain that became progressively rougher.

But for all the fact that Rogue felt no hurry to confront Krell, the young man's hunger drove him toward their destination. It was not logical; there was not even an offer of food once they got there. Be that as it may, his eyes hungered for the hump on the horizon that would make an end to their journey.

He saw no building, though, and the horizon itself became bumpier and bumpier, rolling with hills and jagged cliffs. Their progress became slow. From where the trail led past a hill's crest, he could look down and see the sea glistening ahead of him. Still, no kind of tower presented itself. "These men are playing with us," he murmured to himself. "I wonder where we really are going."

The trail wound down the hill, and they found themselves marching toward a bleak bluff of streaked marble. It was hard to make out much because the sun was getting so low, but metal gleamed in the hollow ahead of them. Then he saw men lighting torches and realized they were marching toward a pair of looming bronze doors set into the foot of the cliff. Several guards stood in front of the doors, dressed the same as Rogue's captors. The two groups hailed each other as they drew close.

"Where are we?" Rogue asked.

"The Tower of Krell," Gar answered.

"What tower? All I see is a couple of doors."

Gar laughed. "You forget you're dealing with men who don't think the way you do. What makes you think you always have to start at ground level and build upward to make a tower? Why can't you start at ground level and build downward?"

Rogue stared at the man in the gathering darkness. "You're crazy. You're all crazy."

Gar laughed. "Suit yourself. At least my hands are free." He walked away, still chuckling at what seemed to Rogue a pretty thin joke.

"Welcome," one of the guards at the door said. "It looks as if you've come back with something."

The leader of Rogue's captors clapped the man on the shoulder. "It went perfectly. We got the horses, we got enough salt to serve an army, we even got a nice string of . . ." He paused and glanced at the captives. "Human property," he finally said with a wink.

"You did yourself a favor," the other guard said. "Krell will be here tonight. He's brought a guest, too."

"An important guest?"

The guard nodded. "The most important there is. Horyk."

The officer whistled. "Horyk the Archpriest. Back on Kolpos. Yes, it's a good thing we brought back all we could get. I suppose there'll be a lot going on tonight." He eyed the captives. "Krell and Horyk—they'll want these men, probably all of them."

"Without a doubt."

"What's Horyk doing back, anyway?"

"State visit, they say. They stayed at the Local Order's temple in Touros for a night, but Krell always wants to show off this place." He shrugged. "If you're looking to work your way up, you invite the head of the Order to your special retreat."

The officer nodded. "We'd better get these fellows put away for the night." He turned toward his men and the captives. "Come on, you. It's getting late. In with you, and we'll get you cleaned up."

The huge doors swung open with a groan. The guards prodded the captives with sword and spearpoint, herding them through the looming gate like so many cattle. Torches lined a high passageway, carved into the living stone of the cliff. A little way along, they came to a lofty chamber, out of which branched several more passages. Rogue looked about in awe and wondered how long it had taken to carve all this and how many men had slaved their lives away doing it.

They turned down one of the tunnels. A new set of guards

went with them now, but they wore the same kind of leather armor the others had. They passed into a long, low chamber that smelled of sweaty bodies and stale urine. Several men in plain, white robes came through a doorway and eyed them as they plodded in.

"Hold it right there," a guard yelled. "Form a line in the middle of the room. Stand up straight and try not to look too stupid."

The prisoners shuffled to a halt. The long march without food had taken all the spirit out of them. Even the Old Prophet looked around the space with dead eyes and hardly even seemed to notice the attendant who looked them all up and down. "A pretty sorry lot," he said in a nasty voice. "I've never seen a group of men this filthy." He walked back and forth in front of them, looking them over with a jaundiced eye. At last he stopped in front of Rogue. "This one looks interesting," he said.

Rogue looked back at him hopefully. "I could be a guard," he offered. "I'm strong and I know how to fight."

"Perhaps," the attendant said with a sniff. "But you're stupid, or you wouldn't be in fetters. And you're ugly as sin." He turned to the others. "Ah, well," he said. "He's far the best of a poor lot. Put him in a separate cell—we might find a use for him. As for the others, get them some clean clothes and take them down to the next level."

"Should we feed them?" another attendant asked.

"No food. No water, either, until we know when we need them. With Horyk the Archpriest coming, it might be tonight."

"Oh," the Old Prophet said. "I'm hungry." Others protested, too, but if did them no good. Guards and attendants forced them from the room with kicks and shoves.

Two more men took Rogue down a different tunnel, to a series of small rooms with hardwood doors. One man pulled the first door open. "Go in there," he said. "You'll find a washbasin. Use it. You'll also find robes like I'm wearing. Put them on." Before Rogue could respond, they shoved him through the door and locked it after him.

He tripped and sprawled on the marble floor. "But my hands are tied," he yelled. "How can I do anything with my hands tied?"

"You're young and strong," came a voice back through the door. "You'll get them untied."

Rogue rolled onto his back and looked around the room. "Why bother?" he said to himself. Then he saw why. At one end of the room stood a ladder a few cubits high, which led to a platform. On top of the platform sat three loaves of bread and three pitchers. A stubby spur stuck out on top of one ladder rung—the rungs were close together, but the spike plainly could be used to pick apart the knots at Rogue's wrists. He smiled grimly. "Pretty sneaky," he said to himself.

Plainly, whoever had designed the cell knew that, sooner or later, his hunger and thirst would force him to work out of his bonds and climb the ladder. The spur was set so he could use it for nothing more than that. He sighed, squirmed to his feet, and made his way across the room. Moments later, he had freed himself, climbed the ladder, and was feasting on stale bread and water. He had never realized stale bread could taste that good.

He ate two of the loaves and drank a full pitcher of the water, all so fast he almost choked himself. Then he lay atop the platform and closed his eyes. He saw the washbasin below him and the clean robes, too. A wash would feel good. He could take his sweet time getting around to that, though.

He slept awhile, then climbed back down the ladder and performed his toilette. Then he slept again. By this time, he had no idea how long he had been in the cell. He ate some of the remaining bread, and after a long time an attendant unlocked the door and came in.

Rogue looked down from the platform and debated whether to try to overpower the man and escape. His expression must have shown his thoughts, because the fellow said, "It will do you no good to fight me. There are two guards waiting outside this door and a lot more between here and the outside. I myself am trained in hand-to-hand combat. Your only course is to obey."

"Thanks," Rogue said. "That's what I really wanted to hear."

"You've done well," the man said. He picked up Rogue's old clothes and handed them to someone outside the door. Then he did the same with the basin of dirty water and the towel that lay beside it. "Some people don't bother to clean themselves as long as they have something to eat."

"It felt good to wash," Rogue said. He climbed down the ladder and faced the man. "What are you going to do with me? Whatever it is, I probably won't like it, will I?"

"You're very lucky. Horyk the Archpriest will arrive in a short while. You will be the archpriest's personal slave."

Rogue frowned. "Why me?"

"Does it seem too good to be true?" The man shrugged. "You're young, you're strong. The archpriest likes to have a young, strong man about to follow orders. Don't question your luck, just follow me." He turned toward the door, then looked back when Rogue did not move. "Follow me," he repeated. "If you refuse, you won't like what happens next."

The two men locked eyes for a moment. Then Rogue shrugged and followed the attendant out of the room. As he had been warned, two armed guards waited for them, along with another attendant. They made their way along corridors the youth had not yet seen, then along runways and down spiral bronze staircases, deep into the bowels of the Tower of Krell.

Chapter Sixteen:
New Landings

THE CITY OF Guelt was unlike any other city in any other land about the Thlassa Mey. Ringed on three sides by rugged mountains and on the fourth by an easily defended harbor, it was a place of mystery, intrigue, and wonder, accessible only to friends or peaceful traders.

As they clambered from their smelly roundship into the barge that would haul them to shore, Rinna and Lissa gazed in wonder at the city's skyline. Above the city wall towered spires, steeples, minarets, all painted the brightest reds and blues and greens. "There's got to be magic in a place like this," Rinna breathed. "I never knew such a place could even exist."

"There's magic here, all right," Geryam said. "But you'd best beware of it. It's not often the kind of magic that'll leave you happy memories."

"Have you been here before?" Owras asked.

Geryam looked puzzled. "I can't say for sure. But it all looks familiar, and I have . . ." He hesitated. "I just have a feel for the place."

"Is this where you had your ... your adventure?" Lissa asked.

Geryam shrugged. "I couldn't tell you."

"Probably not," Owras said. "There isn't a lot of arable land around Guelt; it's too mountainous. And for all the strange and wonderful things that happen here, cockfighting isn't the popular sport it is in other places." His mouth twisted in irony as he used the words "strange" and "wonderful." Guelt could be a dangerous city for travelers. Still, the Dark Order was not strong here, because the place was so isolated. Therefore, it was a good port by which to enter the mainland.

Owras, Rinna, Lissa, and Geryam had parted company from the pilgrims with many hugs and tears. But the Local Order on Artos had made life too hot for them to stay together. They had broken into groups, had wandered to the villages and cities along the seacoast by dribs and drabs, and had fled to a dozen different places. Most had journeyed to the island of Muse. Some had taken ship to Carea, or to Oron or Danaar. The four questers had sailed south, toward Guelt.

"The Order may think they've ground us out, but they're wrong," Owras had said. "They've dispersed our sect to many different lands. What they don't understand is, when you disperse the truth, you just make it spread faster. Every place one or two of us go, the truth will spring up like new flames. They can't ever make us go away."

For their part, the four had decided to follow Geryam's vision. They would go where the Fates led them, wander until they found the priest who had put the warrior through his ordeal. If that was the Maiden's wish, then there was more need for it than just one man's revenge.

"Far as I'm concerned, I don't really have any ill feelings toward the man," Geryam would say. "He's not the first who ever tried to kill me, and he most likely won't be the last. He was just the most novel about it."

Owras's voice cut him off. "If the Maiden told you to find him, it wasn't for your revenge."

"That's what she told me, too," Geryam said. "But I wish I knew what she did have in mind."

"No one can know the answer to a question like that. She has to have reasons of her own."

Geryam nodded. For all his blunt attitude, his faith in the Maiden was plainly complete.

The barge made its slow way to the dock, rowed by two stolid watermen who seemed as oblivious of their passengers as if they had been in another world. When they had finally tied up in the inner harbor, Owras paid the two men, and all the passengers climbed onto the stone jetty.

"What a place," Rinna breathed. From the waterfront, Guelt looked even more striking than from the outer harbor. Faces and clothing unlike anything she'd ever seen paraded along the docks. She saw sailors, merchants, soldiers, courtesans, and the most unusual men and women.

"Take care for your money," Geryam cautioned. "Any waterfront has more thieves than honest people, and this one is worse than most."

Like the others, Rinna carried a purse with several coins. Hers was tied to her girdle, under her outer gown, but she still slipped her hand under her clothes and held it. She looked all around her and knew every word Geryam said about this place had to be true.

A wizened old man in silk robes stared at her, then came closer. "My, my," he said, gazing at the two maidens. "What loveliness. You two girls have all the charm of youth and all the loveliness of your femininity." He turned to Owras. "Let them go with me to seek their fortunes. I guarantee you'll have enough money to last the rest of your life."

"You've got to be joking," Owras said.

"In no wise. I'll make women of them, and we'll all reap the benefits of their beauty."

"Get lost," Geryam said.

"Be reasonable. Look at me, look at the priceless clothes I wear. I'll see them outfitted in garments even more exquisite. They'll learn to sing, to dance, to play the lute and the cittern. They'll meet all the finest people."

"I said for you to get lost," Geryam repeated. Then he shoved the man so hard the fellow staggered and almost fell.

"That was a mistake," the man said. "You're all fools. I could have made life easy for all of you." He glared at them, then shook his fist. "You'll be sorry, just see if you aren't." He watched them walk on, then faded into the crowd.

"What was that all about?" Lissa asked with an incredulous smile. "You'd think he wanted to make us into princesses."

"You're already princesses," Owras said. "Never mind scum like him."

They walked on. The two maidens stared at every sight, sniffed every odor, and strained to hear every sound. Owras and Geryam marched stolidly along, paying little attention to the city's bustle and hubbub. They came to a high archway that formed a gap in the endless line of buildings facing the waterfront. Beyond lay a square packed with people, noisy with drums and music.

"What's in there?" Lissa asked.

"It's a bazaar," Owras said. "A thriving one, by the look of it."

"Can we go see?"

Owras looked up at Geryam; then they both shrugged. "I suppose we can pass through. One route is about the same as another right now."

They made their way into the square and found a hustle and bustle that made the waterfront look tame. Rows of tables and stalls filled the center of the space, and vendors hawked every kind of ware: fruit, vegetables, jewelry, knives, lamps. Gamblers rolled dice on the cobblestones or laid cards down on ornate tables. Vendors worked their way through the jammed crowd, carrying baskets of candy, racks of fruit, every kind of ware.

Around the square stood ramshackle wooden buildings, all painted bright colors, with bright cloth posters advertising entertainments or services. In front of some, men played music or women danced to draw a crowd. Some were no more than closed booths and boasted only one exhibit: a demon's live hand or a talking dog or a child with two heads. Others promised sizable entertainments: a troupe of acrobats or a band of singers and musicians.

"That one's different," Lissa said as she looked up at one of the posters. "And there's no one at all in front of that building. No one harangued the crowd at this attraction, no dancers or musicians drummed up business. There was only a huge poster, which covered the entire front of the frame structure. PAL-DAN, THE HUMAN WORM, it read. FEATS OF MAGIC, WONDER

OF THE WORLD. SEES THE UNSEEN, HEARS THE UNHEARD. ADMIS-
SION, A FARTHING. In the center of the poster was a rude paint-
ing of a worm—more like a snake, really—with a man's
mustached face.

"Who needs someone to shout his talents to the square when
he does all those things," Owras said with a smile. "Sounds
like a real miracle man."

"When it costs that much to get in, he'd better do miracles,"
Geryam said. "The place looks awfully quiet. I wonder if
there's even anyone in there."

"I'd like to go in," Lissa said.

"Oh, Lissa," Rinna said with a toss of her head. "If you
want to see a show, there has to be a better one than this."

"Maybe, but this is the one I want to see."

Owras and Geryam looked at one another. "Should we in-
dulge such a fancy?" Owras asked with a smile.

"I don't see why," Geryam replied. "We've only got so
much coin."

"This will be worth it," Lissa said. "I know it will."

Owras's smile faded as he studied the maiden's face. Finally,
he pushed aside the drapery that hung across the building's entrance. "Come along, then," he said.

They walked along a corridor made of lath that had stained
cloth laid over it. After a few paces, the passage made a couple
of turns; then they found themselves in a little tent theater. A
circle of wooden benches surrounded a sandy space. In the
space stood a couple of chairs, a ladder, a drum, a rack on
which hung some articles of clothing. A low wooden tunnel,
made of old barrels fastened end to end, led from the center of
the circle to the far side of the tent.

"Who do we pay?" Geryam said. "There's no one here."

"Looks as if you put your money here," Rinna said. Behind
each bench stood a stout pole to support the tent's cloth top.
On one of the poles hung a bronze canister with a slot in the
top. Painted in white on the front were the words ADMISSION,
ONE FARTHING EACH.

"How do they make a living out of something like this?"
Geryam said, knitting his brows. "Most places like this, they'd
have a half-dozen people grabbing for your money by this
time."

"Maybe you just put your money in the box and when no one shows up, you finally leave," Rinna said with a smirk. "That'd turn them a nice profit."

"They don't do it that way," Lissa said. "Not this one—put some money in, Owras, and you'll see."

"I don't doubt you're right," Owras said. "But it's a curious operation, all the same." He untied his purse from his belt and pulled out four farthings. When he dropped them into the container, they landed with a clang. To the surprise of all, the metal bottom dropped open with a tinkle of bells and the coins landed in the dirt below. "Humph," he said. "That's novel."

"Thank you, friends," came a hollow-sounding voice. They all turned, but saw nothing.

"Where are you?" Geryam said, looking about uncertainly.

"Right here." This time, they could tell the voice came from the wooden tunnel. An instant later, a face appeared, followed by a misshapen body. The man lay between the ages of Owras and Geryam and possessed the face shown on the poster. His body looked human, however, not like the snake's body they had pictured. He had neither arms nor legs, only little appendages that looked like flippers.

He wore a sort of knit wool garment with holes where his arms and legs should have been. All four visitors stared at him. "What do we do with these coins?" asked Owras, who had picked them up from the dust.

"Throw them to me," the fellow answered. "One at a time."

"Give me a coin," Lissa said. Owras handed her one of the farthings, and she tossed it toward the deformed creature. She missed her aim, but to the surprise of all of them, the man wriggled under the falling coin and caught it between his teeth. With a deft motion, he twisted his head and slipped the farthing into a little pocket knit into the front of his garment.

He looked up at them from where he lay, plainly amused by their expressions. "Now the next coin," he said with a smile. Rinna tossed the next one, then Geryam, then Owras. He caught all three as nimbly as he had caught the first. Once he had tucked them into his pocket as quickly as a frog tucks flies into its belly, he said, "I am Pal-Dan. Prepare to be amused."

They seated themselves on a bench and watched while he performed feats one would have thought impossible for an armless, legless man. He climbed up and down the ladder in the center of the ring, wriggling up from rung to rung even better than a worm. He played the drum, holding the drumstick under each stub where his arms should have been. He used flint and steel to make a fire, then played a little melody on an odd tin whistle while the smoke rose to the top of the tent. At last, he sat himself up on his buttocks, leaned back against the tent pole that rose from the center of the ring, and smiled. "Thank you for coming and seeing me," he said. "I hope you have been amused."

"You said you could read minds and do all sorts of other things," Lissa said. "We want to see that, too."

"Ah," Pal-Dan said. "That costs extra."

"That's a swindle," Geryam said.

"I am grieved, friend. Didn't I show you marvels already, worth more than you paid? You'll remember this for the rest of your days."

"He's got you there," Owras said to Geryam with a smile.

Lissa fished her purse out of her clothing, opened it, found another farthing. "Here's more," she said, tossing it to the performer. "Now read my mind."

Pal-Dan caught that coin just as he had caught the others. "Very well," he said with a smile once he had tucked the farthing away. "You want to know how I became the way I am, and you want to know what other miracles I can perform?" His smile became a grin. "That's what's in all your minds right now."

"You tricked me," Lissa said in a scandalized voice. "That didn't take any special powers."

Pal-Dan laughed. "Lots of men know how to see into the souls of others," he said. "No one ever said it took magic."

"It's still not fair," Lissa repeated. "Tell me something more."

"You're young. You see from your heart because you haven't yet learned to see with your eyes."

This time it was Owras who laughed. "I've been telling her that much myself," he said.

"Then you're a wise man," Pal-Dan said.

"You still haven't told me anything special," Lissa cried.

"Nothing that's worth a whole farthing. I'm a nice person, so you have to give me my money's worth."

Pal-Dan cocked his head to one side. "I believe you are," he said. He crawled back toward the fire and eyed her again. "Protests and insults wouldn't have gained you anything—I've been argued with and insulted a million times in my life. But—" He paused to breathe, because the crawling was plainly hard work for him. "—because I believe you're as nice as you say you are, I'll tell you a little something to nettle you."

He paused for a moment as if in thought, then peered at them through the rising fumes from the fire. "You come from a far place," he said at last, quietly. "You're running away from something. You are also hunting something, all of you. But that man"—he jerked his chin at Geryam—"is hunting the most of all."

Lissa's mouth fell open. "How did you know that?" she cried.

Pal-Dan made a motion that would have been a shrug in any person with arms. For him, it just turned into a funny little wiggle. "I looked at you and that's what I saw."

"Tell us more."

Again, there was a pause. Finally, Pal-Dan said, "You two girlies have lost your parents."

This time, little sounds of amazement came from all four. "By the Maiden," Owras said. "How did you know that?"

"The same way I knew the rest. I see by your faces, I've earned that last farthing. Now I bid you all a good afternoon." With that, though they shouted for him to stop, he wriggled with lightning speed into his wooden tunnel.

The four looked at one another after he had gone. "That was strange," Owras said.

"It had to be some kind of trick," Geryam said.

"Doubtless. But very impressive, all the same."

"Quiet," Lissa said. "He can probably hear you."

"No doubt," Owras said. He stood. "It's all been interesting, but we've spent a lot of time here, and we still have far to go. It's time to leave."

"I don't want to leave," Lissa said. "I like him, and I want to ask him more questions." She stepped toward the tunnel's entrance. "Mister Pal-Dan," she called. "Please come out. I just want to talk."

"Oh, come on," Rinna said. "Let's just go."

"No, no, and no again," Lissa said. "We don't know where we're going anyway. He's really smart. Let's ask him some questions, maybe he can give us some kind of hint that'll help."

"He's just putting on a show," Rinna said. "We're not going to learn anything useful from him."

"Oh, foof."

"Skeek," Rinna said.

"Wait," Owras said. "Lissa's got a point," He put his hands on Lissa's shoulders and faced her. "I'm inclined to humor you this time, little princess. But Rinna's right, too—we have to talk to him in private."

"I wonder where a man like that can even live," Rinna said.

"Follow the tunnel," Geryam said, pointing toward the back of the tent. "Let's give it a go."

They went back outside but found they could not reach the rear of the tent from the square where they had started. The booths, displays, and stages formed a solid wall all around the bazaar. The four of them searched for a break in the wall of booths, and at last they found a narrow alley. They followed it and found themselves in a filthy, litter-strewn space. The sky was growing dark by this time, and Lissa flinched as a huge rat scurried along a ramshackle building ahead of them.

"Be careful," Geryam said. "No telling who you might run into here." He put his hand on his sword hilt and loosened the weapon in its scabbard.

"I'm glad you're here," Rinna said to Geryam. Lissa gave her a look but said nothing.

They followed and followed, tracing their way past old buildings and stone walls. Some of the buildings plainly had people living in them. Others looked deserted. The rears of the booths and tents on the bazaar side formed a patchwork of bare wood, mended canvas, ropes, rags, and stakes. At last, they passed a low wooden opening. "That's it," Lissa whispered. "It has to be."

"Sure enough," Geryam said. A path led from the opening to one of the old buildings. Worn earth did not mark the trail as much as the fact that the space had been cleared of debris. It looked as if someone had swept it with a broom.

The path led to a weathered door in a teetery old building. Cut into the original door was a smaller opening with a wooden panel hung on rings so it could swing back and forth either way. "That has to be it," Lissa said.

Geryam pounded on the main door. "What is it?" came a voice from the inside.

"We'd like to speak with you," Geryam called back.

"Go away."

"Just for a little while," Geryam called.

No answer came. At that moment, a pair of rough-looking men swaggered around a corner in the alley. They stopped when they saw the four, and one of them grinned. "Look at that," one said. "Two winsome little wenches and an old codger—and a big, ignorant lout. Just the way Moreere said it would be. Come on, lads, we've found them."

More men appeared, until six walked slowly toward the staring quartet. Geryam drew his sword, but the six also carried weapons. They pulled them from their hangers: clubs, swords, a rusty mace. "You'd better just give the girls up," the man in the lead said. "No sense dying for them. Moreere is going to get them anyway."

Lissa remembered the man who had accosted them on the waterfront. "What do you want us for?" she asked in what she hoped was a brave voice.

"You'll find out soon enough," the man in the lead said. Then he and the others leaped at Geryam. Steel clashed on steel, six to one. Rather than run, Owras scooped up a handful of dirt and sand and threw it into the eyes of the attackers. Men cursed, a couple turned away coughing; one fell as Geryam's sword found its mark. "You old devil," the leader shouted. "You'll die for that."

"Rinna, Lissa, run," Owras shouted. Even as he did, the mace found his shoulder, and he cried out in pain. Before Rinna and Lissa could even think about flight, two of the men tackled them and hauled them to the ground, screaming and struggling.

Above the sound of the fight, a whistle rang out from behind the door. A commotion started up somewhere down the alley; then the sound of running feet echoed off the faded buildings. Four men, almost as scruffy as the ones struggling with Rinna and Lissa, threw themselves into the fray. They had only bare hands against the swords and cudgels of the others, but surprise was a great advantage. They beat two of the men to the ground while Geryam's sword put another down.

More people ran up from both directions, until fifteen or twenty bodies filled the narrow space. They grabbed the attackers and pinioned their arms behind them while they cursed, spat, and struggled. "Who are you men?" one cried. "What did you want in the Quarters Gallery?"

"They wanted Rinna and Lissa," Owras said. He was rubbing his bruised shoulder where the mace had struck him, and his words came out from between clenched teeth. "Some man on the waterfront wanted them—for who knows what."

"Who are you?" the man asked Geryam.

"They're friends of mine," came a voice behind them. Everyone looked and there lay Pal-Dan, his head cocked to one side. To Rinna's eye, he looked as perplexed as anyone else. That didn't express itself in his voice, though. "They were coming to my house at my invitation when these others attacked them."

"Will you be responsible for them, then?" the man asked. "You know no stranger can walk the Gallery without a sponsor."

Pal-Dan nodded. The gesture looked strange when he did it. "I'll sponsor them, yes."

The man turned to the leader of the thieves. "As for you, sirrah, prepare yourselves to taste Gallery justice. What makes you think you can attack our guests and live?"

None of the thieves replied. Some darted fearful eyes about, while others looked sullenly at the ground. The people of the Gallery hustled them away with shouting and jeers. Other men hauled away the body of the man Geryam had slain.

"Come into my house," Pal-Dan said. "Make yourselves as comfortable as you can."

"You were the one who whistled, weren't you?" Rinna asked. "Why did you save us?"

Pal-Dan's broad mustache lifted at the ends as he smiled a broad smile. "I couldn't let you be robbed or killed, now, could

I? Mostly, I remembered hearing one of you girlies call me 'Mister Pal-Dan.' " He shook his head with amusement. "I haven't been called 'mister' in a long time. I could hardly let you get beat up after that. Now, come into my house, and we'll talk."

Chapter Seventeen:
The Human Worm

IT HAD GROWN all but dark as Pal-Dan wriggled back through the little passway fit into the bottom of the door. For an instant, the four travelers stared at one another in the gathering gloom; then they heard a loud click. The main door swung open. "Come in," Pal-Dan said.

As they walked in, Rinna saw he had used his teeth to pull a cord that hung from the door. The cord tripped a latch and allowed the door to open. She could see how a man like him would be choosy about his guests.

She looked around. The inside of the place looked well painted, in fine repair, and neat as a pin. A little mat in a corner showed where the human worm slept, and another mat with bowls on it showed where he ate. A cozy fire smiled from the little hearth, and a couple of samplers even hung on the walls. Doubtless, Rinna guessed, the samplers were gifts.

Owras and Geryam followed the two maidens in and latched the door behind them. The two men looked badly beaten about, especially Geryam. Rinna felt sorry for them. "Again, we must thank you," Owras said. "You saved us from . . . great inconvenience."

Pal-Dan smiled. "You're welcome."

"What's going to happen to those men?" Lissa asked.

"Why should you care?"

"I don't know. But I guess I do."

Pal-Dan made a face. "You needn't worry about them. They'll get a good beating and a coating of dirt and hot grease. Then they'll get escorted to the waterfront. They dared enter the Quarter Gallery of Guelt's Great Bazaar without permission." He eyed his guests. "The same thing could have happened to you, you know."

"I apologize," Owras said. "We're newcomers to Guelt."

"I know you are. What do you want?"

"How did you know those things about us?" Lissa asked.

"By watching you," Pal-Dan said impatiently. "I have peepholes cut in my tunnel. I watch people carefully, I learn things. You two girls aren't related to these men, they didn't act like father or uncle or brother or grandfather. Yet you were traveling together. Therefore, it was safe to assume you had lost your real parents." He took a breath. "Your clothing, your mannerisms, your speech—all told me you were not from here. I study things like that. I'd guess you were from one of the outer islands—except for him." He jerked his head at Geryam.

"Remarkable," Owras said.

"Too simple for words, really."

"And those things you do, all without arms or legs. How did you learn them?"

"I had to learn them, didn't I? I didn't ask to go through life without arms or legs, and I do intend to survive. You might just as well ask me why I keep my floor so clean. I have to— it's where I spend all my time." He crawled to his sleeping mat, which plainly doubled as the only chair he could comfortably use. He lay back on it, put his head on his pillow, and sighed. "I asked you before and you didn't answer. What do you want with me?"

The travelers looked at one another. "I wanted them to ask you for help," Lissa blurted.

Owras and Geryam stared at the maiden. "Lissa," the old man said. "Take some care."

Pal-Dan ignored Owras. "Help doing what?" he asked. "How can the Human Worm help real people, girlie?"

"I don't like being called that," Rinna said.

"That suits me," Pal-Dan replied. "I don't like being a freak." His mustache moved with his grin. "Girlie."

"That's not fair," Rinna said.

"I didn't ask you to come here, so I'll call you what I want. Girlie."

"Then call us anything," Lissa cried. She looked at all of them, then back at Pal-Dan. "The poster in front of your tent says you know all."

"Pshaw." Pal-Dan sneered.

"She's young," Owras said in an embarrassed voice. "She believes what she reads."

"It was as good an idea as any of you had," Lissa said hotly. "So don't go looking down your noses at me."

"Foof," Rinna said, but no one answered.

"What are you looking for?" Pal-Dan asked Geryam with a veiled expression.

"Wait a minute," Geryam said. "Why do we have to answer that question?"

"You're in my house," Pal-Dan said. "I get to know why you're here."

"That's fair," Owras said. "May we sit?"

Pal-Dan nodded. "Sit anywhere."

They all looked about. The room had no chairs, so one by one, they finally seated themselves cross-legged on the floor. The boards felt smooth, polished by constant stoning and brushing. Rinna looked at Pal-Dan. How many hours had he spent with a brush or floor stone between his teeth? For the least instant, she felt an inkling of the life the Human Worm lived. She flushed and decided she would not again bridle at any disrespect he showed.

"We're looking for a man," Owras began. "We don't know who he is."

"How old is he? Where does he live? What does he look like?"

"We don't know any of those things," Lissa said. "We only know he's a priest high in the Order."

Silence filled the room as everyone stared at her. Owras put his fingers to his temples and slowly shook his head. Pal-Dan smiled. "Thank you, girlie," he said. "At least someone is willing to say something, to move this conversation along. I see the old gentleman is afraid to tell too much—but you needn't be afraid of me, friend. I have no love for the Dark Order."

"Thank you," Owras said, his voice thick with relief.

"But how do you hope to find someone when you don't even know who you're looking for?" Pal-Dan asked.

"That's what we're asking you," Lissa said.

Pal-Dan laughed. "And I'm supposed to know? Come on, girlie, let me admit my failings. There are lots of things I don't know, for all my posters may say. What plans do you have with this priest once you know where he is?"

"We don't know that, either," Geryam said. "We're just supposed to find him."

"Hmm. Strange errand. I won't ask you who sends you on this quest."

"Does it matter?" Owras said.

"I suppose not." Pal-Dan sighed and stared up at the ceiling. "I've had dealings with the Order's priests," he said in a dreamy voice. "One in particular."

Geryam eyed him. "What did he do to you?"

Pal-Dan stared back at the warrior. Their eyes met and locked from across the room. "I wasn't born this way," he finally said. "I was a merchant's son: young, handsome, wealthy. Then I fell in love with a maiden—tall, red-haired, eyes green as a forest lake."

"Go on, please," Geryam said in a strange voice.

"Not much to go on about. Turned out she was married, though she didn't tell me. Her husband was high priest of the Local Order on the island of Touros. A bad one, he was, and very powerful. Knew magic. All the Dark Order's priests know magic."

The room had gone silent as a tomb. Pal-Dan sighed and went on. "He had me kidnapped right off my father's boat and hauled to some secret room he used for his dirty work. Full of beakers, books, stuffed animals."

"That's it," Geryam said in a deadly voice. "What was his name?"

"Don't you know? Guess you've never been to Touros—everyone there does. He's called Krell."

Geryam let out a breath. His face grew red in the firelight. "That's him," he finally said. "That's the name."

Owras's eyes landed on the warrior's strained features. "You mean that was the man who . . . who changed you?" the old man said.

"Yes." Geryam's voice was hardly a whisper. "He was the one. I remember it now, as clear as if it were an hour ago. He was a heavyset man, balding, with just a tuft of gray hair above his ears. He had me thrown into a cell, and when they hauled me out, they conked me on the head and I woke up in a room."

"Metal wall, shelves full of books and instruments, with long tables in the middle of it," Pal-Dan said as if he were telling the story himself.

"Yes," Geryam said again. "Yes. There were cages with strange animals and jars full of things I couldn't even name. The place smelled like a nightmare. Spicy, sweet, rotten, all kinds of smells, all mixed up."

"I went through that room ten years ago," Pal-Dan said.

"Tell me your story," Geryam said.

"If you'll tell me yours."

Geryam repeated once more the tale of how he had met the lovely Nyala and how he had seduced her. He told how it had turned out she was Krell's bride and how the dark priest had learned of the affair.

"So it was with me," Pal-Dan said. "Exactly so. I sang in the marketplace and sometimes for nobles and clergy for my bread. She heard me at a party and told me she liked my voice. Reddish brown was her hair, a great, long streamer of it, down to the small of her back. She couldn't have been twenty yet."

"That's impossible," Geryam said. "She was just that age when I met her, and that was years later."

The two men stared at one another, the warrior and the freak. Owras cleared his throat. "Seems to me you were both trapped," the old man said. "You thought you were gaining a prize, but I think it's more likely you were walking just the path Krell laid out for you, for reasons all his own."

"I'm sure you're right," Pal-Dan said slowly. Then he

laughed until his sides shook. He lay back on his mat and shook his head. "Either he laid the trap or she did, I'm sure of it, now. Oh, my, if they planned to make me feel foolish, they've done a good job."

"More likely there was a darker reason," Owras said.

"I'm sure of that," Geryam said bitterly. "Oh, I wonder— how many men have been had the same as we were?"

"However many it was, we all walked down the path willingly," Pal-Dan said. "And *there's* a lesson." He glanced at Rinna and Lissa, then took a breath. "So, my friend. Tell me the story of what you became under Krell's care. And how did you come to be as you are today?"

Geryam started talking again. The story took time in the telling, and Owras and the two maidens had heard it all before. Geryam and Pal-Dan swapped memories until late at night. By the time they had finished, Rinna and Lissa had fallen asleep, and Owras's head nodded every so often.

At last, Geryam said, "I want to find Krell. The Maiden told me to do it, but I want to find him for my own sake, too. I want to look him in the eye."

"You want vengeance, then?" Pal-Dan asked, his eyes bright.

"I don't know what I want. I just want to look him in the face. I want him to see me, too."

"*I* want vengeance," Pal-Dan said. "I'm willing to put a name on what I want. I want to see him bleed for what he did to me." He scowled.

Owras's eyes opened and he gazed at the freak. "Vengeance is a long and narrow path," he said slowly. "It turns back on itself sometimes."

"Maybe so, but that doesn't mean I wouldn't like some all the same." Pal-Dan looked at Geryam, then at Owras, then back again. "I have a favor to ask."

Owras looked at him narrowly. "What?"

"I want to go with you."

"How?" Geryam asked. "You don't have arms or legs. How could you travel? How could you defend yourself if trouble came?"

"And trouble will come," Owras said.

"Who was it who saved your bacon when trouble came to-night?" Pal-Dan asked.

"This is different," Geryam said. "You've got friends here in Guelt. Out there . . ." He waved an arm to indicate the unseen world beyond the walls that enclosed them.

"I know, I know," Pal-Dan said. "I'm just a freak, I can't take care of myself. Let me show you something I've never shown any other man. When Krell took my arms and legs away, he didn't use knives and saws, you know. He used his art, the dark secrets he's learned. But I don't think he knows all he did to me. I don't think even he knows just how much he changed me."

The freak looked again from one face to the other. Then he whispered, "Watch and wonder." He closed his eyes and they heard his breath quicken. The flesh at his shoulder squirmed, writhed; a lump formed, turned into a tentacle that grew, hovered in the air over their heads. From his hip grew another tentacle, pushed aside the breechcloth at his waist, formed and moved with a fluid motion that made their skin crawl.

Owras watched, eyes wide. "Why don't you use that in your act?" he asked.

"And take a chance on the news getting back to the Order?" Pal-Dan shook his head. "Not likely. Besides, how many coppers do you think I'd pick up by scaring everybody to death? I've watched myself do this many times, and it even gives *me* the creeps. The people would run screaming from my tent, and I'd starve to death."

As he spoke, one tentacle rose to the room's lone window. "It's warm in here," he said. The tentacle pulled the pin that held the shutters latched, pushed the wooden screens open, and let a soft breeze into the room. At the same time, the other tentacle hovered over Rinna's head. The tip of it descended and tousled her blond hair playfully.

The maiden's eyes popped open. She saw the tentacle, flinched, and let out a gasp. "Easy," Geryam said in a low voice. "Don't you touch those two."

"Wait a bit," Pal-Dan said with a grin. "You just said I couldn't defend myself. Now you're talking as though I'm someone people have to be defended *from*. You can't have it both ways.

Rinna edged away from the freak and bumped into Lissa, who woke up and also gasped to see how their host had changed. Owras studied the scene with pursed lips. "There's more here than meets the eye," he said quietly.

"You have to take me with you," Pal-Dan said. "I've waited a long time for this chance."

"Yes, let him go with us," Lissa said. "He can help us."

Owras studied her. "Are you sure, little princess?" he asked.

"Every inch of me." Her eyes showed her sincerity.

"You wanted us to talk with this man right from the start, didn't you? Do you want him in on the quest now?"

Lissa turned her head to one side. "I don't know why, but I feel sure we need him. And I knew from the start he would go with us."

Owras watched her, then said, "That's interesting. Well, for my part, I have no objection. What about you, Rinna?"

Rinna shook her head. "I don't mind. He just gave me a turn, that's all."

"Then it's voted on and decided," Geryam said. He smiled at Pal-Dan. "I guess you've made your point."

"Thank you," Pal-Dan said. He retracted the tentacles so quickly his guests blinked. "I don't deny I have trouble getting around, but I'll see to it you don't regret your decision."

Rinna stood, then yawned and stretched. "I'm tired," she said.

"You all can sleep here," Pal-Dan said. "I have extra mats. It's not much, but it's shelter."

"Thank you," Rinna said. "Right now, I don't care where I . . ." She glanced out the open window as she spoke, then threw her hands to her face and screamed. "It's *him*." She backed away from the window until she tripped and fell over Pal-Dan.

"What's going on?" Geryam cried. He leaped to his feet and stared out the window at what the maiden had seen. They all did. On the ground outside, framed in the feeble square of light the low-burning fire cast, sat Rinna's old pet, Fuzzy Waddles. It had grown huge, a gleaming black apparition with fangs that stuck down from its upper jaw like knives. Its eyes glowed red as evil embers, and its laugh chilled them like a cold wind.

Geryam jerked his sword from its sheath. "Get ready," he

said. But the beast unfolded its huge bat's wings, flapped them until choking dust blew in through the window, then rose as lightly as a dandelion wisp. It hovered an instant, then shot off toward the east at a speed that staggered the mind.

Geryam coughed from the dust, and everybody in the room had to wipe their eyes. The warrior pulled the shutters closed and latched them. Everyone in the room looked badly shaken. "What in the world was that?" Pal-Dan asked.

"An evil messenger," Owras said.

"Yes," Geryam said. "And a murderer in the night. I don't know where we're going to sleep tonight, Pal-Dan, but it's not going to be here. I hope your friends are as generous with sleeping space as they are in a street fight."

Chapter Eighteen:
Horyk the Archpriest

ROGUE FOLLOWED THE two guards and the attendant through an endless maze of ramps, runways, and corridors. The Tower of Krell was an immense labyrinth, which must have taken generations to build. As they descended a series of gleaming bronze staircases, it grew warmer and warmer until the heat became oppressive.

Rogue used his forearm to skim away the sweat. "It's hot down here," he said to the attendant. "Why? Shouldn't it be cool in a cave?"

The attendant looked over his shoulder and smiled. "Not this one," he said. He stood as if making a decision, then said, "Come. We'll make a side trip and I'll show you something."

They turned back from the door they had reached, followed still another corridor, then clattered down steep bronze steps that gleamed with an eerie glow. Rogue stared around him. Metal chambers hung like a series of bronze boxes, fastened in place with shining bands. The stairways, ramps, and runways that stretched between the buildings helped stabilize the mass, but he could feel the structure vibrate with every step.

"This place gives me the creeps," he said. "How many of those metal bands would have to break before it fell?"

The attendant smiled. "The structure is strong," he said. "The chambers and the reinforcing bands are made of iron, with the bronze only as a veneer. It's all inspected from time to time." As he spoke, they reached the bottom of the spiraling steps and walked out onto a landing. "You have reached the bottom of the Tower of Krell," the attendant said. "Now you may look down on what warms us."

The metal plates beneath Rogue's feet were almost too hot for him to stand on. If he hadn't been wearing heavy sandals, he would not have been able to stay where he was. The heat drove the sweat down his body in a steady stream as he moved to the bronze railing at the far side.

The blast of hot air that issued from below took his breath away. Around him stretched an immense, black cavern, a night sky of darkness but all underground. Far, far below, a massive pool, red and silver with heat, formed the cavern's floor. Rogue could only look for an instant before the heat forced him back from the landing's edge.

"You're looking at the very bowels of the world," the attendant said. "That stuff is melted stone, boiled up from the center of all things."

"How far below us is it?" Rogue asked.

"We don't know, exactly. No way to measure. Stories have it that at least one workman fell into that magma for each level of the Tower of Krell when this place was being built. It's said that you could hear them screaming for a long time as they fell." He smiled as he eyed Rogue's expression. "Come," he said. "I'll take you back up to wait for Horyk."

They made their way back up the circling bronze steps. Rogue found the climb exhausting in the heat, and the walk back up the slanting runway that followed was no better. "What holds this place up?" he asked as they went. "And who in the world would want to stay here in this heat, when the whole thing might land in that magma any time?"

"Long, long ago, the first builders set great rods of carbonized iron into the stone far above. There are many such rods, each named for one of the dark gods. They never rust, they never weaken." He stopped for a breath. "As for the heat, if you're lucky, you'll get used to it. Krell adores the heat of this cavern, and so does Horyk. The archpriest has often visited our wonderful tower."

They started up again. As they arrived at the door before which they had paused earlier, trumpet notes sounded softly from far, far above. A long fanfare, as from many instruments, wafted down through the cavern, along with the sound of cheering as heard from far off. The attendant looked up, though all he could see was the level above them. "That will be Krell and Horyk," he said. "We have to hurry."

He took a huge key from his belt and unlocked the door. When he pushed it open, he revealed a large room with walls of pure, polished bronze, inlaid with tracings of silver about the doorways and fittings. Rogue caught his breath. Never in his life had he even imagined such splendor. Candles gleamed from holders of glittering gold. Their light reflected off the gleaming walls until it was bright as day inside.

"This is the apartment Horyk uses on visits," the attendant said. "You should be reverent in here—or anywhere in the tower. But especially here, because Horyk is only a little below the Dark Ones themselves."

He pulled open a gleaming cabinet and removed clothing. "This is the robe you will wear in the presence of Krell or the archpriest," he said as he handed the garment to Rogue. The youth whistled. The robe was made of silk and cloth of gold, sewn together into panels that dazzled like a sunset sea.

"Put it on," the attendant ordered. Rogue did so. The attendant tied the sash, adjusted the way the garment hung, then nodded. "It looks good on you. There's a mirror over there—go look at yourself."

Rogue walked to the mirror, a full-length glass set into the bronze wall with gold scrollwork inlaid all around it. Looking back at him was a tall, broad-shouldered youth, surprisingly attractive, except for a long and knobby face. He liked the way he looked, though, with the robe's gleaming folds hanging from his shoulders like a prince's raiment. He smiled and shook his head. "I never dreamed I'd be dressed like this," he said. Then he laughed.

"You fill the robe well," the attendant said. "Perhaps, if you live, you might do something worthwhile someday." He smiled. "Horyk will notice you, that's for sure. Now come with me. We must go back up and meet the procession."

They walked from the gorgeous room and climbed farther up the Tower of Krell. The attendant unlocked another huge door—double doors this time—pushed them open, then led Rogue into a chamber even larger and more opulent than the first. In the middle of the room stood a sort of fountain. Water streamed through holes in the ceiling, each carved to look like the mouth of a different beast. The streams squirted out at angles, crossed one another, splashed together, then landed in a marble-lined pool sunk into the floor.

The attendant looked at Rogue, then at the fountain, and smiled. "It's cooler over there," he said, pointing. Rogue moved toward the fountain and stood. It was, indeed, cooler where he could feel the spray. The whole room was cooler than the outside, in fact.

"You are more blessed than you know," the attendant said. "Many slaves carry the water which fills the reservoir above this level. Others have to pump the spent water back up so it can pass through the fountain over and again." He looked at Rogue. "Don't defile it, by the way. Any water you drink in these lower levels has passed through this room. The fountain itself is used only when Krell has an important guest."

"Like Horyk the Archpriest?" Rogue asked.

"Exactly."

They stopped speaking as they felt the room vibrate like a ship sailing into high seas. "Someone's coming," the attendant said. "That will be them."

Trumpets sounded outside the tall oak doors, so loud they caused Rogue to jump. The doors swung open and revealed a knot of people on the landing outside the chamber. "All hail the most high," a herald shouted. "Their worships Horyk, arch-priest of our Order, and Krell, high priest of the Order at Touros." Several people entered by pairs.

At the center walked two figures in pale, hooded robes that covered every part of their bodies. Rogue stared at them and wondered how they could wear clothing like that in this heat. Then he felt the attendant's hand on his shoulder. "All kneel," the attendant whispered. The man knelt, then Rogue and the guards knelt beside him.

One of the robed figures threw back his hood and revealed a tall, balding man with beaming face and wisps of grizzled hair at his temples. "Ah, Rigard," he said to the attendant. "You have prepared all things well." The churchman's eye lit on Rogue. "What's this?"

"A new face, Holy Eminence," the attendant replied. "He was brought in just yesterday by slavers, which I took as a sign. I had him cleaned, dressed, and instructed, and I brought him to this place for you to dispose of as you think best."

The other hooded figure, which Rogue took to be Horyk the Archpriest, approached and stood over Rogue. It was a tall figure. The hood shadowed the face, which looked as if it was also covered by a dark veil. "You have homely features, lad," came a sonorous voice. "But you look strong." Horyk the Archpriest turned to the others. "He shall be my body servant during my stay at this tower."

Krell looked at Horyk and a vexed expression flicked over his face. Finally, he smiled and said, "As you direct, your Worship. The youth is yours to do with as you please."

"And I thank you," Horyk replied. "As always, my noble Krell, you are a thoughtful and generous host."

"If the holy party would like to dine," Rigard said, "I have made the arrangements."

"You may dine at your leisure," Horyk replied. "I do not choose to sup at this time. I will do so later, in my own chambers."

Rigard nodded and pulled a gilded rope that hung from the ceiling. In a moment, more slaves appeared, bearing large trays of food. A pair of them rolled up the heavy, knit carpet before the fountain, released a series of catches, and tugged at the bronze handles that sprang up. In a flash, a whole section of floor pivoted down and a long, silver banquet table with upholstered oak benches wheeled up in its place. The slaves set the dishes on the table, brought goblets from cupboards and filled them. The party seated itself with little conversation and the meal began.

Horyk was seated at the head of the table, with Krell at the archpriest's right hand. "Let my new body servant be seated on my left," Horyk said through the veil. "Let him eat and nourish himself with you here, for he will be required to serve me later on."

"As you wish," Rigard said, and lightly pushed Rogue onto the bench at Horyk's left. The youth marveled at his good fortune and acceptance into the same Order that had so recently tried to kill him. Life was strange and he was past trying to understand it all.

In deference to the heat of the Tower of Krell, the food was all served cold: heaping platters of cold, spiced roast; game birds; dried fish washed down by wine; and an endless variety of pastries, breads, and cheeses. The tastes all delighted Rogue. Whoever had prepared this meal was a genius of a cook.

As for Horyk, the archpriest did not even touch the wine. The veil never came off the face, the hands never left the lamp. This dark presence seemed to dampen the spirits of the dinner guests. Even Krell himself acted subdued. Conversation passed in low tones, mostly about religious subjects Rogue didn't understand. At last, the slaves cleared the dishes away and a final round of drinks was consumed. Horyk stood.

"My dear Krell," the archpriest said, "I thank you for your kind invitation to this place and the opportunity to renew our friendship, which has been sadly neglected these past three years. But I am weary from my journey and would retire to my own chambers, there to dine and rest."

"As you wish, your Worship," Krell repeated. He waved to Rigard and the two guards. "Go with them."

Rigard bowed low, and the two guards pushed open the room's doors. Heat welled in through the opening, reminding Rogue of the inferno that boiled far below this bizarre retreat.

Horyk touched Rogue lightly on the shoulder. "Youth, you will accompany me as well." The archpriest walked from the dining hall with supreme majesty of bearing.

They walked back down the ramps and terraces that led to Horyk's chamber. "Have you seen many of the wonders of this place?" came the melodic voice.

"Only a few, your Worship," Rigard answered in Rogue's place. "I showed him the lake of stone below us and not much else."

"I see," Horyk said. "Then we shall have to show him more sometime."

"Do you want to do that before you dine?" a guard asked.

"I believe so, but I will change out of this heavy clothing before anything." With these words, they came before the door to the guest chamber. "You three may wait outside," Horyk said. "My attendant will dress me."

Rigard nodded, unlocked the door, and pulled it open for the pair to enter. Rogue followed Horyk through. "How do you stand it as hot as it is down here?" he asked as the door closed behind them.

"Don't make such quick judgment," Horyk said lightly. "Heat like this has its benefits."

"I can't dream what they might be," Rogue said.

Horyk laughed a high, musical laugh. "Now you will help me change into clothing I can relax in. Go to that wardrobe and bring out the gown hanging farthest to the left."

Rogue did as he was told. He opened the silver door and found a line of exquisite clothing, each article hung on a copper frame. He pulled down the one ordered, a shimmering, filmy puff of pale blue silk. "I've never seen anything like this," he said in wonder. "But isn't this a woman's clothing?"

Again Horyk laughed that same laugh. Then the archpriest pulled away the filmy veil, threw back the pale hood, and shrugged the heavy cassock from the shoulders. There before the astonished youth, auburn hair shining to the middle of the back, eyes flashing, shoulders soft, round, curved, breasts light and uplifted as magical things, stood a strikingly beautiful woman.

Chapter Nineteen:
The Idol Yron

ROGUE COULD HARDLY catch his breath. "You see something other than what you expected," Horyk said with a smile. "Have you ever looked upon the like of me before?"

The young man shook his head. "By my name, I have not." He had seen unearthly beauty before—that one time, so long ago, in the streets of Oron. But that beauty was different from this. Horyk's beauty was sensuous, voluptuous, demanding to be touched.

"You expected an old man, covered with wrinkles and head bald as an old turnip, eh?"

"I don't know. I didn't expect . . ."

"A young and beautiful woman." Horyk laughed as she finished the sentence for him. "You can't imagine how one as young and comely as I am could have risen to the top of the Order. Believe me, young one, there are more things in this world than you yet know."

Rogue swallowed. "What do you want from me?"

"What do you think I want? You're young, you're strong."

Rogue turned away, but a wide grin clamped hold of his features. "I don't believe this."

"Are you sorry it's happening?"

Rogue turned. "Me? No."

"Then come give me a bath. Slide back the panel there, you'll find the water already drawn."

Rogue did as he was told and drew back the bronze panel to reveal a magnificent, marble-lined bath. Gold and silver inlay accented the purity of the stone, and when he dipped one hand into the water, he found the liquid scalding hot. "You don't want to get into this," he said. "It's hotter than you can stand."

Horyk smiled. "Let me see," she said. Before Rogue's awestruck gaze, she walked in, made her way down the three marble steps at one side of the bath basin, then lay back in the scalding water. "You have much to learn," she said with a smile.

"How can you stand it that hot?"

"I like the heat—Krell and I both do. That's why he keeps this tower in this volcanic cavern, and that's why I visit him." She leaned back until her hair floated about her face and only her mouth and nose remained above the water. At the same time, she put up one tapered leg. "Begin by bathing that," she said with a smile.

Rogue took up the cloth and lotion that lay ready at the side of the water, and began. He scrubbed between her toes, up her calf, up the wide part of the thigh. He was finding it hard to breathe, but she only smiled. He suspected it was partly from pleasure, partly from amusement.

"That feels good," she said. "Now wash the other leg the same way." She switched legs and wiggled her toes with pleasure. "You show promise, I'll say that for you. Ah, no, Krell and I have known one another a long, long time. Longer than you might suspect from looking at me. We were lovers once, does that surprise you?"

"I don't know," Rogue said. "Yes, I suppose it does."

"That's because he looks so stodgy. Well, he's a surprising fellow. We made a game up—I would meet some man and take him to bed, then arrange to get caught. Krell would then 'punish' the poor fool by performing some experiment on him." She laughed. "It gave us both great amusement."

She rolled onto her belly with a splash. She looked both playful and dangerous with her head and shoulders out of the water and long, dark hair drawn to one side. "Now my back," she said. "All of it, everything."

"Yes, your Worship," Rogue said. He used the form of address he had heard others use during the dinner.

"But Krell became too powerful," she went on as Rogue worked his way down her back and buttocks. "I couldn't trust him; we had a falling-out. Only in the last couple of months have we made amends and arranged this visit." She turned her head, smiled, and looked at the youth out of the corner of one eye. "I never missed him, but I certainly did miss this place."

Rogue looked at her. "Is he going to be your lover again now?"

She laughed. "What's it to you? My little man isn't growing jealous, is he? Is that a place you'd like?"

"No, I only . . ."

"Don't worry. Once I finish with a man, it's over. Krell lasted longer than any other has, but I can no longer trust him. *He* wants to be archpriest of the Order, you see, which makes lovemaking a little difficult."

"You sound as if he'd kill you to make it that far."

"I'm sure he would. There are no secrets between us. He knows I don't trust him, and I know he knows it."

"And you came here anyway?"

Again, she laughed. "Don't look surprised. It's a typical enough attitude between priests of the Order. The strongest advance, the weak fall and are sacrificed to the Dark Ones. It's pleasing to the Great Powers, and it keeps us strong." She eyed him, and her lips curled into a sensuous smile. "You have much to learn. I may enjoy teaching you."

She rolled over once more, sat up, and locked her arms behind her head. "Now the front," she said. "Everything."

Rogue breathlessly obliged. He scrubbed her with all the technique he could muster while she talked of life as archpriest of the Order. To him, her life seemed a morass of intrigues, thwarted plots, and assassination attempts. He wondered how anyone could live such a life, but she spoke with relish of her vengeance on those who had tried to overthrow her, kill her, or take her place.

Then she stood. He toweled her dry and she let him rub her body with perfumed oil. He knew he was clumsy at that, but she guided and advised him, and he congratulated himself that she seemed pleased with the result. "Maybe you'd like to lie down now," he said, indicating the huge bed that lay in the main chamber.

She smiled. "Later. For now, help me dress and I'll show you the wonders of Krell's retreat. Not many get to see this place and still fewer get to learn its secrets."

He helped her slip on new clothes; then they stepped outside. Out on the landing, it seemed hotter than ever, but the heat seemed to affect the woman not at all.

She explained in more detail than Rigard how water circulated through the place in pipes of copper, how the cavern had been formed out of magma aeons ago, and how the place had been built over generations. It had taken many lifetimes to build this place, yet she spoke of it all with a clarity and currency that puzzled him. Perhaps knowledge of the place had been passed down from generation to generation as level had been hung from level, as gold and silver and bronze had been brought from far countries to find its place in the bizarre complex.

They climbed runways and stairs until Rogue felt out of breath and weak from the heat. For her part, Horyk showed no more strain than if she had been strolling through a meadow at sunset.

They came onto a knot of priests in conversation. By the gleaming sweat that popped from his bare pate, Rogue knew before the men turned that the tallest was Krell himself. The high priest faced them, his eyebrows lifted in surprise. "How do you do, your Worship?"

"Well," Horyk said with a smile. "Your tower agrees with me."

He smiled back. "It always has done. We have missed you the last few years."

"I bet you have," she said. By this time, they were smiling at one another so brightly Rogue wondered if their faces would crack. Plainly, there was no love and less trust between them now, no matter what they might have done together in the past.

"Is your body servant making himself useful?"

"Most useful, and a fast learner," Horyk replied. "Thank you for providing him."

"The Great Ones provide."

"Ah, yes. Be that as it may, I was showing him the beauties and a few of the secrets of your wonderful retreat."

Krell's eyebrows knit in mock sorrow. "Oh, not all the secrets, I hope. I'd hoped to keep a few."

"There are so many, the lad couldn't live long enough to see them all. And that's only the ones I know myself."

"Oh, you know them all. I've never hid anything from you."

Horyk laughed while Rogue watched in wonder. He could tell they were playing a delightful game that could turn deadly any instant. And for some reason, Horyk's burst into laughter had given Krell an instant's advantage. The youth could see it in their expressions and in the way Horyk cut her laughter off. The game was leagues over his head, he could tell.

Krell never wavered. "Come, let me be the lad's guide, too," he said pleasantly. Then he winked at Horyk. "I hope you've left a wonder or two for me to show him."

"Many, many," Horyk said. Her smile had faded.

"Come this way," Krell said in a high-spirited voice. He led them back the way they had come, pointing at doors and describing the nature of the room that lay beyond each. One, he unlocked. "This is my study," he said to Rogue. He gestured through the door at long tables, at towering bookcases, and at cages of animals and cupboards full of strange items. "I have spent many an hour in this place, I can tell you." He looked into Horyk's face. "How I'd love to show this youth some of the wonders I've gleaned from endless study in here."

"That wouldn't be proper," Horyk replied. She didn't smile this time and looked uncomfortable. At last, Krell locked the door back up and they went on. As they made their way back down toward Horyk's chamber, Rogue began to understand at least part of the game's nature. The guided tour they were giving him—that was nothing but a veneer over something serious. In showing him around, Horyk had also been testing her freedom of movement in this place. In continuing the tour himself—and at the same time, escorting them back toward Horyk's chamber—Krell was showing that her movement was, indeed, limited. Did that mean the archpriest and her body servant were prisoners in the Tower of Krell? Rogue couldn't guess. But from the look of the woman, he guessed she had many tricks up her sleeve. It looked as if Krell had surprised her, but Rogue did guess she had surprises of her own.

They passed Horyk's room and climbed down the ladder to the landing below. This, as Rigard had showed Rogue, was the lowest point in the whole structure. "Now, young man, I will show you my greatest artifact," Krell said. He pulled a lever in the deck plating and a section of the metal itself slid back, revealing a hole in the center of the platform.

Hot air blasted through the hole, so hot it took the youth's breath away. Even Krell and Horyk looked uncomfortable, and the wind howled so loudly, the high priest had to shout to make himself heard. "Look down, if you can," he said.

Rogue steeled himself to peer down through the opening. Below them, hanging from chains of bronze, was the immense metal statue of an owl. The thing gleamed eerily in the reddish light and looked so lifelike it seemed about to fly. "That is the Idol Yron," Krell shouted. "Look well on it, lad. You have never seen its like in all your life."

Rogue did his best to study the hanging statue, but the hot air coming through the opening forced him to pull his head back. "I don't know what to make of it," he said.

"He's young," Horyk said to their host. "There are things which escape him in his youth."

"May he live long and gain the insights he needs," Krell said with a smile.

"Yes, may he." Horyk did not smile back. "You yourself do much to determine his future, my dear Krell."

Krell shrugged. "That's as it may be, too." He put his hand on Rogue's shoulder. "Now look again, youth," he said. "Look down at the Idol Yron as it swings, look at the great stone which it holds in its talons."

The youth did so, even though his eyes watered from the hot air that met them. "Yes, I see it," he finally said. "It's dark and pocked with holes, like a piece of lava rock."

"Good lad, and thoughtful, too," Krell said. "But it's not

lava. It had different metals in it, along with other minerals I can only guess at. It came out of this cavern when we first started building my wonderful tower. But it was a thing of legend long before you or I or even our dear Horyk were born. It has been worshiped down the ages, sometimes even when men did not know what they were bowing before."

"What is it, then?" Rogue asked.

"It is called the Stone of Ending. It comes from a time before ever there were men on the shores of the Thlassa Mey. Its origin is with ancient gods, but we do not even know which gods they were. It is said that anyone who actually touches it will die."

"Considering where it's hanging, I believe that," Rogue said, then looked up at the sound of Horyk's laughter.

Krell only went breezily on. "A wise observation. But if you found it, its effect would be the same, even in a green, rolling meadow. That's why we keep it here, far from the eyes and hands of men."

"But someday, a man will touch it without dying," Horyk said behind them. "Why don't you tell him what will come of that?"

"Ah, yes," Krell said. "It will happen, though who can know when that day will come or who the man will be. Or woman, your Worship," he added looking up at her. Then he turned back to the youth. "But on that day, the world will end."

"How do you know?" Rogue asked.

"We know," Horyk said. "It's our business to know."

"Be patient with the lad," Krell said to her. Then he turned back to Rogue. "There are many ways to learn these things. When you are wiser, you will learn some of them. For now, make note of all we tell you." He smiled, looked from the youth to the beautiful woman, then said, "But you must be tired from your journey. Although you would never know it in this place, the hour is late. Perhaps you'd like to retire."

Horyk's smile returned. "Perhaps I shall."

Krell gestured toward the ladder. "After you, your Worship."

"Nay, dear man. As host, you have privilege of being first."

Despite the smiles and sweetness, Rogue could tell the two were playing their game in deadly and intense earnest. For his part, Krell shrugged, levered the decking back into place, then climbed up the ladder to the next level. Rogue followed, then the archpriest.

Their host saw them to the door of Horyk's suite. "Rest you well," he told them as they went in. "Whatever your new servant cannot provide you, your Worship, be assured my people will come even at the wiggle of your little finger."

"I know it well," Horyk replied. "You have always been an attentive host." With that, she slid the stout door shut in the high priest's face. When she turned from the door, her own face had turned into a mask of anger and frustration. "That leering criminal," she said in a low voice. "He thinks he can cut me off from my own people, hold me against my will in this lair of his. I don't know his whole game, but it's plain he thinks he's gotten stronger than I am."

She walked to the middle of the room, stroked her chin; then a smile crawled back onto her features. "Yes, he's found some new skill or some new ally. He's turning it into a war of nerves. The more he can worry me, the more he can puzzle me, the weaker I'll be."

She turned toward Rogue. "But, dear boy, there are things I've kept from him, too. I've never shown him the extent of *my* powers, either." She looked at the youth's expression and laughed. "Poor boy, what have you gotten yourself into, hmm? But be of good cheer."

She studied him narrowly. "There's something different about you, I can sense it. I don't know if I like it." She looked thoughtful for an instant, then went on. "No matter. In a way, you'll play a crucial role in this test. In fact, if Krell had dreamed what an important player you might become, he'd never have let you near me."

She turned toward the bed, humming a little tune to herself. "The games begin," she said over her shoulder. "Good. Life gets dreary if it lacks excitement." She patted the bed. "Come sit here. Let me look at you."

Rogue did as she told him. He swallowed as she untied the belt to his garment, pulled it open, and removed it from his shoulders. She placed a hand against his chest, forced him back onto the bed, then pulled the rest of his clothing from him. "My, you're strongly built," she murmured. "Your face is so homely it's interesting, but your body is interesting in the accepted manner. Move over."

He slid to the middle of the bed, and she lay on her side facing him. "Now," she said in a voice that was half command, half laugh. "Tell me about that nasty little incident before the temple at Oron."

His mouth fell open, and he tried to slide away from her. Her hand clamped about his arm like a vise and the pressure stopped him. "Didn't you think I'd know each little thing that takes place among my children?" she said. "Don't insult me, boy. You'd better tell, and tell honestly."

Her voice sounded low and sweet, but he heard a hard edge to it that told him there would be no use in trying to lie, or even to shade the truth. "It was a prank," he said. "Another fellow and I, we were in a contest to see who could come up with the wildest plan."

"So you desecrated the temple and humiliated my priest," she said with an amused smile. "Was that your idea, or his?"

Rogue swallowed again. "Mine."

"And I take it you won the contest?"

"I suppose I did."

"You disappoint me, do you know that? You were meant for greater things than petty pranks and insults." She smiled. "But it's all the same for that. I should punish you severely, you know, but I need you too badly, what with Krell proving an onerous host. Lie on your back, relax, try to forget I know your shameful past."

He did as she commanded. Her hands flitted down his chest and belly and he felt the bed's vibration as she slid toward him. Then a rapping came at the door, a sound as if someone were slapping a branch against the hardwood. Horyk sat up. "Who's there?" she called. "Don't you know I'm not to be disturbed?"

The slapping continued, and with it a high-pitched babbling. "Oh," she said, and stood. "Cover yourself," she said to Rogue. "Just slip under the blankets. This could be important."

Rogue pushed the silk and fur coverings back and slipped beneath them just as she pulled the heavy door open. A dark shape loomed on the platform outside, a shadow against the cavern's uneven light. "Come in," he heard Horyk say. Then he saw her step back into the room and heard her laugh. "You've grown a new fur coat," she said merrily. "I like it— you look huggable, now."

A frightful creature crawled into the chamber, huge, batlike, catlike. Feet scuffled and wings rustled as it moved past Horyk. But it was bigger than any bat or cat. It was the size of a wolf, with a cat's head, fangs to slash and tear, claws that looked like curved dagger's blades, and fur as black and gleaming as the oil at the bottom of a lamp.

Horyk pulled the door shut and walked back toward the bed. "This is my pet," she said, stroking the vile-looking black head. "It is loyal to me and does my bidding with great intelligence and insight. And it's always trying some new strategy." She leaned closer and spoke to the monster. "I don't like you combining with mortal creatures, you know that. Some new quality might change you in a way that could make things—complicated. And you can't ever take the changes back."

Having scolded the beast that much, she grinned and gazed into its yellow eyes. Its black lips pulled back, and it chattered into her ear in some language Rogue couldn't understand.

She lifted her head and smiled at the youth. "For months, it has been watching people dangerous to me. There is a forbidden cult which despoils the purity of these lands." She looked at Rogue, and dark laughter danced in her eyes. "They are far more dangerous to us than dirty boys throwing stones at my temples." She listened to the beast again. "And it seems our friend, Krell, is chief among their enemies. That poses me a question, doesn't it—shall I let them come to this place and accost him? There's risk in that, but the inconvenience to him might make it useful."

The creature purred at her again, licked its meaty tongue across daggerlike teeth, then gazed at Rogue through yellow eyes. She turned and smiled at the youth. "It likes you," she said. "Who knows, the two of you might become very close friends." Her laughter rang through the chamber.

Then she pulled herself farther onto the bed, gazed deeply into Rogue's eyes, and placed her fingers on the material covering him. She pulled it slowly down, revealing him in all his nakedness. "But now it is time for us," she said with a smile.

She snuggled close to him while the candles in the bronze chamber dimmed as though on cue. The youth looked into her face and tensed under her caresses. A strange smile curled her lips, and they turned soft and pouty, as if sweetened by passion. From the side of the bed, her strange beast watched them, its yellow eyes gleaming.

His mind wandered as her hands massaged his arms, his neck, his chest. If the lads of his old group could only see him now, he thought, lying beneath the passionate caresses of the most powerful person on the banks of the Thlassa Mey. He smiled to think of it—they'd be drooling with envy. Then again, all the lads of the old gang were probably dead by now, killed or sacrificed by priests of the order Horyk ruled.

That put a pause into his enjoyment. Had they all met their fates at the hands of this deadly cult? He looked into Horyk's eyes and saw them blazing into his, her face a mask of evil, greed, passion, and lust incarnate. Her mouth opened and her lips pulled back from her teeth. With a motion more like a snake striking than anything human, her head snapped forward, and she buried those teeth in his shoulder.

Pain lanced through him. His back arched, and he screamed at the top of his lungs. "Don't move," she growled in a guttural voice that was more animal than human. "This is what you were made for. You silly little boy, you thought you'd escaped the Order."

"What are you doing?" he shouted. "This is crazy." He struggled, tried to pull away from her clutching fingers and her gnawing mouth, but her arms gripped him like iron bands. He flailed with his own arms and struck her on the side of the head. Her eyes blazed hotter than ever, she screamed in rage, then she struck him so hard his head swam. The bed shook as the winged monster leaped up beside them.

"You fool," she said. "Who do you think you are, to strike Horyk? You are my meat, my food—didn't it occur to you to wonder how Krell and I could both be young and fair of face while this retreat we built together is generations old?" She laughed, but her laughter sounded far away to him. He felt as if he had been drugged.

"My years number close to two hundred," she said. Then she bent her neck and licked the blood that oozed from the wound she had made in his shoulder. When she looked into his face again, blood was smeared on her lips. "It's good," she said with a smile. "You may be young and foolish, but you're also young and strong. Your life essence will add years to my span. What greater honor could there be for a person like you?" She lifted the arm that had pinned him down and stroked her pet. "Come, my friend," she said. "Let us dine."

The room pulsed around Rogue. He felt, rather than saw, as Horyk and the awful creature crouched over him. He felt her smooth lips against the blazing pain of his wound, then the rough tongue of the beast. They took turns lapping up his life fluids.

Horyk's body stiffened as if in ecstasy. She lifted her head again, clenched her teeth, and screamed at the top of her own lungs, a scream that made his own cries sound like a whisper. Strange words broke from her lips, words of the language he had first heard in the grotto below the Dark Order's temple in Oron. The candles flicked out as if all snuffed by the same hand. The room vibrated and rumbled, then took on a strange, greenish glow.

Rogue's head swam. The room floated about him as if none of the walls connected with each other, as if the bronze had turned to liquid—both more and less than liquid. Corners appeared where there shouldn't have been corners, like glimpses into places that weren't real. Long, lolling tongues licked out of the shadows, slobbered over him, tasted him, and coated him with strange, pungent-smelling slime.

Each time one of the horrors touched him, he felt himself weaken, as if they licked power from him the same way Horyk licked his blood. The room echoed with the sound of the licking, the feeding. And over all trilled Horyk's laughter. "Feed well, feed well," she shouted, then laughed harder than ever. "And you, my pet, your thirst is slaked. Fly you, fly you back and accost my enemies. See to it they never reach this island, that they do not trouble me ever."

The sound of beating wings filled the room and a black shape rose above the bed, blacker than the walls or the feeding things that bobbed and licked and hauled at the hapless youth. Up and up the beast rose, and still no ceiling stopped it. Farther and farther away moved the beating of the wings, higher and higher, until the sound faded away entirely. That left only Horyk's laughter, the touch of her mouth, the endless gobbling that flooded over him. Pain swept over him, his body arched and jerked on the mattress. But at the same time, it was a sweet pain, which filled him with a strange pleasure. After what seemed the longest time, merciful darkness finally closed down on him.

Chapter Twenty: Over the Altines

BEFORE DAWN, PAL-DAN had left his little house forever. The questers, their number now grown to five, had obtained a push-cart from one of the freak's friends and started on their way. They brought all the blankets Pal-Dan owned, for it was known to be cold in the mountains east of Guelt. They loaded him into the cart, covered him over, and began their trek, as helpless-looking a party as had ever started out on that treacherous road.

Whatever Fuzzy Waddles was, not a one of them doubted the hideous beast was evil. Geryam ventured to say the thing was a minion of the Dark Order. Owras wasn't sure. But it had listened to them making plans, that was beyond doubt. They left the city with hardly any sleep.

By midmorning, they had journeyed well into the foothills and the highest peaks stood before them, the tallest still wearing their winter coats of snow. A spring sparkled in the sunlight ahead of them. It was a bright jet of water that flowed straight out of the hillside, plunging into a pool beside the road in an aurora of white. A freshet danced out of the pool, trickled across the trail, then plunged down the mountainside, toward the stream at the bottom of the canyon on their right.

"Ah, me," Owras said. "That water looks like a gift from the gods themselves. I vote we stop for a breather."

"Vote seconded," came Pal-Dan's voice from below the blankets. "Can't I lift my head and look about a bit? I feel like a turkey trussed for the market."

"Might as well," Geryam said. "I haven't seen a soul for leagues." He reached down with one hand and yanked the blanket back.

"Ouch," Pal-Dan said. "That sun hurts the eyes. But what a view." He craned around, looking from side to side, rolling back and forth with such enthusiasm that he looked as if he might roll right off the little wooden cart.

"Watch out," Geryam said. "Don't rustle about so, or you'll tip this thing over. It's hard enough to push as it is."

"Oh, sorry," Pal-Dan said. "I'll be more careful. You see, I don't get out much."

"I can see how that might be," Lissa said. "How do you stand it?"

Pal-Dan laughed. "I stand it because I have to, girlie. You'd be amazed what you can stand when you have to." His eye twinkled so brightly, Lissa ignored the disrespectful word he used to address her. He only did it to tease—she had figured that out a long time ago.

"Oh, me," Owras said as he threw himself down beside the pool. "I'm getting too old for this fugitive life."

"Where are we going from here?" Rinna asked.

Owras leaned over, cupped his hands full of the pool's clear water, then drank. He took two or three handfuls of water, then ran his fingers through his white beard before he answered. "We had to get out of Guelt, that was the main thing," he said. "There were getting to be too many people who knew us. But this trail leads over the mountains, toward a city called Ourms."

"Worms?" Lissa said with a laugh. "Who would name a place that?"

"Ourms, my little princess," Owras corrected. "There, we'll take ship for Kolpos."

"That's where the fun will really begin," Geryam said.

"If we get to Kolpos," Pal-Dan said with a smile.

"Is Ourms as dangerous as Guelt?"

Pal-Dan made the funny little wiggle that passed with him for a shrug. "It's not a lot better. But this trail is worse than either, from all I've heard. Bandits, animals, you name it. It's a wild land, this stretch of the Altines. Wolves, giant condors—and humans can be worst of all."

"What a song of gloom," Geryam said. "If it's such a nasty route, what are you doing here?"

"Don't get me wrong," Pal-Dan said. "I'm happy to be here. If I fell down that cliff and breathed my last this instant, I'd die happy. I'm doing what I've wanted to do for ten years."

"Go after this Krell, you mean?" Rinna said.

"That's it exactly. By all that's bright and beautiful, I know it's dangerous. Getting killed quick instead of slow is probably the best any of us has to look forward to. Even so, it's better than a life of waiting and wiggling."

"What an attitude," Geryam said with a laugh. "Try not to cheer us up too much, will you?"

"That's me," Pal-Dan said with a wink. "Always good for a laugh."

"I'm tired," Lissa said. "When can we rest?"

"We'd better press on," Owras said, getting another drink from the pool. "We can't stop too long here—it's too close to the road and there's no kind of cover."

Lissa groaned. "How can you say that? I'm tired." She drew the word "tired" out into a sound of pure misery.

"Don't talk that way," Rinna said. "You know just as well as anyone that we have to keep going."

"Oh, foof," Lissa said.

"Skeek," Rinna shot back. The others grinned at the banter and the group struggled back onto the trail.

The trail grew steeper beyond the pool, until it became an exhausting climb. Though he was tall and powerfully built, Geryam's arms finally grew so weary he could no longer push the cart that carried Pal-Dan. The two maidens replaced the warrior, one holding on to each handle.

The trail turned into a series of stone ledges, barely wide enough for two men to pass. The cart took all the room there was in some places, and when the two maidens had to push it over rough places, the single wheel would catch and the contraption would tip and teeter as if it might go over the cliff and take both of them with it. Owras and Geryam both had to help more than once.

For his part, Pal-Dan kept up a string of banter and song that would have kept the rest of the party in stitches, had they not been working so hard. Since his lack of arms and legs kept him from helping, he seemed determined to hold up his share of duties by entertaining the rest. As for the danger of the cart dumping him and itself into the nearest canyon, he did not show any sign of minding. "Oh ho," he would say with a laugh. "You can't scare old Pal-Dan that way. With the life I've lived, I'm too tough for your puny little rocks to harm."

At last they topped the pass that wound between two snow-covered peaks. Away and away in the distance, they could see the blue of the Thlassa Mey spread beneath a glaring sun. "Somewhere in all that blue is the island of Kolpos," Owras said.

"We're so close," Rinna said. "It feels as if we're almost there."

"That's just because you've had a rough climb," Geryam said. "It's still far off, believe me."

They passed on down the trail and, after a long walk, dropped back down to timberline. "Those trees look so nice," Lissa said. "I could just lie down under one and go to sleep."

"That's not a bad idea," Owras said. "What do you think, Geryam? It wouldn't do any harm to find a secluded spot and rest."

Geryam agreed and struck out through the brush to find a place. Before long, he came back. "I've found a perfect spot," he said. "Follow me."

He led them to a tree-shrouded hollow between towering boulders. In no time, they had spread themselves out on the soft grass, eaten loaves, and poured down refreshing wine from a skin Pal-Dan provided. A soft breeze slipped through the treetops, and one by one they fell asleep.

When Rinna woke up, the sky had grown almost dark. She looked about and saw the shapes of Lissa, Pal-Dan, and Owras stretched on the ground around her. All slept. But as she looked sleepily about, she had no idea where Geryam might be. "Oh," she said softly. She threw her blanket back and walked down to the stream's edge to look for him.

She did not see him there. She knelt, scooped up a drink from the flowing waters, then stood. The light was failing rapidly, but she at last spotted his dark mass seated on a great boulder that overlooked the clearing. He was looking back at her, she could tell. She waved and he waved back.

She made her way up the brushy slope. As he watched her climb, he smiled and shook his head. "You are a determined little lady, Rinna."

"Oh, bosh," she said as she seated herself beside him. "I'm not little, I'm almost as tall as most men. Don't look down your nose at me just because I'm younger than you are."

"All right," he said, tilting his head to one side. "You've knocked down the 'little' part. What about 'lady'? Are you not one of them, either?"

"I am when I want to be."

He chuckled. "What is it Lissa would say to you about now? 'Foof,' is that it?"

She nodded with a smile. "Yes. And then I'd say 'skeek' back. We've been doing that ever since we were little. It just got started. My father used to tell us our foofing and skeeking would drive him crazy someday." Her smile faded. "Now I wish that was all he'd ever had to worry about."

"Poor Rinna," Geryam said. "You've had to grow up very fast, haven't you?"

"I was grown-up already."

"Maybe. But you've had some hard knocks. The world shouldn't be that way."

Rinna frowned. "But it is that way, isn't it? What would Owras say to that—he'd say it's up to us to change it, wouldn't he?"

"I suppose he would. But it doesn't matter. People won't change." He spat into the grass below the rock. "The world will always be a place where bad people do things to good people."

"Well," she said. "I don't know what Owras would say to that. I'd say it doesn't matter. Someone else's evil doesn't stop me from trying my best to do what's right."

"You're a good person," he said with a nod of his head. "I wish I'd had your wisdom when I was your age."

"You're sorry for things you did? The fighting and . . ."

He nodded before she could finish. "Yes, and the women and the gambling, too, I suppose. I had a right to go out and have good times, didn't I? But I didn't have the right to hurt other people. I did that, and I wish I hadn't. But I can't change it, can I? All I can do is go on from where I am." He looked at her. "You're so pretty and so innocent. Oh, don't look at me as if I've insulted you. You've seen bad things, but believe me, you haven't seen many of the ways a man and a woman can be bad to each other. Sometimes I wonder what you and Lissa must think of a man like me."

She tossed her head. "You don't care what we think. We're just little girls to you."

"Oh," he said. "You're wrong there. I care very much what you two think. And Owras, too. And Pal-Dan. You people—my friends—you're the best things to happen to me. You've taught me what real friendship is."

She stared at him. "I wouldn't have believed it. Not as much as you argue and boss us around."

He shrugged. "I have a job to do. But I still care. I've learned to listen to you more than you think."

She smiled. "We care for you, too. And as for what Lissa and I think, she thinks you're . . . very handsome."

"And you? Maybe you think so, too, just a little?"

She shrugged, but did not answer. "Well, I'll tell you what I think," he said. "I think you're both quite beautiful."

She pierced him with an appraising look. "Which one more? You've looked on lots of women, so you must have an opinion."

"You're both beautiful," he repeated

"Both exactly the same."

"No, not the same. Both beautiful in different ways. Don't try to trap me, Rinna."

Without thinking about it, she leaned her head on his shoulder. "I won't try."

"And watch out." He shifted beneath the pressure she put on him. "That could be dangerous, too. I'm only a man, after all."

She sat up straight. "Oh, sorry. It's just that I feel safe with you."

He put his hands out, turned her face toward him, looked straight into her eyes. "You're not safe. The man I was lurks just under the skin, leering at you, watching you. Believe me, you're not safe at all."

She grasped his hands and held them to her. "Then I don't want to be safe." The next thing she knew, his arms had surrounded her, and their lips pressed together. For a moment, the sweetness of his breath was hers, the luxury of his touch, the warmth of his skin. Then the kiss ended and he stood.

"I shouldn't have done that," he said.

"It's all right. I wanted you to."

He eyed her for an instant, then began to walk down the hill. "All right, be that way," she said.

"It's time to wake the others," he said. He did not stop walking. After a moment, she rose and followed him, wiping her hands on her blouse. The sun had set so low in the west, she could hardly find her way down.

Chapter Twenty-one:
The Writing Trees

BY THE TIME Rinna caught up with him, Geryam was talking with Owras. "I don't think we should camp here tonight," he said. "It gets cold fast in these mountains. It's already chilly. We'd better lower down. Besides, we're rested now."

"All except for you," Rinna said.

Geryam turned and looked at her. His face wore a funny expression. "I'll be all right. I'm rested enough to push the cart."

Owras's eyes moved from the warrior to the maiden, then back. "I agree it would be well to move on," he said. "But travel at night is dangerous. Night is the Order's time."

"That's true. But the sky is clear and the moon's coming up. It's almost full. At least we'll be awake. We'll have our wits about us if something happens."

They rolled up their blankets and their meager supplies and put them onto the barrow. Then they helped Pal-Dan in. The moon had not yet grown full and her glow provided barely enough light for them to walk. Rinna and Lissa walked ahead of the barrow to keep an eye out for treacherous spots in the trail.

Far below and beyond them, the Thlassa Mey stretched toward the curve of the world, black and silver in light from the rising moon. Where it stretched away to south and north of the rising orb, it was a dark wonder. But the party had to watch the mountain crags around them and the trail before them. Even Pal-Dan no longer sang and joked.

"Rinna," Lissa said in a quiet voice.

"Yes," Rinna said back.

"Why did Geryam give you that funny look? What did you say to him before he came back?"

"I didn't say anything."

"Oh." Lissa's voice told Rinna the other girl did not believe her. Rinna sighed. Life could be complicated sometimes.

Off in the distance, one wolf, then another howled. "Oh, my," Lissa said. "I hope they don't get any closer."

"I wouldn't worry about them," Geryam said. "We're too many for them unless they're starving. And that won't be a problem this time of year."

"Geryam's right," Owras said quietly. "By and large, animals won't be the danger tonight—if danger there is. The danger will come from men."

"It's such a beautiful night," Rinna observed. "I grant it's getting chilly, and the trail's treacherous. But it's lovely to the eye. You wouldn't think the Dark Order could reach this far."

"They can reach anywhere," Owras said. "You know that, Rinna."

"Yes, I do. I know it in my mind. But in my heart, I guess it's too awful to really believe."

They walked on and on, down a trail that wound across meadow, along cliffside, and through patches of forest. In steep places, the fronts of their legs became as weary from holding back as the backs of their legs had gotten from climbing upward the two days before. When the trail took them through trees, they had to pick their way almost by feel. In fact, they stopped at one point, and Geryam cut down branches for Rinna and Lissa to use as walking sticks, probing the dark, rocky road in front of them.

The moon passed over them, toward the peaks they had left behind. As they wound their way out of the trees once more, toward cliffs of night-darkened limestone, Owras said, "We won't be able to walk much farther. When the moon sets, it'll just be too dangerous."

"Look up," Pal-Dan said just then. "I thought condors only flew in the daytime."

"They do," Geryam said. "What did you see?"

"Something big, flying west. Too big to be a bat or a night-hawk."

"That cursed thing that follows us," Geryam said. They heard him hitch his sword in its scabbard to make sure it would come free if needed. "If it's spotted us, it has all the advantage." Almost as commanded by one voice, they all sped up. Rinna stumbled in the darkness and almost fell. She heard Geryam curse behind her. "Head toward those cliffs on the right," Owras said. "That's a little shelter, at least. The thing can only come at us from one way."

They turned off the trail, across stony ground that made the walking rougher than ever. "What's that noise?" Lissa said suddenly. From the peaks behind them came a strange buzzing, whooshing, squeaking sound, borne along on the breeze like a ghost to the ears. It quickly grew louder.

"I can't guess," Owras said. "But it gives me the shivers." A shape hurtled out of the darkness and struck Rinna on the back of the head.

"Ow," she cried. "What was that?" She didn't get the whole sentence out before another shape struck her, and another and another. She screamed. Out of the moonlit darkness swooped a cloud of the shapes, clattering against all of them, forcing them to duck their heads.

"Bats," Geryam cried. "It's a swarm of bats." The little creatures rained out of the dark like a shower of little fists, forcing them to their knees. Geryam shouted in rage and anger, drew his sword and swung it through the air over his head in a wide arc. But the things avoided the keen blade with ease and kept right on striking the humans.

Rinna gasped against the onslaught and she heard Lissa shriek in fear and anger, hair stirred to a froth by the attack. "The cliffs," they heard Owras shout. "Run toward the cliffs. It's our only hope."

Rinna saw Owras snatch his valise from the cart and yank something from it. Then she ran, stumbled, fell, got up and ran again. Furry bodies pummeled her and panic swept over her in a cloud. Nothing mattered except to get away, not the cuts and bruises, the pain of falling time and again, nor the blood that trickled down the back of her neck where one of the little things had bitten her. Her friends didn't matter, either. She ran as if possessed. Then the moon passed behind a tall peak behind them and everything turned black as the inside of fear itself.

The cliff wall loomed ahead of her, a dark mass that blotted out the stars. "This way," she heard someone yell, and she followed the voice. She ran full tilt into a stone. Her head exploded into lights, and she felt herself go down. She tasted blood where her mouth had whacked against the boulder in the darkness.

The bats tore at her as she lay there. Her fear was even stronger than the pain and the weariness. She clambered back to her feet and staggered on. "Over here," the voice shouted again. It was Owras's voice, and she followed the sound as a foundering ship would have followed a range light.

Blindly, she stumbled on until the cliff wall loomed all around her, until the mass blotted out all the sky that was left. The ground was no longer uneven, but had turned smooth and sandy. And the next time Owras called, his voice was straight ahead and it echoed eerily.

The bats did not come from as many directions now, though they still pummeled her back and hair. Only then did she realize she was in a tunnel. The floor felt too smooth and even for it to be any cave. "Where are you?" she called.

"I'm up here," Owras shouted. "Don't slow down, don't give up. They'll kill you if you do."

She ran on, even though her body begged her to simply lie down and die. If she did lie down, she knew, she really would die. So she plodded on, sometimes glancing off the twisting tunnel wall, while the attack grew weaker.

She heard a scream in front of her, then the sound of a struggle. "What's there?" she called. No answer came.

Next thing she knew, the floor beneath her feet gave way in a sandy rush. She heard herself scream, felt herself struggle against the sliding sand that carried her downward. She rolled a way, then fell into empty space with a gasp, then glanced off a slanting slope. By the time she rolled to a stop at the foot of the slope, she could barely breathe.

A violent wind blew sand in her face, forcing her to close her eyes and hold the hem of her torn robe over her face. But at least the bats no longer attacked her. They had not followed her, apparently unable to fly in the face of this gale. "Owras," she called. "Where are you?"

"Up here," came the reply. "Be careful, it's still dangerous."

She crawled toward him on her hands and knees, still holding the cloth over her mouth so she could breathe. The blowing sand blinded her and forced her to clench her eyes. Not that that mattered: she couldn't see a thing in this darkness anyway.

She bumped into something soft, and Owras's hand reached out and clapped onto her shoulder. "Oh," he said. "This is awful, isn't it?"

"What place is this?" she asked. "Where are the others?"

"I don't know. I've no answer to either question."

"It's a miracle we found this place."

"Not quite a miracle," he said. "There's a philter I've been working on for years, ever since my eyes started getting old. I just had time to snatch the vial out of my bag and drink it before we got hit. Far from perfect, mind you, but it helped enough for me to spot this cave in the darkness."

"Can you see anything now?"

"No," he answered. "It only lasts a few moments. And I only had the sample."

"Ah, me," she said. "Lissa and Geryam and Pal-Dan. Where are they now, I wonder? What if they're all dead?"

"Hush, child." Owras reached into the darkness and put a palm to her cheek. "Things will all come out right." He coughed because he had breathed in a little of the sand. "But maybe we should try to find a place that's not as windy. This cavern is like the inside of a bellows."

Above the shriek of the wind, they heard a cry behind them. "Over here," Rinna cried. "Who is it?"

"It's me," Lissa's voice called back. "How did you get to such a strange place?"

"Same way as you," Owras yelled back. "Can you find us in the dark?"

By way of an answer, Lissa's hand found Rinna's shoulder. "We're trapped in here," the maiden said breathlessly. "We could never climb up that hole, even if we could see."

"Then let's move toward the wind," Owras said. "It has to come from somewhere—there has to be an opening to the outside."

They crept into the teeth of the gale, slowly, like turtles. "Be very careful," Owras said as the gusts picked up. "There's no telling where we might go—" He cried out and disappeared from beside the two females. An instant later, Rinna felt the sand slip from under her and she was falling again, down a straight, narrow stone chimney, glancing off the rocks, but falling so slowly, held up by the wind that screamed past her, that the blows did not hurt.

She landed on another slope, a hard, full one this time, and rolled down and down until she collided with the old man in a jumble of arms and legs. An instant later, Lissa landed on top of them with a grunt. They separated themselves; then Owras shouted, "Look. There's a light."

Sure enough, off in the distance glowed an indistinct line of light, like a candle viewed from inside a wicker basket. "Something's moving out there," Lissa said. "I can see it."

"You're right," Owras breathed. "By the Twelve, this is a strange place." There was no harsh wind in this cavern, only a sprightly breeze that flicked at them on and off. But from all around them came a wondrous creaking and groaning, like the timbers of some scaffolding under a great weight. Above that came a continual howl, as from a thousand souls in torment.

They crawled toward the light until Rinna bumped into something hard. "What's this?" she said. "Why, it's a tree standing here. Still rooted. And it's shaking, Owras. How can that be?"

"I've no idea, child. I've witnessed more wonders on this night than I'd wish in a lifetime."

"I hope it's not some new evil," Rinna said with a shudder. "Some new wonder from our friends in the Dark Order."

"Hello," came a voice out of the darkness. "How did you three get here?"

"By the wondrous gods," Owras said. "That sounds like Geryam."

"It is Geryam," the warrior's voice said. "Though by these gods of yours, I don't know how I got here myself. This whole cliff must be honeycombed with caves and wind tunnels."

"But what about Pal-Dan?" Lissa cried. "We're all here but him. He didn't have a chance against those bats. He's probably lying dead up there somewhere."

"Don't fuss your head, girlie-cue," came Pal-Dan's voice. "I told you once and over again, I can take care of myself."

"But how?" Lissa asked in wonder.

"He put out those tentacles of his," Geryam said. "I grabbed him, and we took off for the cliff behind all of you, him using the tentacles as feelers."

"But you couldn't have gone fast," Owras said. "How did you get away from the bats?"

"I'm a man of many talents," Pal-Dan said. "Hear that?"

"Hear what?" Lissa said. "I don't hear a thing."

"Of course not," Pal-Dan said with a laugh. "It's too high-pitched for you to hear. But the bats can hear it, and it drives them crazy. It's a way I whistle—I have the best ears of anyone I know, but I can barely hear it myself. Dogs hear it, though, because I can watch them turn and look at me when I do it. And those bats didn't like it. Besides," he said with a chuckle. "I think they were hottest after you two girlies. And who could blame them?" He laughed again.

"So we went along behind you," Geryam said. "Neat as you please, but slower than you. We lost track of you in the darkness, then found a tunnel. Fell, started rolling and bumping off things . . ."

"Got sand in our faces," Pal-Dan chimed in. "Blessed near killed both of us, it did. Then we wound up here, with these weird trees."

"But we must have been in a different tunnel than you," Geryam said. "Or else, we wouldn't have got past you without running into you."

"I wouldn't be so sure," Owras said. "Anything could happen in this darkness, with all this wind and sand. But where are we, I wonder?"

Just then, a brilliant light flashed through the cavern, as if the sun itself had bloomed beside them. The cries of the wind increased, along with the groaning from the dark tree trunks around them. Rinna had to put her hands over her eyes, it had grown so bright.

Pal-Dan whistled. "By all that's a wonder," he said in a hushed voice. "I've never seen anything like this. And I'll never tell anyone I saw it, because they wouldn't believe me."

The sun must have risen in the east and flashed its light in through the cavern's opening. The top of the space loomed fifty fathoms above them, lined with a mineral that reflected and accented the light, made the place so brilliant they all had to close their eyes to keep from being blinded. When their eyeballs adjusted and they finally looked about, they saw a space thick with towering trees—trees with long, limber branches and huge, dark leaves. Like tormented souls the trees stood, waving their branches back and forth, up and down, wood striking wood, like a crowd of mad, giant boxers.

"It must be the wind," Owras said. "The wind makes the branches move that way. See, it blows through the mouth of this cave, across the top of the trees, then up through all those shafts which open above us. We must have fallen down through one of them."

"And they're worn smooth by sand blowing through them for all the ages," Rinna said. "That makes sense, but who would have expected it? How do these trees grow in the dark? The sun can't shine in here very long each day."

"And why doesn't anyone know about this place?" Lissa asked. "You'd think it would be famous all across the Thlassa Mey."

"We'll find answers to our questions," Owras said. "But for now, we'd better walk toward the opening, while we can all see it."

"That's right," Geryam said. "Let's get out of here." Then his eyes fastened on Rinna's face. "But by the gods," he cried. "You poor lass—you've sopped up more hurts than ever I did in battle or street fight. Look at the poor girl, Owras." He rushed to Rinna, threw his arms about her shoulders, and held her to him.

Rinna managed to reach her hand up. Her face had hurt ever since she had run into the boulder earlier. Now, when she touched herself, she found her lips swollen and cracked, her nose and cheeks scratched and cut, and her whole face covered with dried blood. "Oh," she said. "I must look awful."

"Don't worry about how you look," Owras said. "You've taken a worse beating than any of us."

Geryam released her in a way that told her he would like to have held her longer. "Do you feel like walking?"

"Of course I do," she said.

"Well, you're not going to for a bit," Owras said. "I've still got my bag, and I have salve in it. Sit down and we'll take care of you." Rinna did as he told her. He pulled a vial of ointment and a soft cloth from the valise and began cleansing her. "This may hurt," he said. "But at least the wounds look clean. I don't think they'll leave permanent scars."

While he worked on her, the sun rose past the cavern's entrance. The light faded, became gentler, but the place remained about as bright as a cloudy day. "There's the answer to one of your questions, Lissa," he said. "See? Those trees have some special kind of leaf, very large and very pale green. And the roof of this place must be some special kind of mineral. It stores and holds the sunlight for a long time."

"What a wonder," Lissa said. But Rinna noticed the other maiden avoided looking at her.

Once Owras had applied his medicines to Rinna's wounds, they all rose and started toward the entrance. It was a long walk between the writhing trees, a good part of a league. The cavern was immense, which made the brightness of it all the more wondrous.

Owras walked in the lead, with Geryam behind him, carrying Pal-Dan over one shoulder. "This is an insulting way to travel," the freak said. "But I guess it's better than rolling, or humping along like a worm. I'll not complain."

"You'd better not," Geryam said. "Think how I feel. I have to do the work."

They walked toward the cavern's entrance; then Rinna stubbed her toe on something. "Ow," she said. "What's that?"

Geryam peered down at the pale objects in the half-light. "I'll tell you what it is," he said slowly. "It's bones. You've tripped over a skeleton, Rinna."

Rinna nodded—she could tell what it was now. In fact, it

looked like two bodies instead of just one, lying where they had fallen. "People have died in here," she said softly.

"Let's get on," Pal-Dan said. "Won't help us to worry about that—better those two fellas dead than us five."

"He's right," Owras said. "Let's move on."

They started up again. Rinna held back until she and Lissa brought up the rear. "So," Lissa whispered. "There's nothing going on between you and Geryam, is there? I saw the way he looked at you. I saw the way he grabbed onto you, so don't tell me fibs. You've caught his fancy, haven't you? Just you remember, you're not the only woman in this world. I'm not just going to let you have him without competition."

"Oh Lissa, hush," Rinna shot back. "He thinks I'm just a little girl. I wish you were right, but I think he fancies that sword of his more than he fancies me."

"Don't tell me that. I saw the way he looked at you." Rinna laughed. "This will be fun. But we have to make him decide between us before we get to Kolpos. After all, he might be all scarred up from fighting by then, and neither of us will want him."

"You're just making this into some kind of game."

"Well, isn't it?"

"Maybe not to him," Rinna said.

"Oh, foof," Lissa said.

"Skeek," Rinna said back, but her heart wasn't in the usually good-natured exchange. What if Lissa was right? What if Geryam really did fancy her? Did she want that as much as she had thought she did?

Chapter Twenty-two:
Images

As THEY MADE their way out of the cave, Rinna watched Geryam in spite of herself. Thoughts of romance dropped from her mind as they emerged onto a little stone shelf a hundred fathoms above a broad beach. On the other side of the beach rolled the shining waters of the Thlassa Mey.

"Answer to Lissa's second question," Owras said. "No one's made a fuss about this cave because you can't reach it from below. Those bones we found—they must have reached it from the caves above, same as we did. That's why it's been a secret until now."

"But how do we do any better than they did?" Geryam asked. "No one but an ant or a lizard could climb that cliff."

"And what about *that*?" Lissa asked, pointing upward. The rest followed her gesture and all eyes fastened on a black, hovering shape.

Rinna groaned, then said, "Not again."

"Fuzzy Waddles, was that what you called it?" Pal-Dan said in a soft voice. "Strange name for a critter like that."

"It fit it when I gave it to it," Rinna said. "That was a long time ago."

High-pitched laughter sounded as the thing spiraled down toward them. Geryam drew his sword as it lit at the far end of the ledge. It leaned its head to one side and eyed them. It released a scornful little cough, and a tiny lick of smoke puffed from its mouth. "Why don't you just leave us alone?" Rinna called. "We don't want you anymore."

"Fools," the creature said in its piping voice. It giggled, sniffed, then opened its mouth and yawned. Its huge teeth formed a hideous smile; then it closed them together with a loud snap.

"It's as if the thing was smiling at us, just plain gloating," Geryam said. "You sent the bats to do us in, didn't you?" he said to it. "But they didn't do the job. If you've come to finish it yourself, you'll have a fight on your hands." He waved the sword at it.

As quickly as a snake striking, the beast leaped at him, bowled him over, and almost knocked him off the ledge. He rolled back away from the edge, and his sword's blade clanged against rock as he struck and missed. The thing turned with a snarl and charged again, wings spread, jaws agape. It lashed at Geryam with one taloned paw, knocking him back against the stone behind him. "You'll die last, little man," it said. "I'll let you linger awhile."

"Quick, Rinna, Lissa," Owras yelled. "Run. Run for your lives, back into the cave." He grabbed the young women by their robes and shoved them in the right direction. As soon as they fled, the winged monster turned toward them, roared a fearsome roar, and reared onto its hind legs. Geryam shot to his feet and swung his sword again. The blade caught the thing in the back; it screamed in pain and toppled over the cliff's edge.

"Keep running," Owras yelled. "Don't look back." The two young women did run, but Geryam looked over the cliff's edge to see the beast open its wings and soar out over the ocean. Up and up it flew, until it was just a speck against the pale blue of the sky. Then it dived, growing larger and larger, folding its wings and shooting into the cave with such speed it actually whistled as it went by.

The warrior scrambled to his feet and ran after it. As he leaped through the cavern's mouth, he saw Rinna's and Lissa's backs. They were still running, leaping over tree roots and stones. Then he heard a scream of rage and pain and looked up. The howling wind at the cavern's roof had caught the cat creature and had hurled it into one after another of the flailing trees. It thrashed and tried to escape as it was pounded from branch to branch, then fell like a stone, its wings broken and bleeding.

"Keep away from it,"Geryam yelled. "It's not dead, yet." In an instant, he had reached the creature and, before it could turn to face him on its broken legs, thrust his sword's blade between its ribs.

It roared and lashed out at him, but he danced backward, out of reach. The sword pulled from his fingers, and blood spurted around the wound, splattering over his arms and face. He screamed in pain—the blood burned like acid. The thing writhed on the sandy soil. It covered itself with grit and dirt, which stuck to its blood and made it look filthy and pitiable. Finally, it quivered and lay still.

Gasping with pain, Geryam inched closer and stared at the thing. It did not move, not even when he grabbed his sword and wrenched it from the carcass. The blade had turned black and the beast's juices had pitted the metal. "Is it dead?" he heard Owras call.

"I think so," he answered. "It's not moving or breathing." He touched one open eye with the tip of his sword. The creature did not blink, and the eyeball quickly lost its glitter as it dried. "It's dead as anything can be," he finally said. "But my sword didn't kill it. These trees did."

Owras and the two young women cautiously approached. "Don't get too close," Geryam said. "The gods only know what this thing can do, even when it's dead."

As if to confirm what he said, the creature began to vibrate, to shimmer in the cavern's reflected light. "Get back," Geryam yelled, and backed away himself.

It shook, quivered, then went all but transparent, as if it were fading away before their eyes. Instant by instant, it faded until Geryam could clearly see the soil beneath it. After a moment, the image clouded as if it had filled with fog.

"Geryam, get away," Rinna shouted. Geryam did back farther away from the creature as it turned pure white. The wings, broken by the writhing trees and its fall, shifted and became whole again. The bones that had protruded were now sheathed beneath gleaming white fur. Blood and dirt no longer matted its coat. It had become as clean and white as newly washed linen. He looked at his forearms in wonder—the blood had faded from his skin, the burning pain was gone.

The eyes blinked. The creature looked about, then rolled to its feet and gazed at Geryam. "Hello," it said in a soft voice. Geryam brandished his sword. "Get back," he cried. "The trees may have done for you last time, but I'll fight you to the death if I have to."

The creature did not advance toward him, but it did not back away, either. He stepped toward it, blade raised. This time, it did back away. "Head back toward the cave mouth," he said. "I don't know what it's going to do, but I'll keep an eye on it."

"Be careful," Owras said. "It probably won't make the same mistake twice, getting caught in those branches."

"I know it well," Geryam said. "But go ahead. We can't stand here and stare at it forever." He blocked the creature's way as they edged past him, toward the mouth of the cave. It never made a move toward them, but watched as they passed away from it. Its look seemed intent, but appeared more confused than vicious.

Once they had made it past, Geryam backed toward the cavern's mouth himself. The creature sat on its haunches and watched him for a moment, then stood and padded after him. "Back, you," he yelled. It sat on its haunches and looked at him. "I don't know what to make of this thing," he yelled toward the others. "It makes no move toward attacking, but it won't go away, either."

"Let me look at it," Lissa said behind him. He heard her footsteps as she walked back into the cavern. "Nothing's the same about it," she said. "Why, even the color of its eyes has changed. They were yellow as a bee's tail before, and now they're blue."

"That doesn't make it your friend," Geryam said.

"It doesn't make it our enemy, either," she said. "Who are you, animal? What's happened to you?"

The creature looked at her. "Hello," it said again. Then it began to purr.

"What a sound," Lissa said with pure pleasure. "I think it's turned into a friend."

She started past Geryam, toward the creature, but the warrior reached out a hand and stopped her. "You can't go up to that thing," he said. "It'll slash you to ribbons."

"No it won't," she said. "Let me go."

"You're crazy."

"It's not what it was before."

"Let her get closer if she wants to," Owras said in a strange voice.

She crept closer, and reached out her hand and touched it on the nose, between its eyes. It jerked its head back at first, then, like a curious kitten, nuzzled her fingers. She knelt beside it and rubbed it between the ears. It rolled onto its back so she could stroke its belly. "It's not what it was before," she said again. "It's a whole new creature. It's as if Fuzzy Waddles has come back in a way. That awful black thing, that wasn't Fuzzy Waddles—but in a way, this is." She looked up at Geryam. "Maybe it all happened when you killed it. You changed it somehow, and some other part of it is alive now."

"That's impossible," Geryam said.

"Nothing's impossible before the gods," Owras said. "I wonder if it can change into a regular cat, the way it could before."

"How about it, animal?" Lissa asked. "Can you become a Fuzzy Waddles again?" She looked back toward Rinna. "But I get to name him this time. I don't think Fuzzy Waddles fits anymore, do you?"

"No," Rinna said with an incredulous laugh. "Fuzzy Waddles doesn't fit at all. You tamed him, you name him anything you want to."

"I'm going to name him Image," Lissa said. "Because he's only an image of what he was."

"I can't believe you're doing this," Geryam said incredulously. "Remember what it did. It made people sick and it killed them. It followed us—it spied on us and set those bats after us."

Lissa shook her head. "He didn't do any of that. His image

did." Her arm slipped around the beast's neck and the thing laid a huge, white paw against her thigh.

"I'm inclined to trust Lissa on this," Owras said. He turned to the maiden. "You've just got a feeling on this sort of thing, haven't you?" he asked with a smile.

"Yes."

Owras advanced cautiously, stuck out a hand, and stroked the animal. Its back arched beneath the rubbing. "I think your 'feelings' are pretty reliable," the old man said.

Geryam, Rinna, and Pal-Dan all shook their heads or looked at the old man and the maiden as if they were out of their minds. But they didn't argue. Then Lissa said, "I'm going to climb onto his back and ride him down from this ledge."

"Now wait a minute," Geryam said. "You really are crazy if you're going to do that."

"Try me," Lissa said. She slid onto the animal's back, wrapped her arms about its neck, and cried, "Fly, Image. Fly me down from here." Image leaned its head to one side, looked at her from the corner of one eye, then spread its great wings. Before anyone could stop them, it had leaped from the edge of the precipice.

Lissa screamed. Whether the sound came from excitement or terror, none of them could guess. The white wings flapped mightily, but the creature did not gain altitude. Rather, it spiraled down and down until the two of them disappeared into the treetops at the base of the cliff. "By all that's a wonder," Pal-Dan said. "Will we ever see them again?"

"I wish I knew," Owras breathed. They all craned their necks to see down into the trees, but the animal and the maiden had vanished. After a few moments, Image spiraled back up from the green canopy and landed at the other end of the ledge.

The four humans stared at it. "What did he do with her?" Rinna asked.

"I don't know," Owras said. He moved gingerly toward the winged feline. It made no move to stop him and allowed him to touch it. Its mouth opened. "Trust and come," it said.

"Is Lissa all right?" Rinna asked, half in suspicion and half in wonder.

"Come," the beast repeated.

"He must have carried her down there safely," Rinna said. "Can I go next?"

"This is dangerous," Geryam said. "Owras, how do you know all this is on the level?"

"How do you know your hand is really at the end of your arm?" Owras replied. "But you stay, Rinna. I'm old and creaky, so let me take the next ride. If I'm all right at the end of it . . ." He hesitated, then whispered into Geryam's ear. Then he climbed astride the smooth shoulders, clasped his arms around Image's neck the way Lissa had done, and cried out as the beast leaped over the cliff's edge again. "This is scary," he yelled. Then he also spiraled from view.

Geryam shook his head, and the three who remained watched as Image's white shape and Owras's dark clothing vanished into the leaves. A moment later, the beast once more flew from the trees, circled above them three times, then landed. It walked to Owras's bag, grasped the leather top in its jaw and took off once again.

Geryam stared after it, openmouthed. "That's what he said it would do," he said. "Maybe the whole thing is on the level."

"I want to go next," Rinna said. When Image once more landed on the ledge, she ran to him, climbed on, and held on tight. The ride down was breathtaking, with wind in her face, the trees rising toward her at unnerving speed, then a gentle landing while Owras and Lissa stood and grinned at her.

"Have you ever had a feeling like that in your life?" Lissa cried. "I thought my heart was going to pop right out through my mouth."

"That's just the way it felt," Rinna said. She released the smooth, white neck, rolled off Image, and lay in the grass. "Oh, me. I don't want to get up for a while."

"You can see why he spirals that way," Lissa said. "He's not strong enough to go anywhere with someone on his back. All he could do was carry me down here—he could never have carried me back up." She laughed incredulously. "Are we ever lucky we needed to get down off a cliff, rather than up out of a pit."

"The gods always provide," Owras said with a smile. "But what a curious creature he is."

"I'm sure we can trust him, now," Lissa said. "If he'd wanted to hurt us, he'll never have a better chance."

Image padded over to the young woman, looked up at her, and allowed her to rub its head. Then it took off once more and a moment later reappeared, carrying Pal-Dan. Geryam had used his belt to tie the freak to the creature's back. Quickly after that, Geryam had joined them, though his landing was a rough one because he was by far the heaviest of the lot.

"I wouldn't have believed it if I hadn't seen it," he said as he sat on a rock and rubbed a bruise he received on landing.

"It's a mystic creature, indeed," Owras said. "He can be of great help to us, and Lissa seems to have all the knack for controlling him."

"But can we ever completely trust him?" Pal-Dan asked.

Owras released a long sigh. "I don't know the answer to that. I fear we can never be sure. But for the moment, his new color seems to reflect his new way."

"I won't sleep soundly while he's around," Geryam said. "I don't care how friendly he acts. He was friendly before, until he started bleeding people dry."

"Oh, you," Lissa said. "Don't listen to them, Image. I know you're true to me, and you can stay at my side as long as you want."

"Well enough," Owras said. "But tell me, young lady, how do you propose to get this creature into the city of Ourms or onto a ship? Our aim is to get to the island of Kolpos, and as you've told us yourself, he can't just fly us there."

Lissa stared at them. "I don't know," she said slowly. Then she brightened. "But Fuzzy Waddles was just a cat. Surely, they'd let a cat onto a ship—you know, they catch rats and all." She turned and looked into the china blue eyes. "Image, can you become just a plain cat?"

Before their eyes, the animal yawned, then shimmered, changed, and shrank. The great wings folded, softened, became tiny, then shriveled to no more than tiny lumps on the shoulders of a large tomcat. "How wonderful," Lissa shouted. "And there you are, all of you. Now who's to object?"

"Certainly not I," Owras said with a smile. "Your animal seems to have an answer for every objection, Lissa. Very well, then, we've had a nerve-shaking adventure, but we're still on the course we chose. Let me pick up my bag and we'll set off for Ourms."

Chapter Twenty-three:
The Clutches of the Order

ROGUE'S SENSES ASSAULTED him like a mob storming a manor house. His belly heaved and tossed, his head hurt, and his tongue felt as dry as the inside of a flour barrel. Tears and pus had glued his eyes shut, so tightly he actually had to pry them open with his fingers. When he did get them open, he found himself still inside the bedchamber of Horyk the Archpriest. It looked just as it had when she had . . . when strange creatures had joined her in consuming him like an after-dinner snack.

The thought turned his stomach and made him gag. He put his hands over his face, rolled onto his stomach, and gritted his teeth against pain and nausea. The spasms finally subsided, and he rolled onto his back once more. Sores covered his body: great, red splotches of raised skin. The sight of them and the thought of what they meant would have made him gag once more, but he just didn't have the strength.

He tried to sit up but he couldn't. "Don't try to move," a voice said. "It'll just make you feel worse."

He looked toward the voice and saw Horyk herself, watching him with a secret kind of smile on her lips. "If you can move at all, you're better off than anyone has a right to be," she said. Then she laughed. "The Dark Ones appreciate your vigor. They look forward to another visit."

He groaned and put a hand over his eyes. "Why don't you just kill me and get this over with?" he said.

"Don't be theatrical," she said. He heard her leave her seat and walk toward him, but he made no move to attack or resist. He couldn't. Then he felt her hand beneath the back of his head, lifting. "Drink this," she said, putting a metal goblet's cold rim against his lips. "Don't be afraid. It's excellent spiced wine, some of the best in the world."

He drank without speaking. It was either that or drown in the scented fluid. It burned its way down his gullet and into his belly. He could feel its heat spread through him, making him feel warm and dizzy. "How long have I been here?" he asked.

"A while. Time will never mean anything to you again, so don't ask."

"Why not?"

"You don't have much. Then again, you have all eternity. When you have regained enough strength, the Dark Ones will feed on you again. That will be the last you will breathe in this world, but you will be one with them forever."

He didn't reply, so she went on. "You pleased their palates—I could tell by the way the sacrifices went this morning. You have great strength and vigor." He felt her fingers trace their way down his chest and belly. "It's almost sad not to use you for more earthly purposes."

Even as weary and awful as he felt, the teasing lightness of her touch made him tingle. He wondered if she really was as old, as ancient as she told him she was. Then again, there was no reason she should lie to a condemned man. And Krell, too, surviving by magical artifices—the Dark Order was even more awful than he had thought before, ruled by human monsters who held their unspeakable rites and revelries and used the world's population as an endless sacrifice.

That made him think of something. He opened his eyes and looked at her. "How are Krell and you getting along?" he asked.

"What do you care?"

He sighed. He felt too weak and dizzy to shrug his shoulders. "Just curious. I don't know anything about this place. No reason you shouldn't tell me what's going on, is there?"

"No reason." Her voice turned cold. "Krell thinks he's got me where he wants me—or at least he did before you came along. You changed that. The Dark Ones are strong with me, now. He knows that. I'm stronger, too, thanks to you." She sat beside him on the bed, brushed his hair away from his forehead, and smiled down at him. "I really have to thank you. Right now, it's a standoff. Krell smiles and flatters and gives me gifts, because he knows I'm still stronger than he is. Still, here I am, trapped in his lair." She smiled coldly. "Fascinating, isn't it?"

"More strange than fascinating."

"That's because you're a silly boy and you don't know much. That's too bad, considering the fact that you are a key player in this drama. You still live. You can still provide sustenance. I will please the Dark Ones again and gain still more strength from you. After that, Krell will be destroyed and this . . ." Her smile vanished and she looked pained.

"What's going on?"

She shook her head and looked away. Then she stood. She crossed the room, then braced her hands against the bureau and made a little sound of agony. She stood a moment longer, then released a deep sigh. "The lucky fools," he heard her say under her breath. "They don't know their good fortune. Now I've lost them."

"What's going on?" he repeated.

She turned and glared at him. Then her look softened, and she returned to his side. "A tragedy," she said. "I've lost a dear friend, a strong and cunning friend. But I can get him back, the little meddlers don't know what I know. They don't even know what he can do for them while he's theirs." She shrugged. "That's a minor struggle right now, though it could prove bothersome later. For now, I have to watch Krell. Only when I've destroyed him can I turn to them."

She sat in silent thought a moment, then smiled at him once more. "So you're the key," she said, touching him again. "You'll receive my eternal gratitude. But first you'd better rest and eat and drink and regain your strength." She stood and walked toward the door. "Food is coming," she said as she went out. "Eat all you want, drink all you want. Enjoy every morsel." Then the bronze panel closed behind her and she was gone.

He watched her go. The wine had made him so dizzy, he couldn't have gotten up even if he had felt strong enough. Later, though he had no idea how much later, a pair of servants came in with a large platter. It held pastries, at least three different kinds of meats, plus breads and rolls, tubers, all kinds of garden vegetables.

The servants did not speak to him, only looked at him with a sort of pity mixed with disgust. They pulled a little stand over to where it touched the bedside, laid the platter on it, then left as silently as they had come. The aroma made Rogue feel like throwing up at first, but as he grew used to the smells, they became inviting to him.

Still, he hesitated to take any of the food. He felt so weak, surely starvation would be a quicker, easier ending than the fate Horyk promised him. Why should he regain strength, only to be a sacrifice in another orgy of obscene chants and tongues? Then again—and this thought made him angry—how could Horyk be so very sure he was not capable of escape? To give up without a struggle, that was not the way he had learned in the streets of Oron. If he could find a way to fight back—better yet, if he could find a way to kill her or kill Krell before he himself died—that would be enough. He rolled over, picked a piece of meat from the platter, and ate.

His stomach bucked against the food he swallowed, but he kept it down. He did not eat much, and he avoided the sweets. He had never cared for his body before; he had always eaten and drunk whatever had pleased him. But this time, he took great care not to partake in a way that would make him sluggish or drowsy.

He slept awhile. When he awoke and found himself alone, he searched the chamber for some way out besides the heavy bronze door. He pulled open drawers, examined the bath, and looked beneath the bed. He even tried to pry the mirrors and decorations from the walls and look behind them. He found nothing.

After what seemed a long time, Horyk returned. She seemed

pleased to see he had eaten a little and not angered by the obvious evidence that he had searched the room. "You're a fighter, then, aren't you?" she said with a smile. "You'll make yourself strong, if only to take a last chance at escape or combat. That's good. I will gain as much from the strength of your spirit as the strength in your body. Not one in a hundred offers me what you do."

To his amazement, she disrobed down to a sheer, white sheath, snuffed the candles, and crept into the bed next to him. She rolled onto one side, faced away from him, and quickly went to sleep, her parted lips releasing the light, airy breaths of a sleeping maiden. He watched in disbelief until he felt sure she really was asleep, then slipped from the bed. He crept unsteadily to the bureau, picked up a heavy jewelry case and brought it down on her skull.

Her hand flew up as if shot from a ballista. She caught the case before it could strike and hurled it into a corner, where it crashed with a tinkle of stone and glass, leaving a dent in the chamber's metal wall. Just as quickly, her hand snapped back and struck him a thunderous blow to the chest, knocking him backward, into the bureau.

Pain lanced through him, both from his breastbone and from the welts the bureau left in his back as he crumpled. He could barely breathe. Still, no matter how much it hurt, he refused to groan. He would not give her that satisfaction. Asleep or awake, he would not let her hear him admit pain. He lay on the cold floor in the darkness and waited for her to wake up.

He must have fallen asleep at last, because he woke up to find himself alone, the chamber once again brightly lit by candles. He tried to stand and made it to his feet. He felt stronger than he had before, though his body ached all over from the blow Horyk had dealt him. A new platter of food lay on the stand beside the bed, still hot.

He walked over to the food, lifted a morsel, then sat down on the bedside and wept. Be a man, a voice inside him shouted: fight back. But despair washed over him like a flooding river washing over a sandbar. Still, even in the midst of despair, anger and a cold sense of the situation's logic fought their way to the front of his mind. He would not surrender. He would not give up, to Horyk or to despair. He would find a way out of this place, and if worse came to worst, he would find a way to do himself in before she could make another meal of him.

She was full of surprises, though—he had to consider that. She would take him before he was ready, that was almost certain. He had no time, no way to prepare. He sat and seethed, then forced himself to eat.

Horyk returned after a while, full of little jokes and sweet remarks. She acted like a maiden of fifteen, sweet, innocent, and lovely. If he had not seen and felt her in action, he could never have believed the evil of which she was capable. Krell dropped by for a moment, too. He and Horyk traded smiles and polite banter, but Rogue could sense the tension between them, the double edge beneath their witty remarks.

They talked as if Rogue were not even there. The youth noticed that Krell carefully kept the door open while he sat with Horyk, and several armed men stood on the landing outside. Even the youth had to smile. There could be no mistaking the fear and distrust that lay beneath the smirking priest's genteel manners.

Before Rogue realized it himself, he was on his feet, running toward the doorway. He could hardly keep his balance, his legs felt like rubber, but he made it through. He bowled past the first guard before another tripped him up and he sprawled on the hot metal deck. He cried out at the pain of hot bronze against his bare flesh; then two more guards hauled him to his feet and turned him around.

Krell and Horyk strolled to the door, their faces covered with amused contempt. "Kill me now," Rogue shouted. "Before she uses me as her sacrifice."

"Soon enough, dear boy," Horyk replied. "I'm afraid the high clergy doesn't listen to the advice of green-witted street urchins."

"Krell, can't you see what she's doing? Once she feeds me to those long-tongued gods of hers, she's going to be even stronger. She'll tear this place apart and you with it. You've got to have it out with her, now or never. You won't get another chance, you fool."

Krell smiled a rubbery-lipped smile as he walked toward Rogue. "You know nothing of our dealings," he said in a silky voice. "Horyk and I are the most intimate of friends and have been since before you were born." He turned toward Horyk and laughed. "Long before." They both laughed merrily.

Krell slapped Rogue, harder than the youth would have believed possible. The lad's ears rang and stars exploded into clusters of light. "But don't ever talk to me that way." He turned to the guard. "Get him out of here."

"Leave him," Horyk said. "He's mine. He was always mine, before he even breathed."

Krell's head snapped around, and he stared at her. But his smile never faltered. "He's troublesome. Surely you've no use for him."

"Leave him. I like trouble."

The two stared at one another, smiles frozen in place. The guards held Rogue uncertainly, waiting for instructions. With a cry, the youth threw an elbow into one guard's midriff. When the man doubled over, the youth broke away from the other who held him. He bolted down the nearest runway, then down a spiral of steps.

He found himself trapped on the little observation deck, the lowest level of the entire complex. The round door in the deck hung open. Beneath him, he could see the Idol Yron hanging from its chains, the Stone of Ending still clutched in its great claws. Guards clattered down the steps behind him, and he could hear both Krell and Horyk shouting orders. He faced the guards; the hot air blasted through the opening; then he grew dizzy and his weakened legs buckled. He found himself falling, toppling through the opening, landing on the great bronze owl.

He screamed. The heat smothered him, overpowered him. The hanging idol tipped and teetered in its chains, and he felt himself roll the width of one great, bronze wing. His hands clutched wildly as he slipped downward, tried to grasp a metal-feathered leg and failed, then clawed against the hot stone.

The Stone of Ending. Rogue's eyes clenched, he howled in pain, and he felt the stone grow soft and mushy in his grasp. It melted around his hands like hot wax, filled him with searing pain. This was the end that had begun when he had thrown rotten fruit at the Order's temple in Oron.

But he did not die, much to his amazement. The stone grew hard again, and cold, like concrete manacles, molded so tightly he could not have let go if he had tried. The owl's mighty bronze head turned; the yellow eyes opened, and stared at him. A wing moved, shook, flapped. Chains snapped like threads.

The thing swung crazily, Rogue felt the power as it twisted and flailed its wings. More chains parted. He hung with his hands imprisoned by the Stone of Ending and plummeted toward the magma below, screaming, his hide baking from the heat. The bronze wings lifted him, then carried idol and stone and human prisoner upward, past the astonished faces on the ramps and terraces of the Tower of Krell, up toward the opening at the top of the great cavern.

Chapter Twenty-four:
Ourms

THE FIVE QUESTERS found Ourms to be a fishing and trading town of moderate size. It was not nearly as large and exotic as Guelt, but then it was not as dangerous-looking, either. They arrived about sunset, and since their bodies ached from their long walk and harrowing adventure, the first place they sought was a suitable-looking inn.

They found one not far from the city's inland gate. It looked small but clean, with three levels of rooms built around a lovely courtyard. Fruit trees bore up heavy loads of quinces and pears just a few cubits from where they would spend the night.

Owras put down money for two rooms. "We men can sleep in the one," he said. "You two ladies can have the other—and your privacy."

"I won't sleep much, knowing that animal is in there with them," Geryam said.

"Oh, bother," Lissa said. "He'll protect us, not hurt us."

"You can't know that," Geryam said. "How do you know

what he eats? Remember how you learned what he ate when he was black?"

"That's not fair," Lissa said. "That wasn't him—this is a completely different creature."

"Hush, both of you," Owras whispered loudly. "You're attracting attention."

"I don't care," Lissa said. "Geryam's just not being fair."

"At least I'm not going to chew you full of holes and suck all your blood out during the night," Geryam said. He glanced at Owras, who was still motioning them to be quiet, and his face grew red as he tried to argue without making noise.

"That's a problem, too," Owras said, pointing to a sign posted on one side of the room. NO PETS, the sign read.

"All right," Rinna said. She turned toward Lissa. "Looks as if Image just wasn't meant to stay with us tonight."

Owras looked at Lissa with sympathetic eyes. "I'm sorry, little princess," he said with a rueful smile. "Would it be too much bother to send him off somewhere for the time being?"

"That's not fair."

"Perhaps not, but it'll do him no harm. I'm sure he can take care of himself for one night."

Geryam laughed a nasty laugh. "That's got to be the truth," he said.

"All right, all right," Owras said. "How about it, Lissa, just while we're around people? It would look better."

"Oh, all right," Lissa finally said. She knelt and rubbed the cat's back. "Image, I want you to go back and wait in the mountains for the night. Don't go sprouting wings or anything where anyone can see you, all right? Will you be able to find us in the morning?"

The cat rubbed against her calf and purred. "I knew you would," she said. "Now, off with you, and be a good cat." She stood up and watched as the animal ran from the courtyard, and darted between astonished patrons in cat fashion, its tail straight up in the air. Once it was out of sight, she glared at Geryam. "I hope you're happy," she said.

"I feel safer," he replied. "For you and me both."

They had water sent up to their rooms so they could wash; then they walked down to the inn's common room for dinner. The meal was simple travelers' fare: capons, roast beef, bread, and a robust pottage, but it tasted like heaven after all they had been through over the last few days. They did not stay up to talk and sing with the other guests, but rather climbed the stairs, went to their rooms, and crawled into their beds.

When Geryam woke the next morning, his head felt as if a hundred slaves stood inside it, beating at the walls of his skull with heavy hammers. He started to sit up, then fell back, groaned, and rolled over. He held his arms over his head for a moment, trying to still the horrible throbbing.

Then he rolled over again and looked about in spite of the pain from his throbbing head. The sun had already flown high into the sky. Its rays filtered down through the shuttered window and threw ladder patterns across the floor. Again, he started to sit up; again, he had to fall back because of the pain. "Owras," he cried. "Owras, Pal-Dan, wake up already."

No one answered. He heard only the snores of the other two men. Geryam finally did sit up, then padded over to Owras's cot and shook the old man's shoulder. "Wake up. We overslept."

He did the same for Pal-Dan, then went back to sit on the edge of his own cot and hold his head between his hands. Pal-Dan rolled over and looked at the window with a grimace. "Oh, me," the freak said. "I feel as if I've been on a three-day drunk. Did one of you slip something into my ale last night, or what?"

"I didn't," Owras said. "But my head hurts, too."

"It stinks in here," Pal-Dan announced. "Smells as if somebody's been burning something."

Owras sat up gingerly. "It does, doesn't it? I wonder if there's been a fire."

"I didn't hear an alarm," Geryam said. "Then again, I was sleeping so soundly, I wouldn't have heard it if they'd knocked the building down." He took a deep breath. "Do you have anything in that bag of yours for this head?"

"I don't know," Owras said. "I'll see what I can throw together." He reached down and hauled the leather bag up onto the bed with him.

"Meanwhile, I'll go check on the ladies," Geryam said. "They must have slept just as late as us, or they'd have been at us like harpies by now." He slid on his clothes, laced up his sandals, and unbolted the door. He walked the few cubits down the corridor to the next room rubbing his eyes, then half staggered when he saw the door to Rinna and Lissa's chamber. The latch was shattered and had been pulled out of the wall.

Ignoring the pain in his head, he rushed into the room. The two cots lay tipped over on the floor, their quilts strewn across the hardwood. A bureau on one side of the room also lay on its front, with washbasin, pitcher, and mirror lying in shards on the floor. Geryam looked in disbelief, then thundered back to his own chamber.

"Trouble," he shouted as he burst back through the door. "Someone's broken in. The women are gone."

Owras sprang to his feet. "Who?" he cried. "Why?"

Geryam had already run back out. Owras plodded after him, followed by Pal-Dan, wriggling along like a snake. "That blasted cat," Geryam cried as he stood beside the overthrown washstand. "I should have killed it while I had the chance, should have run it through and cut it into a million pieces." He groaned, then leaned down, picked up one blanket, and held it to his chest. "Oh, Rinna, what's happened to you?"

"You did kill the cat," Pal-Dan said. "You couldn't hardly just keep on killing it. Besides, why did the cat do it—it could have killed at least one of them easy enough yesterday." He peered around on the floor as he spoke. "Why didn't it just fly through the window, 'stead of breaking the door down?"

"He's right," Owras said.

"And lookie down here," Pal-Dan went on. "This didn't come from any white cat." They looked down on the floor and saw him staring at a shining object. Owras bent down to pick it up, but Pal-Dan snapped at him. "Don't touch it. Sorry, but it's better to just leave everything where it is. Better to piece together how it all happened, don't you know?"

He stared at the thing. "I'm low to the floor, so there's not much I miss. Besides, I've learned to watch things close—it's part of my act. Now, this here's a brass ring, torn right out of someone's ear, I'd say. And lookie here—couple drops of blood on the sheet next to it."

"By the gods," Geryam said.

"Looks as if the girlies put up a struggle, and they weren't the ones takin' all the licks, if you know what I mean. Look here, too. Dark hairs; there was some hair pulling going on and that hair didn't belong to Rinna or Lissa. Didn't belong to that cat, either."

"The innkeeper," Geryam said. "I'm going to talk to the innkeeper."

"Be careful," Owras said. "We're strangers to this town. The authorities won't want to listen to three outsiders like us."

"Blast the authorities," Geryam said. "The innkeeper'll listen to us, or he won't live to see any authorities."

Owras and Pal-Dan trailed back into the corridor while Geryam went back into their own chamber and buckled on his weapon. "This is interesting," came Pal-Dan's voice from the hall. "Look at this pot. Been something burning in here. That's what I smelled."

"It's like incense," Owras said. "But it's not." He stuck his finger into the ash. "Unless I miss my guess, that's why we slept so late."

Geryam came out of their room, glanced at the pot, then stormed down the hallway and down the stairs that led to the courtyard. He found the innkeeper wiping down the tables in the common room. "Remember me?" he said when the man looked up. "There were five of us: three men, two women. Someone's taken the women. What went on around here last night?"

The innkeeper stared up at him. "I run a regular business here, mister. Things like that don't happen in my place."

Washcloth and water bucket went flying as Geryam grabbed the man by the collar and dragged him out of the room. "It happened last night," the warrior snarled.

The man struggled, but Geryam hauled him close. "We got drugged last night, my friend, and it gave me a headache you wouldn't believe. I'm in real pain. I get mean when I hurt—I get very mean." With his free hand, he hauled his sword from its scabbard. "You'd better become helpful, and you'd better do it fast. If you don't, you'll be hurting just as bad as me. Difference is, I'll recover."

"All right, all right," the innkeeper said. "Show me what you're talking about. I'll go, you don't have to get rough."

Geryam shoved the man toward the stairs. They climbed to the second level, then walked to the chamber where Rinna and Lissa had slept. "Oh, my," the innkeeper said. "This is terrible. This sort of thing just doesn't happen in my house."

"It happened last night," Geryam said again. "See this pot?" He kicked the earthenware pot Pal-Dan had spotted. The vessel rolled onto its side, and gray-green ash strewed over the floor. "They burned something in this pot to drug us, so we wouldn't wake up while they were breaking into the other room."

The innkeeper stared. "Yes, I saw the pot. Four men insisted on renting this room." He pointed to the next room down the hall. "One of them carried that thing—I couldn't help noticing that."

"One of them have an earring?" Pal-Dan asked.

The innkeeper looked down at the freak with distaste. "Yes, one of them did. Rough-looking chap with a dark beard."

"Bingo," Pal-Dan said. "We got our kidnappers."

"Do you have any idea where they might have come from or where they might have headed?" Owras asked.

"No real idea," the innkeeper replied. "Then again, I just might. Two of them wore sailor's jackets. They weren't just overcoats, they were sailor's jackets. They must have been sailors."

"Let's get out of here," Geryam said. "We've got to get down to the harbor—it's our only hope." He started down the hall, and Owras started after him.

"Hey, wait for me," Pal-Dan yelled. Geryam retraced his steps, picked up the freak with a grunt, and the three of them hurried toward the stairs.

"Wait a minute," the innkeeper cried. "Who's going to pay for this damage?"

Geryam stopped, turned, and glared back at him. "I don't really care," he finally said. "Why don't you take that pot there and sell it—maybe that'll pay for the damage." Then he turned on his heel and he, Owras, and the freak disappeared toward the courtyard.

They hurried down toward the harbor of Ourms. The harbor was not a large one, but still held a half-dozen merchant vessels and a good-sized fleet of fishing boats. They headed for the harbormaster's large stone house. It stood at the end of a long, stone breakwater that stretched far into the harbor. They pounded on the door, and a servant let them in. The fellow was a foppish-looking sort, dressed in velvet doublet and spotless tights, and he looked down his nose at them. "What can you want?" he asked.

"We have to speak to the harbormaster," Owras said. "It's urgent."

"Sir Gaddeau can't help if you want to book passage on a vessel," the servant said. "You have to make your contract with the master of whatever vessel sails to your destination. It's not our affair."

"We're not here to book passage on anything," Owras said. "It's my . . ." He hesitated. "It's my daughter. She and her . . . her cousin were kidnapped last night. We think she might have been taken aboard one of the ships in the harbor."

"That hardly seems likely," the servant said. "But even if something like that did happen, this isn't the place to come. You need to go back down this lane, turn left, and then walk eight blocks. You'll find the constable's house. This would be his affair, not Sir Gaddeau's."

"He'll be in the Local Order's pocket," Pal-Dan whispered to Owras. "They're sure not about to help us."

"The constable doesn't have the authority to board ships and inspect cargoes," Owras said. "Only the harbormaster can do that. The constable can't help us."

"The constable has to investigate the crime to show if any ship needs to be boarded," the servant said wearily. "Only after the proper procedures have been followed . . ." He stopped short and swallowed hard. The point of Geryam's sword was suddenly pressing hard against his side.

"You'd better be a nice man and just let us in," Geryam said with a nasty smile. "Or someone's going to have to call your constable over here to investigate a very violent and bloody crime. Only you won't do the calling yourself, because you'll be the victim."

"You can't just walk in here and . . ." The servant's voice trailed away as the blade's pressure increased.

"Whatever they do to me for this," Geryam said, "you won't be around to enjoy it unless you let us in. And if I get arrested later on, you'd better make sure I get executed. That's because I'll come looking for you when I get out." He smiled even more broadly. "Now, do be a nice man and let us in."

The servant stepped away from the door. "First door to the right," he said in a croaking voice.

"Diplomacy's not your strong point, is it?" Pal-Dan said as they rushed in.

"Sometimes yes, sometimes no," Geryam replied as he put away his blade.

They found the harbormaster talking to a pair of wealthy merchants. He was a tall man who wore rich clothes— probably paid for from bribes—and sweet perfume. He looked down at the strange trio, and his eyebrows lifted. "Who might you be?" he asked.

Owras put on his most solemn face. "I know this is a bad time, your Excellency," he said. "But my daughter's been kidnapped, along with her cousin, and we fear they may be on one of the ships in your harbor."

"What about the constable?" Sir Gaddeau asked. "You should have seen him first about something like this. I'm surprised my servant even let you in."

"We thought about the constable," Geryam said blandly. "But your servant told us you were a man of extreme wisdom and kindness and you would help us if you could."

"Hmph. I'll have to speak to that man." He looked them over again, with plain disapproval. "Well, tell me your story and I'll do what I can. But make it quick. I'm a busy man."

Owras quickly related what they found at the scene and the innkeeper's description of the abductors, then asked if any ships were scheduled to depart that day.

"By the powers," one of the merchants cried. "I know one of the men you describe. He was third mate on my own vessel. Up and quit my captain as if we all had the plague, just yesterday afternoon."

"Where did he go?" Geryam cried. "Did he tell you?"

"Said he had some wealthy offer going, aboard the *Far Lands*."

"What ship's that?" Geryam asked.

"She's a contract trader," the merchant said. "Small ship,

sometimes she runs a regular trade route, but mostly they put her under charter to independent shippers."

"Something must have come up," the other merchant said. "I had a half-dozen men miss muster this morning."

"She usually anchors off the breakwater," the first merchant said. "You can probably see her from that window, if there aren't any houses in the way." He stepped to the window himself. "By thunder," he said suddenly. "She's getting under way."

Geryam stepped up behind him. "They are," he cried. "That has to be the ship." He turned toward the harbormaster, shouted a hasty thank you, then he and Owras headed for the door, Geryam still carrying Pal-Dan.

"Thaddeus," Sir Gaddeau called. "Who are these people and why in the world did you let them in?" They could hear the harbormaster berating the hapless servant as they rushed out of the building and down the hill.

As they hurried along, they caught occasional glimpses of the ship in question as it made its way toward the harbor entrance. "What are we going to do?" Geryam said in anguish. "We don't even know where they're headed."

Owras thought, then said, "We have to charter a boat ourselves. It's the only way. If we don't follow them, we'll lose them forever."

"If we're going to charter something, it'd better be small," Geryam said. "We aren't rich, you know." He was beginning to pant from the strain of carrying Pal-Dan.

They found a few fishing craft moored in a row, so that a person had to cross the deck of each one to get to the next. The one farthest out was a sizable craft, and they saw a man sitting in the bow. "Let's ask him," Geryam said.

They shouted and motioned until the man saw them. He looked, then finally rose and walked boat by boat toward the jetty. "What do you want?" he asked in a surly voice.

"Your boat's free," Geryam said. "We need to hire it."

"What, to the likes of you, when I don't even know you?" He looked them over. "You're a queer-looking lot, you are. Why should I? What can you offer?"

"We need you to follow that ship," Owras said, pointing toward the *Far Lands*, which was just clearing the breakwater.

"Two young ladies have been kidnapped and we think they're aboard her."

"And they're kin of yours?" The man looked sympathetic. "I'd like to, but I've got a responsibility to my own kin. Can't just let you have my craft for nothing."

Owras rummaged around in his robes for his purse. "Here," he said. "You can have this—it's about five talents, all I have in the world."

The man took the purse, hefted it, then looked back at the old man. "That's a good sum, but I don't know if it'll pay me and my brothers for time and craft and all."

"Then take my purse, too," Pal-Dan said from where Geryam held him. He ducked his head and used his teeth to pull a large purse from his blouse. "Owras, you take your money back. No sense you making yourself poor over this. I'll pay this time."

The seaman took that purse and handed the other back to Owras. "Five talents, ten, almost fifteen," he counted. "Yes, that'll do it, all right. More than enough, more than we'd make fishing in a couple of months. When do you want to get under way?"

"The sooner the better," Geryam said.

"I'll go get the others."

"Leave the purse with us till you get back," Geryam said.

"Sure, right," the man said, plainly impressed by the weight of Pal-Dan's gold. "I'll hurry."

He took off down the jetty at a run, and Owras turned to Pal-Dan. "Where did you get that kind of money?" he asked. "You're very generous."

"I'm not generous," Pal-Dan said with a laugh. "The harbormaster's generous—only he doesn't know it. The purse is his."

"How?"

"Just a quick snitch when no one's watching me," Pal-Dan said with a grin. "Nobody wants to look at you when you're a freak, so you can get away with murder."

Owras stared at him. "My friend, you are a wonder, indeed. And here comes the shipmaster and his friends at a run. Well you've saved the day. Now I only hope we can get outside the breakwater before the harbormaster calls the constable himself and has us all thrown into some dungeon for life."

Chapter Twenty-five: Aboard the *Far Lands*

WHEN RINNA WOKE up, she felt as if her skull were going to explode. Then she realized she felt sick everywhere else, too. At first she thought she had burrowed under the blankets on her bed so far she had half smothered herself; then she remembered what had happened.

She remembered the stinking fumes that had crept under her door at the inn. They had made her feel sick, then groggy and giddy. Still, when the men had beaten their way through the door, she and Lissa had fought like wildcats. The men had worn kerchiefs tied over their faces, which must have filtered out the worst of the fumes. Though the young women had bit, clawed, and pulled hair, they had been clumsy as drunks in a barrel. The men had yelped with pain and cursed, but in the end they had bound and gagged the two, then had hauled them out of the room like pieces of furniture.

Now she hurt all over and felt sick to her stomach besides. Part of the stiffness, she decided, was due to the fact that her arms were still tied behind her back. And rather than being under blankets, she was bundled inside some kind of wrapping, a bag of some sort.

She could tell from the feel of the floor beneath her that she was lying on rough wood planking. Worse, she could feel the pitch and roll and hear shouts and echoes of feet on the decking above her. With sinking heart, she realized she was once more on a ship.

She heard a sigh behind her, followed by a groan. "Lissa," she called softly. "Is that you?"

"Where are we?" came Lissa's voice. "This is awful. I'm going to throw up."

"Quit wrestling around like that and just lie still," Rinna said. "You'll feel better."

"I want out of here," Lissa said. Then she shouted, "Let me out of here!"

"Don't yell like that. They're not going to answer, unless it's to put a gag in your mouth. And don't struggle so. Lie quiet. If you lose your supper, it's a sure thing I'll lose mine."

Lissa quit struggling. "Foof," she said after a while.

"Skeek," Rinna replied softly. At least Lissa had kept her sense of humor. Rinna loved her like a sister.

The footsteps above them slowed down until they heard only an occasional thump. The rolling kept on, though, and so did the creaks and groans of the timbers as the ship made its way through the tossing sea. Rinna knew the feeling and the sounds from voyages she had made before, but being bound and stuffed where she couldn't see a thing made it all very unpleasant.

After a long time, she heard footsteps in the hold. "I stowed 'em behind those barrels," came a man's voice. "See, there they are." He must have been holding a lantern, because Rinna could see the light through the cloth over her head.

"Open the bags," came a high, wizened voice. "Let's have a look at them."

Rinna couldn't tell how many men there were. But they must have decided to look at Lissa first, because Rinna heard them fumbling with the other maiden's bag. "Ah," the cracked voice said again. "She's a young beauty, isn't she?"

"Ugh," came Lissa's voice. "Not you again."

"Oh, yes, dearie. You didn't think I'd give up, did you? Fact was, you made the whole sale cheaper for me by running away. Saved me shipping. You two are a rare pair, I'll tell you, and I know where I can unload you. I'm assuming you're both virgins, of course."

"Get lost," Lissa said.

"She's got to be," a third voice said with a laugh. "They never give you a straight answer if they really are."

Men laughed; then the one with the old, nasty voice said, "Open the other bag."

Rough hands grabbed the cloth that held Rinna, pulled her around, then undid a knot above her head and let in light and the sour smells of the ship. "By all the dark wonders," the old man said. "Look what you've done to her."

"Not us," a man answered. He was one of the sailors who had grabbed her the night before, who had lost an earring and part of an ear in the bargain. "She had that scab on her nose and those scratches afore ever I laid a hand on 'er. Though to tell truth, she deserved that and more for what she did to me."

Rinna looked out and saw five men. Four she had seen the night before, and the fifth—she groaned. The fifth was the old man who had spoken to them on the streets of Guelt when they had first landed. "You," she cried. "Don't you ever quit?"

"Course I don't," he said. "Moreere's the name, young women's the game. I supply pretty faces to rich men who can afford them." He leaned down, looked at her closely. She would have hit him if her hands had not been bound behind her. "I can see it, now," he said. "The scab's an old one, and I doubt it'll leave a permanent mark. Good thing. You two are a big investment. I wouldn't like it if you lost your value. Marks on the face are bad."

"Where are you taking us?" Lissa asked.

"To a fancier of young flesh," Moreere replied. "I doubt you'd know the name. But don't worry, you'll be treated well. I think," he added with a laugh. "You know, that crusty old man you had with you should have taken me up on my offer when he had the chance. As it is, I've still got you and he gets nothing at all." He shook his head with a smile. "Bad business for him."

"Our friends will find us," Rinna said. "And then you'll pay."

"Not likely," the villain replied. "Unless I miss my guess, they'll be crying after you through the streets of Ourms for a long time. I have friends in high places, you see—a man in my business meets all the high and mighty. By the time they get any idea where you're going, you'll already be there."

Lissa groaned. When Rinna looked at her, she had tears in her eyes. "Don't fret," Moreere said. "It'll be a jolly life for you where you're going, and your hulking lug of a friend and the fuddy-duddy old man you had with you will get over it before long. Who knows? By the time you see them again, you both might be ladies of high estate." He smiled at both of them, then turned to his henchmen. "Feed them and take them up to the captain's cabin. I want them to be comfortable through this trip."

He turned on his heel and walked past rows of crates and barrels until he disappeared from view. The other four hauled the young women to their feet and dragged them to the forward section of the hold, then hauled them up a ladder to the ship's deck. It was a humiliating journey, with men gawking at them and their captors grabbing them wherever it seemed most convenient.

They soon found themselves in the master's cabin, with the door to the deck latched and locked and the cabin windows open, showing the ship's wake streaming after them. "Oh, my," Lissa said. "Why does he keep picking on us? Who is he? Doesn't he ever give up?"

"Apparently not," Rinna said. There was a desk built into the cabin's forward bulkhead with a stool attached to the deck in front of it. She sat on the stool and leaned her head on the desk in despair. Then she brightened. "What about Image? I wonder if he could fight those apes?"

"Who knows? Besides, I sent him away. How do we know if he even cares where I am?" A wood-framed bed had been built into the bulkhead before Lissa. She slumped into it and wept bitterly.

A knock sounded on the door. "Make yourselves decent if you ain't," a voice said. "I got vittles." They heard the latch trip, then the door opened and a sailor stuck his head in. It was one of the same sailors who had broken into their room the night before. He looked at Lissa and his rough face fell. "Now, don't you be down in the mouth, lass," he said. "That Moreere fellow, he promises you're going to be right well took care of."

"What do you care?" Rinna shot back at him.

"Oh, lass, if I'd ever suspected this was going to bring any real harm to you, I'd never of been a part of it. I'm an honest seafaring man, I am. Here's a plate of salt pork and fried taters and even some wine and water from the captain's own stock. You have a bite, and you'll feel better."

"I don't want anything," Rinna said. "I'm seasick."

He looked sympathetic. "That's a pity, and I'm sorry to hear it. If you gots to heave, well, lass, you'll do better for having something in you to get rid of. Now, don't pull a face at me—it may sound disgusting, but it's the very truth. It'll settle your stomach more like than stir it up—it's real good officer grub, it is. Now do be good and eat a little. I wouldn't want you to sit and pine. No good cryin' over spilt milk."

The fellow did seem to be a good enough soul, though not very bright. But when Rinna sniffed at the food, the very smell drove her away. "Set it on the desk," she finally said. "How about you, Lissa, do you want some?"

"Ugh, no," Lissa replied. She groaned, rolled over onto her stomach, and pulled a blanket over her head.

"So much for food," Rinna said. "Well, leave it. Maybe we'll feel better later on."

"That's the way, lass. You'll feel better by the time we reach Kolpos, and my heart'll feel better for seeing it?"

"Kolpos?" Rinna said. "Is that where we're going."

The sailor straightened and looked worried, as if he'd caught himself making a serious blunder. "Lass, you'd better forget you ever heard that from me. I didn't ever mean to tell you that."

"If that's the case, I'll forget it as quickly as possible. Why shouldn't I know?"

The sailor looked over his shoulder, out the open cabin door. "Mister Moreere doesn't want me telling you things."

"I see," Rinna said. "If you're the honest, upright man you say you are, then why in the world are you working for him?"

"I have a pretty wife and three bubs of my own at home. He comes up to me in the street a coupla days gone by and offers me big money to work for him. Lyles, too—that's the fellow you pulled the beard and earring on. Well, it's as much money as I can make in a year. I got family to think about, I tell you. I'm not sure about the look of it, but he swears you'll not be hurt. You'll be helped in the long run, he says. So I pitches in."

"And is this Moreere's ship?"

"No," the sailor said. "This here's a vessel of independent registry. Moreere chartered her."

"Why?" Rinna cried. "Why are we worth all the money he's paying to get us to Kolpos?"

"I guess someone there's got an interest in you," he said with a shrug. Then he looked over his shoulder again. "I need to be gone. Wouldn't be right for Moreere to see me chatting too long." He stepped back to the deck outside, then leaned back through for a last word. "Now, you young ladies do be reasonable and eat a bite or two. Won't you, please? It'll do you good, and you shouldn't be losing strength."

"He's got that much right," Rinna murmured as the door closed and latched. "I suppose we can look on the bright side. Kolpos is where we were going anyway."

"That's wonderful," Lissa said bitterly. "It makes me feel so much better."

Rinna picked at the meal the sailor had brought, but couldn't work up any interest in it. Finally, though, after dark had fallen, both she and Lissa felt well enough to eat some of the food, by now long grown cold. A short time later, the sailor came in again, with more from the ship's galley. They talked again. He seemed happy that they had eaten something, and told them his name: Macound. But they weren't able to get any more information out of him about their destination or the reason Moreere was willing to pay so much to capture them.

The following morning found them gazing out the cabin windows, toward the wave-tossed horizon behind them. All at once, Lissa stood up straight. "Look there," she said. "There's a sail. Is someone following us?"

Rinna looked. Unmistakable on the horizon, the triangular sail was a flash of white and gold in the rising sun's rays. On a closer look, she could tell it was some kind of fishing boat. "You're right," she said. "I wonder . . ."

"The same thing I wonder, I bet," Lissa said. "Are they coming after us?"

"It's our only hope," Rinna said. "Even if we could get off this tub, there's no place for us to go except into the water. I wish there were some way we could get them a message."

"How about in a bottle?" Lissa said. "Just like in stories."

Rinna turned and eyed the other young woman. "Oh, sure. But first, find a bottle. Second, find a way to make it drift exactly where they'll see it from their boat. No, there has to be a surer way than that. And you can bet, we'll only get one chance. But let me think . . . I might have a plan."

They whispered together for a moment; then the cabin door rattled. They heard the familiar sounds of latch and lock before the door creaked open and Macound carried in a platter of food. "Now, ladies," he said. "I know you're going to make a show of not eating, but you know as well as I, it's bad for a body to let good grub go cold. So won't you please have a taste? The cook's half off his head trying to find a way to please you."

Rinna nodded. "We're sorry, Macound. I know you mean well, and Lissa knows it, too."

"That's right," Lissa said. "If we have to be here, it won't do us a bit of good to starve ourselves."

"That's better." Macound beamed as he put the tray down.

Rinna picked up a spoonful, only to put it down again. "But I just can't eat, I just can't."

"Aw, lass, don't be that way, Now you will, now you won't . . . it'll make us all daft. Moreere's getting after me already about you not eating."

"How can we eat when we're unhappy?" Lissa asked.

"But you said . . ."

"It's not just being here," Rinna interrupted. "We've resigned ourselves to that. But we're worried. Poor Owras and Geryam and Pal-Dan. They're going to be frantic with worry."

"You can't help that, lass."

"That's just the point. We don't want them to worry, but there's no way we can help them."

"If only . . ." Lissa said, staring at the platter.

"If only what?" Macound asked.

"If only someone could get word to them that we're all right," Rinna said. "So they wouldn't worry."

Macound looked indignant. "You're being pretty foxy, aren't you? Well, it won't work. Besides, how could I get word to them? I don't even know them."

"Oh, you couldn't miss them," Rinna said. She described them carefully, especially the fact that Pal-Dan had neither arms nor legs. "And they'll probably show up in Kolpos before long—that's where we were going anyway, before all this happened."

"Ah ha. Are they following us in that . . ." His voice trailed off.

"Is there someone following us?" Rinna asked innocently.

The conversation went on; the poor seaman wavered as he parried the two maidens' verbal thrusts. Finally, he left with food barely touched and scratching his head. Rinna looked at Lissa and they both laughed. "I think he'll actually do it if we keep working on him," Rinna said.

They did keep working on him, for the next full day. They refused food until he begged them to eat. Then, when he seemed on the verge of tears, they would extract a hint of a promise from him—to "at least think about it"—after which they would eat a few bites.

Once not eating became part of their strategy, their appetites returned with a vengeance. Still, they managed to survive on only a taste here and a sip there, until the lights of Touros, Kolpos's largest city, rose up before them. Again, they heard the shouts of officers and the noises of men working the rigging. After a bit, a loud rattle shook the timbers. The ship lurched, heeled over, then drifted to one side.

"What's that?" Lissa asked.

"I think they dropped the anchor," Rinna said.

They heard a noise outside the cabin; then the door flew open. Before them stood Moreere, with a black cape wrapped around his shoulders. Behind him stood other men, one of whom gripped a lantern. To Rinna's disappointment, Macound was nowhere to be seen.

"It's time for you to leave this ship," Moreere said with a smile. "For your own safety, I ask you to come quietly."

"Where are we going?" Rinna asked.

"Don't be curious. Curiosity's a bad habit."

"What about all the sailors?" Lissa asked. "What's going to happen to them?"

The man eyed her with a puzzled look on his face, as if he had no idea why she would ask such a stupid question. "I've paid them all off," he finally said. "Whether they'll stay with the ship, or how many of them will, isn't important. Not to me, at least. Come along, both of you."

They left the cabin, and the night breeze kissed their faces as they walked across the deck. A few sailors stared at them as they moved past, but they didn't see Macound's face any-where.

The lights of a city blinked in the distance, beyond a league of surf. As Rinna had suspected, the ship rolled at anchor. The sailors had broken out the ship's crane and they had swung the captain's gig alongside the gunwale. Now it hung there, gently bumping against the larger vessel. A crew of oarsmen had already entered the boat, and stood in two neat rows. "Step into the boat, ladies," Moreere said. "Mind you be careful. We don't want you damaged in any way."

Rinna looked about. She toyed with the idea of jumping overboard and knew from Lissa's look that the other young woman was thinking the same thing. But she decided not to. There would be no hope of escape, and probably none of survival, once they struck the water. Besides, Moreere would be ready for such an attempt. So she stepped into the boat, putting out one arm to steady herself. One man caught her hand to keep her from losing balance, and she looked up to see Macound looking back at her. She took her eyes off him immediately; then she and Lissa sat on a thwart amidships.

Moreere climbed into the boat and sat between the two maidens. "How nice," he beamed. "For a fancier of flowers like myself to be surrounded by such pretty blossoms."

Rinna ignored him and so did Lissa. "Lower away," the captain shouted. Sailors chanted at the lines, ropes creaked through sheaves, and the captain's gig dropped toward the tossing waves. They settled into the water with an awkward lurch, sailors at bow and stern cleared away the falls, and the oarsmen started pulling toward shore. As soon as the boat cleared the ship's side, they heard the captain give the order to raise anchor.

The oarsmen strained at their task, the boat plowed through the waves, and the breeze blew spray into Lissa's face. They watched a shadowy headland slide past them in the darkness, and the lights of the city grew closer. Rinna sighed and tried to feel warm in the salt air's chill. What might await her on the island of Kolpos, she had no idea.

Chapter Twenty-six:
The Captives

IN DARKNESS, RINNA and Lissa found themselves hauled out of the captain's gig of the *Far Lands* and hustled along the breakwater of the harbor of Touros while that rough-looking city slept. The fresh wind blew the waves in the harbor white and black and sent them smashing into the stone of the jetty. It tossed the hair of the two maids and sent the spray flying into their faces.

A posse of men waited where the breakwater met the dock, dark-robed against the wind and the spray. A couple of lanterns peeked out from between the massed cloaks. As the party from the ship drew closer, Rinna could tell the waiting men wore armor and that attendants held horses in the darkness behind them.

Moreere walked up to one of the men. "I've delivered them, just as I said. It was at great expense, as you can imagine. Krell owes me."

"Krell?" Rinna and Lissa looked at one another in horror and surprise. Fate was strange.

"He'll see you well rewarded," the officer said to Moreere. "He always does."

"Couldn't you give me something on account? I spent nearly everything I had just getting here."

"I don't deal in your kind of money, worm," the officer said. "People like you disgust me, with your groveling for whoever'll pay for the girls you seduce. I said you'll get your money, but you won't get it from me."

Moreere laughed. "Aren't we mister high-and-mighty? Don't forget, friend, you work for Krell same as I do. You take his money."

"It's not the same. I'm not his pimp, the way you are."

"Tell that to these two girls while you're hauling them to the Krell's tower." Moreere started to laugh. He kept the noise up even as the officer pushed past him and confronted Rinna and Lissa.

The two maidens stared at the rough-looking man. He gazed back at them with eyes hard and cold as flint. "So you're the ones," he said. "It's pretty girls you are, and I can't say I'm glad to be part of this. But I have my orders." He turned to one of his men. "Bring them each a blanket. They look as if they're freezing."

Men brought robes and wrapped them around the girls. Then they hustled them to the horses and mounted them onto two that had been equipped with sidesaddles. "Don't try to escape," one of the men said matter-of-factly. "There are twenty of us, the best riders in Krell's whole guard. And we've been ordered to kill you, rather than let you get away."

Rinna and Lissa watched the officer talk to Moreere another moment. Their words were apparently angry ones, because the weasely man finally wheeled away from the soldier. "All right, get out of here," Moreere yelled at the sailors and henchmen who had come with him from the ship. "I can't pay you any more than I already have. Blame him, not me."

The men buzzed angrily. Then the officer climbed onto his horse, and the mounted company clattered away before the two maidens could see the scene between Moreere and his hirelings played out to its end. They turned down a dark street and rode through the dark city at a steady pace.

They rode into the countryside beyond Touros, a land where

trees tossed their dark heads in the wind and night-blackened hills rose against the starry sky. After a time, they stopped, dismounted, and made camp. The soldiers put the two maidens into a tent and let them know sentries would be stationed at every corner.

The sun had risen by the time the soldiers woke them up. The wind had died down to a breeze. Meat was already cooking over a low campfire, and one man was passing around fresh biscuits. Rinna couldn't help comparing how much better the soldiers ate in their camp than she and the other questers had in theirs. "Perhaps there's an advantage in working for the Order," she whispered morosely to Lissa. "They have the food."

"Foof," Lissa said. "I'll eat their food, but I hate them anyway."

They ate a leisurely breakfast, then mounted their horses. By afternoon, they reached a higher range of hills. Over one of them, the air shimmered the same way air shimmers over a hot stove. "What's happening up there?" Rinna asked one of the soldiers. "I've never seen anything like that."

The officer looked at them over his shoulder. "You've never been to this part of the island before, have you, Miss?"

"We've never set foot on Kolpos at all," Lissa said.

"Take the northern trail," the officer ordered. "They might just as well see a sight or two before we deliver them."

"Oh, thanks," Rinna said sarcastically. "At least I'll die after getting a guided tour of the island. That makes me feel lots better." She saw the officer's ears redden, but he did not turn around again.

These hills were rocky and all but treeless. As they rode higher, Rinna could see the blue of the Thlassa Mey sparkling off to the north. From the summit of one hill, they looked down into a dark crater from which hot breezes issued like bad breath. On looking into the rift, the two maidens could see a lacy webwork of metal tracing its way down along one wall. Beneath that, so far below them it looked as if it lay at the center of the world, a lake of red glowed like an evil eye.

"That's the Tower of Krell," the officer said. "You can barely see it from up here, but you'll see it well enough later." He explained how the Order had built the tower in that cavern over the generations, and how the molten lake below heated it. "That's what you saw this morning," he said. "The heat waves rising from this hole."

"It's an infernal place," Rinna said. "Only infernal people would stay there."

"Maybe they're infernal," the officer said. "But they run this island."

This time it was Rinna and Lissa who did not answer. The company rode down a ravine and through the great, bronze doors that formed the entrance to the Tower of Krell. In a huge, underground stable, they dismounted, and attendants came to claim the two young women. As they climbed down from their sidesaddles, Rinna and Lissa saw the officer staring at them. "I feel sorry for you," he said. "I know you're in for a rough time. I just want you to know I wish you the best. I'm only following orders."

Rinna looked back at him. "If we were more careful about whose orders we followed, the world would be a better place," she said. "But if it makes you feel any better, I don't suppose I hate you for being a part of this." Then the attendants marched her and Lissa through a doorway and down a corridor.

"Don't speak for me," Lissa whispered as they walked along. "I hate all of them enough for both of us."

The attendants led them into a large chamber. "Take off your outer robes," one old man said. "Where you're going, you won't need them."

Rinna looked into Lissa's eyes. Lissa looked back. As one, they threw the heavy robes up over their heads, then flung them into the faces of the men who held them. They turned and fled together, toward the corridor from which they had just come. A few paces down the hall, a half-dozen armed guards hurtled out of a side corridor, bowling them over like blocks of wood. One hit Rinna with the full force of his body and knocked the wind from her. As she fell, she saw three more pounce on Lissa before she could get back up. They bound her hands, then jerked her back to her feet. They did the same with Rinna.

Once more, the two females found themselves in the long chamber. "Don't try that again," the old man said. He looked angry, and his face had gone red. "Krell has gone to a lot of trouble to have you brought here. He doesn't want to be disappointed by your death now that you've come this far."

"You're all worms," Rinna shouted. "Worms to work for people like this."

"Gag her," the old man ordered. Though Rinna kicked and struggled, two guards forced a gag into her mouth. They did the same to Lissa, then started off with the two maidens, down through the maze of bronze chambers and platforms that was the Tower of Krell.

They wound their way down until they reached a large, circular chamber, where panels of glass alternated with panels of finely polished metal to form the walls. A huge, bald man in white robes stood there, arguing with a beautiful woman.

He turned and smiled at them, a blubbery leer of greed, lust, and savagery. "So there you are," he said. "Come in. You're lovely, just as I heard. And so young." He turned to the woman. "What do you think, Madame Horyk? Aren't they the most precious morsels you ever saw?"

Horyk gazed at them and smiled. "They're quite lovely, Krell. Are they from some finishing school? Perhaps your nieces, or the daughters of a friend. So sweet, so simple-looking."

He laughed a nasty little laugh. "Not quite. They arrived here a day ago, all the way from the island of Artos."

"Artos?" She stared at them. "Then these are the girls . . ."

"Correct. You haven't paid attention to your duties, my dear Horyk. These maids—especially this one—" Here, he laid a palm on Rinna's shoulder. "—are high in the destiny of that little cult you find so threatening. The Cult of the Twelve."

"Ah," she said. "Let me send them to my castle on the Stilchis. I'll make it worth your while."

He shook his head. "That's not possible," he said. "As the young ruffian you kept down in your chamber was yours, so these two are mine."

"Don't be presumptuous. You know I can take them by force."

"Perhaps, perhaps not." He turned to the guard. "See to where they stand." To Rinna's surprise, guards shoved both her and Lissa sideways, until they were both standing on circular silver plates set into the floor. The plates looked about the diameter of fruit baskets.

Horyk smiled, but her smile dripped with anger and cruelty. "If you won't hand them over to me, then they'll die here. You won't use them for your own purposes." She lifted her hand, and a bolt of light pierced from her fingertip as if it were a taper. But Krell was just as quick. He placed one hand over the head of each girl and from his palms dropped two cylinders of crystal. The glass drifted down over them like sand sprinkled from a jar, and the light glanced off the shining surface and struck the bronze wall. It left discolored places in the metal where it hit.

"I've learned much, good Horyk," came Krell's voice from outside the cylinders. "I'm flattered that a man of my weak talents can surprise you." He laughed as the silver disks dropped Rinna and Lissa into tubes below the floor. As they moved downward, the crystal around them dissolved, leaving them free to slide down the tubes.

Down they slid, through spirals and twists, until the tubes opened out and they both flew into a dimly lit chamber. They rolled across the floor, amazed but unhurt, and stared at one another. "What was that all about?" Lissa cried.

"I've no idea," Rinna replied. "What a pair."

"And here we are in this room. Was ever a prison a drearier place?"

Rinna stood and looked around. A candle glowed from behind a glass set into one wall. The chamber was smaller than the other, not made of the shining bronze she had seen before. She reached out and touched the wall, to find it hot and metallic. "Iron, I think," she said.

"What are they going to do with us?"

Rinna made her way all around the room. There was no door. "I don't know," she replied. "But from what we saw of that pair, I don't think we're going to like it."

Chapter Twenty-seven:
Sails and Wings

FOR A DAY and a night and a day, Owras, Geryam, and Pal-Dan followed the *Far Lands* eastward across the Thlassa Mey. Though they hung back in the larger vessel's wake so that they could only see the top of the mainmast above the horizon, they knew any lookout aboard that ship had to have spotted them alone in the broad blue sea. A couple of times, they changed course to change positions with the ship ahead of them, but when they dropped back astern of her, they found themselves so near that even someone standing on the deck could have spotted them with the naked eye.

As evening fell on the second day, the broad, gray hump that was Kolpos rose out of the sea ahead of them. And as the sun drove his chariot below the horizon and the sky grew dark, the mass grew broader and higher and specks of light sparkled against the hills the same way starlight twinkled in the sky.

"They're making for Touros," the fishing boat's master told his passengers. "This is the quickest approach from the west. In a while, they'll change course to the left, you just watch."

That was just what happened. A dented moon rose out

of the sea, and the dark cliffs of Kolpos drifted to the left of them. Then the headlands fell away, and the ship ahead of them steered toward a cluster of lights on the far shore of a broad bay. "That'll be Touros up there," the master said.

The moon brought with it a brisk breeze, and the fishing craft took a tack that put them a far piece to the left and downwind of the larger craft. Still, they could see the great lantern at the stern clearly. Their course and the fact that they did not have to keep to the middle of the channel allowed them to pull farther into the bay than the larger, slower merchant vessel.

"That's good thinking, my friend," Owras said to the master. "We may even be able to reach the harbor before she does."

"Almost certainly," the master said. "She'll have to heave to until morning and take on a pilot. There's shoal waters in Touros and their own skippers guard their charts the way an old carpenter would guard a young wife." He nodded with satisfaction. "See there, see how she's falling back. He's dropped anchor."

"That's good," Geryam said. "This way, we can be there and watch any people they send to shore. They can't hide from us, now."

"Hmm," Owras said. "Who knows what more tricks they may have up their sleeves."

They sailed on a broad reach, far up the bay, until they could watch the white waves beating on the shore and the ship's lantern glittered a league southeast of them. It was an exciting time, almost like a race, and Owras found himself warmed by a thrill he had thought reserved for younger men. Then, while he watched, the fishing boat's master stepped to the transom and stared at the larger ship. "Something's wrong," the fisherman said.

"How do you mean?"

"She's falling away too much—her position's changing. That means she's raised anchor. And what's worse, the wind is shifting, starting to blow up the bay."

"She's getting away, then," Geryam said. "By the gods, we were fools. We knew they saw us, yet we let them lure us into this bay."

"With the wind between her and us, now," the master said. "That captain's a foxy one."

"Can you catch up with them again?" Owras asked.

"It's going to be a nasty game, trying to get out of this bay with the wind in our faces," the master said. "We've still got room for a reach into the wind. But it'll be short reaches at best. Our only luck is that their tub won't sail into the wind at all. I don't think they'll be able to get so far we can't spot them again once daylight comes."

"You'd better get to it, then," Owras said. "Ah, I should have known this was going too easily."

"Bring her about," the master yelled. "Tiller to the right, luff sail, and bring her into the wind as far as she'll go." Like madmen, the crew heaved against the tiller and hauled at the rigging. They tugged the mainsail's long boom inboard. Soon, the breeze refilled the sail and the slender craft heeled over until Owras and Geryam had to hold on.

It was a long, slow process to make their way back out of the bay, and the ship they pursued had vanished around the eastern headland long before they made it. "He played it perfectly," the fishing boat's master said.

"We—I—took the bait hook, line, and sinker. Now, if he gets a little help from the morning wind shift, we'll play hob trying to catch him."

"Do your best," Owras said. "This is still, by far the faster vessel."

They didn't make the mouth of the bay until well after sunrise. Once they finally reached past the headland, though, they did spot the *Far Lands*, hull down on the eastern horizon. "You've done it," Owras said to the master. "My congratulations to you and your crew."

"And our thanks, too," Geryam said.

"It was a hard night's work," the master replied. "My men are tired, and I am, too." He eyed his passengers. "I wonder how long this voyage is going to take. My bargain with you may not have been a good one, after all."

"You did make it, though," Geryam said grimly.

"Now, Geryam," Owras said. "There's no sense antagonizing these men. They have worked hard for us." He laid a hand on the master's shoulder. "Please know, we do thank you, and we'll do our best to make things right with you, whatever happens."

"I appreciate that," the master said. "But it looks as if a long day is ahead of us. I'm going to get some rest." He stepped toward the craft's tiny cabin, and so did one of his crewmen. The other two hands remained on deck, trimming the rigging and watching the three passengers.

"That's a good idea," Owras said. "I could use some sleep, too. Staying awake all night doesn't agree with me."

"Wait on," Pal-Dan said. "Look up there." During the whole night, the freak had lain on the deck, bracing himself in the space between the rail and the stern hatch. A person would have thought him asleep all that time, except each time one would look at him, it was to see his eyes wide open, looking out to sea between the stanchions, or up into the sky. Now, as Owras and Geryam turned, it was to follow his gaze upward.

Soaring out of the west on broad wings was what at first looked like a huge albatross. But an instant's careful gaze showed it was a far different creature. "It's that cat-thing," Geryam said. "I wonder what it's after."

"I don't know," Owras said.

The man at the tiller stared up at the strange creature as it dived toward the boat, circled it at close range, then flew off toward the west a little way. It gazed back down at them, then flew over the boat once more.

"What is it?" the tillerman asked. "I've never seen anything like that in my life."

"I wish I hadn't seen it, either," Geryam said.

"Don't be hasty," Owras said. "It may mean us good instead of harm. I wonder if it's trying to tell us something."

"More likely, it's trying to figure a way to do us in."

"I'm with Owras," Pal-Dan said. "But what the thing's got to offer is more than I can guess. What is it, Image? Are you swearing at us, or singing us a sweet, old song?" He tilted his head to one side as he studied the animal. "Who knows? He might miss the girlies just as much as we do."

Geryam set his jaw and said nothing. As for Image, the beast circled the sail a couple of times at close range, then set its head against the top of the canvas and pushed, flapping its wings with obvious effort. The vessel leaned farther to leeward. A high-pitched wail came from the creature, carried softly on the wind. "No, no, no, no, no," it seemed to say.

"I don't understand this," Geryam said.

The creature hovered over the boat, studying them all with a keen eye. Suddenly, with terrifying quickness, it dived toward them. "Look out," Geryam yelled. "Here he comes." The warrior dived to one side, and Owras had to scramble to the other as the creature swept past them.

Owras half expected to feel the great claws rake his back, but there was only a wafting breeze as Image swept by, banked to the left, and snatched between its iron jaws the leather bag the old man kept for emergencies. With a curse, Geryam leaped after the parcel, but he was too late. Image's wings carried the beast out over the water; then it beat its wings hard to gain altitude.

They climbed to their feet and stared as Image circled the mast a couple more times, then headed for land. It quickly became a shrinking speck. "This is crazy," Geryam said. He watched the creature with hands on hips.

"We have to go after him," Owras said.

"That's foolish. That's just what he wants us to do."

"Maybe. But everything we have is in that bag, all our money, all my salves and remedies."

"We can get more money," Geryam said. "We can live without salves and remedies."

"I want to go after him anyway," Owras said. "Something funny's going on."

"Look," Pal-Dan said. "He's landing on that hilltop."

Owras peered out over the water, shading his eyes with one hand. "I can't tell. My old eyes are too foggy."

"He might well be," Geryam said. "He's teasing us, then."

"I'm going to get the master," Owras said. He stepped below for an instant, then returned with the other man. The fellow wore a curious expression. "Put this craft about," Owras said. "I want to go ashore."

The master gave the orders, the tillerman pulled hard, and the ship's head swung to the northwest. In moments, they were racing before a following breeze, heading straight toward Kolpos. "I can't carry you all the way to the beach," the master said. "I'd be blown aground. I'll take you into the bay a little way, and you can catch a ride in on the pilot boat."

"This is ridiculous," Geryam said. "We're losing time."

"Maybe," Owras said. "Maybe not. Either way, I want to reach that hilltop—and as quickly as possible." As they neared the shore, they could quite clearly see the white speck that was Image.

"All right, look," Geryam said. "I'm a strong swimmer—get me in close, and I'll get ashore by myself. If we take the pilot boat, it'll be all day before we get there."

Owras looked at him, then rubbed his white beard. "All right," he finally said. "But that animal's not the one you killed up in the cavern. Don't assume it's out to do us harm."

Geryam let out a breath. "If it's a fool's errand, I'll wave you off," he finally said. "You get back after that ship. But . . ." He hesitated. "But if I don't wave you off, then I guess the best thing for you to do is get into the harbor."

So it was agreed. In a trice, Geryam had stripped off his jerkin and his boots. Keeping only a knife as a weapon, he dived into the water. They watched his broad back for a long time as he battled the waves, then finally crawled out onto the pale sand of Kolpos.

For his part, Geryam felt exhausted by the swim. He walked up the beach slowly, trying to catch his breath. It was by now almost noontime, and the sun had warmed the sand until it felt hot to his bare feet. Still, he made his way up the hill toward where Image had landed. Even though he could not see the great cat because of the hill's curvature and the brush that coated it, he remembered the general direction.

It took a while, and he was sweating and swatting flies long before he reached the top. When he reached the stony promontory that was the hill's crown, he found himself surprised. Owras's bag rested in plain sight. Beside it lay Image, once more turned into a plain, white housecat. He drew his knife as he approached, but the animal did not move, nor did it make any attempt to change back into its fearsome, winged form.

"You're brazen, aren't you?" Geryam said. "You're telling me I can attack you and you won't attack me, is that it? But how do I know your game's a fair one? How can I trust you when I don't know anything about you?" The cat did not answer, but only stared up at the warrior with its pale blue eyes.

Then Geryam found himself staring down at the ground, at the dust beside Owras's bag. In the dust was drawn an arrow, which pointed back along the promontory, northwest, toward the city of Touros. At the pointed end of the arrow were the words, "LISSA. RINNA."

Geryam stared at the arrow, then at the words, then back at the cat. It still looked at him with nothing more than a cat's unreadable expression. Then he wheeled and ran down the hillside a little way, stumbling, almost falling. "Hey," he yelled, even though he knew they would never hear him over the expanse of tossing waves. "Hey, I'll meet you in Touros. Don't even stop at the pilot boat, put in at the harbor."

He turned around in disgust. "There's no way I can signal them," he said. "Not to do that." His eyes lit on the cat once more. "But you can," he said. "Look, I still can't say I like you, and you probably don't feel any better about me. But if you're loyal to the girls, you'll help."

He snatched open Owras's bag and pawed through the contents: little cloth bags full of twigs and leaves, clay vials stopped with wooden stoppers, a small purse with Owras's five talents in it. Finally, at the bottom, he found a few scraps of paper. He found neither quill nor ink, though. He looked around, then stared at the animal. It looked as if it were laughing at him. "Wait a minute," he said. "You can talk when you have wings. Change back, then. Go tell Owras to meet me in Touros as soon as he can. I'll be waiting at the waterfront."

The cat stared at him with its head tilted to one side. "Come on," the warrior said. "Do something. I feel like an idiot standing here."

More quickly than Geryam's eye could follow, the cat leaped past him, then shot into the brush. In the blink of an eye, the animal had vanished from view. Geryam stood and eyed the brush where he had last seen the white tail. "Well, that's that," he said to himself. "Did I make a fool of myself for nothing, or what?" He sighed and picked up the bag, then started the long walk toward Touros.

Only after he had walked a few paces did he look down the hillside and see the large, white form burst from the brush in a flash of broad wings. Once more, the creature had become a thing of dreams and nightmares. With great, pumping strokes of its wings, it climbed toward the pale blue sky. He saw it soar toward the fishing boat, which lay off the point; then he stepped up his own pace as he saw the craft turn its prow toward the city. White or black, trusted or feared, the creature was a mystery and a wonder.

The walk toward Touros was hard on Geryam's feet and doubly wearing on a man already weary from nearly two days without sleep. Still, the warrior kept up a good pace, stopping only at a spring he found bubbling from the hillside. The gray stone walls and the houses and towers behind it loomed ever closer. By the time his feet found the grimy, cobbled streets of his youth, they were covered with shadow.

He knew Touros well, both the halls of the nobles and the dives where he and his warrior friends had once caroused. He turned his steps toward the waterfront. He knew Owras and Pal-Dan would make their appearance from that direction. Besides, he had friends in that district. It was practically dark by the time he came to the familiar door of a tavern he had once frequented.

The Gold Miner, the place was called, though the only gold anyone had ever seen mined there had come from the coin unsuspecting strangers laid down on the gambling tables. But the owner had long been Geryam's friend. The two had done one another many a good turn over the years.

A long counter of spruce formed the tavern's rear wall. Beyond, Geryam could see into the dark, steaming kitchen and smell roast beef, boiled fish, and all the staples of the rough man's diet. A lean, sallow fellow Geryam did not know polished the shining wood with a cloth. "Wot's your pleasure?" he asked without even looking up. He looked as if he had forgotten to shave.

"I need to talk with Clank," Geryam said. That was the proprietor's nickname, from the none-too-polite way he always had of setting a guest's table.

"Not likely," the fellow said.

"Why? I'm an old friend of his."

The man laughed a nasty laugh. "Not no more. Clank ain't got no friends. He's been dead as a hammer for a year and a half."

Geryam's face fell. "What happened to him?"

"It's not healthy to ask."

Geryam nodded. The Dark Order had great strength in

Touros. An accidental slight to any of the cultists, or even to one of their housecarls on an errand, could be fatal. When a person was told not to ask about an accident or a death, that was what it usually meant. He set his jaw. That was one more debt laid against Krell's door, as far as he was concerned.

"All right, then," Geryam finally said. "Does Meenah have anything to do with this place?" Meenah had been Clank's wife, at least in all but name.

"Who's askin'? Won't do you no good to suck up to her." The man blew his nose into his wiping cloth. "Her share in this place already passed into other hands."

"Nalord, don't be such a stuffy old fart," came a woman's voice. The sound was loud and brash, like a load of pots being dumped onto pavement. "Don't listen to him, Geryam. He's so full of himself he'd bust like a boiled sausage if I didn't take him down a peg once in a while."

"Meenah," Geryam said. "You look the same as always." He began to reach toward the woman, to clamp her in the familiar old embrace, then hesitated. "I'm sorry to hear about Clank."

The huge, red-haired woman shrugged and spread her hands wistfully. Then she grinned once more and threw her arms around Geryam, almost smothering him. "I've done with mourning, and I'm glad to see you. That's all that matters." She gestured toward the man who had spoken. "My only mistake was getting so lonely I up and married this old piece of liver pie while my dear old fellow was still warm in his grave. This one wanted my share in the tavern, he did, and once he got it, he's been about as good a husband to me as a pig sittin' on a nest of hen's eggs."

"If you weren't a nagging, ugly witch, I'd be pleasant enough," the man snapped back.

"The last time you were pleasant is when your mother died and you got to collect on her will, you grubbing old fool. Oh, forget him, Geryam. Come on into the kitchen and we'll stuff some chowder and ale down you. You look as if you just crawled off a sinking ship."

"Mind you, not the good ale," Nalord said.

"Stuff a boot in your mush," Meenah tossed back with a laugh. "This man was a friend long before I met you—and he could whittle you down to a sliver before you blinked if he took a mind to. So tend to your guests and leave the kitchen— and *my* guests—to me." With that, she led Geryam around the counter and into the steaming kitchen while the tavernkeeper muttered to himself.

They talked over old times, and Geryam explained a little of how he had escaped the clutches of the Local Order and made his way to the island of Artos, only to come back home. He told only enough to keep her from being suspicious. It wasn't good to let anyone know you had escaped one of the Order's punishments.

As for Clank, her dead husband, his end had come about as Geryam had surmised. A few mercenaries had tried to riot in the tavern, and he had unceremoniously dumped them into the gutter outside. As it had turned out, they had been in the employ of Krell himself—and the high priest didn't take to having his people roughed up, even when they deserved it. A few days later, Clank had disappeared as completely as if he had never existed.

"Meenah," Geryam said after a moment's silence. "I need your hospitality. I have friends coming into town—most likely, they're already here. I need food for them and drink and a place to hide and get some rest. And I'm looking for two young women, the sweetest, most innocent and precious little ladies anyone ever looked after."

"What?" Meenah said with a twinkle in her eyes. "So you can take a personal hand in denting that innocence? You haven't changed a bit, you old dog."

Geryam smiled back, but it was a wistful one. "No, those days are behind me. This is on the up-and-up. Will you help me?"

Her face grew serious, too. "This has got something to do with the Order, hasn't it? You can't vanish into their clutches the way you did and just come back." Her eyes narrowed. "Are you working for them now, or are you crazy enough to try and pull something on them?"

"What you don't get into won't dirty you, my girl. I just need your help."

"Oh, pshaw. You know I've never been able to say you nay. But stay clear of that persimmon of a husband I've got. He'll sell you to the Order, or them to you, or anyone to anyone if there's a farthing in it. I'll help you but you can't stay here. If you did, and he got wind of it, he'd be falling over himself to tell someone with money."

An uproar from the tavern's common room made their heads turn. "I saw him go back there, you old guffer. I gots to talk to him."

"You don't talk to anybody," Nalord's voice returned.

"Then call him out to me. I recognized him and I got some word for him, and he'll be needin' to hear it."

"You're here to have a drink or some beef, but not for talk," Nalord roared. "Now get out."

Geryam rose to his feet and walked toward the man. The fellow was a simple-looking sailor, with a patch over one eye. "What's going on?" the warrior asked.

" 'At's him," the sailor yelled. "C'mere, sir, and let me whisper in your ear. I'm an honest bloke, I am, an' you can believe any word I give you is truth itself, good as gold and just as pure. I may not be much to look at, but I'm still my mother's son, I am."

Perplexed, Geryam kept his hand on his knife blade as he stepped outside with the man. He quickly learned the fellow had served on the ship in which Rinna and Lissa had been transported, that he was very taken with the two young ladies, and that he had developed second thoughts about their capture. "Man named Moreere nipped 'em," the sailor said. " 'E's a bad 'un. Deals in human stock, you might say, finds live bodies for anybody as wants 'em, and for any purpose."

"What's going to happen to them?" Geryam asked. He grabbed the man by the shoulders. "Where are they taking them?"

"North," the fellow said. " 'At's all I know. Don't know who they're going to, don't know why. Just know the fellow's got more money than anyone, and he's willin' to spend it to get a look at those two." The old tar shook his head. "It's a raw deal as far as I'm concerned. For my part, I'm sorry I ever had a hand in it."

"Don't be," Geryam said. He reached into Owras's leather bag, which he still had with him, and drew out a pair of coins. "All my thanks," he said, clapping the man on the shoulder with one hand and pressing the coins into the man's palm with the other. "Don't tell a soul you talked to me. You never saw me, you don't know who I am. Understand?"

"So I do," the man said. He turned away; then the light from the tavern door glinted on the coins Geryam had handed him. He looked over his shoulder at the warrior. "Good luck, you hear."

"Thanks," Geryam said, and went back inside. His mind raced. He still had to find Owras and Pal-Dan, that was most important. And there would be no time to accept Meenah's hospitality, other than the food and drink she could provide. Weary though he might be, they had to set out toward the island's interior, in hopes of finding Rinna and Lissa. So intent was he on his own thoughts as he walked back into the building, he did not notice Nalord's dark face watching him keenly from the corner behind the door.

Chapter Twenty-eight:
Old Friends

GERYAM COLLECTED THE goods he needed from Meenah, then bade her good-bye with a hug and a few words of thanks. He paid no heed to the huge woman's husband, but he did follow her advice to leave by the back way.

He hurried down to the waterfront of Touros and did not have to search long before he found Owras and Pal-Dan, standing beside a fishmonger's cart, munching on salted chubfish and drinking watered ale. The old man had hired a perplexed sailor to carry the freak.

Geryam paid off the sailor from Owras's coin purse, then took up the burden himself. The three of them started off down the waterfront, each telling a different tale of what had passed since they had separated.

With the help of more friends from Geryam's mercenary days, they quickly got well set up with weapons and supplies Meenah might have overlooked or had not had on hand. Geryam even got hold of a large leather harness, with which he improvised a kind of backpack for Pal-Dan.

Evening found them making their way from Touros by way

of the town's northern gate. Geryam walked along with both hands free and Pal-Dan strapped to his back in such a way that the human worm could keep an eye on the trail behind them.

"It's a wonderful ride you're giving me," Pal-Dan said. "But it must be wearing you out."

"It's good exercise," Geryam replied. "By the time we get out of this, I'll have legs like tree trunks."

"You have them already," Owras said with a little smile. "That's why Rinna and Lissa both fancy you so."

Geryam frowned. "Don't tease me, Owras."

"Odd you should think I was. It's not my intent."

"The young ladies are too special for me. Both of them."

"Rinna doesn't think so," Pal-Dan said. "I've watched her. She looks at you and her eyes get as big around as saucers."

Geryam sighed. "Leave me alone, you two. I'm fond of both of them and I won't deny it. But . . ." He looked ahead and shook his head. "At least let's make sure they're still alive before you make fun of me any further."

"Quiet," the freak suddenly whispered. "There's somebody out there. I saw a light."

"Are they following us?" Geryam whispered back.

"Of course they are. Did you think they might be out here for a healthy stroll?"

"Let's be ready," Owras said. He reached into his robes and brought out a new dagger. Geryam loosened his sword in its scabbard.

"They're still back there," Pal-Dan whispered a moment later. "I saw it again."

They saw another glow through the trees ahead. Then a tall man in chain mail stepped out from behind a spreading elm. "Halt right there," he said in a commanding voice. "You have no right of night passage in these woods."

"Rullo," Geryam cried. "Who posted you out here?"

The stranger stared at Geryam; then his mouth fell open. "But I thought you were . . ."

"Dead?" Geryam answered. "Never quite, though I was as good as. More than once. Come on, Rullo. I'm an old friend. Can't you let us through? We're on an important errand."

"Can't do it." Rullo shook his head, and three more men

came up behind them. Then brush crackled behind the questers, and another three men appeared from that direction.

"Seven against two and a half," Pal-Dan whispered to Geryam. "Do we stand a chance?"

"Hard to tell," Geryam muttered. Then he said in a louder voice, "Look, Rullo, we're not doing any harm to your blessed woods. We'll just pass through and go our merry way. You'll never even know we were here."

"I know where you're going," Rullo said. "You're chasing two girls."

"Say what?"

Rullo drew his sword. So did the other soldiers. "You're trying to reach the two girls who passed this way last night, aren't you? Sorry, old pal. They're Krell's guests by now, which is what you're going to be in a bit. You've gotten foolish in the last three years, Geryam. Krell has eyes all over Touros, all over Kolpos. Now, why don't you all be good fellows and come along quietly?"

Geryam's mind raced back to the tavern and Meenah's new husband. Was he the stool pigeon? It didn't matter; someone had informed on them. The warrior set his jaw and slipped his own sword out of its sheath. "You know who I am and why I'm here, then," he said quietly. "You shouldn't be working for Krell, you know. He's a slimy worm."

"You worked for men who were just as bad or worse," Rullo shot back. "You used to say it yourself: a man's sword belongs to whoever sets his table."

"I was wrong," Geryam said. "There has to be a better way." He eyed all the warriors who surrounded him. "Come on, all of you," he said. "You're true blades. This world's got to be changed—you're all going to have sons someday. Do you want them to grow up in a world where people like Krell run things? Band with me, with us. We'll make it a world where a man sets his own table—he doesn't have to let the Dark Order do it."

"Nice speech," Rullo said. "But no takers."

"All right, then." Geryam rubbed his chin with his free hand. "Take me, but let my friends go."

"No deal. All of you."

"Rullo, you know what I was like with a sword. You could never beat me; neither could anyone else we knew."

"There are seven of us," Rullo said with a smile. He glanced at his cohorts. "Take them," he cried, and leaped forward with a blow at Geryam.

Quick as a flash, Owras's dagger flicked out and cut the straps holding Pal-Dan to Geryam's back. The freak fell to the grass with a grunt, then rolled to one side, putting out long tentacles as he went, catching two soldiers by the legs and dumping them onto their own backs. At the same time, Geryam leaped at Rullo with a cry, parried the warrior's first blow, and aimed a return cut at the man's neck. Blood flew and Rullo dropped to his knees. Just as quickly, a second man took his place.

Another soldier clubbed Owras in the face with the pommel end of his sword. The old man was no match for trained warriors—he cried out and went down. Pal-Dan managed to trip another soldier, then had to roll away as one of the first he had surprised regained his feet and aimed a deadly cut at one tentacle. Pal-Dan snatched the member back just in time, but the fellow pursued him. More joined in the fight with Geryam. It was plain that the battle would soon be over.

A scream from the sky made them all look up. A white form fell out of the darkness like a fury, wings beat the air, and talons slashed at the heads of two men who fought Geryam. They screamed, dropped their swords, and clutched their bloody faces. It took only a couple of slashes for Geryam to finish the creature's work.

The other four watched in panic as the white apparition wheeled, banked, attacked once more. They threw down their swords and ran, ducking as the beast flew over their heads. "I'll be blessed," Geryam cried as he stared at the disappearing backs. "It's that Image cat again."

Pal-Dan worked his way through the long meadow grass until he was at Owras's side. He, too, watched until the white form disappeared into the night sky. "Friend or no, he showed up at the right time," the freak said. "Lissa did a good lick when she cuddled up to him."

"I guess she did," Geryam said, still looking up.

"Help me with the old man," Pal-Dan said. "We've got to get him moving. Those bruisers will come back."

"You take care of him," Geryam said. "I know Rullo. He's a horse soldier and the rest were, too. There have to be horses around here somewhere." He picked up one of the lanterns the soldiers had set down and went seeking into the darkness.

A few moments later, Geryam came back, leading seven tall stallions. "Found all of them," he said. "We might just as well take every one. Krell knows we're here—we can't be in more trouble than we already are."

Owras sat up with a groan. "What's going on?" he asked as he rubbed the side of his head. His face was already swelling where the soldier's sword hilt had struck him on the jaw.

"We won," Pal-Dan said lightly. "Your girlie's cat saved our bacon." He looked at the old man sadly. " 'Fraid you weren't cut out to be a warrior, friend."

"I could have told you that," Owras said. He stood up unsteadily. "How is Pal-Dan going to ride, Geryam?"

"I'll hold him," the warrior said. "Either that, or tie him across the saddle like an old blanket. Come on, let's get out of here."

They picked up another lantern and loaded themselves onto two of the horses. Then they rode into the night, leading the rest of the animals. Somewhere above them, Geryam guessed, flew Lissa's winged friend.

They rode the space of a league, which took a fair amount of time. Then Owras said, "We're going to have to stop, friends. I just can't go any farther. I've been awake for two days and beat in the head into the bargain."

"That's fair," Geryam replied. "I'm not feeling so fine myself. We'll do better if we're fresh."

"Do you object, Pal-Dan?"

"I doubt he minds," Geryam said. "He's already asleep. In fact, you're going to have to get him down."

They stopped beneath a tree and lowered the snoring freak to the ground. Then, while Owras unrolled blankets, Geryam tethered the horses between two more trees. The most gentle of breezes whispered among the leaves above them as Owras and Geryam stretched out on the ground, one on each side of the sleeping Pal-Dan.

"I wonder if we should set a watch," Geryam said drowsily.

"I'm sure we should," Owras replied. "But I'm just too beat. I couldn't have gone another step."

"If Krell still has men in this neighborhood, they'll just have to surprise us."

"I wonder," Owras replied. "I don't think that'll happen. From what we've seen tonight, we may have a sentry after all, a dedicated and keen-eyed one. He's probably hovering somewhere right above these trees." They spoke no more. Danger or no danger, only a moment or two passed before they joined Pal-Dan in healing slumber.

Chapter Twenty-nine:
New Allies

WHEN GERYAM WOKE up, the sun had already risen. "By the gods," he whispered to himself. "We need to be on our way." A sound caused him to look toward the place where their packs lay, beneath the tree to which the horses had been tethered. A naked young man was standing there, staring back at him. The youth was tall, broad-shouldered, and had one of the homeliest faces the warrior had ever looked at. Geryam found himself staring so hard, he did not even think to speak for an instant.

"Get away from those packs," he finally yelled, then shot from beneath his blanket, his sword already in his hand. The young man backed away, then tried to turn and run. His feet tangled and he fell with a cry just as Geryam reached him.

"I wasn't taking anything," the youth yelled as Geryam put a knee in his back.

With practiced ease, Geryam grabbed the youth's shaggy hair and pulled his head back. With the warrior's knee in the small of his back and his throat exposed to the sword, the lad

251

was helpless and plainly knew it. "Who are you?" Geryam asked. "What are you doing here?"

"Don't you know?"

"Why should I? What's that thing you dropped?"

"It's a piece of rock, just what it looks like."

The lad looked at him out of the corner of one eye. "I'll trade it for something to eat."

Geryam looked around. "We'll feed you soon enough. Are you from around here?"

"If I were, would I be butt-naked, walking through these hills? How does a fellow get off this stupid island? Every time I turn around, someone grabs me. First crazy religious freaks, then slave traders, then Krell and Horyk and all that lot . . ."

"Krell," Geryam said. "How did you get away from Krell?"

"None of your business. How do I know you're not working for him?"

Geryam pulled back on the lad's hair till he cried out. "You better talk, or I'll break your neck right here." To his surprise, the youth managed to writhe from under him. Rather than cut the lad down with the sword, Geryam tried to get a new grip, but the youth kicked out with one foot, then scrambled to his feet. In the blink of an eye, he was running through the grass with Geryam after him.

The youth quickly tired, however, and Geryam caught him easily. "What's wrong with you?" Geryam shouted. "For all your strength, you ran like an old codger." For the first time, he noticed the sores up and down the youth's thighs and belly. "By the gods," Geryam said. "Who did this to you?"

"Horyk." The youth lay back, shut his eyes, and panted.

"Who's Horyk?"

"The archpriest," came Owras's voice. "Leader of the Dark Order. What's he doing on Kolpos, lad?"

"She. Horyk's a woman."

"A woman? I didn't know that." Owras rubbed his bearded chin.

"She's more monster than woman, I can tell you." With Geryam's help, the young man climbed to his feet. As they walked, he told of his escape from Oron, of how he came to the Tower of Krell.

"That must be where they took Rinna and Lissa," Geryam said. "How do we get there?"

"You don't," the youth said. "You'd have to be crazy."

"We're crazy, then. Is there any way we can sneak in?"

"None. The doors are too stout. And if Krell hadn't been wrong about his idol and the Stone of Ending, I wouldn't ever have got out, either." He told them how Horyk had dined on him, then told how he had escaped. When Geryam looked doubtful, the youth showed him a little gold owl that hung on a chain about his right arm. "That's all he left," he said. "He dropped me on the other side of that hill, then flew off. I couldn't even get up, I was so sick. I just lay there until I fell asleep. When I woke, all I had was the Stone of Ending and this . . . this charm."

"I've never seen anything like this," Owras said, touching one of the sores lightly. "This Stone of Ending, where is it?"

"He dropped it over there," Geryam said. "Wait, I'll get it."

"No, don't touch it." Owras looked serious.

"You believe him?"

"I don't know the name Yron," Owras said. "But the Bronze Owl is sacred to Pallas, one of the highest of the Twelve. If this lad speaks true, then he has been touched by the true gods." He glanced at Geryam. "Same as you."

"How can we believe that?"

"It's hard to believe a stranger," Owras said. "I found it hard to believe you at first, Geryam. We don't have time to get to know this lad. But we have to work together." He looked at the youth again. "We don't even know your name. What is it?"

"They call me Rogue."

Owras shook his head. "I don't want to know what 'they' call you," he said. "I want to know what name your mother and father gave you."

"They're long dead. They named me Parthelon—but the fellows on the street always laughed at it. Besides, I like Rogue. It's easier to say."

"So's the word 'fool,' " Owras said with a smile. "But you don't want to be called that, do you? My young Parthelon, you have been touched by Pallas, which is a good sign. A very good sign. Pallas's sacred owl carried you to safety."

"What was Pallas's owl doing in Krell's tower?" Geryam asked.

"The Dark Order knows few of the mysteries of the true gods," Owras said. "That's why the Order is doomed."

"Krell said they found it when they dug the tunnel into the cavern where the tower hangs," Parthelon said.

"Ah. He doesn't know what he found."

Until now, Pal-Dan had only been listening to the others. "What about this Stone of Ending?" he asked.

"That, I cannot explain," Owras said. "But Krell may not be completely wrong. Parthelon touched the stone, and lived, yet the world did not end. Yet perhaps a world *will* soon end—his world of lust, torture, and blasphemy."

They walked to the place where the stone lay. Owras stood and looked down at it. "Seems innocent enough," he said. "Ore-bearing rock, it looks like. Very regular, circular shape, though."

"You can have it if you want it," Parthelon said.

"I think not. It came to you under circumstances which could best be described as—unique." Owras smiled. "You'd best keep it."

"We'd best find him a pocket to put it in," Pal-Dan said with a wicked grin.

"That's true," Owras said. "These horses' packs might have some spare clothing in them. Look through them, lad. While you're at it, we'll find you something to eat."

"Are we going to give him weapons, too?" Geryam said.

Owras looked from him to Parthelon, then back. "We'll see," he finally said.

"I don't care about that," Parthelon said. "If there's clothing and food, I'll be happy with that. Then I'll be on my way."

"On your way? With the Dark Order after you?" Owras smiled. "What makes you think you'll ever escape them? You never could before, and they're more interested in you than ever, now."

"What am I supposed to do? Just lie down and let them sacrifice me to those bloodsucking gods of theirs?"

"Fight them," Pal-Dan said.

"That's right," Geryam said. "With us."

"Wait a bit." Parthelon put his hands on his hips and looked at the warrior. "You haven't trusted me since I got here; now you want me to pitch in with you. Make it worth my while and maybe I will."

"We'll give you food and clothing," Owras said.

"I can get them anywhere."

"Just try," Pal-Dan said. "You're a marked man."

"You're not a street ruffian anymore," Owras said. "You're a man—a man named Parthelon—and you've been touched by the gods. You might just as well face Krell and Horyk alongside us. It's no more dangerous than running away from them."

Parthelon stared at him, then shrugged. "Who cares?" the youth finally said. "I've been in plenty of fights. Feed me, and I'll go with you."

The three men stared at the youth. His face had turned into a smiling mask. Finally, Geryam knelt and pulled open a pack. "We have biscuits," he said. "We have wine and water." Then he pulled open one of the captured food pouches from the horses. "Looks as if Krell's soldiers were kind enough to leave us dried meat, as well—and some cereals for eating on the march." He looked up at Parthelon. "See if you can find yourself some clothes; then we'll feed you and be on our way to have a look at this Tower of Krell."

Parthelon looked through the bags and found a few things he could wear. Soon, he had clothed himself in a crazy costume of oversized breeches, sandals, and a floppy leather hat with a bright feather in it. He also found a belt and scabbard that were to his liking. But for the moment, Geryam vetoed the idea of him actually wearing a sword.

When he ate, it was with all the gusto of a famished pig, gobbling down great handfuls of food, followed by gulps of watered wine. It was plain to see he had not eaten for a long time. They all joined him in a late breakfast, but each of them had to pause from time to time to watch in amazement the quantities of food he could put away. And his manners were just as unpleasant to watch as his face was to look upon.

Once they had eaten, they saddled and mounted the horses. As a guide, Parthelon showed insight and effort from the first moment. He suggested that, since they had extra horses, they leave some tied to trees halfway to the tower. The extras would make good remounts, should the party be pursued and need fresh animals.

While they rode, he described what he had seen of the Tower of Krell. His description of one room struck a chord with both Geryam and Pal-Dan. "I remember a place that looked just that way," Geryam said. "That was where Krell laid his curse on me. He didn't kill me, but he came close."

"You?" Pal-Dan cried. "What about me? You have a man's body once more, but I'm still just half a man."

"No matter," Owras said. "No sense competing for who suffered the most at Krell's hands. Let's just see that such a room never claims another victim."

"He called the place his laboratory," Parthelon said. "Horyk always said that was a sign of weakness. She said she didn't need beakers or potions."

Owras shook his head. "Sounds as if they're both deadly. We'll need help from the gods to defeat them."

"Maybe so," Geryam said. "I hope the gods are listening." While he spoke, he thought of Rinna and Lissa. The two maidens were in grave danger. He did not speak again for a long time.

The trees thinned out, the ground grew rough and ledgy, and they finally rode up a ridge Parthelon had described. "That's it," he said. "On the other side is a hole, the most awful crater you've ever seen."

"I see it now," Geryam said.

They rode closer; then their horses began to rear from the sulfur and brimstone stench that rose out of the crater. They dismounted and hobbled the horses, then crawled to the edge of the hole and peeked in.

Pal-Dan whistled. "Maybe I've been in Krell's grip, but I don't remember this place."

"Maybe he still had his laboratory in Touros back then," Parthelon offered. "They told me, he's been working on this place for ages."

"Maybe," Geryam said. "Or maybe you were like me, Pal-Dan. Maybe you were drugged when they hauled you down there. I don't remember how I got into that room, or how I got out of it. I only remember what went on in there."

"It doesn't matter," Owras said. "All that matters is, we have to get down there."

"How?" Parthelon asked. "The inside is shaped like an egg-shell with a hole broken in the top. How in the world can we crawl down the overhang? And the doors are guarded by half an army."

"We have to get down this way. We have to find a way," Geryam said. "We just have to get down there."

"I'll get you down there," Pal-Dan said matter-of-factly.

Parthelon stared at him. "How? You can't even sit on a horse by yourself."

Pal-Dan smiled at him. The youth's mouth fell open when leathery tentacles came growing from the freak's shoulders and hips. "There are things you don't know, sonny. You don't know I've been living for this moment for the last ten years. And you don't know how old Krell gave me a gift by accident when he took away my arms and legs."

Parthelon stared at him. "I guess you're right," he whispered.

"I've been thinking this out for the last two leagues," Pal-Dan said. "Geryam, you fix up a pack from one of the horses. Tie it around my shoulders and my waist. Then hang on for dear life while I carry you down." He peered over the edge again. "The walls of that cave, they're rough enough I can hang on to them." He looked at them. "It's the only way."

"Blamed if I will," Parthelon said.

Geryam looked at Pal-Dan, then back into the rift. Finally, he said, "All right. If Rinna and Lissa's lives weren't hanging in the balance, I wouldn't even think of it. But if you say you can get us all down there, I'll risk my life on your word."

"Not all of you," Pal-Dan said. "I'm no fool, I'm not going to promise what I don't think I can do. I can carry two, I'm sure of that."

Geryam looked at Owras. "You stay, old man. The youth and I are the fighters."

Owras looked longingly into the hole. "All right," he finally said. "But that's only if Parthelon wants to go."

Parthelon took on the same breezy expression as before. "Sure," he said. "Why not? My life's not worth a thing out here, as you said,"

Geryam quickly made a harness for Pal-Dan's shoulders. They pulled two of the girth belts from the horses, then secured loops for them and cut slits for wrist thongs. That way, Geryam and Parthelon could tie onto their wrists in case one of them slipped and lost his grip. They put the wide straps around Pal-Dan, and the freak crawled near the hole.

"Are you fellows ready?" he asked with a smile.

"Not yet," Geryam said. "Parthelon, if you look at my saddle, you'll find an extra sword there. It's not the best, but it's sound, and it'll do the job. If you're willing to climb down into this hellhole with us, I guess you're true enough to deserve a sword."

Parthelon turned and trotted to the warrior's horse. He found the sword and buckled it on. He also put on a leather pouch into which he put the Stone of Ending. "If it's a gift from these gods of yours, I'm going to keep it with me," he said half-apologetically. "It's not very heavy."

Owras nodded. "That's good reasoning," he said. Then the old man shook hands with Geryam and Parthelon and clapped Pal-Dan on the shoulder. "Good luck," he said.

"We don't need luck," Pal-Dan replied with a grin. "We need a blessed miracle." He uncoiled two of his sinewy tentacles, gripped projections down inside the crater, and pulled himself toward the edge. Geryam and Parthelon watched until the last instant, then got down and locked their fingers into the hand grips. Pal-Dan pulled himself and the other members of the awkward-looking trio over the rim and down into the venomous rift.

Chapter Thirty:
A Duel

THERE WAS NO guessing how long Rinna and Lissa had to wait in the sealed chamber. They sat and talked for a while, then dozed off and slept on the bare metal floor. A whirring sound woke both of them up. They looked about like dazed chickens until they found their eyes drawn to a flashing light. The brightness twirled and altered, like a shiny coin being spun on a tabletop. It moved slowly toward them. "Come in," it said.

"We're already in here," Lissa said grouchily. "There's no door. How can we come in there if we can't leave here?"

The light spun and flickered. "Come into me. Into the light."

Lissa glanced at Rinna. Rinna shook her head. "No," she said.

"Fine. I'll come into you." The light shot toward Rinna like an adder striking. Before she could even flinch, she found herself enveloped, surrounded, blinded by the flash and glow. Then, as quickly as it had surrounded her, the light flicked off and left her sitting in a chair.

She found herself in a large, gray room. Shelves along the

walls groaned beneath the weight of urns, bronze pots, and wooden boxes heaped with every kind of material and debris. There were bookshelves, too. Across the floor stood long tables, loaded with beakers, glass carboys, stuffed animals, and all kinds of odd items. Krell stood beside one of the tables and smiled down at her. "Hello," he said in a friendly voice. "Do you feel well?"

"Not really," Rinna said. Another flash of light blinded her and made her jerk her head around. When the light faded, she saw Lissa sitting in a chair next to hers. She tried to get up, but found herself unable to move, as if her arms and legs had been strapped to the arms and legs of the chair. Lissa acted bound, too. "What are you going to do with us?" Rinna asked.

Krell's smile broadened. "You're going to help me," he said. "I'm having a professional disagreement with Horyk and you're going to help me resolve it." He made a gesture with one hand. "Rise."

The chair to which Rinna was bound floated upward. Lissa's chair did the same. The two maidens found themselves looking down at the table before Krell and saw an immense sword lying there. Long it was, as long from hilt to tip as he was tall, and decorated with ornate engraving the full length of the blade. Even from where she hovered, she could see tiny animals, scenes of hunts, revels, and battles. The hilt looked broad as a man's chest, made of bronze and decorated with jewels and burnished silver inlay.

"This weapon represents a life's work," Krell said. "I've paid artisans all across the Thlassa Mey to forge the blade, to polish it, to hone it, and decorate it. Others made the hilt and soldered it onto the tang. Nice, eh?"

"I don't know much about swords," Rinna said.

"Me, either," Lissa said. "What's it got to do with us?"

"You're going to help me consecrate it," Krell said. "I'm sure you've noticed by now, I master many arts. I make you rise, I make you fall." He gestured and the chairs bobbed up and down. "I take people into my study here, and I transform them as I see fit."

"We know about that," Lissa said. "We have friends who've been through this place."

Krell studied her. "Oh, really? Who might they be?"

"Geryam and Pal-Dan," Lissa said.

"Oh, Lissa," Rinna said. "Hush."

"No need for her to be quiet," Krell said. "You have no secrets from me here. Anytime I want, I can wring every thought from you." He paused for a moment. "Yes, I remember both of them, now. Both fell for a little ruse Horyk and I used to work together—you don't need to know the nature of it. I have to admit I'm surprised they're still around."

He turned from them and ran his fingers the length of the blade. "No matter now. We have bigger game afoot. You see, I've studied for many years. I know all any man could learn in the time I've had. I can change men into animals, and then back again. I can turn the darkness into light, and then back again." He smiled a crooked smile. "With a little hard thought and the right hand movement, I could blast either of you from existence.

"But I'm still frustrated," he said. "The Dark Ones speak only to one person: the archpriest. That gives her a great advantage."

"I suppose it would," Rinna said sarcastically.

"I plan to replace her as archpriest. Of course, she's not about to die and let me have it. She's been around for generations, and she's still stronger than I. It's her hold with the Dark Ones versus my command of my art. She can't leave this place unless I let her, but her power is still strong. I can't overcome her yet. Stimulating impasse, isn't it?"

The two maidens did not reply, so Krell went on. "This blade is the answer. I will enchant it and consecrate it to the Dark Ones. It's the masterwork of an entire world, so they'll be pleased. Their loyalty to Horyk will waver. At that moment, I'll carve my way into her chamber and slaughter her like a shoat. I'll become the new archpriest and I'll be more powerful than she ever thought of being."

"Oh, Krell, how you ramble," came a woman's voice. "You should have remained my ally and not become my rival. Life was so enjoyable when we did things together."

Krell's gaze shot around the room. He snapped his fingers and light sparked from the place where his fingertips met. "You're spying on me, aren't you? That's not polite."

"Plotting to kill me isn't polite, either."

Krell clapped his hands. A flash of light flew from the impact, bounced off the nearest wall, then rebounded off the floor. It continued to bounce around the room, off wall, floor, ceiling, another wall, like a stone skipping waves. Suddenly it struck something invisible, stopped, and formed an expanding glow. To the maidens' astonishment, Horyk's fair face hovered where the light faded. The face glowed as though lit from within. "No sense hiding," Krell said. "If you're going to eavesdrop, you might just as well be where I can see you."

The face smiled a caustic smile. "Well done, Krell. But these games and tricks have gone on long enough. It's becoming tiresome."

"Not for me," Krell said. "Why don't you just retire as archpriest. Sign the job over to me, and we'll be friends again."

"I wouldn't force you to shoulder such a tiring responsibility."

"Sweet of you," Krell said with a sour smile. "You'll yield it soon enough, I warrant." He pulled open one of the table's drawers and drew a large dagger.

"Come," he said, pointing a finger at the chair that held Lissa. While the maiden squirmed, the chair drifted toward him, then gently lowered until her feet hovered at about the height of his chest.

"What are you doing?" Horyk's face demanded. Her expression showed real worry.

"One last, great experiment," Krell said in a bursting voice. "The Dark Ones will enjoy a meal from me as well as from you, when it's as delicious as these two maidens. Their powers will flow into this blade and then I'll carry it down to your chamber, my dear Horyk. I'll come visit you."

"Krell, you're crazy."

"That's rude," he said. "I would have thought better of you."

"I'm coming after you, Krell. You've gone too far, this time."

"You can try. Your chamber's sealed from the outside. I did it just before I called these little lasses here. You've been unfortunate, dear Horyk. That lad who was going to help the gods replenish your powers? He's gone, now. He's gone but these ladies are here." Krell smiled sweetly. "Advantage to me, don't you think?"

Rage filled Horyk's face—rage and fear. "You'll never succeed," she fumed. "Better men than you have tried."

"Don't interrupt me," Krell said. He reached toward Lissa's ankle, which hovered before him. "Now, my young lady, just let me have your little foot."

Lissa kicked and fought. That made her chair rock back and forth, but Krell only laughed. "You're a scrapper," he said. "But that's what the formula calls for. A virgin, pure of heart and pure of soul, full of courage and faith. Your blood will quench my blade." Even as he spoke, the great sword on the table began to turn red, as if heated in some invisible forge. Rinna imagined she could even hear the gasping of distant bellows.

"Hold," Krell shouted. Lissa's foot stopped moving as if locked in iron, even though the rest of the chair swung more crazily than ever from her struggles. Krell slipped her sandal off like a lover and dropped it to the floor. Rinna could hear his breathing. The tip of his knife slipped along the foot's white side, and the dark blood followed after. Lissa screamed as the pain lanced up her leg, and cursed him, but the droplets spattered and steamed on the red-hot blade, all as accurately as if they had been poured through a funnel.

Krell turned toward Rinna, his smile evil and bloated across his face. "It's a great, huge blade," he said. "Much pure blood is required. Come."

Rinna's spine chilled as she felt her chair move toward the evil man. It settled beneath her; she felt his hand on her foot, but no matter how hard she struggled, she could not free herself. She felt the icy tip of the blade touch her skin, then felt searing pain. She heard herself screaming.

Horyk screamed, too. "You fool," she shrieked. "You're upsetting the balance."

"That's my aim."

"I'll fight you."

"You can try."

"I'll destroy you. There are still things you don't know. Prepare yourself, Krell, my patience has worn out."

Krell laughed. "You can't even get out of your chamber, my

dear. I had it welded up solid while you slept. While you're sorting *that* problem out, I'll finish my business here, then come to see you."

Rinna felt herself weaken, and as if she were looking on the scene from afar. She watched her blood and Lissa's spatter over the ornate blade, smoking, steaming, leaving behind stain and residue. Slowly, the metal cooled back to a steely gray.

"There, now." Krell squeezed her ankle, then wrapped a cloth around the cut in her foot. "It won't do for you to lose too much strength. If the Dark Ones like this sample of your fluids, it might be well to save the rest for later." He smiled and looked up at her; then he put on a huge pair of black gauntlets and reached for the deadly-looking weapon.

"Krell." Horyk's voice was a shriek, a shrill command. They all turned and looked at the archpriest's disembodied face, and Krell's own face went slack with surprise. The lovely features had swollen as if a bellows had pumped the woman full of air. Her bulging lips parted in a hideous grin. "You are a silly man, to think you could defeat me. You left me a way out. For shame."

The swelling face burst and bright, yellow fluid streamed forth, congealed, and formed a pillar in the middle of the room. It took shape in an instant, and Horyk stood before them in the flesh. "You are the most brilliant of all my minions, Krell, but you've outsmarted yourself. You have that sword now, you've done well. But you have those huge gloves on, too. You can't practice your art with your fingers bound in leather." She laughed. "Prepare to die."

She began to chant, her voice going faster and faster until it was a high-pitched scream. The chamber filled with little eddies of air, as if breezes were blowing out of each corner. "There," she shouted. An opening formed in the center of her forehead and from it issued a writhing ball of darkness, which shot toward the man at the table.

Krell snatched at the sword and lifted it just in time. The ball glanced off the blade, shot to the floor, and spread like a pool of blood. The metal plate grew red-hot, then melted and sagged away. Through the opening, Rinna and Lissa could see walkways, walls of bronze, even the cavern wall, all bathed in a red glow.

Krell did not have time to recover before another projectile hurtled toward him, this one green. Again, he managed to deflect it. It struck a shelf, shattered urns and beakers, and a blaze sprang up.

His sword began to glow, and he lunged toward the woman. "It absorbs all the mystic force it touches," he cried. "Keep trying, Horyk. Do your best. You make my weapon mightier with each bolt."

"Then I won't use bolts," Horyk said. She spread her arms with a cry, and the table on which the sword had lain uprooted itself from the floor. Beakers, tools, and implements fell and shattered as the huge, heavy object loomed toward the man. He dropped to the floor, and the table passed barely over him. He scrambled back to his feet and shook a glove from one hand. A beam of light shot from his fingertips, spread, and formed a wall of crystal. When the table swung back toward him, it struck the crystal and rebounded with a horrid noise.

"Well done," Horyk shouted. Then she laughed. "You parry well. Now see if you can fight without the very air you breathe." She made a complex, twining motion with her fingers, and the table began to spin. It moved faster and faster, turned on end, became a blur, whirred, and whistled. Rinna could feel the air drifting past her, toward the spinning table, as if it were a breeze blowing down a tunnel.

Suddenly, with a flash of light, the table disappeared. Air collapsed into the empty space with a sound like thunder. Rinna's chair tumbled and rolled with the turbulence. There was no air anywhere. Krell managed to get his free hand up once more, and gestured, causing a cylinder of crystal to form in the middle of the room where the table had been. Air screamed in through the hole in the floor, and Rinna felt the tightness in her lungs relax.

Krell turned back toward the archpriest. "Now it's my turn," he said. He gripped the sword's handle, and his brows knit. Flame spurted from the tip and bathed her in eerie light.

The flame surrounded her, swept by her, then scorched the chamber's far wall. "This is child's play," she said. She smiled and put her hands on her hips. "Surely, you can do better than that."

Krell's lips writhed, and a shaft of green light eddied around his hands, shot along the blade, and lanced toward her. This time, she dodged, and when the shaft struck the wall behind her, it blew the scorched portion of wall completely away. Her eyebrows lifted. "You are deadly indeed," she said. "I'll not play with you any longer."

She screamed, and the room filled with deafening noise as every beaker and urn and vial on every shelf shattered. Shards, chips, and slivers of glass shot toward the man at the center of the room. Quick as thought, Krell spun like a dervish, so quickly that he and his sword became a blur. Pieces glanced off him and careened against wall and floor and ceiling.

Rinna and Lissa watched the battle helplessly. Through gaps in the floor and the wall, they could see people gather and stare at the chamber in dismay. Horyk and Krell struggled on, angled around the room until the archpriest stood close to the two maidens. "As for these little bits of fluff, they shall not be yours," she shouted. "You shall not use them to curry favor with the Dark Ones." With a stroke from one hand, she sent a gust of wind toward the maidens. The air sent them spinning toward the gap in the end of the building.

Krell cried out and threw up a wall of crystal, but he was too late. The two chairs had already passed through. As soon as Rinna and Lissa passed out of the chamber, their chairs dropped from beneath them and they fell toward the molten stone hundreds of fathoms below.

Chapter Thirty-one:
Escape From the Tower

THE CAVERN WALL was a cascade of rough stone. Knobs, bulges, and sags made it a complex maze of odd shapes, so Pal-Dan found plenty of purchase for his downward climb. Geryam still hated the ride, though. Hanging on for dear life to the leather harness they had rigged was not his idea of a good time—all the more so when they were lowering themselves into such a pit of fiends as this one.

When the warrior caught a glimpse into Parthelon's eyes, he could tell the youth was every bit as unnerved as he was. As for Pal-Dan, the freak went about his terrifying business as coolly as a farmer counting beans for planting. The sweat poured from him and dripped into the abyss. His breath came in long, even drafts. His eyes remained riveted on the rock knobs from which he hung. He never spoke a word.

The climb became more straight down as they moved toward the shining buildings below them. From what Geryam could see, the place was a marvel of the architect's work. Huge rods of iron had been set into the stone, and everything hung from them. The warrior whistled beneath his breath. "I've never seen a place like this," he said.

"It gets worse," Parthelon said. "The people in there are all crazy, the craziest I've ever seen. Those girls you're talking about could be anywhere. I hope you know how to find them."

"Krell's laboratory," Geryam said. "That's where I want to go first. Can you find it?"

"I don't know," Parthelon said. "They showed me so many different places, I don't remember where they all are. I think it's toward the bottom." He paused and stared downward. "Hey, what's going on?" he said. "Look at all the people running around."

Guards in chain mail and attendants in white robes flocked along the walks and terraces like ants atop an anthill. They were so taken with what was going on inside the complex, they didn't even notice the trio hanging over their heads.

"Something big's up," Geryam said. "Hurry and get us down there, Pal-Dan."

"Bother you," Pal-Dan replied in an out-of-breath voice. "You try keeping a grip on this rock. I'm going just as fast as I can."

"Look," Parthelon said. "They've spotted us." Soldiers stared up at them, pointed, then went for their weapons. One grabbed a dagger from his belt and hurled it upward with a wide sweep of one arm. The weapon clanged off the stone a handsbreadth from one of Pal-Dan's tentacles.

"Blast," Pal-Dan said. "That's scary." Another dagger glanced off the same tentacle. A third struck the end of one of his snaky coils, and with a cry he released his hold. They dropped down and, for an instant, swung out over the molten rock far below. Then, despite the pain, Pal-Dan managed to grab a stone knob with his injured member and swing them back in, toward the bronze runway.

"I can't hold on," he shouted. They swung, spun, and plummeted toward the runway three fathoms below. Soldiers and servants scattered, but not fast enough to keep the trio from landing square atop a knot of people. They went down in a screaming muddle of arms, legs, and bodies while the runway bounced with the impact.

Geryam shot to his feet, snatched his sword from his scabbard, and cut down the soldier facing him. More men ran up, but Parthelon took on one with mighty sweeps of his weapon. Pal-Dan wrapped a tentacle around the sword dropped by the fallen man and used it to deadly effect.

The freak turned out to be a fine warrior. The fact that he could absorb and extrude his tentacles at will made them all but impervious to wounds. He had already absorbed the tentacle wounded by the dagger, and now it issued from his shoulder once more, good as new. He caught hold of the structure above him and heaved himself up, slashing down at his enemies.

People screamed and ran from the three invaders. A dozen spear-carrying guardsmen came up, then slowly advanced on the trio. "Quick," Pal-Dan yelled. "Grab hold of me." When Geryam and Parthelon gripped his harness, he wrapped his tentacles around the railing to the runway above them, and hauled them up. Before the astonished guards could react, the three had climbed to safety.

There was no one on this landing, at least for the moment. "Come on," Geryam yelled. He and Parthelon took off at a run, toward the other side of the complex. Pal-Dan snatched up a fallen sword with a tentacle, then followed them as best he could, swinging along on beams and supports like an acrobat on trapezes.

The runway they were on took them close to the cavern wall, then swung under a series of structures, led between a couple more, and ended at a long ladder. Below them, they could see many people gathered on a large landing. "That's it," Parthelon said, pointing with his sword at the long, low building at the center of the landing. "That's the room he said was his study."

"Something's going on in there," Geryam said. The building, in fact the whole structure, shook with crashes and explosions. The bronze wall turned red-hot at one point and melted away until a large hole appeared. The crowd gasped in fear and horror. Some people fled back up ladders and staircases, but more of the curious gathered from above and below.

Parthelon and Geryam threw themselves down the ladder and landed atop the structure. Everything inside this hellish cavern felt hot to the touch, but the metal top to this room was even worse. The place shook like a drumhead. "You, there," a guard shouted up at them. "What do you think you're doing?"

"Uh-oh," Pal-Dan said. "We're in for it now." A couple of guardsmen tried to reach them by climbing on one another's shoulders, while a half-dozen more dashed up a catwalk to the level above them.

Suddenly, the room below them trembled so hard it threw them from their feet. A huge hole appeared in the wall just below them, and to his amazement, Geryam saw two young women in chairs float out of the building's dark interior. "It's them," he cried.

People on the landing below screamed and scattered. The two maidens drifted over the landing; then the chairs on which they sat plummeted as if ropes lifting them had been cut.

With a shout, Pal-Dan shot out his tentacles to their farthest limits. One wrapped about Rinna's arm like a whip cracking around a post; the other clutched onto Lissa's waist, then wrapped back upon itself, forming a knot. The jolt of the load pulled the freak toward the edge of the roof. "Help," he cried out. "They're beauties, but they're heavy as horses."

Parthelon leaped and grabbed one tentacle before Pal-Dan could slide any farther. Geryam jumped on the freak's back, held him down, and felt the muscles beneath him surge as the human worm hauled the two young women upward. "Get off me," Pal-Dan shouted. "You're crushing the life out of me."

Geryam reared back onto his knees and helped Parthelon pull. For his part, Pal-Dan hauled Rinna and Lissa up, over the railing and onto the landing. People fled this way and that. One man in white attendant's robes ran full into Rinna as she was being dragged over the rail, knocked her down, and broke Pal-Dan's hold. As for Lissa, the freak managed to pull her onto the rooftop.

"Rinna," Geryam yelled. "Run and jump." The young woman dashed across the landing amid fleeing bodies, then leaped for her life. Geryam reached down with all his might, felt the warmness of her palms clamp onto his wrist, then pulled up. A man in armor saw what was going on and ran toward her, sword drawn.

Another explosion, even larger, shook the structure as if it were a child's toy. The force of it knocked the guard off his feet, and Geryam hauled Rinna onto the roof with the rest. "Let's get out of here," Parthelon yelled.

A couple of soldiers had made it to the top of the building by then, but Geryam cut one down while Parthelon bowled into the other, knocking him over as if he were a house of cards. They threw themselves onto the ladder and scurried up it like rats up a mooring line.

Still another explosion shook them, and they heard tortured metal twist and bend. Rivets and forgings screamed and popped; iron beams and support rods groaned and buckled. The ladder tilted at a crazy angle. Geryam felt the place quiver as the wrought iron pulled out of the metal roof below. The lower portion of the complex swayed wildly, dropped downward, then ripped loose and fell.

People screamed as they went down. Some even leaped from rooftops and handrails, then fell alongside the doomed structure, their wails adding to the cacophony until the whole mass faded and shrank with distance. When it struck the seething lake of rock, it disappeared in a fountain of red, yellow, and silver.

The fugitives had no time to watch. They scurried up the ladder and reached a landing in time to run headlong into a pocket of guards who had climbed up and cut them off. Swords and curses flew; men fell. Rinna and Lissa snatched up swords and also fought. Faced by wildly fighting opponents, one of whom had arms and legs like snakes, the soldiers dropped back.

"We'd better get to the top as fast as we can," Parthelon cried. "Look at those supports—this whole place is going to give way." Even as he spoke, one of the great support rods pulled from the cavern wall with a sound like thunder. Stone fragments shot past them and the deck canted at a steep angle.

Soldiers and slaves scrambled up the doomed structure. Like sheep, they clogged the galleries carved into the stone above. Rather than facing warriors now, the fugitives found themselves up against a mass of pushing, shoving backsides. They skirted the fleeing crowd, then ran out along a walkway that wound along the hard stone for a distance.

"There's no time to fight our way through that," Geryam said. "Pal-Dan, can you get them out the way you got us in?"

"If they can hold on," the freak said. "I've still got my harness."

"We can't leave you," Rinna said. "That's not fair."

"Pal-Dan can't carry all of us," Geryam said. "You'll be lucky if he can even carry the two of you back out of this hole."

"Don't be insulting," Pal-Dan said. "Tie their hands to the harness so they can't slip off."

Geryam put out a hand and cupped the side of Rinna's face. "It's the only way," he said. "You two have to survive. You have to found a movement and do away with this whole rotten order. Far as I'm concerned, I've done more then I set out to. Krell went down with his study."

Rinna swallowed. "Geryam, you have to get out of this place. I love you."

Geryam smiled and patted her shoulder. "What a lovely fool you are," he said softly. "But let's tie you to Pal-Dan's harness. You both look so weak, I don't think you can hold on by yourselves." Hurriedly, they used leather straps to tie the two maidens fast. Then Pal-Dan wrapped tentacles around projections in the stone and pulled the three of them up, off the walkway. Like a great, slow spider he went, the two maidens hanging from his back.

Geryam and Parthelon made their way back along the walkway. "This is bad," Geryam said as another support rod pulled out of the stone and the walkway shook like a ship's deck in a gale. "Why did you ever let yourself in for this?"

Parthelon laughed. "Let myself in . . . you talked me into it, that's why." He shook his head. "Besides, the Order has had me cornered so often, I've been living on borrowed time ever since I left Oron."

"Look up there," Geryam suddenly cried. "What are those holes?"

They stopped and stared at a series of round openings cut into the stone. "I've no idea," Parthelon said. "But if we can get to them, they're safer than this deck." Even as he spoke, the structure shifted again. More people screamed and a few toppled over sagging, slanting railings and fell to their doom.

A series of boxlike bronze cabins faced the edge of the top level where it met the stone. Between them was a large, high gallery jammed with people pushing, shoving, trampling one another in their fury to get out of the death trap. "No one's going to worry about stopping us," Geryam said. "Let's climb up there."

A quaking ladder led up to a catwalk, which went along the tops of the cabins. "Blast," Geryam said when they reached the walkway. "The lowest one is still just out of reach."

"Climb onto my shoulders," Parthelon said. He helped the warrior up, heaved, and Geryam managed to scramble into one of the tunnels. The walls had been carved smooth, and the passage extended back into the stone. A rat's hole of a tunnel stretched as far as the eye could see. Geryam managed to work his way around, then reached back, extended a hand, and helped his partner up after him. "These might be ventilation tunnels," he said. "If that's so, maybe we're going to get out of here after all."

They started crawling along the tunnel, then heard a commotion behind them. Apparently, someone had seen them escape and he, too, was trying to climb up to the round shafts. "We better hurry," Parthelon said breathlessly as they crawled. "This could get crowded."

They went on their knees and elbows, sweat pouring from them. After several moments, they found their way blocked by a heavy grating. "Great," Parthelon said. "Maybe we're not going to get out as easy as we thought."

Geryam looked down between the slots in the metal. Below them, in a huge, dim chamber, he could see horses, cattle, and men moving about in a frenzy. Chickens squawked and scrambled out of the way, men saddled palfreys, others dashed through the gallery as fast as they could go. "So that's it," Geryam said. "This isn't a ventilation shaft at all. It's a heating duct. These tunnels bring warm air from the cavern into the stables. Pretty cunning."

"What about that grating? Can we knock it loose?"

"Maybe. Try to get turned around, then get up beside me and we'll kick." The two men writhed about in the narrow passage until they could both get their feet against the metal. They both pushed and kicked with might and main. Just as the metal groaned and started peeling out from the stone at one corner, they felt a vibration as if the whole mountain would turn to dust. Up the tunnel behind them came a grinding groan, a sound of cosmic tearing, and the wailing cries of doomed souls.

"There it goes," Parthelon said. "I can't say I'm sorry about it, but we'd better get this grating the rest of the way off."

They redoubled their efforts, and at last the metal peeled back far enough that a man could crawl down between it and the stone. "Lower me," Geryam said. "I'll find some way to get you down after."

"Promises, promises," Parthelon said with a dry smirk. But he did grasp Geryam's wrists and lower the warrior down as far as he could. They released one another; Geryam dropped and rolled, then shot to his feet and hid behind a stack of hay just as one last contingent of guards hustled past. When they left, the stable became empty. Apparently, everyone else had perished when the last supports to the Tower of Krell had given way.

Geryam darted about the empty stable like a giant mouse and finally found a coil of rope hanging on a peg in one of the horses' stalls. He returned to Parthelon and threw the coil up to the younger man. "Tie it onto the grating," he shouted. "Then climb down."

It took only instants for Parthelon to hitch his way down. As his feet neared Geryam's head, the grating pulled the rest of the way out of the stone, and sent him sprawling, then landed a handsbreadth from his head on the straw-strewn floor. "That was close," he said with a whistle. "Now, let's get out of here."

They scrambled down the huge passage. Some refugees still remained in the place, but everyone ignored the two strangers as they ran out through the towering bronze doors, which now hung open and unattended. The warm afternoon breeze kissed their faces, welcoming them back to the world of life and humankind.

They ran breathlessly up the rocky hillside and in a few moments saw the first of the horses they had left hobbled. An instant later, they spied Owras, Rinna, and Lissa kneeling in the grass. "Hurry and untie the horses," Geryam shouted as they ran up. "We have to get out of here before something else happens."

Lissa looked up, and there were tears in her eyes. "Let it rest, will you?"

"What's the matter?" Geryam asked. Then he saw Pal-Dan lying on the stony ground. The freak's tentacles stretched out, deflated and flaccid, and the eyes smiled up at him weakly.

"Those are some heavy girlies," Pal-Dan said in a soft voice. "But it was a pleasant load, by my faith—the most pleasant I've ever lifted." He looked at Lissa and grinned as the maiden touched him lightly on the face. "I'd fight for the chance to do it again."

"The strain of climbing back up burst his heart," Owras said. "There's no hope."

Geryam stared down at the man, but could think of nothing to say. All he could do was step forward and kneel at the fallen hero's side, like the rest. "Bless you, Pal-Dan," he said softly. "We'd have all died if it hadn't been for you."

"I love flattery," Pal-Dan said back. "Keep it up." But for all his wit, his face showed he was in pain.

Geryam felt the ground quiver beneath him. "What was that?"

The quiver turned into a heave that all but threw him and Parthelon to the ground. "Feels as if the pot's boiling down there," Pal-Dan whispered. "Dropping Krell's palace into that molten pool down there—no surprise that would give these hills indigestion."

Geryam ran the rest of the way up the hill and peered into the great pit. Far below, the molten stone bubbled and roiled, with a million little flashes of yellow light. Explosions burst here and there, throwing up great heaps of lava. Clouds of steam and gas billowed up toward him. "This is bad," he whispered.

Something else also flew upward, clothed in robes of flame. As the object neared, Geryam could make out a face and eyes that burned upward. "What's this?"

Rinna let out a cry behind him. "It's Horyk. And she has that sword."

They all recoiled from the crater's edge as Horyk shot out, face alight in a fury of hatred and triumph. Flames swirled around her until even her face looked red with the fire element. "You," she cried, sweeping toward them. "Your challenges are nothing beside Krell's—and he's dead as ashes." She laughed and hovered over them. "What, one of you dead already? Take cheer, the rest will soon follow. None of you have seen my real powers."

Owras glanced about wildly. "Parthelon," he said in a soft voice. "Your stone, the Stone of Ending. Throw it. Now."

Parthelon snatched at the bag that held the stone, but before he could lay his hands on it, a white shape shot from the clouds above them, toward Horyk. "Image," Lissa cried.

The beast plainly tried to crash into the archpriest, but she was too quick for it. With a snarl of rage, she swung the great sword. The blow caught Image in the middle, slicing the beast in two as neatly as if it had been a sausage. With a little gasp, the two sections plummeted into the crater below. "Image!" Lissa screamed.

Horyk's gaze fell on her and the evil eyes glowed with cruelty. "I'll deal with you first," she said with a sneer.

By this time, Parthelon had snatched the Stone of Ending from its leather pouch. With a grunt, he heaved the fist-sized stone as hard as he could. Horyk's savage eye caught the motion and she turned, catlike, to deflect the missile with the big sword.

When the Stone of Ending struck the blade, it burst with a crash loud as a thunderclap. The stone turned molten as wax, flowed along the blade in a half instant, turned it red-hot, melted and changed it. The shock of the explosion knocked the questers all off their feet and hurled Horyk through the air like a crossbow bolt. Her scream filled their ears while the blade itself fell harmlessly to the ground beside Parthelon.

"She's falling," Rinna cried. The young woman scrambled to the crater's edge and watched Horyk shoot downward like a comet out of the night sky. Flames wrapped round her and black smoke streamed back and left a trail of her downward plunge even after she had faded from view. An explosion greater than any before shook the magma below as she struck. Jets of steam, smoke, and ash shot upward, and the ground heaved so hard the horses downhill from them screamed and reared in terror.

Parthelon snatched up the sword Horyk had dropped. "It's changed," he said softly. "The Stone of Ending has reforged it." Indeed, the engraving and inlay were gone from the blade and the handle, so the weapon had a simple, clean look to it. Around the pommel, inscribed in tiny letters, were the words *Spada Korrigaine*.

"The Blade of the Fairies," Owras said as he looked over Parthelon's shoulder. "Bear that always, for it's a gift from the gods. You're a man of destiny, that much is plain to see. Your fate is bound up with ours, now."

"That's wonderful," Geryam cried. "But we'd better get out of here." Even as he spoke, the ground heaved again. Jets of ash shot out of the opening, and the fine powder began to settle around them."

"What about Pal-Dan?" Lissa cried.

"He's dead," Owras said. "Let this place be his tomb, and honor a noble memory."

Lissa turned to give the dead freak a last caress as the surviving questers started down the hill at a run. They cut the hobbles off the horses, swung into their saddles, then set off down the hill at a gallop. Behind them, the eruption became more violent and threw up clouds of steam, ash, and hot gases hundreds of fathoms into the air. As if to vomit out the foul mass of the Tower of Krell, the magma rose to the surface of the crater and poured out. Over the next weeks, months, and years, it would form a mountain, a volcano that would be called Mount Jephthys by the shipmen across the Thlassa Mey.

And with the smoke and gases rose a strange creature, a huge, winged cat, large as a tiger and black as the ash from which it emerged. While the questers fled toward the city of Touros, the creature circled the rising plume for a moment, gnashed its huge teeth, then flew out over the Thlassa Mey's sparkling waters. Steadily, it set its course toward the sea's southern shore and the great temple complex that stood at the mouth of the Stilchis River.

DENNIS McCARTY'S
FANTASIES

They Can't
Get
Much Better